Mother

Praise for Thorne & Cross

"*Mother* is about as disturbing as one can get. Thorne and Cross are seriously twisted individuals who know how to horrify and entertain at the same time." - **Fang-Freakin-Tastic Book Reviews**

"A delightfully sinister walk up the shadowed staircase to the room Mother arranged especially for you. So, what's in the cupboard? What's she hiding in the basement? Inside the garage? Under the floorboards? With *Mother,* Thorne and Cross reanimate the "familiar," leading you down a path of familial treachery that gets midnight-dark all too quickly." - **Michael Aronovitz – author of *Phantom Effect***

"*Mother* is a thriller in the truest sense of the word. What begins with a walk through a nice neighborhood in a nice town quickly becomes a chilling and unnerving descent into madness that is harder and harder to escape. Because I wear a fitness tracker I have scientific proof that the finale is a wild ride. Although I was curled up on the couch reading, *Mother* caused my heart rate to go up ten points! I'll never look at a neighborhood block party the same way." **- QL Pearce, bestselling author of *Scary Stories for Sleep-Overs***

"Thorne and Cross bring the goods with THE CLIFFHOUSE HAUNTING, a clockwork mechanism of gothic chills designed to grab the reader by the scruff and never let go until the terrifying conclusion. Atmospheric, sexy, brooding, and brutal, the book manages to be simultaneously romantic and hardboiled. Highly recommended! - **Jay Bonansinga, the New York Times bestselling author of *The Walking Dead: Invasion*, *Lucid*, and *Self Storage*.**

"In *The Ghosts of Ravencrest*, Tamara Thorne and Alistair Cross have created a world that is dark, opulent, and smoldering with the promise of scares and seduction. You'll be able to feel the slide of the satin sheets, taste the fizz of champagne, and hear the footsteps on the stairs." -**Sylvia Shults, paranormal expert and author of *Fractured Spirits* and *Hunting Demons***

"In this classic-style gothic, young Belinda Moorland takes a job as governess for the children of Eric Manning, whose family mansion, Ravencrest, was reassembled stone by stone after crossing over from England. Now stalked by a bevy of quirky, shady characters ... the sinister estate and its naughty nightside hijinks take center stage in this expert tale of multi-generational evil - and love. *The Ghosts of Ravencrest* will chill you and make you hot and bothered at the same time. There's nothing like a stay in a California town created by Thorne and Cross!" - **W.D. Gagliani, author of *Wolf's Blind* (the Nick Lupo Series)**

"Alistair Cross' new novel THE CRIMSON CORSET ... is taut and elegantly written taking us into the realms where the erotic and the horrific meet. Reminiscent of the work of Sheridan Le Fanu (CARMILLA, UNCLE SILAS) in its hothouse, almost Victorian intensity, it tells a multi-leveled story of misalliance and mixed motives. The language is darkly lyrical, and the tale is compelling. Read it; you'll be glad you did." - **Chelsea Quinn Yarbro, author of the *Saint-Germain Cycle***

"Tamara Thorne is the new wave of horror - her novels are fascinating rides into the heart of terror and mayhem." - **Douglas Clegg, New York Times bestselling author**

"Tamara Thorne has become one of those must-read horror writers. From her strong characters to her unique use of the supernatural, anything she writes entertains as much as it chills." - **Horror World**

"I was open-mouthed as the plot unfolded. This deeply psychological novel contains truly appalling revelations, and is certainly not for the faint of heart. If you are looking for an unforgettable and heart stopping read that explores the depths of human depravity then this is the book for you." - **A Reader's Review Blog**

"In their riveting new stand-alone, Thorne and Cross deconstruct the classic tropes of the Gothic thriller into a Freudian nightmare. Alfred Hitchcock would have loved MOTHER! Highly recommended!" - **Jay Bonansinga, New York Times bestselling author of *Self Storage* and *The Walking Dead: Search and Destroy*.**

Mother
Text copyright ©2016 Tamara Thorne & Alistair Cross
All Rights Reserved
Published by Glass Apple Press
Cover Design by Mike Rivera

First paperback edition May, 2016

ISBN-13: 978-1533074393
ISBN-10: 1533074399

Mother is dedicated to our own mothers,
Louise Curry and Linda Anderson,
who thankfully, are nothing like the mother in this book.

And to *her* … the mother of all mothers,
who made this novel possible.

Acknowledgements

We'd like to thank the following people, without whom this novel would not be the same.

Q.L. Pearce, for listening to us all day and always being there for us.

Berlin Malcom, for all the hard work she does on our behalf.

Libba Campbell, for being our eyes.

Mike Rivera, for waving his magic wand and turning our ideas into true works of art.

Jay Bonansinga, for being a great friend, and welcoming us into the *Walking Dead* family.

Mark Hein, for being absolutely brilliant.

Douglas Clegg, for feedback and good times.

Heather Anderson, for her impeccable attention to detail and for supporting this ongoing venture.

Robert Damien Thorne, for his infinite patience, his wonderful cooking, and his cat-daddy skills.

Chelsea Quinn Yarbro, without whom the writing world would be a very different place.

Mike Aronovitz, for rocking our blog and writing such great reviews.

Andrew Neiderman, for setting the bar ... and for being wonderful.

Kevin O'Brien, for saying yes.

Sven, for that unbreakable spirit ... you will not be forgotten.

Our feline companions, our muses: Riki, Pawpurrazzi, Sir Purrcival, Mikey, and the rest of the the feline gang, for their conditional love and scratching ability..

Gold Country, for its majestic beauty, its mists, and its inspiration.

All the guests over at Thorne & Cross: Haunted Nights LIVE!, for sharing their wit and wisdom, and being a pleasure to know.

And most of all, to *you* ... our readers.

And they say writing is a lonely business ...

The Players

**Repeat Offenders (characters who have made appearances in other Thorne & Cross novels)

CLAIRE HOLBROOK, web designer
JASON HOLBROOK, flight instructor

Residents of Morning Glory Circle
PRISCILLA MARTIN, mother to Claire and Timothy
TIMOTHY JACOB MARTIN, Priscilla's son, (deceased)
FRANKLIN MARTIN, Timothy's father (deceased)
FREDERICK MARTIN, Priscilla's husband, Claire's father, brother to Franklin Martin
BARBARA (BABS) VANDERCOOTH, friend to Priscilla
CARL VANDERCOOTH, her husband
AIDA PORTENDORFER, neighbor, friend
STAN PORTENDORFER, her husband, retired
HANK LOWELL, neighbor, owner of motorcycle shop
CRYSTAL LOWELL, his wife
HARLEY LOWELL, their son
DAVID LOWELL, their son
PHYLLIS STINE, neighbor
CLYDE STINE, her husband, retired
GENEVA-MARIE COLLINS, neighbor
BURKE COLLINS, furniture store owner and husband to Geneva-Marie
CHRIS COLLINS, their son (8)
BARRY COLLINS, their son (16)
LANCE (ACE) ETHERIDGE, neighbor, editor of the Snapdragon Daily
IRIS ETHERIDGE, neighbor, his daughter
CANDY SACHS, neighbor
MILTON SACHS, neighbor, attorney, husband to Candy
BILLY SACHS, their son
RODDY CROCKER, neighbor, police officer
BETTYANNE CROCKER, his wife
EARL DEAN, neighbor, owner of candy store
EARLENE DEAN, his wife
DELPHINE DEAN, their daughter
DAPHENE DEAN, their daughter

DUANE PRUITT, neighbor, contractor
JERRY PARK, neighbor, Duane's husband
NELLIE DUNWORTH, neighbor
BERTIE DUNWORTH, neighbor and Nellie's sister

The Church
ANDREW PIKE, priest
DAVE FLANNIGAN, retired priest and friend to Andrew
MABEL THOMPSON, church organist
FATHER PHILIP, Andy's assistant

Ladies Auxiliary
MARY BELL, Ladies Auxiliary member
LIZZIE KNUDSEN, Ladies Auxiliary member
MRS. HANNAH DEXTER, Ladies Auxiliary member
JANE, Ladies Auxiliary member

Airport
PAUL SCHUYLER, pilot, owner of flight school
BRIDGET, flight school secretary

The Doctors
STEPHANIE BANKS, psychiatrist, ex-girlfriend of Timothy's (from Brimstone)
DR. EUGENE HOPPER, physician
DR. LIGHTFOOT, physician
DR. LARA PUTNAM, physician

Around Town
QUINTON EVERETT, bank president, Little League coach
PALMER MCDONALD, mayor of Snapdragon
CHASTITY MCDONALD, his daughter
TRACEY WEATHERS, girl scout
GIUSEPPE BARTOLI, deli owner
JIMMY BAXTER, Little League member
COACH ZELLNER, high school coach of Timothy's
MRS. JOHNSON, maker of baby blankets
MR. LINDON, maker of wooden toys
TONYA WATSON, Clyde Stine's high school sweetheart
JAKE FAIRVIEW, a pilot at Schuyler's Flight School
LOUIS CANNON, founder of Snapdragon (deceased)

KELLY PORTENDORFER, Stan and Aida's child
RAYMOND PORTENDORFER, Stan and Aida's child
MRS. CROTCHLER, school teacher
MR. XTRA BIG, a phone sex client
DETECTIVE LOGAN. a local detective
BART UNDERHILL, mortician

In Pleasanton
BLANCHE, Babs' sister
DOROTHY WINCHESTER MEYERS, Babs' sister

On the Air
**COASTAL EDDIE, radio deejay
**REVEREND BOBBY FELCHER, evangelist

In the Pages
**KATHRYN MCLEOD, novelist

Honorable mentions
**GLADIOLA GELDING, friend to Phyllis Stine from Crimson Cove
SHELLY MARTIN, first wife of Frederick Martin (deceased)
**JUSTIN MARTIN, cousin to Claire (from Madelyn) (deceased)
**CONSTANCE WELLING, authoress, sister to Phyllis Stine (from Cliffside) (deceased)

Mother

by

Tamara Thorne & Alistair Cross

Glass Apple Press

Prologue: Timothy Martin

"No more," he whispered. "No more."

At twenty years old, he'd had enough. Enough pain, enough heartbreak. *She* had traveled a thousand miles to find him. And now he was once again *her* prisoner.

He stared at the prescription bottles in his hands. There were enough pain pills and tranquilizers to send him on a permanent vacation, as long as *she* didn't discover what he'd done before the train left the station.

He stared down at his broken leg. He and Steffie had been hiking one of the steep hills in Brimstone when his foot caught on an exposed root, sending him down the incline in a shower of rocks and dirt. His own body had betrayed him and when *she* came, he knew he was finished. He'd been looking over his shoulder since he'd left home, and he was tired. He would never be free.

The cast ran from his knee to his ankle, and he'd wanted crutches, but she'd insisted he use his stepfather's old wheelchair because it was a compound fracture. Half an hour ago she tried to force him into bed, saying she knew best, but he refused, claiming he wanted to look out the window.

Fuck you, Mother.

Now he turned and peered at the bedroom's open doorway. She'd had the door removed the minute she'd dragged him home, saying it was for his own safety and that she needed to keep her eye on him. His privacy was gone. Again. No freedom, no say in his own life. He thought of Steffie, her long auburn hair and deep green eyes. Hot tears burned and he wiped them away.

Mother had unplugged all the phones, but even if she hadn't he wouldn't try to call Steffie. He was humiliated, resigned. Steffie deserved better than a life with a broken man and his overpowering mother. *This isn't the way I planned it. I'm so sorry, Steffie.*

He stared at a bottle of vodka on his bedside table. *Grey Goose, nothing but the best.* The alcohol was one of the reasons he'd left in the first place - he knew he had to quit. And he had, for nearly two years. But there it was. *She'd* brought it to him, saying it would help his pain. *This time she may be right.* He shook a handful of pills onto his palm, grabbed the vodka from the table, and swallowed them. The burn satisfied. Motionless, he waited. And waited. But nothing happened. He didn't even feel sick, but he knew he'd taken enough to do the job. More than enough.

At last, he felt the first buzz of the drugs and rolled himself into the closet. He pulled the door closed behind him, and as drowsiness began its dance, he fashioned his leather belt into a noose. Where the pills might fail him, the noose would not. She would find his body before long, but he didn't care; his soul would be free. And all that mattered now was that *she* couldn't follow him.

Part 1:

The Beginning of Always

"Abandon all hope, ye who enter here!"
-Dante Alighieri, Inferno

At the Rat Trap

"I can't believe you've been talking to her behind my back." Claire Holbrook glared at her husband. "I told you, I never want to see her again!"

Jason set a stack of bills on the kitchen table. "We have a lot of debt built up. A hell of a lot."

Claire's eyes flitted to the pile of envelopes.

Jason leaned back and blew out a breath. "Our unemployment checks cover some of them, but ..." His gaze moved to Claire's abdomen.

Instinctively, she touched her stomach. He could see she was fighting back tears.

"I don't know what other choice we have." Jason stood and put an arm around his wife, surprised when she stiffened against his touch. "It would be temporary."

"She's crazy, Jason. You don't understand. There's a reason I never talk about my mother. She's certifiable."

"We'd only be there until we can get back on our feet, Claire. She's already lined me up with a job at a flight school. It's not as much as I was making as a pilot, but it's a lot better than waiting tables. I'm not in a position to turn it down."

An airline pilot working out of San Francisco International, Jason Holbrook had been living the dream until he had a small seizure - on the ground, fortunately - and was subsequently diagnosed with a mild form of epilepsy. Very mild, but still, it *was* epilepsy ... and Jason would never fly another plane. It was the greatest disappointment of his life. "We deserve better than this." He looked around the studio apartment, at the stained walls, the ratty carpet, the drooping cabinets. "This is an opportunity to start over. I think we should take it. We have to."

"But to go back to Snapdragon. To go back to ... *her.*" Claire's gaze touched the stack of unpayable bills on the chipped table top.

With her glossy chestnut hair, fair skin, and clear blue-green eyes, she looked out of place here, a sparkling diamond in a tarnished setting. "I don't want to pressure you, sweetheart," said Jason. "But we're out of options."

"I won't subject this child to her. I won't. You have no idea, Jason." Claire's hand returned to her stomach. "Your family was so nice, so normal. Mine wasn't."

Jason winced. "Well, if Mom and Dad were still around, I know they'd be happy to help, but ..." His parents had been killed in an auto accident two years before; it was a wound that had barely begun to heal.

"I wish they were around."

"Me too. But they aren't." He sighed. "We can be out of your mother's house before the baby comes. It'll be smooth sailing."

"Nothing goes smoothly with her, Jason. Nothing."

He shrugged. "Maybe she's changed. Age has a way of mellowing people. You haven't talked to her in-"

"Ten years."

"That's a long time, Claire. People change."

She shook her head. "Not her. She'll never change. Trust me on this."

"Claire, sweetheart. We've gone from living in a beautiful little house of our own in Berkeley to renting this scuzzy apartment in Oakland. We can stay here and keep looking for work-"

"I can work from anywhere, Jason. I already have a couple of clients that followed me from IMRU." When IMRU Designs shut down, Claire and Jason had taken it as a sign she should follow her dream and start her own website design business. Plus, with a baby on the way, she couldn't go job hunting. Dr. Lightfoot had warned her to take it easy - her pregnancy was moderately risky - and that meant no unnecessary stress.

"I know," he said, leading her to the couch. They sat and he put his hand over hers. She started to pull away, then stopped. A good sign. "I know, and I have every confidence that you will have a fantastic business, but it'll take time to get off the ground, and I haven't been able to find work here." *No one wants a pilot who can't fly.*

Claire looked up at him and he saw her lip tremble. He wanted to kiss it, to hold her, but knew she wouldn't like it right now; strength was too important to her. Finally, she spoke. "You said she got you a job at a flight school."

"Yes, teaching. Simulations. Everything but actual flying."

"What's the name of the business?"

"Schuyler's Flight School, and-"

"Wait, stop. Paul Schuyler?"

"You know him?"

"He was Tim's best friend. They grew up together." Claire shook her head.

She rarely spoke of her older brother. Jason knew virtually nothing about him; it was a sensitive topic, so he didn't pry. "I'd be doing what I love - or the next best thing. After I get some experience, I can parlay that into being an instructor at a big airport, or even at one of the military bases in northern California. We might be able to move back to Berkeley eventually."

"Yes, but that takes time, and I don't want to stay that long. I don't even want her to *see* our baby. Ever."

He found it hard to believe anyone could be as horrible as Claire claimed her mother was. He thought perhaps the two of them simply butted heads; it made sense that the mother would be as headstrong as the daughter. "Claire, I'll make enough money at this job in Snapdragon that it won't be too long before we can rent a place of our own. Someplace *nice*." He looked around the shoddy one-room apartment. "Not like this. A place we can live in happily with our baby until we can move back to the city."

"You don't understand, Jase. She'll do everything in her power to keep us with her."

"We won't let her, it's as simple as that." Jason took Claire's hand. "It's been a long time. She's not the woman you remember. She'll be thrilled to see you again, she told me so. She misses you - she hasn't laid eyes on you since you were seventeen!"

Claire looked unimpressed.

Jason leaned in. "We're a great team, Claire. I think we can take her." He gave her a grin, pleased when she smiled back.

"She'll try to divide us, Jason. That's what she does."

He shrugged. "We can survive her." He squeezed her hand and saw something change in her eyes. Her resolve was melting away. "It's our best move. Right now, it's our *only* move. And there's something else."

Her eyes flashed. "What?"

"It's good, don't worry." Jason smiled at her. "We wouldn't actually be living with her. She says she understands that we're a married couple and that we need our privacy, and has offered us the apartment above her garage, *rent-free*, until we're back on our feet!"

"I see." Claire looked him in the eye. "Please tell me she doesn't know I'm pregnant."

Jason took a slow breath. "I'm sorry, but I did tell her. It was a slip." He paused. "But, Claire, she was really happy about it."

Claire's eyes went dead. "No. If she didn't know, it would be bearable for a couple months, or at least until I start showing. But I can't ... I just can't." Her voice was cold, distant. "You shouldn't have told her. That was out of bounds, Jason."

"I'm sorry, sweetheart."

Her eyes blazed. Claire was hard to rouse, but her fury was god-like when ignited.

"I was wrong to say anything. It just slipped-"

She glared at him for long moments, then her expression softened. "I'm sorry, too. I've only been thinking of myself. You've been through hell.

You've had your life ripped apart." She sighed. "I wish you hadn't said anything to her about the baby, but I guess I can understand." She paused. "She probably wheedled it out of you."

"She was pretty charming, but it's my fault. I'm sorry. I would never intentionally betray our trust." He meant every word. Ever since the epilepsy diagnosis, he hadn't been the sturdy, reliable guy Claire had fallen in love with back in college. He was an emotional wreck, fighting depression from day one. He looked at her. "I'll never betray you again."

She took his hand and pulled him down to sit with her on the sofa. "Maybe we could rent a house near the airport and not tell her. It's a lot cheaper to live in Gold Country than it is in the Bay Area."

"Maybe ... but with the foreclosure, our credit is shot. We're down to one car and can barely make the payments on it. Hell, we can barely afford this rat hole. But with the new job, we can save, and rent a place before too long - six months, max."

"Six months?"

Jason nodded. "Without credit, we need to pre-pay at least that much rent, but I think we can save up *and* be out of your mother's house in that time."

She blinked at him and he saw something in her eyes he hadn't seen in months: hope. "Do you promise? Six months at the most?"

"You have my word. You're eight weeks pregnant now," he added. "That means we'll be in our own place, away from your mother, before the baby comes."

She nodded then looked around the small apartment. "We'll need a contingency plan."

"What do you mean?"

"As soon as we get there, I'm going to start looking at new places. If she tries anything, *anything* at all, we'll have an escape plan, even if we have to rent another rat trap by the week over by Snapdragon Airport." She watched a shiny brown cockroach scuttle into one of the cupboards and shivered. "Anything would be better than this."

Relief crashed over him. "I think that's a great plan, Claire." He pulled her close and kissed her forehead. She didn't pull away, so he grazed her lips with his. She put her hands on his cheeks and held him there, relaxing in his embrace. The months of worry, of constant anxiety, melted away in the span of that kiss. For the first time since losing his job at the airline, Jason Holbrook felt hope for the future.

At 3,500 Feet

"So you grew up here," Jason said as they passed another sign announcing the turnoff for Snapdragon Caverns.

"I did," Claire said. "Right here, in the middle of nowhere." On the radio, John Denver started singing about country roads taking him home. She turned it off. *Home,* she thought. While John Denver's childhood home may have been all rainbows and roses, hers was the last place she wanted to be. *Jason has no clue. How did I let him talk me into this?* The reply came unbidden: *Because there's no other choice.*

"It sure is pretty up here."

"Yeah, I guess so." Claire looked at the oaks and pines that surrounded them as they drove the twisting road through the forest. They'd reached Highway 49 nearly an hour before, passing famous gold rush towns like Sonora and Angel's Camp, then turned east on Highway 4. Just after Murphys, they'd turned off on Snapdragon Highway and were now winding further into the hills. It *was* beautiful, but with each passing mile, the knot in Claire's gut tightened and writhed.

All she could think about was seeing Mother for the first time in ten years. She hadn't planned on ever laying eyes on that woman again, let alone living on her property. Suddenly, from the dark recesses of her mind rose memories, fragmented flashes of sensations rushing her: the pungent smell of bleach, her big brother Tim in tears … and then a feeling of falling, falling. *Falling!* Instinctively, she clutched the armrest. *Slow deep breaths,* she told herself. In moments, it passed.

"You okay?" Jason glanced at her.

"Just a little nausea. It'll pass."

She looked out the window. *At least I'll get to see Dad again.* She felt bad about the way she'd treated him as a child; she'd been afraid of him because of his handicaps and she wanted to make up for that.

And then there was Aunt Babs. Claire looked forward to seeing her, more than anyone. Babs Vandercooth, a neighbor and friend of Claire's mother, was the only person in Snapdragon that Claire had kept in touch with; she was more like a mother than Priscilla Martin ever had been.

"Look!" Jason pointed. "A deer." He grinned. "Did you see it?"

His optimism was making it hard to be so glum. "I did."

"I'll bet you hiked the caverns," he said.

"Yes, but never tell Mother. When Tim was in high school, he and his girlfriend took me along on a tour. It was so much fun."

"Why can't your mother know?"

"She forbade us all to go."

"Why?"

"She claimed there was poison gas in the caverns. Even now, she'd throw a conniption if she knew we'd gone."

Jason laughed. "You're kidding."

"I swear it." She paused, fond memories of her big brother returning. "If it hadn't been for Tim, I'd never have gotten to go to a parade or a carnival or a rodeo. Having an older brother who knew how to sneak around was really great. He made life bearable. Even fun."

"I'm glad you had him as long as you did. But your mother forbidding you to go to tourist attractions? That really *is* crazy."

She smiled. "You have no idea, Jason. None."

"It wasn't all that bad, was it?"

Claire watched the trees pass by. "We'll see what you have to say about her a few weeks from now."

He chuckled and squeezed her knee. She wished she felt playful enough to squeeze his, but between the stress and the ache in her shoulder, she didn't have the energy. She winced and rolled her shoulder.

"Is it bothering you again?"

"A little." She'd had trouble with her right shoulder for as long as she could remember. It was worse when she sat still too long. "I'll take some ibuprofen if it gets worse."

She turned the radio back on and the Wilson sisters were belting out *Magic Man*. "It's your song, Magic Man," she said, cranking it up.

He laughed and gave her a wink.

When she'd met Jason in college, he really had seemed magical to her. He'd been gorgeous - he *still* was gorgeous, with broad shoulders, a sandy-blond brush cut, dimples, and blue eyes fringed by dark lashes she'd always envied. He'd been a senior, she a sophomore, but the moment they met, their chemistry had been undeniable. He was five years older, a pilot in the Navy Reserves, and he'd come back to college because he needed a bachelor's degree to follow his dream of becoming a pilot for a major airline. Claire herself was carrying a heavy class load and working full-time - she had been ever since running away from Mother the day after she received her high school diploma. Her field was art and design, and she was good at it, in part because Mother used to go through her room and throw all her drawings in the fireplace. In retrospect, she knew it had been a good thing - it had fueled her desire to be the best graphic artist she could possibly be - but she still resented Mother's invasions of her privacy ... and wasn't looking forward to more of them. She shivered.

Claire and Jason had moved in together six months after meeting, and got married as soon as Jason graduated and landed a full-time job at the airline. She continued her studies, graduated with honors, and was soon employed as well. Two years after college, they bought their beautiful little cottage in Berkeley and two new cars. Life was good, and the future was bright.

And then, IMRU, the Silicon Valley company she worked for, went out of business and laid off a hundred graphic artists and designers, herself included. It didn't seem so bad at first, because Jason made good money and encouraged her to start her own business - he knew that was what she really wanted - so they tightened their belts a little and worked hard.

And then, last June, Jason had his first seizure. That was a death sentence for a pilot. They soon lost the house and sold nearly everything they owned trying to pay bills, eventually ending up in the scuzzy Oakland apartment. Jason was working as a waiter in a posh San Francisco restaurant and she took a waitressing job nearby because they'd sold her little white Neon to make a few more house payments. They'd been fools to do that.

Now everything they owned was in the Prius and the small U-Haul trailer they towed. The last of their furniture had been sold before leaving Oakland - they didn't want to bring any cockroaches along.

She glanced at Jason. His medication nearly guaranteed he wouldn't have another seizure, but that meant nothing to the FAA. He'd become depressed, so she'd put on a happy face - even tried to convince him - and herself - that a little adversity would be good for them. There was unemployment, and her business was coming together, after all.

And then she'd missed her period.

That changed everything.

Magic Man wrapped up as they passed the exit to the caverns and Jason turned the volume down. "Are you nervous?"

It wouldn't be long before they hit the town limits. "Yes. I just keep telling myself it's for six months or less. Preferably a *lot* less."

"Remember, if it's intolerable, we'll find an apartment."

"And we won't tell her where it is, right?"

"That's the deal." They were at 3,500 feet now - the sign said they were at Snapdragon Summit - and they began a slow descent into the valley. He took two more curves and then Snapdragon came into view at the 2,800-foot mark.

Claire's stomach roiled and her heart pounded in time with a sudden headache. The pain in her shoulder flared hot and bright.

"I'm sorry we have to do this, sweetheart."

Father Andy's Fundraiser

Father Andrew Pike strolled among the booths set up in the Holy Sacramental Catholic Church's school auditorium, smiling and nodding, greeting and talking. His congregation was nothing if not loyal, and many had turned out to sell their wares to help raise funds for new hymnals, bibles, and choir robes. He was very proud of his flock.

All around him, pies and cookies were flying off tables. Homemade jams and chutneys were selling like bibles in purgatory, and Mrs. Johnson's hand-stitched baby blankets were nearly gone - and it wasn't even three o'clock yet. Mr. Lindon's wooden toys sold well even though Christmas had just passed, and Babs Vandercooth's patchwork animals were selling out. She'd even sold two of her beautiful patchwork quilts before noon.

Truly, the economy had improved. Just a few years ago, the Winter Wonderland Charity Sale had brought in only two hundred dollars. Today, the sellers had surpassed that in less than an hour, probably because Priscilla Martin had taken over the Internet and newspaper publicity for the event this year. She'd even talked Ace Etheridge, the *Snapdragon Daily*'s publisher, into donating ad space in every issue. It didn't hurt that he was a nominal member of the congregation, of course, but he'd never been so generous before Priscilla twisted his arm. Father Andy smiled. Priscilla had recently taken a class on building websites so that she could turn Holy Sacramental's outdated site into an attractive, welcoming place for online visitors. He was sure the new website was another reason the Winter Wonderland sale was so crowded. Even out-of-towners had come this year.

As he neared Priscilla Martin's jewelry booth, he was surprised to see Phyllis Stine, in her signature jangling plastic bracelets and calf-high go-go boots, manning the table. He was even more surprised to see that Geneva-Marie Collins' counter neighbored Priscilla's; it seemed a sign they might be getting along. Priscilla had been the president of the Ladies' Auxiliary and leader and organizer of most of the charity work done in the name of Holy Sacramental since the time of Andy's predecessor, Father Dave Flannigan. This did not please Geneva-Marie, who wanted to guide the Ladies Auxiliary herself.

A spicy, seductive aroma brought him to a stop. He greeted Giuseppe Bartoli, who was selling pasta salads and fine deli meats imported from his store in town.

"Father Andy, come have a taste of my antipasto salad. I know how much you like it."

"Gladly!"

Giuseppe scooped a big spoonful of salad into a sample cup, stuck a spork in it, and handed it to Andy, who tasted it and closed his eyes. "It's heavenly, Giuseppe. Please save a quart for me, won't you?"

"I will, Father." Giuseppe smiled, then went to help a customer.

"Father!"

The priest turned at the sound of Quinton Everett's voice. "Why Quinton, how good of you to come today!"

"My pleasure, Father Andy." The president of Snapdragon Bank and Trust had forsaken his usual charcoal suit and silk tie for Dockers and a Ralph Lauren Polo shirt. He smiled, showing even white teeth. His dark hair had such a perfect sprinkling of gray at each temple that Andy suspected he had it done at the barbershop.

Father Andy smiled. "And what are you shopping for today?"

"I'm afraid I don't have time to shop - I'm taking the Little League out for pizza. We're going to do a little pre-season planning - but I have something for you." Quinton reached into his back pocket and extracted his wallet. "This is for new surplices for the altar boys." He handed a check to Andy. "We can't forget them, now can we, Father?"

Andy accepted the check, shocked at the amount. "Quinton, this is *very* generous of you."

"I want them to have the best." Quinton smiled. "The very best."

"This will buy at least fifty surplices. May we use the overage toward choir robes?"

Quinton Everett's eyes darted back and forth in that odd way he had. "As long as it's for the boys, Father, use the excess however you see fit."

"I'll do that, Quinton. Thank you." He watched the banker head for the exit. The man often made Andy uncomfortable in a way he couldn't quite define. He wished his mentor, Father Flannigan, was here to discuss it but since he'd resigned he avoided most events. Though Andy had been in charge of the church for several years now, he still felt wet behind the ears, and his boyish looks didn't help any.

He headed over to Priscilla Martin's jewelry table.

"Hello, Father," said Phyllis Stine. She was a gangly woman who favored puffy platinum hair and the mold-blue eye shadow of the sixties. Her face was stretched so tight it was alarming. He suspected it was as plastic as her bangle bracelets.

"Good afternoon, Phyllis." Andy looked at the stack of brightly colored booklets at the table's edge. The top one's title was *Kiss of the Wild Crystal*, the author listed as Constance Welling. It showed a woman touching her lips to a purple hunk of quartz. "What are these, may I ask?" He picked up the top one. The next one down was called *My Crystal and Me* and showed a poorly drawn child peering at a glowing stone.

"Oh, I hope you don't mind, Father. I'm trying to sell some of these - for the charity of course. My little sister died earlier this year - she was *murdered!*"

"I'm so sorry."

"Anyway," Phyllis plowed on in her mile-a-minute way, "She was a writer and she had this huge estate that she left to me but after paying off all her bills, all they had left to send me were a couple pallets of her books."

Father Andy eyed the stack dubiously. "Of course. I'm sorry for your loss."

"Oh, it's okay, Father. Constance was probably asking for it. She never was what you'd call a 'good girl.'"

"Still, she was your sister. And murdered. I'll say a mass for her if you'd like."

"That's very sweet of you, but she'd hate that. She was one of those New Age nuts, you know?"

Ill at ease, Andy changed the subject. "Is Priscilla on a break?"

Phyllis shook her head, plastic hoops clicking. "No, she left early. Her daughter's coming to town."

"I didn't realize she had a daughter."

"Oh, yes. Her name is Carlene. She moved away long before you were on the scene. It's been ten years since any of us have seen her. Hopefully, she's better behaved these days. Prissy said she was *quite* a trial back then."

Father Andy nodded and looked down at the chunky jewelry on the table. Jewelry-making was Priscilla's hobby and she was good at it, though it wasn't to his taste. Unlike Phyllis' plastic persuasions, much of Priscilla's jewelry involved large beads that he privately thought were better suited to Wilma Flintstone. And the rest of the accessories, well, honestly, he found them unnerving.

As a priest, he possessed intimate understanding of relics, religious and otherwise, and Priscilla's human hair necklaces and bracelets reminded him of such sacramentals. She did beautiful work, beading the hair with complimentary colors, showing it to its best advantage, but she always wore one piece that put him off: a necklace made from the golden locks of her long-deceased son, Timothy. Andy knew she missed the boy, but it didn't seem healthy - he'd been gone for twenty years.

Priscilla's hair chain was slender, braided and studded with tiny gold beads. Fourteen karat. He wished she hadn't told him she'd crafted it *after* Timothy died.

Andy had been squeamish about physical relics ever since he was a boy, and he knew it was irrational. He told himself Priscilla was simply a woman who kept a reminder of her son near her heart, that it was an example of her ability to create beauty where others found only darkness. His own church was laden with sacramentals and relics far more gruesome. But somehow, it didn't seem like the same thing.

Resisting the urge to cross himself, Father Andrew moved on, smiling and nodding, greeting and talking.

Mark Twain Slept Here

The voice came at her from blackness, insistent, and hissing: *"Touch them! Touch them!"*

"No," Claire said. Images flashed: nylon rope, a looming black shadow, a tear slipping from a frightened blue eye.

"Touch them!"

Someone yanked her arm. Claire pulled back. *"No!"*

"Touch them, Carlene! Touch them!"

Another hard yank, and searing pain shot through her arm, blazing into her shoulder. In the dream, Claire screamed. But still ... she would not touch them ... whatever *they* were.

"Touch them!"

"No!"

A new voice, louder and deeper, snapped her eyes open. "Claire? Are you okay, sweetheart?"

Cool sweat chilled her forehead. She was in the car. With Jason. She was safe. *Just a dream.* But it was more than that. Something dark and unsettling hovered just beyond her reach. And then ... it was gone.

Jason glanced at her. "I think you were having a nightmare, sweetie."

"I'm fine." Her voice was thin.

"We're in town."

She sat up and loosened the seat belt, ignoring the tremble in her hands, the ache in her shoulder.

Snapdragon looked as quaint and lost in time as it had a decade ago. As they left the highway and turned onto Main Street, a blast of nausea hit her. She uncapped a bottle of ginger ale and took a long pull, her shoulder aching more now than it had in years. Bruce Springsteen sang about taking *Thunder Road.* Inspired, she rolled down the window and let the wind blow her hair back. The cold air felt good on her face.

"You okay, honey?" Jason glanced at her.

"I'm fine," she lied.

"I'm pretty anxious myself," he said. "How's your shoulder?"

"I'll live."

"You look a little-"

"It's just morning sickness. Afternoon sickness, actually." She knew he was only trying to be supportive. "I'm sorry, Jason. I know I'm terrible company. I'm just so tired all the time. And really nervous right now." She stifled a burp then took another big swallow of ginger ale, concentrating on the feel of the bubbles burning in her throat. "Sorry," she said, and let the burp go free.

He laughed. "I dare you to do that in front of your mother."

"I just might. What's in it for me?"

"The pleasure of pissing her off."

"I could do that anytime." She laughed. "But let's not talk about her anymore. Let's talk about something fun."

He pointed at the festooned banner bridging Main Street. "We could go to the Valentine's Day Rodeo," he said. "Watching cowboys breaking their necks sounds pretty fun to me. And romantic." He wiggled his eyebrows. "What do you think?"

Claire snorted and squeezed his hand. "Now I remember why I married you. You're insanely romantic."

Jason shrugged. "I just know how much you love dead cowboys. Do they have a lot of rodeos in Snapdragon?"

"They're constant. The four biggies draw the tourists, though. Valentine's Day is one of them." She nodded at the next banner. "It's one of our many Gold Rush Days."

"Isn't it a little chilly for a rodeo?"

"It doesn't matter because it's the celebration of a historical event. January 24th, 1848," Claire recited. "James W. Marshall found gold at Sutter's Mill in Coloma. Then, on January 22nd, 1849, Louis Cannon found gold here in Snapdragon. Christ, it seems like that's all we ever heard about in school." She pointed at one of the looming false front buildings lining downtown Main Street. "Right there, in front of the bank. See him?"

"The statue of the man and the mule?"

"The very one. That's Louis Cannon."

"Kind of a reprobate-looking fella."

"You bet. It's said Snapdragon became a town so quickly because he spent so much money on whiskey and hookers that the town became incredibly prosperous while it was still made mostly of tents."

"Seriously?"

"That's what they say."

Jason drove slowly, minding the speed limit and gawking at the Old West architecture. Old Downtown, she had to admit, was scenic. Snapdragon was proud of its past, proud too of its survival when so many other boomtowns had turned into ghosts. Then the bright yellow arches of a McDonald's appeared, the restaurant itself hiding like a hermit crab in an Old West building.

Icy dread touched Claire's spine. She hated McDonald's, and it wasn't the food, it was Ronald McDonald himself. She'd been terrified of clowns since she was a child, thanks to the garish portraits Mother had hung in her room. Every night, she'd felt their big, glinting eyes on her when the lights went out. She shuddered.

"Don't worry. We won't eat there," said Jason, grinning.

That was another reason she'd fallen for the guy: When she'd told him all about her idiot fear, back when they were dating, he never made fun of her for it. "Thanks." Claire cleared her throat and continued on, tour-guide style. "Anyway, Snapdragon was part of the gold rush in the mid-1800s. After its short days as a boomtown, the lake and railroad kept it from becoming a ghost, and while it had dwindled to a few hundred souls, it never entirely died. Then, in the late 1960s, builders came in and established new neighborhoods full of curving streets lined with expensive tract houses and well-behaved trees."

And it was then that Mother and her husband bought the biggest house on Morning Glory Circle, the best cul-de-sac in town.

Naturally.

Jason laughed. "I see."

"And there's the Snapdragon Hotel." She pointed at a big red brick and yellow clapboard structure on the corner of Main and Magnolia. "It dates back to 1857 and it's claimed that Mark Twain slept there regularly."

"We're in Calaveras County ... Maybe he did."

"Maybe." Claire concentrated on history, trying to keep her mind off Mother, who was barely a mile away now. Her stomach was a twisting snake pit. "The hotel also claims Wyatt Earp gambled there on numerous occasions."

"Yeah, but is there *any* place out west where Wyatt Earp *didn't* gamble?"

"Nope. I don't think so." Claire sipped the last of her ginger ale and admired the old building. "I went inside once with a friend, back in elementary school. Lori's mom took us to lunch there at the Daffodil Grill. They had glass lamps hanging above the tables, all painted with flowers - snapdragons, daisies, lilies, roses; they were all different - and they had long glass crystals hanging from them that cast rainbows on the carpet and tablecloths. I was entranced."

"How was the food?"

"Divine. We had burgers and old-fashioned ice cream sodas in silver goblets. I felt like a princess."

"That settles it." Jason pulled a quick right on Magnolia and parked. "We're having lunch at the Daffodil Grill."

"We can't afford to, can we?"

"If your mother is as horrendous as you say, we can't afford *not* to. We need sustenance to face the beast." He gave her a peck on the cheek. "I love you, you know."

"Back at'cha, Magic Man." Claire rubbed her shoulder.

"I'll give you a shoulder rub tonight." Jason grinned.

"That would be awesome."

The Lawn Wars

"That's not even Pookie Bear's poop!" Aida Portendorfer huffed. "I think that's Waldo's."

"Waldo?" Stan couldn't identify his own dog's droppings, let alone keep all the neighbor dogs' names straight.

"Oh, Stan, you know!" She pointed at the pale olive two-story traditional on the other side of the street. "Waldo is Duane Pruitt's golden retriever. His poops are bigger than our Pookie Bear's! And paler, too. I wonder what Duane feeds him. Maybe I should suggest he take Waldo in for a checkup. He might be having another bout of pancreatitis."

Stan stifled a groan. He dearly loved his wife of forty-odd years, even though Aida couldn't resist sticking her nose in everybody's business. Gossip was her lifeblood and everyone on the sac knew it. She'd asked for binoculars for Christmas again this year and, reluctantly, he'd finally buckled.

Just as he'd expected, she now spent a lot of time upstairs, peering into neighbors' windows and commenting on the state of their housekeeping and the color of their furniture, which was never right for the carpeting.

"Are you listening to me, Stan?"

"I think Duane can take care of his dog without your advice, Aida."

"Hmm. I suppose. He's very handsome, isn't he? He takes good care of himself and that must mean he takes good care of Waldo."

"I'm sure." Stan stared at Duane Pruitt's house. Aida was right: Duane - who had recently married a nice Korean man named Jerry - was very neat. Before Jerry came along, Stan hadn't even suspected the ruggedly handsome contractor was light in the loafers. His husband Jerry spent a lot of time jogging shirtless, even in winter. Stan liked him, too; he was always smiling and friendly.

"Stan? Are you listening to me?"

"Yes, Aida-honey. Duane keeps his yard very nice."

"No, I asked you to go make sure Waldo is in Duane's yard. I think this is his poop and it's not like Duane to let him run around loose."

"Then how do you know what his poop looks like, honey?"

She sighed. "Because we talked about it, Stan. Don't you remember? At the Morning Glory Street Fair last October. You were there."

"Sorry, I guess I wasn't listening." He needed a respite from his wife. Now. "Aida-honey, I'm going to take a little walk. I need some exercise."

"You go ahead without me," she said, as if she ever came along. "I'm getting the snapdragon bed ready now, you know that. Our seeds have sprouted and I want to get them into the ground and out of the guest room as soon as the weather permits. We're going to win first prize in this year's Morning Glory Circle Snapdragon Contest." She put her hands on her plump hips and turned to stare three doors down at Prissy Martin's big white house. She eyed the freshly-painted shutters edging the windows, stared at the tall flagpole that waved American, POW, and MIA flags. Below those were California's golden bear flag and the Snapdragon flag.

Stan suppressed a grin. Aida wanted to win that Snapdragon flag more than anything, but if she won it, she'd insist he erect a flagpole. *Probably an inch taller than Prissy's, too.* When it came to pissing contests, his Aida had more to prove than any man. He glanced at her half-hoed flower bed and wondered if the dog with the pale poop liked to dig up gardens, too.

"We'll win, Stan," she said. "Oh, we'll win big this year." She smiled proudly. "Red, white, and blue snaps blooming in the biggest American flag on the block! Prissy Martin will turn purple with envy." She looked at the huge rectangular patch of garden that had replaced the lawn. "It will be grand."

"Okay, Aida-honey, that's nice. I'm going for my walk now." He turned.

"Stan?"

"What?" He tried to sound pleasant.

"If you happen to see Burke Collins, would you ask him if he's going to barbecue for the Presidents' Day block party next month?"

"Sure," he called over his shoulder. Burke Collins was a little too full of himself for Stan's taste, but he supposed he was a nice enough guy, especially if you enjoyed your liquor. Burke's Kalamazoo barbecue cost thousands and he liked to show it off. He called it the Rolls Royce of grills.

"When you pass Prissy Martin's house, see if you can tell if she's fertilized her flower beds yet."

"Okie-dokie." He waved without looking back. He passed the Stine home, a neat two-story traditional painted the same blue as the eye shadow Phyllis Stine favored. Well-tended white roses and neat box hedges eased the pain of the color considerably, though Aida vehemently disagreed. Next, as the cul-de-sac began its narrow turn, came the Halloween House - that's what Aida and Prissy called it. Hank and Crystal Lowell, their rambunctious kids, and their standard poodles lived there. Hank owned a motorcycle shop. *Nice guy.* Crystal was nice too, once you got past that lipstick-red dye job on her head. *Nice from the neck down, though.* The mouthwatering scent of barbecue wafted from the Lowell's backyard as *Surfin' Bird* played and the kids whooped and hollered, splashing in the heated pool.

Next, sitting center stage on Morning Glory Circle, was Prissy Martin's coiffed two-story Federalist, white clapboard, red brick chimneys, and classic black shutters fronted by the only green grass in January on the cul-de-sac. *AstroTurf.* It was as neat and clipped as Prissy herself and her flags fluttered so high and proud that the sac called it the White House. He continued on without sniffing her flowerbeds for fertilizer. Aida could do that herself.

He passed Milton and Candy Sachs' two stories of cotton candy fluff. *Poor Prissy, stuck between the Lowells' pumpkiny paint job and Candy's pink taffy apple one. Between the colors and those noisy dogs - not to mention Crystal's hair and tattoos - Prissy must be fit to be tied.*

He passed by Duane and Jerry's home and their pale-stooled dog wagged his tail in greeting from behind the white wrought iron gate. He glanced across the street and saw Aida's broad behind as she weeded her patriotic flower bed. He looked away before she noticed him. Sighing, he thought of those tight, tattered jeans she used to wear with her tight tie-dyed tank tops. Those were the days.

Next came the Collins' huge home and Stan was pleased to see no sign of Burke. Before they'd remodeled, Prissy's house had been the biggest on the street; but Burke and Geneva-Marie had recently turned their two-story traditional into a Spanish hacienda, even adding a second story to their three-car garage. Beautiful as it was, it stood out like a sore thumb on the cul-de-sac full of Federal, Colonial, and other traditional American styles. He nodded to young Billy Sachs who delivered papers, mowed lawns, and washed cars in the neighborhood. Today, Billy was waxing Geneva-Marie's pearl white Escalade.

Billy was a great kid, lucky to be adopted by such attractive, well-to-do parents. His mom, Candy, was as statuesque and beautiful as any model, plus she was friendly, fun, and addicted to soap operas. She didn't seem to have a brain in her head, but she was sweet like a little puppy dog. He liked her almost as much as he liked looking at her, even if she was taller than he was.

Stan continued on, passing Babs and Carl Vandercooth's oyster gray Colonial. They were good people, the Vandercooths. Next was Ace Etheridge's light turquoise house. The editor of the *Snapdragon Daily* was a widower, but his grown daughter, Iris, had been living with him since her divorce five years earlier. Her radio blared and that pretty Adele woman belted out that she was sorry for breaking someone's heart. *Nice voice on that one.*

Iris was watering, her blond hair in a ponytail, wearing denim cut-offs that accentuated her long legs. *Looking good, Iris.* As if reading his thoughts, she turned and waved. He waved back. She wore a light blue sweatshirt in deference to winter. In summer, she was even more fun when she waved.

He crossed the street - Daisy Drive - and passed by the Crockers' corner home. His belly growled as he scented more barbecuing meat. Roddy and Bettyanne had painted their simple home in a green so light it was almost white. It made a nice backdrop for Bettyanne's massive flower beds. Even this time of year, they bloomed in radiant blues and purples. Bettyanne had the greenest thumb in the neighborhood. Not only that, she was a pretty little thing, with golden curls that made her look like an innocent child. She and Roddy - an officer on the Snapdragon police force - had no children, just the flowers, and a pair of fluffy white cats that sat sunning themselves inside their picture window. *Nice people, the Crockers.* It was good to have a cop living on the street, too.

The Dunworth sisters lived next to the Crockers and their yard could have used some of Bettyanne's green thumb. *Nice ladies, the Dunworths. And such sweet voices, too.* He saw Nelly Dunworth - a medically obese woman in her forties at least once a day as she rode her scooter around the cul-de-sac; it was nice she could get out.

Next to the Dunworths lived his own next-door neighbors, Earl Dean and his wife Earlene, and their twin daughters, Daphene and Delphine. "The Shining Twins," Morning Glory Circle called them. Privately, of course. Earl might be the best chocolatier this side of the Rockies - his candy shop, The Fudge Depot, had been written up as a must-visit in *Westways* - but he wasn't a terribly likable fellow. Not only was Earl a grouch, but on more than one occasion, Stan had seen him relieving himself against the wall that separated their yards. Earl had caught Stan staring once and the man didn't even have the courtesy to look embarrassed - he just kept on urinating, whistling *Row, Row, Row Your Boat,* as if it were the most natural thing in the world.

It was a matter of time before poor Aida witnessed Earl's acts of indecency. She'd be scandalized. *My how my girl has changed!* She used to love peeing in the woods and he couldn't help smiling to himself at the thought of her catching Earl hosing down the hedges. All of Morning Glory Circle would know within the hour, of that he was certain. *And that's karma for you.*

Just then, the Deans' side gate opened and the twins came out, holding hands. In their free hands, each clutched a melting hunk of fudge. Daphi and Delphi Dean, in matching white shirts, plaid skirts, and shiny Mary Janes, stared vacantly as Stan strolled past, their cottage-cheese complexions glowing in the afternoon sun.

"Hello, girls."

"Do you like fudge, Mister?" One of them asked.

The other one giggled.

"Why, sure," said Stan. "Everyone likes fudge."

Their smiles fell, their too-close eyes appraising him as if he'd failed to get whatever joke they'd been trying to tell.

The one on the left whispered to the one on the right, and together, they turned and fled.

Sweet girls. Strange, but sweet. Odd little things.

As Stan approached his own home - a nice yellow Colonial - he saw Aida staring at him from the living room window. Once he entered, she wasted no time.

"Did you see Prissy's flowerbeds?" She plunked her binoculars down on the foyer table. Their miniature collie, Pookie Bear, barked and wagged his tail as if Stan had been gone for hours.

Aida followed Stan into the living room. He took the paper off the side table, and settled into his brown leather La-Z-Boy. "Nope."

"Where's Waldo?" Aida demanded. "Is he locked up?"

"I didn't see him, Aida-honey."

"Well, did you see any dog poop on any of the other lawns? Was any of it pale, like Waldo's?"

"Didn't see a thing."

Aida returned to her post at the window. "I just know it was Waldo." She paused. "Stanny, can you smell it? I'm making your very favorite dinner tonight. Beef stew with little red potatoes and baby carrots and okra, just the way you like it."

"That's great, Aida-honey. Thank you." Stan opened the paper to the sports section, his mouth watering. Prissy Martin might have the best snapdragons, but Aida, he was sure, was the best cook on the sac.

Run for Your Life

"That was the best ice cream soda I've ever had." Jason signaled and pulled back onto Main Street.

"It was almost as good as the burger. I won't eat again for a week!" Claire glanced at the clock on the dashboard. "Oh crap, it's past four."

"So?"

"Mother."

"What about her?"

"She'll be making dinner - and she insists five o'clock is the dinner hour. I didn't even think about that."

"Maybe we can talk her into holding off until seven or eight. You're pregnant. You'll be able to eat again by then."

Claire gave Jason a grave look. "Mother serves dinner at five, and there are no exceptions. It's been that way as far back as I can remember. And woe unto anyone who dares challenge Mother's laws."

Jason gave her a sidelong glance and a skeptical smile. "You're a grown woman now. I can't imagine she'll be that uncompromising."

Claire snorted. "You haven't met her yet." She felt better than she had all day. The food had given her a big boost.

"Well, if she is, just tell her to fuck off."

Claire laughed. "Jason! You *do* understand how I feel!"

"I'll support you all the way. You know that." He gave her the sly, sexy grin she'd fallen in love with - the one that still made her heart beat faster. She decided it was good that some things never changed. Claire glanced at the clock again and then out the window.

"You need to give me directions now, sweetheart," Jason said.

"Turn around, get back on the highway, and head for San Francisco."

"Very funny."

"Okay, okay. Stay on Main for another mile. We have to head for the 'new' part of town."

"New? There's something new here?" Jason grinned.

"We're going out to the 1970s new, Mother's neighborhood." She grimaced. "I can't believe you talked me into this." Her mood threatened to go dark, but she steadfastly refused to allow it. "When you see Chrysanthemum Avenue, turn left. It'll wind around; just follow it until we reach the four-way signal. Then turn right on Petunia."

"Jeez, what's with all the flowers?"

"You ask that in a town named Snapdragon? Listen, babe, this place is all about the flowers. They have snapdragon-growing contests on individual streets. Mother always wins. Then they have the Snapdragon Festival. You'll love that. She'll try to make us go because she always enters the town-wide contest too."

"She ever win?"

"Every fucking year."

Jason burst into laughter and Claire joined in until she had to wipe away tears.

"And what happens if she doesn't win?"

"We don't know. We've never seen that. But it would be bad. Apocalypse-bad. There's Chrysanthemum. Make the turn." Her laughter died and the queasiness returned.

Little had changed. The huge old university stood in stateliness in the middle of a massive park full of naked oaks and green pines. Claire remembered the huge white columns fronting the building - and a new memory floated to the surface: Mother telling her they used to tie bad people to the pillars and whip them. This was always followed by a warning to behave. "*Monster*," she muttered.

"What?"

"Nothing."

"Is that a courthouse?"

"No. It's Langhorne University."

"Wow, that's a pretty big deal - I didn't realize Langhorne was in Snapdragon. A lot of famous people have gone there."

"Yeah, it's known for its writers' residency programs. And its art, drama and music colleges are the best. They used to have art shows on the grounds a couple weekends every month. I bet they still do. Snapdragon is a big old artist colony at heart."

"It's beautiful. We should picnic there - look at all the benches." He smiled. "We could feed the squirrels."

"Maybe. Careful, the road's going to narrow and get really curvy in a second."

They left Old Downtown. The neighborhood around the courthouse was still full of the huge Victorians that had fascinated her as a child. She'd begged Mother to let her sketch them, but Mother hated the area and wouldn't take her. It was jealousy, Claire knew. Mother wanted to live there, in a fine mansion, but couldn't afford it - and she hated what she couldn't have.

They drove the winding road through more modest neighborhoods, from smaller Victorians to California Bungalows and then simpler newer homes of stucco or clapboard. Claire closed her eyes, taking deep breaths. *I hope Jason's right. I hope she's changed. Please let her be different.* Finally, they arrived at a four-way signal. "Here's Petunia." She wished she hadn't eaten the ice cream. "Turn right." They were almost there. *Oh God ... I don't think I can do it.* She steeled herself and stared out the window.

Petunia was mostly countryside, dotted with ranch-style homes and small farmhouses spaced far apart. Many had signs advertising fresh eggs or apples and pears for sale. Finally, they came to Daisy Drive. Claire cringed, her panic burgeoning.

"Are you all right?"

She hadn't realized he'd been watching her. "I'm fine." But her hands were tight, white fists in her lap. *What are we doing?* The feeling of dread was overwhelming.

"It's just a few months," said Jason. "I promise."

Claire closed her eyes. *This is a mistake.* She flipped the radio on, countering the heavy silence. *Run for Your Life,* sang the Beatles.

You've got to be kidding me. Claire shut the radio off.

Think of This as Revenge

The instant Jason turned on to Morning Glory Circle, he wanted to hum *Pleasant Valley Sunday*. He cruised the cul-de-sac slowly, heading toward the big white house presiding over the rest of the street. Claire said nothing, but her knuckles were bloodless.

As they approached her mother's house, he saw a portly woman hoeing a huge flower bed where most people kept lawns. He glanced at Claire, then sang, "There's Mrs. Green, she's serene because her roses aren't in bloom. Yet."

Claire didn't crack a smile. Her face was paper-white. He squeezed her hand. "Anticipation is the worst, sweetheart, and the worst is almost over."

She nodded, barely, but said nothing. That was a bad sign. He wanted her to say something caustic about her mother, to come out swinging. When Claire didn't rise to a remark, it meant something was truly bothering her.

"After we get on our feet, you'll never see the woman again if you don't want to. And she'll never lay eyes on our baby. I give you my word."

Claire nodded.

They passed a house the color of bread mold and he began pulling over in front of a dark pumpkin-colored one, then stopped directly in front of Priscilla Martin's stately black-shuttered beast of a home and shut off the engine. "Think of this as revenge," he told his wife, praying for a response.

"What?" she asked. "What do you mean, revenge?"

"We're using her, then we're leaving. That's all this is."

Slowly, her mouth rose in a half-assed smile. She looked him in the eye. "I love you. You always know what to say."

He leaned across and kissed her.

Claire straightened her spine and opened the car door.

The first thing he noticed was the lawn. It was as green as shamrocks.

"It's AstroTurf. It'll really skin your knees," she said, her tone was flat and dry. She wavered and steadied herself against the car.

"Are you okay?"

"It's just the pregnancy. It always happens when I stand too fast."

"Low blood pressure?"

She nodded, got her bearings, and squared her shoulders.

As they walked toward the house, Jason put a hand to her back. She was rigid, her eyes fixed and her chin raised. Passing a freshly painted lawn jockey, they ascended several broad cement stairs. Jason gave her a reassuring look.

At the door, Claire thunked the golden eagle knocker down hard. Jason wasn't sure she was breathing. Despite all his efforts to assure Claire that they were doing the right thing, it occurred to him now that perhaps they weren't, that Priscilla Martin might be a monster after all … that they might be making a grave mistake.

When the door opened, Claire stiffened.

Priscilla Martin stood, eyes wide, hands raised to her mouth. She was much smaller than Jason had expected; maybe five-feet four-inches, with coiffed black hair, flawless makeup, eyes wet with tears, and smooth pale skin like Claire's. In her powder blue blouse and matching pants, she didn't *look* like a monster.

"Oh, Carlene." Priscilla stepped onto the porch and embraced her daughter, tears rolling. "Carlene, oh, Carlene. My baby."

Claire was as rigid as a metal beam. "It's Claire now, Mother."

Priscilla nodded. "Yes. Of course." She squeezed her daughter hard. "I promise I'll do my best to respect your wishes. You never did like the name I gave you. I wish I'd made a better choice."

To Jason's surprise, Claire gave her mother an awkward pat on the back before breaking the embrace. Priscilla appraised her daughter, and in the strained silence, Jason heard *Don't Sit Under the Apple Tree* playing softly within the house.

Priscilla turned soft, watery eyes to Jason. They were a disturbingly pale shade of amber. Despite them, the woman had surely been a beautiful young girl. Priscilla opened her arms. "Jason," she said. He hesitated, then stepped into her hug and she embraced him. The powerful smell of *Opium* perfume overwhelmed him. "It's so nice to finally meet you in person. You're as handsome as you sounded on the phone." Priscilla patted his back then stepped aside. "Come in, come in."

Claire and Jason stepped into Priscilla Martin's living room.

***

And the Oscar goes to Priscilla Martin for best use of waterproof mascara in her flawless performance of The Saccharine Symphony for a Son-in-Law. Claire watched Mother flutter around Jason - the way Tinkerbell fluttered around Peter Pan - then looked over the big living room. It hadn't changed any more than Mother had, though it was obvious that the cornflower-colored rug had been upgraded, the creamy walls kept freshly painted, and the furniture - stark 1970s-style couches and chairs she remembered from her earliest days - had been reupholstered with fabrics and colors matching the originals. From Mother's record player, the Andrews Sisters droned on and on. Claire had forgotten that staple of her childhood.

The same Colonial maple coffee and end tables gleamed with lemony polish that vied for dominance with Mother's perfume, and the table and pole lamps were pristine with the same plastic-covered ballerina-ruffled shades that were popular generations ago. The shades were many and all were yellow, cornflower, or cotton-candy pink, just like the furniture. The walls were covered with paintings and needlework featuring snapdragons in colors as pastel as the lampshades and rug. Bouquets of silk snapdragons were placed wherever there was space. It looked like a clown had thrown up in the living room.

Being here was like stepping into the past, and in the periphery of her mind, a vague and unsettling memory played hide-and-seek with her. Her stomach twisted as the acrid scent of bleach overwhelmed her senses. She glanced at Jason - he was oblivious. And then the odor was gone - as if it had never existed. *Just my imagination.*

She looked at the mantelpiece over the red brick fireplace on the narrow end of the room. Above it was a gold-bronze metal bald eagle clock. The wingspan was at least a yard and its talons clutched an enameled green laurel. Its breast was emblazoned with an American flag which was mostly hidden by the clock face. Hideous didn't begin to cover it. When she was little, it had terrified her. She was convinced the eagle flew through the house at night and peeked in everyone's bedrooms. If it caught you awake, it would peck your eyes out.

The long-forgotten memory emerged unbidden - Mother had told her that to keep her in bed at night. And Claire'd told her big brother about it. One day when Mother wasn't home, Tim had taken the eagle off the wall and showed her the back, where it had batteries and said, "Made in Taiwan." He'd told her that if she was still afraid, he'd take the batteries out every night so the eagle couldn't come after her. She glared at her mother. *Monster.*

And then there was Tim. She tried not to think about him because when she did, tears came, and she did *not* cry. Would not. He was ten when she was born and after her father's accident, Tim had become a father figure. He'd kept her sane - until he lost his own sanity.

Tears imminent, she turned her gaze to the mantelpiece. The soldiers - little hand-painted porcelain figurines dressed in Naval blues and whites - were complete with gold detailing and red piping. Lined up by the dozens on either side of the framed veteran burial flag resting directly beneath the big eagle, the soldiers stood at attention, honoring the dead. *Not a speck of dust.*

Claire glanced at Mother, who was clutching Jason's arm and looking up at him with adoring eyes. *Nothing changes.*

Tim's father, Franklin, had never met his own son, dying in Vietnam a month before he was due to come home. *Her* father was Franklin's identical twin, whom Mother married a few years later, after Frederick's first wife died. *It's all so ... incestuous.* Her dad, Fred, had had his accident when Claire was only three, so neither she nor Tim ever really had a father.

"Carlene?"

Claire didn't turn around.

"I mean Claire! I'm so sorry, darling, I'll get better at this, I promise."

Claire turned and blinked. *Another apology? From Mother?* She didn't think she'd ever heard the woman apologize in her life. "Yes?"

"I was just telling Jason all about your apartment. Would you like to go see it before dinner?"

Black-Eyed Children

Priscilla Martin paused at the doorway to the above-the-garage apartment. "I was using this as my jewelry studio, but as soon as I knew you were coming, I moved everything to the guest room and had this all fixed up for you." She smiled at Claire, then Jason. She really was trying hard. "I hope you like it. If you don't, you can redecorate."

She unlocked the door. Claire had told Jason that Tim had begged to live here when he'd turned twelve, but Mother wouldn't hear of it, saying he was too young to live on his own. The real reason, Claire said, was because it was filled to the rafters with junk. It was hard for Jason to believe Priscilla, with her military neatness, harbored such chaos behind closed doors.

The lock clicked and Priscilla stood back. "Go on in, you two, and tell me what you think."

"Thanks." Jason followed Claire inside. Priscilla brought up the rear.

Seeing Claire's expression, Jason smiled. "This is really nice, Mrs. Martin."

"Oh, please, call me Prissy. Or Mother."

"Okay … Prissy. This is great."

"Car- Claire?" Prissy asked in her peculiar nasal tone. "Will this do? I tried to furnish it with things you'd like."

Claire turned. "It's … It's nice. Thank you."

Jason could see she had trouble getting the words out. He took her hand and squeezed it.

"I had them paint all the walls in Navajo White. I remember you always liked that shade, Car … Claire. I hope you still do."

Claire nodded. "I do."

Jason crossed to the tweedy couch - browns, blacks, oranges, whites - and sat down. "This is really comfortable." It faced a wall-mounted flat screen TV.

Claire nodded. He could tell she was shocked that her new living room wasn't done in pastels. She loathed what she called "wimpy" colors and, after seeing Priscilla Martin's living room, he understood why.

"And I got this recliner just for you, Jason." Prissy pulled a throw off the chair. "And I hope the television is big enough. It's thirty-six inches. We have cable."

"The chair looks great."

"If you don't like it, the salesman assured me we can exchange it. Try it out."

Jason sat in the dark brown recliner. It was a little stiff, but he'd break it in in no time. He really liked the nubby upholstery. "You didn't have to do all this, Prissy." 'Prissy' was awkward in his mouth but 'Mother' would be worse.

"I wanted to." Claire's mother smiled.

Natural bamboo blinds covered the big window that looked at the rear of the main house and a sturdy pine coffee table fronted the couch. Matching end tables held lamps - thankfully without frilly ballerina shades - and a wooden magazine rack and a brass pole lamp with an amber shade stood next to his recliner. "This is really nice," he said again.

Finally, Claire looked at her mother and nearly smiled. "Thank you. You've been ... thoughtful."

"Let me show you the dining area and kitchen." Prissy led them past the couch, through a wide doorway that opened on the tiny dining room. A modest round maple table and four chairs were installed there. Claire made an approving noise. Beyond that was the kitchen. "I had them install this fridge and stove just last week." The white appliances were sized to fit the petite yellow-walled kitchen. "There's no dishwasher - if you want one, we can have some cabinets removed. Just say the word."

Claire spoke up. "We rarely used a dishwasher when we had one." She smiled and opened one of the cabinets by the sink.

"Everything's new," her mother said. She looked at Jason and he saw tears of joy in her eyes. She wanted Claire's approval badly and now she finally had it. It would be a downhill battle from here.

"Jason, aren't these pretty?" Claire showed him the dishes stacked in the cupboard. It was Corelle Ware, tan with a subtle flower border. There were tumblers, coffee mugs, juice glasses. In the drawer was a gleaming set of silverware, and on the Formica countertop were a toaster, a small microwave, and a coffeemaker.

"There's a mixer and blender in the bottom cabinet. If there's anything else you need just let me know."

"This is perfect, Mother." Claire smiled at her. "Thank you."

"We'll just go to the market for a few things tomorrow and we're all set." Jason felt the best he had since everything had gone to hell.

"No need." Priscilla opened a cupboard, revealing cereal, soup, spices, flour, canned vegetables, fruits, and other basics. "Look in the fridge, Claire."

Claire opened the freezer first, revealing frozen veggies, a couple TV dinners and raspberry Toaster Strudel, which Jason knew was Claire's absolute favorite thing in the world. She looked at him. "Did you tell Mother I love these?"

"No-"

"I remembered you love them all on my own, honey."

"That's nice."

Mother nodded. "There are only a couple things in the fridge. I didn't want to stock it until you got here, so everything will be nice and fresh. I'm taking you two to the market tomorrow, my treat."

"You don't have to do that," Jason said.

"I don't have to, but I want to." She smiled at them both. "You'll let me, won't you?"

"Yes," said Claire before Jason could. "Thanks."

"I'll pay you back out of my first check."

"No you won't, Jason. You'll save every cent to get back on your feet, and I'll help you however I can. By the way, are you excited about starting your new job next week?"

"I am." Jason, overwhelmed with gratitude, searched for the right words. For days now, every time he thought about his sudden good fortune - thanks to the woman standing before him - relief threatened to overwhelm him. It was as if all the anxiety of the past months was melting away. Finally, he and Claire had a chance at happiness again. Tears pricked his eyes and for a moment, he thought he might lose it. "Thank you." His voice quavered.

"You're welcome. Let's see your bath and bedroom, shall we?" Priscilla led them from the kitchen into a small laundry area built into the hallway. A brand new washer and dryer awaited them. There was a built-in ironing board and shelves that held detergent, fabric softener, and bleach. Beyond that was the bathroom. Small, but neat and clean. The shower/tub combination had a striped blue and white curtain that matched the small one on the window. "I like this apartment because it's circular - you don't have to go back and forth to get to where you want to go," Priscilla told them. They turned into another short hall. "Now, here's the bedroom. I tried to make it extra cheerful. I used a few things from your old room, Claire, to decorate."

The room was spacious for such a small place. A double bed rested beneath a large window through which the last golden rays of sunlight shone. There were two dressers against opposing walls, a beige rug, and paintings of children and grinning clowns on the walls. The children, with their large, black eyes, were even creepier than the clowns.

Jason glanced at Claire, who stared at the demonic children and oily clowns with a look of horror.

"These were your favorites, remember, darling?" Prissy admired the artwork.

Claire swallowed hard.

"Maybe the baby will like them, too."

"These things gave me nightmares, Mother. I hate them."

Prissy's mouth became a little O, and she brought her hand to her breast. "You never told me that, Carlene - Claire. Why didn't you ever tell me?"

Claire's jaw flexed. "I did."

Prissy gave Jason an imploring look.

He put his arm around Claire's shoulders.

"You may re-decorate however you want. I just thought you'd like them." She clasped her hands and wrung them, and Jason felt a stab of pity for Prissy. She was trying so hard, and Claire was giving her so little. He pushed away his irritation.

"We'll buy you better paintings tomorrow when we go out," said Prissy. "There's the best little art shop downtown. They'll have something you like more."

Claire nodded.

"Well then," Prissy said, "why don't we go back to the house and have dinner? I've made your favorite - manicotti with extra ricotta. That *is* still your favorite, isn't it, darling?"

Claire blinked and smiled weakly. "Yes. I still love manicotti. But-"

"I'm afraid we've already eaten, Prissy." Jason smiled. "It's all my fault. I just had to try the burgers and ice cream sodas at the Daffodil Grill." Despite Claire's claim that her mother was rigid about dinnertime, the woman's smile never faltered.

"Of course, we can keep it warm." She turned to Claire. "I didn't know you'd ever been to the Snapdragon Hotel, let alone their restaurant."

Claire nodded. "It was a long time ago. With a friend."

"Did you?" Prissy blew out a breath and looked around. "At any rate, I should leave you two alone now. I need to feed your father, and I'm sure you kids want some time to yourselves to settle in. Just pull your car up next to mine in the driveway." She looked from Claire to Jason. "If you need anything - anything at all - don't hesitate to ask. I'll see you for dinner at seven."

Claire cleared her throat. "How is Dad? I'd like to see him."

Prissy frowned. "No better, I'm afraid. He's had quite a bit of excitement today. Let's wait until morning for visiting, shall we?"

Claire nodded. As soon as Mother left, she started opening windows. "I hate her perfume. It gives me a headache ... and it makes the dizziness worse."

"You should tell her."

"I will."

Marble Madonna

"This all looks so delicious!" Jason deposited a big spoonful of chicken Alfredo next to his cheese manicotti. Caesar salads and garlic bread accompanied each plate. At the center of the polished cherry wood dining table, four tall white candles burned in a gaudy silver candelabrum. Their dishes rested on fancy silvery placemats and Claire couldn't help noticing Mother had broken out her best china - the same china neither she nor Tim had ever been allowed to use. Even at Thanksgiving dinner, the kids had been relegated to a card table set with plastic dishes.

"Would you like to say grace, Jason?" Mother asked.

Jason fidgeted with his linen napkin. "Um, won't you do it tonight, Prissy?"

"Of course." Mother closed her eyes, bowed her head, and clasped her hands in front of her. For a very long moment, she was as still as a marble Madonna. Jason and Claire exchanged glances.

Mother sighed. "Our Father in Heaven," she began. "Bless us this day. We give You our thanks for the meal we, Your unworthy servants, are about to enjoy." There was silence and just as Claire unclasped her hands, Mother continued. "Lord, thank You for the opportunity You've given me to spend time with my daughter, Carlene - who calls herself Claire now, just so You know - and her husband, Jason Holcomb."

"It's Holbrook, Mother."

Mother took no notice as she plowed on. "Oh, Lord ... we have so much to be grateful for, and we know that Your graciousness is beyond our capacity to understand, even though we don't know what Your Grand Plan really is ... Oh, Lord ... "

Claire rolled her eyes at Jason. He was holding back giggles.

"Bless these children that they may find the Path of Righteousness, lead them into the light of Your Eternal Love, and bless their unborn child, that he ..." she paused. "Or *she* ... will be a Lamb of the Lord and serve You well on earth as he ... or *she* ... shall in heaven."

Claire shivered at the words.

Mother silenced. Claire sighed. *Finally!*

"Deliver us from evil, Oh Lord."

Oh, crap.

"Keep us from the grasp of Satan's servants, wherever they may be lurking. We know that Lucifer wears many disguises, and we ask that You, in Your righteous almighty wisdom, steer us away from all of that which You do not condone."

There was a long pause, and Jason spoke up. "I'm starv-"

Mother shot him a dirty look, then reclosed her eyes. "We ask this in Your holy name, Amen." When at last she unclasped her hands and reached for the salt shaker, the sudden motion was startling. "Well," said Mother. "I think the Lord won't mind if we eat now." She shook salt over her plate. Enough to banish demons.

Sitting next to Jason, with Mother in her usual position at the head of the table, Claire was half-surprised she allowed them to sit so close to her. She remembered the days when she and Tim were placed a good six feet down the table because Mother didn't like to listen to her children chew. There'd been advantages to that; this close, it was clear that mother had dipped herself in a fresh layer of *Opium*, and Claire's head was beginning to ache from the cloying stench. It added to her dizziness, bringing on small waves of nausea.

Claire almost told Mother she didn't think she could bear the perfume, but now wasn't the time. She was determined to give Mother a chance since the woman had tried so hard to impress her. She knew Mother's kindness was just an act but held her tongue for Jason's benefit. He'd figure it out soon enough.

"Well." Mother looked at Jason. "What do you think of my cooking?"

Jason had taken a large bite of pasta and held his finger up while he chewed. After swallowing, he said, "It's fantastic, Prissy."

Mother beamed, then looked at Claire. "Are you going to eat, honey? You haven't touched your manicotti."

Claire gave her a weak smile and pushed the pasta around on her plate. "I'll eat. I guess I'm just not that hungry yet."

Jason smiled. "We ate too much at the grill, but given how good this is, I'll find room no matter how full I am." He took another big bite. "Why didn't you tell me what a great cook your mom is, Claire?" He grinned at Mother, who radiated pride.

Claire knew damn well that the woman didn't deserve any praise. She took a bite of manicotti. *Yep. Straight from Bartoli's Deli.*

While they ate, Mother sat there, poking at her meal and watching the two of them. It was nerve-wracking and Claire almost told her to quit staring.

"You should try some Alfredo, Prissy," said Jason. "It's fantastic."

"I'm watching my figure. At my age, everything goes straight to my hips."

Jason laughed. "Nonsense. Your figure's great. You should at least enjoy your own cooking."

Claire managed not to choke.

Mother laughed and waved the compliment away. "Here." She picked up the dish of manicotti. "Have some more." As she leaned forward to hand the manicotti to him her long silver and gold beaded necklace dipped deeply into the Alfredo bowl.

"Oh, dear." Mother snatched it up and sucked the locket clean, then laved it with her tongue. The cheese sauce was gone in an instant. She picked up her napkin and dried the necklace, inspecting it for missed cheese. Satisfied, she tucked it back into her blouse. "This necklace," she told Jason, "is very precious to me."

"It's- it's lovely, Prissy," Jason managed, as he dished manicotti onto his plate.

"Would you like more Alfredo, Jason?" Mother asked. "It looks like Carlene hasn't been feeding you enough."

Jason had the audacity to dimple up at her. "No, thank you, Prissy. After this, I'll be so full I might pop." His eyes went back to his meal as he lowered his head and continued eating.

"Very well," said Mother. After a beat, she asked, "Do you know what you're going to name the baby?"

Claire dropped her fork.

Jason cleared his throat. "We haven't talked about it; we don't even know the gender yet. We've barely found out we're pregnant."

Claire, chewing now-tasteless pasta, fought with herself over her mother's question. She wanted to scream that the baby was none of her business, but she knew that was irrational; if anyone else had asked the question she wouldn't have reacted that way.

"'*We're* pregnant'?" Mother said to Jason. "Oh, dear boy, I hear young men say that nowadays like they have any idea of what we women go through after you plant a baby in our bellies." She chuckled. "It's very nice of you, though."

"If I could, I'd share all the physical problems with my wife." He beamed at her.

Claire gave him a silent smile; she knew it was true.

"Well, you wouldn't say that if you knew how bad those hemorrhoids hurt, would he darling?"

Claire's face turned to fire and she couldn't look at her mother. "I wouldn't know," she mumbled, then forked salad into her mouth.

"I'm sorry, Car-Claire. I didn't mean to embarrass you. Are they bad?"

"I have a little morning sickness in the afternoons. That's all I know about, Mother."

Mother looked at Jason again. "I had *terrible* hemorrhoids, Jason, when I was pregnant with Car-Claire. Just excruciating! They were so bad that I had to have Frankli- I mean Frederick, her daddy, put ointment on my bottom every night until she was born." She winked at him.

Claire's cheeks burned with humiliation and rage and Jason looked a little purple himself. "Mother, please."

"Claire, darling," Mother said. "I'm so sorry. Did I embarrass you?"

"No, but ..." She hesitated. "I mean, yes, Mother. I'm really not comfortable when you talk like that."

Jason nodded. "Some of our friends are very ... open about these things, and it always makes us both a little uncomfortable." He smiled. "We're pretty old-fashioned, I guess."

Mother opened her mouth but was silenced by the doorbell, which chimed out *O Say Can You See?*

Another thing that never changes.

Mother stood, dabbed her mouth with her napkin and fluttered toward the living room. "Comiiiing..." she crooned.

"The *national anthem*?" asked Jason.

Claire nodded. Mother invited someone inside and a moment later she reappeared with two women Claire recognized as Phyllis Stine and Aida Portendorfer, neighbors from down the street. She'd hoped it would have been Aunt Babs.

"Oh, *Carlene!*" cooed Phyllis, her hair as falsely platinum as it had been ten years ago. In a clank of plastic jewelry, she pushed a tray of wrapped cookies into Mother's hands, and came at Claire, intent on a hug. "My, how you've grown up! You look so beautiful! You're just glowing!"

Claire wished she could say the same for Phyllis. The woman still wore blue eye shadow up to her dyed black eyebrows, and looked like a washed up go-go girl with her white hoop earrings, matching white fingernails, pale lipstick, tight sundress under a white faux fur stole, and blue boots the same sickly shade as her makeup.

Claire stood, and Phyllis wrapped her in a bony hug.

Aida Portendorfer, who'd put on another twenty pounds since Claire had left, stood smiling. She'd let her hair go gray and was the embodiment of a sweet grandmother, with rosy cheeks and twinkling eyes. A pair of binoculars hung around her neck. Aida was the neighborhood gossip and Mother had always disapproved of her, but given the fake smiles and superficial tones, no one would have known. *Of course Mother disapproves of everyone.*

"I hope you like the cookies, Carlene," Phyllis said. "I baked them myself."

Aida gave Claire a look that stated Phyllis did *not* bake the cookies. "We're just so excited to have you back ... Claire. All of Morning Glory Circle has been abuzz with the good news! And you're going to have a baby!" She came in for a hug, opening arms that were as big as Claire's thighs.

"Hello, Aida," said Claire.

"I've always loved that name - Claire," said Aida. "It suits you. Did you have it legally changed?"

Claire nodded. "I did. The minute I turned eighteen." She glanced at Mother, expecting to see anger, but to her surprise, there was nothing except pride as she clasped her hands and half-heartedly offered the neighbors some pasta.

"No thanks, Prissy," said Aida, then turned back to Claire. "Have you had morning sickness or any strange cravings?"

"A few cravings. A little afternoon sickness. Lots of dizziness."

Phyllis nodded vehemently, her plastic earrings bobbing. She looked like a dumbed-down Joan Rivers with bad taste. "Make sure your mother gives you saltines and tea. That will fix you right up."

"And you must be Claire's husband!" Aida moved toward Jason who stared with wide eyes at the chubby woman coming at him.

"Yes. Jason Holbrook. It's nice to meet you." He held out his hand. They shook and Phyllis pushed her way between them.

She gripped his hand and with her free one appeared to be feeling his biceps. "Such a handsome young man," she said. "Isn't he handsome, Aida? Such pretty blue eyes!"

Aida nodded. "I'm afraid we've caught them in the middle of dinner, Phyllis."

"We should leave." Phyllis glanced at Mother. "We thought you'd already eaten. You're usually such an early bird."

"I-" Mother began.

But Phyllis steamrolled on. "We just wanted to give your daughter a proper welcome to the neighborhood. And congratulate her." She turned to Claire. "Have you thought of any names for your bundle of joy yet? Are you going to find out if it's a boy or girl?"

Aida spoke up. "When Stan and I had Kelly and Raymond we didn't know what they'd be. Even if we could have known, we wanted to be surprised, so we used yellow and green to decorate their rooms-"

Phyllis broke in. "Can't go having a pink room for a boy, though I think blue would be fine for a girl these days."

Mother cleared her throat and started herding the women toward the front door. "It's too soon, they don't know anything yet. They've been traveling all day and as you can imagine, in her condition, Claire is very tired. You can speak to her after she's had some rest."

"Bye, Claire, bye, Jason," Phyllis and Aida cried from the living room.

"Goodbye," Jason called. "Thanks for the cookies."

Mother returned and before Claire could express her anger about the neighborhood knowing she was expecting, her mother blurted, "I'm so sorry, Claire. I didn't mean to tell anyone about the baby. It slipped out. I'm so proud of you! I'm going to be a grandmother! You can forgive me, can't you?"

Claire stared at her mother, wondering if she'd ever get used to hearing the woman apologize. "Of course, I forgive you, Mother. You're only human." *Barely.*

Mother smiled. "Good! Because I really want to take you shopping for baby things! I would just love to be a part of the baby's life." Her eyes welled with alligator tears. "I do hope you'll consider Franklin for a name … if it's a boy."

Anger spiked. "Frederick's my father. Not Franklin."

Mother sat back down. "Oh, yes, of course, dear. That's what I meant. They're both fine men. Perhaps you could use them both. Franklin Frederick-"

Jason cleared his throat. "I'm not particularly fond of either name, to be honest, Prissy."

"That's right," said Claire. "If we name the baby after anyone, it would be Jason's father, Michael. If it's a girl, we might name it for his mother, Sarah. Both were killed two years ago in a car accident and we were very fond of them." She took satisfaction in Mother's wounded expression. "They helped us out a lot in our early days together." It felt good to twist the knife a little.

"Of course," said Mother. "I didn't mean to overstep my bounds." She smiled. "I'm just so proud that I'm afraid I get a little too excited." She looked from Claire to Jason. "You two must be exhausted. Let me wrap up some pasta for you to take upstairs - I'm sure you'll be hungrier later, Claire. Remember, you must pray over *any* meal, even leftovers." She smiled, her lips thin, like a snake's. "Let's meet at ten tomorrow morning and go shopping. Get your grocery list ready!"

***

"Did you see that?" asked Jason. "That Phyllis woman was totally feeling me up!" He gave Claire a grin. "I think she's hot for me, sweetheart. You better keep an eye on her."

"You think I should be jealous of a mummy?" Claire put the pan of pasta into the fridge. There was no way she was going to eat any tonight, not with the headache burgeoning behind her eyes.

"She is kind of scary looking. I kept wondering how she could even close her eyes with skin that tight."

"She seemed especially impressed with your biceps."

Jason reached for the tray of cookies, grabbed one, and made an exaggerated flexing motion with his arm. "Yep. With guns like these ..."

Claire wrapped her arms around his waist, stood on tiptoes, and pecked him on the cheek. "You *are* pretty hunky."

He took a bite of the cookie and made a face. "Tube cookies," he said.

"Phyllis Stine isn't the baking type. Neither is Mother." She disengaged herself from her husband and began looking in the wooden cupboards that lined the wall above the sink. "You don't really believe Mother made dinner herself tonight, do you?"

"She didn't?"

Claire shook her head as she looked over the rows of canned beets, spinach, corn, and soups. "She bought it at Bartoli's Deli." She took a can of beets, turned it over, and saw that it was expired - by three years. *Just what I figured.* "Mother has never made fettuccine, let alone manicotti, in her life." The corn was even older and she tossed the cans in the trash.

Jason watched her. "I thought you liked corn."

"I do if I don't think it's going to poison me. These are expired. By years. All of them." She continued tossing cans then picked up the bag of flour and opened it. "Look at this." She held the bag out to Jason.

"Yuck! What is that?"

"Weevils. And more weevils."

Jason took the flour and set it in the trash. "Well, at least there's Bartoli's. We'll always know where to get damned good pasta," he said. "What are you looking for?"

Claire sighed. "I need a Nuprin. I was hoping she might have stocked some for us."

"In the kitchen?"

"Mother thinks pills belong in the kitchen. They're part of the five basic food groups. Just ask her, she'll tell you."

Jason tossed the half-eaten cookie on top of the expired flour and vegetables, then picked up a can of soup. "Jesus, this dates back to the last century." He tossed it and the rest without checking further. "You have a headache?"

"Her perfume makes my head hurt." She shut the cupboard. "Did we bring any ibuprofen up?"

"There's a bottle in the overnight case I brought up with the computers. Your pill organizer and prenatal vitamins are in it, too. So is your music box. I figured you'd want that."

"You're so sweet," said Claire. The music box, a gift from Timothy for her ninth birthday, was one of the few things she truly cherished. It had a little plastic ballerina that spun and bobbed on its springs to sweet, tinkling music. It was empty inside. Claire had never worn much jewelry - but that music box ... it was special. When Tim had given it to her, he'd told her that she could tell the little ballerina anything, and she would always keep her secrets. Claire had taken that literally and had often talked to the tiny dancer when she was upset.

"I'll bring up the rest of the bags in the morning," Jason said.

She gave him a flirty smile. "So, we're sleeping naked tonight?"

Jason leaned against the counter. "Sounds good to me. I'll go get your painkillers."

"Thanks. I'll be in the living room checking out that comfortable sofa."

Jason returned with two ibuprofen and a glass of water.

"Thanks, babe." She tossed the tablets back, then drained the glass as Jason tried out the recliner. "Will the TV irritate your headache?"

"No, it's fine."

He picked up the remote, aimed it at the television and clicked it to no avail.

She looked at the clock. It was only nine, but she was tired and Jason looked tired, too. "I think I'll take a shower and go to bed."

"Maybe I'll join you." He shook the remote and tossed it on the couch. "I'll figure the TV out in the morning."

Claire laughed. "That's the first thing you'll learn about my mother, Jason: nothing works. When something breaks, it goes onto the list of things that need to be taken care of, where it stays forever."

Jason frowned. "Well, she's probably been pretty busy setting this place up for us."

He thinks I'm a terrible daughter.

But if that was his thought, he didn't say so. "Speaking of lists, let's make one for the groceries in the morning. Do you think your mother will mind if we get a couple of steaks?"

Claire shrugged. "No. You're in the seduction stage."

"Huh?"

"There are three stages to all of Mother's relationships. The first is that she seduces you. Next, she tries to establish dominance, and that leads to the third stage, which can go one of two ways - either she'll realize she can control you, or she'll stay as far away from you as she can get. Right now, she's seducing you, showing you how generous she is. She'll encourage steaks."

"Cool. Let's try to keep her in that stage. Does she have a barbecue?" His look told her he thought she was being too harsh.

"She has several, I'm sure." Claire stood up. "Are you coming to bed?"

Jason pursed his lips. "I think I'll stay up a while, after all. Maybe I can figure out the TV and see if we have an internet connection for the laptops. It'll be less we have to do tomorrow." His voice was flat.

She was certain now that he thought she was being unfairly critical of Mother. And that meant he'd been sucked in by her charms. *And why wouldn't he be? She's the finest actress this side of Hollywood.* Claire wanted to be angry, but she was too tired. She rose then stooped to kiss her husband on the lips. His kiss was chaste. She headed toward the bedroom, eager to rest her aching head on a soft, cool pillow.

***

After doing a set of nightly push-ups and sit-ups, Jason lay on the couch, thinking. He wondered why someone would hire him, sight unseen. He knew his soon-to-be-boss, Paul Schuyler, was an old friend of Tim Martin's, but it seemed awfully risky to give a job to someone you'd never even met, let alone interviewed. *What if I'm not what he expects? What if Prissy made me out to be something I'm not, and he's disappointed?* Jason decided not to worry about it. He would do the best he could. It was nice of the man to hire him, and very kind of Prissy to make it happen.

His thoughts drifted to Timothy Martin, dead at twenty by his own hand. Claire hadn't told him an awful lot, but he knew Tim had a girlfriend who had moved to Brimstone, Arizona, and he had joined her soon after. Then he'd had an accident and Prissy had brought him home to Snapdragon where she could help him recover. At least that's what he'd gleaned out of Claire's not-so-nice telling of the tale. Surely, he'd intended to get well and go back to Brimstone, back to his girlfriend. *So why did he kill himself?* As far as Claire knew, Tim hadn't suffered from any kind of depression, though he had developed a drinking problem. *Maybe that's what did it.*

Jason wondered what became of the girlfriend in Brimstone. Maybe, if he hit it off with his new boss, Paul would tell him. The whole thing was just so tragic. When Jason himself was twenty, he'd felt like he had the world on a string. Anything was possible. His entire life had sprawled ahead of him, waiting for him to live it. He simply couldn't imagine what would drive someone so young to end his own life. *Tragic. And tragic for Claire. She loved her big brother so much.*

Algebraic Prowess

Jason placed a can of corn in the shopping cart.

"Oh," said Prissy. "I gave you plenty of corn and other veggies. I put them in the cupboard next to the sink."

Jason felt his face heat up.

"It's all expired, Mother," said Claire.

"Of course it is, dear. These things are good far beyond the dates they put on the labels. We mustn't be wasteful." Prissy touched the beaded hair necklace between her pointed breasts. She wore a pastel blue pantsuit dressy enough for a business meeting and matching blue and white pumps. Her hair and makeup were flawless, as if she'd just stepped out of a beauty parlor, and *Opium* hovered around her like a chemical fog. *All this, for a grocery store?* The pumps bothered him the most. He was with Claire on foot comfort and couldn't imagine why any woman would wear heels to the market.

Claire's jaw flexed. "I'm not going to eat corn that expired before I was even married. And even if the spinach and beets were still fresh, you know I don't eat those things. I never did." She added a smile. "Not even Popeye could talk me into canned spinach, don't you recall?"

Prissy stared at her daughter, then smiled. "Of course. I didn't realize they'd been expired so long and that probably wouldn't be good for the baby." Her gaze flicked to Claire's stomach. "I wasn't thinking. I'm so sorry, Claire."

Relief swept over Jason as the women's eyes unlocked. A treaty had been struck.

"Just let me check this," said Prissy, snapping a can of corn off the shelf like a lizard going for a fly. She turned it over, studying the label as she punched numbers into a clunky calculator she'd pulled from her handbag. Satisfied with the equation, she reached for a different brand of corn, punched in more numbers, then did the same with a third. And a fourth. "Just as I suspected," she said, arching her brow.

"What's that?" asked Jason, leaning on the shopping cart.

"Well, this one has more ounces than the other three, but the price of *this* one," she flourished the third can, "is actually lower. While it may have the lowest price, it also has the lowest ounces. So this one," she said, holding up the second can, "is actually less expensive, because while it's priced a little higher, the ounces exceed those of the other three cans." She beamed at him and Jason blinked, unable to imagine going to this much trouble.

He pointed at the price tag on the shelf. "It has the price per ounce right here, Prissy. You don't need to bother with a calculator."

"You can't trust the store itself to be honest. You never know what they'll try to pull. They *rely* on misplaced trust, Jason, sweetheart. *Capitalism* relies on it." Prissy placed the can in the cart and waved a hand. "I know. It's a little more time-consuming this way, but I always get the best bargain possible ... and we *must* keep a close eye on our finances, mustn't we?" There was something in her tone - something close to judgment - that irked Jason.

Claire, however, looked fit to be tied. "We like Green Giant Niblets, Mother." She took a fifth can from the shelf and placed it in the cart. "And if we have to pay for it ourselves, we will, because this is the kind we want. We aren't entirely penniless, you know."

Prissy nodded. "Of course, darling." She replaced the other cans, disapproval on her face.

As the Carpenters sang *Close to You* overhead, they walked down another aisle, filling their cart. Priscilla moved even more slowly than the song, stopping at every item they chose to inspect the labels, and compare the product to its competitors with surgical precision and the algebraic prowess of a 1980s Texas Instruments calculator.

Jason thought Prissy's eccentricity was funny - he couldn't help it. Claire, on the other hand, did not appear amused.

Now and then, as achingly slow melodies dribbled from the loudspeakers, they ran into someone Priscilla Martin knew, though she never bothered to make introductions. There was an attractive thirtyish blonde named Iris, who introduced herself as the daughter of Ace Etheridge, editor and publisher of the *Snapdragon Daily*. She lived at the other end of Morning Glory Circle with her father and taught fourth grade at Snapdragon Elementary. When she invited Claire to come over for coffee, and Claire accepted, Prissy spoke up.

"I don't see any flour or sugar in your cart, dear. Have you already bought your ingredients for our annual yard and bake sale?"

"I'm no cook." Iris smiled. "We'll pick up some cookies or something for your sale."

"Well, we can't all excel at baking, can we?" Prissy said. "So tell me, Iris, have you read any good books lately? I hear you're a fan of romance."

Iris looked perplexed, worried even. "Excuse me?"

"You could sell them at your yard sale to pay for the cookies you're donating."

"I'll keep it in mind."

Prissy smiled. "I mean, I've read romances and they're not the kind of books you want to hang onto or read more than once, are they, dear? You might sell them while you can, you and your father. Such a nice man. Do give him my regards."

"Excuse me, I have to get going," Iris said in a cool tone, without taking her eyes off Prissy. "See you soon, Claire." She pushed her cart briskly away.

Near the bakery, they ran into a tall, distinguished man whose close-cropped dark hair with salt-and-pepper temples, and stylish casual wear made him look like a male model. "Why, Quinton Everett, what are you doing here?" Prissy asked in a breathless tone.

As the speakers began playing *I Heard It Through the Grapevine,* Jason was amused to see his mother-in-law bat her eyelashes and posture like a schoolgirl with a crush. Everett didn't seem to notice. "Just doing my weekly shopping." He turned his gaze on Jason and Claire and smiled, raising his hand, but Prissy grabbed it before Jason could shake it. "You have the best manicurist in town, Quinton," she gushed. "Just the best. I hope you'll come and see us at the Morning Glory Circle Yard and Bake Sale next weekend."

"I'll certainly try." His cell phone rang. "Excuse me, won't you?" He put the phone to his ear and pushed his cart away.

"Busy, busy man," Prissy said. "In fact, he's just about the most important man in town. I nearly married him, back in the day."

Claire looked shocked. "Who is he?"

"Why, only the President of Snapdragon Bank and Trust. He's done me a lot of favors over the years." She looked after him, lashes batting again.

Jason managed not to laugh.

"Let's continue, children. We haven't got all day, you know."

They began trudging after Mother once more.

As the minutes dragged by, and time slowed to a creeping pace that would try the patience of a tranquilized garden snail, Jason began to understand his wife's point of view. *Tick ... Tock ... Tick ... Tock ... Is it possible to doze off in a market? Yes, it is. Tick ... Tock ... But Prissy's helping us,* he reminded himself as they approached the two-hour mark and The Carpenters began singing about being close to you again. She was eccentric, but she was kind. He could see how she could annoy some people, but he still couldn't help feeling that Claire had painted her mother in a worse light than she deserved. *People* do *change,* he told himself.

Forty-five minutes later, as they made their way to the self-checkout, Jason had surpassed his limit and was becoming angry. But he held it in.

"I don't trust checkout girls," announced Prissy. "I prefer doing it myself so there's no risk of being overcharged." She was nothing if not frugal, Jason told himself. *And just a little eccentric.*

Claire leaned against a magazine rack and gave him a satisfied smile. He knew what she was thinking: *I told you so ...*

One excruciatingly precise item at a time, Priscilla Martin began scanning and bagging, stopping on occasion to recheck labels to be certain she'd made the wisest possible choice. She stared particularly long and hard at the Niblets label before letting out an exasperated sigh and sweeping the can across the scanner.

Jason suppressed a groan, promising himself they'd never shop with Prissy again. This foible was just too much. *Tick... Tock... Tick... Tock...*

Against the magazine rack, Claire was swallowing laughter. He leaned over and whispered in her ear, "Why didn't you warn me?"

Claire just smiled.

Terrible Creatures

Babs Vandercooth nibbled an Oreo between sips of coffee. "It's like being a kid again, Pris. Have a cookie."

"Really, Barbara - Oreos?"

"Why not?"

Prissy eyed a cookie like it was a big black bug, then snatched it up. She carefully unscrewed the top of the Oreo and examined the white filling, a dubious look in her eye. Peeling the filling from the cookie, she dropped it on her saucer, a lardy white lump that Babs eyed. "Take it, if you want it," Prissy said. She never missed a thing.

"Don't mind if I do." Babs picked up the disk of filling and popped it in her mouth, feeling ten years old again. It felt good. Aida had told her this morning that Claire and Jason had arrived last night, but Babs hadn't asked about her yet. Pris had no idea she'd kept in contact with Claire all these years, and they'd decided to play it cool to keep her from catching on - but, oh, how she wanted to see her.

"You know that stuff will kill you," Pris said.

"Why'd you offer it to me, then?"

"It's *your* choice," Prissy used her most arched tone. "It's *your* body." She dipped a chocolate disk in her coffee, nibbled it, then set it aside. "Now, we need to make up a list of who is baking what for next weekend's sale."

"What would Morning Glory Circle do without you, Prissy? We'd all be headless chickens!" Babs trusted her friend wouldn't hear the bite in her voice; she never did.

Pris smiled. "Do you have your notebook?"

"Sure." Babs pulled a pen and a legal pad out of her tote.

"You'd be much better at this if you brought your laptop, Barbara. Then we could just print out a list for everyone to follow instead of passing out handwritten notes."

"You know me, I'm kind of a Luddite when it comes to computers."

Prissy sighed. "Only because you choose to be. There's a new computer class starting at the adult school next Monday night. You should go."

"Oh, you know enough about computers for both of us, Pris. And Monday night, Carl and I always play bridge with Stan and Aida."

Prissy looked heavenward. "If that's more important to you ..."

"It is," Babs said firmly. "Much more important." She'd learned to head off her friend whenever a lecture was looming - a frequent occurrence. She picked up the pen. "What's the plan?"

Prissy always had a plan. Back when she'd babysat Babs, she would show up with a game plan. That's what she called it. First they'd play crazy eights, then checkers, then when Babs turned ten, Prissy taught her backgammon. At twelve, Pris attempted to teach her chess, but Babs thought that was about as fun as hygiene films in Mrs. Crotchler's phys-ed class. Prissy finally gave up on that, but still occasionally brought it up, as if Babs' boredom with chess was some kind of handicap. But that was Prissy, and most of the time, Babs let it be. When she and Carl were newlyweds, Pris helped them buy their house on Morning Glory Circle, putting in a good word with the loan officer - Quinton Everett - so they could get the loan. And Prissy'd been there when Carl had his little problem. She could be truly amazing sometimes, though there was always a price. *Oh, is there a price.*

"Barbara? Are you listening?"

"What? Oh, sorry. Gathering wool."

"You need to exercise your mind, Barbara. Otherwise, you'll lose it. I don't want to end up wiping drool off my best friend's face some day, now do I?"

"I was thinking about how good you've been to me and Carl."

Prissy smiled, then snatched another Oreo. "Let's have Aida Portendorfer supply cookies. Tell her we need - hmmm - twelve dozen chocolate chip and another twelve dozen sugar cookies. And the same amount of snickerdoodles. Maybe some brownies, too."

Babs jotted it down. "Duane Pruitt always makes the fudge brownies. Leave those to him. You're asking Aida to make an awful lot of cookies as it is, Pris."

"Oh, Aida loves to show off her cooking. She'll adore it. And we'll sell them for five or six dollars a dozen. If those little hotshot Girl Scouts can charge that much, so can we. This sale will raise enough to allow us to buy three more animatronic Santas for the street this year."

"I don't think Aida will be happy about it. It will cost a lot, too."

"Oh, the Portendorfers can afford it, just like Duane can afford to make the brownies. Put him down for two hundred - make that two-thirds brownies and one-third blondies. And Barbara, everyone will make the cost of ingredients back with their yard sale items, so don't worry so much. After all, they get to keep seventy percent of their profits since they volunteered for the bake sale."

"Virtually everybody on the cul-de-sac always volunteers to help, Prissy. No one can refuse you, you know that." Babs ate another Oreo.

Prissy arched a brow. "Not everyone."

"Who turned you down?"

"The Deans, of course... *and* the Crockers! Can you imagine? The Crockers?" She inhaled. "And I could barely convince myself to ask those lowlife Lowells, but I did, since everyone *must* contribute." Her face pruned up. "White trash. I swear. Tattoos. Hair the color of ketchup! That woman is such a tawdry Audrey! And the man has motorcycles! Not to mention those horrid dogs."

Babs had to work hard to keep amusement off her face. "Well, I'm not surprised the Deans turned you down. They both work at the Fudge Depot all weekend. They always turn you down."

"Yes, but the Crockers?"

"Bettyanne told me she's going to visit her niece in San Francisco next weekend for her baby shower! Isn't that nice? And Roddy is probably on duty. When you're on the police force you don't always know your hours too far in advance."

"Oh, please, Barbara. Bettyanne could spend the morning with us before taking off. Or at least take the time to make a couple dozen chocolate lava cakes before leaving."

"It's a long drive, Pris. Be nice."

Prissy blew air out of her nostrils, like a dragon warming up. "Well, all I know is, until now, Roddy has always been able to schedule around our events. Most likely, he's planning on hiding his car in the garage and watching sports all day while the *rest* of the street *works*."

"Oh, Pris. Give him the benefit of the doubt. You've no reason to think that. And so what if it were true? He works hard. He's one of Snapdragon's Finest. He's allowed to have a bachelor weekend."

"*Everyone* on the Circle contributes. That's what we agreed."

"That's what *you* agreed, Pris."

Prissy gave her that thin-lipped glare that meant she was losing patience, the glare that made Babs want to keep pushing - but she didn't. "Thirty percent of garage sale proceeds go toward our Christmas decorations, and one hundred percent of the bake proceeds do as well. It's *charity*! The Crockers and Deans should at least make a donation if they won't participate."

"Prissy, your blood pressure is way too high right now, I'm sure of it. Ask them for a donation."

"That cheapskate Earl Dean has never given anything toward the street decorations."

"Honey, relax. He doesn't decorate, why should he?"

"He's a horrid little man. You'd think a candy maker would at least allow us to put up a giant candy cane on his lawn. Everyone else does. He decorates his business for Christmas, but won't even put lights on his house. He's a terrible creature. Just like his wife and those retarded children of his." Prissy's face was turning redder by the moment, but she lowered her voice to conspiratorial tones. "But do you know what he and Earlene do, Barbara? Do you know?"

"No." Babs leaned forward. "What do they do?"

"They decorate a Christmas tree *inside* the house - and they string lights *in* their living room too - but they keep the blinds down so the *rest* of us can't enjoy their decorations. They're very selfish."

"Why is that selfish?"

"If they're willing to decorate for themselves, they can at least put the gosh-darn candy cane on their lawn, like the rest of us." She looked like she smelled something offensive. "They're the blight of the street. A mole on an otherwise flawless face! We need to do something about them and, darn it all, if I don't get some cooperation, I just might."

Stop it, Prissy! she wanted to say, but what was the point? Pris never let up once she sank her teeth into something. Plus, Babs was reluctant to antagonize her. She feared what Priscilla Martin could do; she'd seen it firsthand.

"I just might," Prissy repeated.

Babs heard the kitchen door open and close, saving her from having to reply. Prissy's head swiveled. "Car-Claire? Is that you?"

"It's both of us, Mother." Claire appeared in the dining room doorway, her handsome husband behind her. "Aunt Babs!" she exclaimed, her eyes lighting up. "How nice to see you!" She hesitated, taking the enthusiasm down a notch. This is my husband, Jason. Jason, meet Aunt Babs."

"She's not your aunt," Mother muttered. "Barbara, you should never have encouraged her to call you that."

Babs paid no attention, but smiled at the couple as they entered the room, then shook hands with Jason. His grip was as pleasant as his smile. Then she and Claire hugged, long and hard. "Will you be joining us at the bake sale this coming weekend?" asked Babs. "We'll sneak inside and have tea and Chesapeakes, just like we used to when you were a girl."

"That would be nice," Claire said. She exchanged glances with Jason. "We don't really have anything to sell, though. We already did that."

"Perhaps you can get your mother to give you a few items to sell." Babs turned to Prissy, all innocence. "You've been talking about unloading some of your stuff for years, Pris."

Prissy pursed her lips. "I just haven't gotten around to clearing out the garage."

Babs twinkled at Jason. "I have a wonderful idea. This strapping young man could help you!"

Something dark moved across Prissy's face, while Claire's wore a look of amusement.

Jason nodded. "Of course I can help. Just tell me when you're ready."

Prissy gave her son-in-law a false smile. "I'll do that," she said. "When *I'm* ready."

Babs sat back, pleased with herself. Now maybe Prissy would *finally* get around to having that yard sale she'd been talking about for over three decades now. All she needed was a little push.

"Have you kids finished putting all your groceries away already?" asked Pris. She turned to Babs. "We went on quite the shopping trip this morning."

"That we did," Jason said with a twisted smile.

"I filled their cupboards and fridge so they wouldn't have to worry about a thing." Pris sounded very satisfied with herself. "I even bought them some nice steaks."

Babs knew what a trip to the market with Pris was like - she still remembered the time her friend had treated her to one as a housewarming present twenty-five years ago. Babs hadn't shopped with her since. "How lovely." She winked at the kids and Claire and Jason grinned back.

"What can I help you two with?" Pris asked.

"I was hoping to introduce Jason to Dad."

"Oh, well, let's do that later. He's having an after-lunch nap."

"Okay ..." said her daughter.

"Now, why don't you two run along? Barbara and I have a lot of planning to do for the Morning Glory Circle Yard and Bake Sale."

Claire looked annoyed, then she and her husband said their goodbyes and disappeared.

Prissy sighed. "Kids these days!"

"What a fine young woman she's turned out to be, Prissy!"

Priscilla smiled weakly. "I suppose. I only hope she's gotten over some of her ... *problems.*"

"Well, everything concerning her seems to be going along rather nicely."

But Pris wasn't convinced. "Time will tell. Now, let's figure out the rest of our game plan. What is it Geneva-Marie always makes?"

"She's donating six dozen of her wonderful cinnamon-pecan rolls."

Pris clucked her tongue. "Only six dozen? Those sell like mad. Tell her she needs to double that."

Babs looked up. "She already told me all she has time for is six dozen."

"Well, there it is, then. Obviously her dedication to our Christmas decor is half-hearted." She smiled, dry as toast. "No Santa in front of the Collins house this year. Have you talked to the Sachs yet?" Prissy's nose twitched. She had never been fond of Milton and Candy, but once they painted their house pink, she became downright snippy.

"Candy is supplying cupcakes. Eight dozen."

"Out of a box, no doubt."

Babs ignored her. "The Dunworth Sisters are donating a dozen pies, all from scratch."

"What kind?"

"I didn't ask. I was simply grateful."

Pris sniffed. "Make sure and find out. And see if they can contribute at least six more."

"I believe their income is fixed. A dozen is probably pushing their limits already."

Pris sighed. "Very well. What about Mr. Etheridge? I saw his daughter Iris in the market and she had no flour or sugar or even mixes in her cart."

"He's a bachelor, Pris, and he and Iris both have full time jobs. They don't bake, but I'm sure they'll find something nice at Costco to sell. He mentioned they have some lovely popcorn balls."

"Popcorn balls are not adequate. This is a *bake* sale." Pris looked down her nose. "I'm sure Iris can manage a few cakes or something. Make sure and tell them that. Double fudge."

"Pris-"

"They can do it. After all, I'm making eight dozen cannoli!"

You've ordered eight dozen from Bartoli's. Babs just smiled. "The thought of your cannoli makes my mouth water. I don't know how you do it."

Pris snagged a third Oreo. "And what are you contributing this year?"

"I think I'll make two dozen each of lemon, raspberry, chocolate, blueberry, and cranberry bars. My usual."

"Last year-"

Babs cut her off. "I *know* I only did half that last year, but I was still recovering from pneumonia."

"You're an angel. I guarantee you, you'll have one of our new Santas gracing your lawn next season."

"That's nice of you, Pris." Babs hesitated. "What about the Stines and the Lowells?"

"Phyllis will surely contribute more gingerbread than we'll sell; it's not very good, you know, but her heart's in the right place, even if her eyes and lips aren't."

"Prissy!" Babs shook her head. *I swear, no secrets are safe on Morning Glory Circle. None at all. Of course, it's pretty hard to hide all those nips and tucks.*

Pris dipped her cookie in coffee. "As for the Lowells, why don't you ask them for some pumpkin muffins and pumpkin bread? Surely that woman can figure out how to make those."

Babs suppressed a smile. While Pris hated the Sachs and their pink house, she absolutely abhorred the Lowells - her other immediate neighbors. She perceived their burnt pumpkin home as much worse than it was. Perhaps it was the yard full of kids and dogs, Hank's Hawg, or Crys's fire engine red hair - probably all those things - but the Lowells really put Prissy's panties in a bunch. Babs looked down, hiding her amusement. *Poor Pris, surrounded by houses painted in colors like in the old Ticky-Tacky song.* Babs secretly enjoyed the bright colors. If it weren't for Pris, her own pale gray, white-trimmed Colonial would be a lovely bright spring green.

***

Jason brought the last suitcase into the bedroom and dropped it on the bed. "What's in here, sweetheart?" An anvil?"

Claire grinned. "Yep, Wile E. Coyote said we couldn't leave home without it." She hung a dress in the closet, slipping it off a cheap plastic hanger with a broken tip and onto one of the many wooden ones Mother had stocked. She tossed the crappy hanger in a cardboard box on a heap of other discarded hangers. "We brought more hangers than we did clothes," she said. "I wonder how that happened."

"I don't know about you, but I was packing in a hurry. I just swept everything into boxes. Sorry."

Claire laughed. "It's not a problem." They'd sold their good ones at a yard sale they'd held when they were trying to drum up some extra money. They hadn't made much. "I hate those cheap hangers." She glanced at the box. "To the trash with them all! When we move, we'll get some nice ones." She looked at the stack of clown portraits she'd removed. They now rested - face-down - in the corner. "I'll get these. You get the hangers."

Jason picked up the box and they headed outside where he counted six large garbage cans awaiting pickup on Mother's curb.

With great relief, Claire dumped the clown portraits into the large garbage can. "Good riddance." She shivered. "I've dreamed of trashing those horrible things since I was little."

"They are pretty hideous. Good therapy." He went back to work.

"No, no," Claire said when she saw Jason lifting the wrong lid. "The hangers are mostly plastic."

Jason frowned. "Oops." He moved to the recycle bin and began dumping the hangers.

"Jason. Wait."

"Huh?"

Claire felt ridiculous. "Mother has more than one recycle bin."

"This one's almost empty."

"See the white dot she painted on the lid?"

"Um, yeah."

"That means it's for plastic."

"Fine." He started to pour.

"See the blue dot on the next one?"

He nodded.

"Metal. You have to put the metal hangers in there. And the brown dot? That's for cardboard. You put the box in that one."

"Wait, we come from the recycling capital of California. You're saying Snapdragon is pickier than Berkeley?"

Claire shook her head. "Nope. Mother is."

"Let me get this straight. The city sends out trucks just for her, or what?"

"No, they dump them all in the same truck. The collection guys shut her up by claiming there are separate sections inside."

Jason laughed hard and long then dumped the entire box into the plastics bin.

Claire was laughing now, too. "Mother's going to be all over you for doing that. Just you wait. And don't say I didn't warn you, Magic Man."

"She's going to notice? I don't believe it! Who looks in their cans after they're on the street?"

"Mother. She doesn't want anyone stealing out of them, you know."

"You're pulling my leg."

"Look in the other bins." She lifted the brown-dot lid. At the very bottom, they saw several neatly flattened boxes. "I can almost guarantee you that now that she has a cell phone, she takes pictures. As evidence. In fact, I'd bet on it."

Jason snickered and moved to the one with the blue dot and peered in. Claire joined him. Neatly washed vegetable and soup cans lined the bottom. They moved to the green bin and it was empty except for a few small twigs. "Why does she even bother putting these out?"

At the front door, Mother and Babs appeared. They said their goodbyes and Babs smiled as she passed them. "It's wonderful to have you back, Claire. And nice to meet you, Jason."

As Babs headed home, Claire saw Mother standing in the doorway, her mouth a shocked little "O" as she watched Jason and Claire. She disappeared into the house.

"Uh-oh," said Claire. "Here it comes."

"What?"

Before she could explain, Mother was marching toward them, several empty black trash bags in hand. "Wait! Wait!"

Claire sighed and crossed her arms. "Here we go ..." Hopefully Mother would be so concerned with the recyclables she wouldn't notice the clowns in the garbage can.

"Just hold on a minute," said Mother, opening the recycle bin. "Oh, no. Let's not throw these out, kids." She dug several hangers out and stacked them on the ground.

"And why not?" Claire's voice was hard but she didn't care.

"Because," said Mother, "we can donate them. Or, better, sell them at the yard sale!" She reached into the bin and brought more out. "That's as far as I can reach. Jason, would you mind fetching the rest for me?"

"I, uh ... Sure." Jason gave Claire an uncertain glance and started digging for hangers.

Mother crouched and began placing them just so, inside the garbage bags.

Annoyed, but not wanting to make waves, Claire bent to help her, trying not to get too much of Mother's overbearing perfume up her sinuses.

"No, no, no," said Mother, snatching several hangers from Claire. "You have to stack them right or they'll tear holes in the bags. Like this." She demonstrated the correct method.

"Oh, Jesus Christ," said Claire under her breath.

"You mustn't take the Lord's name in vain! You owe the swear jar a dollar!"

Jason snorted a laugh and set the rest of the hangers on the ground as Mother stacked them into neat piles and placed them carefully in the bags.

Claire stood - too fast - and fighting a wave of dizziness, she crossed her arms against her stomach. *God, she's exhausting.* When Jason bent to help Mother, he was given the same reprimand and demonstration; the look on his face warning her that they were moments away from owing another dollar to the swear jar.

They both stepped away as Mother filled the garbage bags, all the while mumbling beneath her breath. When she was done, there were three bags full of hangers.

"I'll just take them inside for now. Surely, someone can use them." Mother looked at Claire and Jason. "I just hate throwing away something that might come in handy for someone else. Charity begins at home!" And she was off, like a little hanger-collecting tornado.

Claire blew out a sigh of relief that her mother hadn't noticed the clown portraits. As Mother disappeared up the walk and went inside, Claire said to Jason, "The hangers will go into the house, all right. And there they'll sit until the day she dies."

Jason looked incredulous. "I thought she'd be happy we were recycling them."

Claire shrugged. "Apparently not."

"But why does she want to keep them?"

"She keeps everything."

"But why?"

"Because she's crazy. Just like I've told you a hundred times." Claire shook her head and sighed. "Now, let's go make sure the U-Haul trailer is empty so you can get it turned in before five. We don't need to pay another day's rent on it."

They headed up the driveway. The trailer was empty. "I need to grab my keys," Jason said. At the foot of the stairs, he paused, eyeing the garage. "So what's in *there*?"

"Shit. Lots and lots of shit. Neatly stacked, but it's still shit. It's probably the same stuff that was in there when I was a kid. And more, of course. Mother likes to use every last inch." She paused. "And now you know why there's no trash, don't you?"

In the Swing of Things

It was nearly four-thirty when Claire rolled up the bamboo blinds covering the picture window to let in what was left of the wintery sunlight. Jason would be back soon and she thought about dinner; they'd grill the little beef filets and have them with baked potatoes and salad. There was plenty of time for that. For now, she wanted more sunlight so she crossed to the narrow wall near the TV and opened the blinds on one of the smaller windows. Below was Mother's back yard.

The AstroTurf lawn was pristine - Mother had a gardener use a leaf blower on it a couple of times a month. He also cared for the rose gardens that grew between the neat, white, garden sheds lining the big rectangular yard. She'd paid to have black shutters attached to the fake windows on the sheds so they'd match the house. There were more sheds than there used to be - several of the rose gardens had been cropped to half their original size, and at least one obliterated. The waterless birdbath - birds were messy and not wanted on Mother's property - still stood in the center of the yard, and off in the far corner was the swing set she and Timothy had played on. Looking at it made her stomach knot and a wave of dizziness passed over her. She had a sudden feeling of falling, and gripped the windowsill to steady herself.

When it passed, she opened her eyes, and stared at the ominous old play set. She didn't know why the sight of it bothered her; she couldn't even remember playing on it except for the times Tim stood behind her and pushed the swing. *God, Tim, I miss you.* He'd been the best part of her childhood.

Claire crossed back to the picture window and gazed down at Mother's big potting shed that Mother actively used. It was huge - hand-built by Dad when she was little. The roof cranked open to reveal a flat Plexiglass inner ceiling that let the building serve as a greenhouse as well. Mother loved to show it off. She started her snapdragon seeds there every year. The roof was open now, and no doubt Mother had an award-winning crop of seedlings going.

Raising her eyes, Claire looked at the back of the house. It was as neat and perfect as the front, with sliders at the kitchen and the den behind the living room. Upstairs, there were two balconies. The far one belonged to Mother's master bedroom. The other, almost directly across from the apartment, was part of a smaller bedroom Dad still lived in, as far as she knew. Even now, she avoided looking at it. She'd found it dark and frightening when she was young, with drawn drapes and handicap bars in the adjacent bathroom and near the bed. It had a medicinal smell. But nothing had been scarier to her than her father after his accident.

As a child, she'd been afraid of him because he could barely speak and when he did, it was garbled. What must have been nerve damage to his face rendered his features frightening to a small child. She'd avoided him, and now felt bad about it. She wanted to get to know him and apologize for having been so distant.

She made herself look at Dad's balcony. The drapes were open, revealing darkness beyond ... and movement.

She stared, thinking she'd imagined it. But she hadn't; slowly, an arm appeared and then, at a nearly imperceptible pace, the slider began to open. She couldn't look away. Her heart pounded.

I'm not a child anymore. There's nothing to be afraid of.

Wispy white hair appeared as the man rolled his wheelchair out onto the balcony. Slowly, he straightened, revealing his entire face. His dark eyes staring at her, boring into her soul. *Boogeyman.* Mother's voice in her head. *Boogeyman! Stay away!*

Even Mother wouldn't say that ... would she? I must have made it up. She wanted to turn, to run, but she didn't. Instead, she waved.

The old man grimaced and she knew it was a smile. She waved again.

Slowly, so slowly, he raised his arm and waved back; she could see his hand tremble with the effort. Joy replaced fear. She returned the wave then gestured at herself, then him, then herself again and pointed. *I'm coming to see you!*

Her father nodded and smiled.

***

Jason pulled the Prius into the drive and looked down at the sparkling cider. Champagne wouldn't do in Claire's condition, but he was feeling festive. After dropping off the trailer, he'd been overcome with a feeling of hope. This was a new beginning and it called for celebration. Killing the engine, he grabbed the bottle and headed toward their upstairs apartment. *Maybe I'll even get the TV hooked up and see what movies are playing.*

A soft sound caught his attention. He turned.

The mumbling came from the potting shed and, through one of the windows, he saw movement. It was Prissy; he could see the outline of her smoothly-coiffed unnaturally black hair on the other side of the glass. She made a broad sweeping gesture with her hands. Then she giggled.

Jason's breath caught when a door slammed. It was Claire at the top of the stairs. "I was going to-"

Jason raised his finger to his lips.

Claire went silent and crept down the steps. "What is it?" she whispered.

Jason pointed to the potting shed. "Your mother's in there. I think she's talking to herself."

Claire raised a brow. "Of course she is," she whispered. "She always needs to be making noise. She doesn't like silence. She says it makes her nervous."

Jason smiled. "Don't be so hard on her. She's probably lonely."

Prissy giggled.

Claire shook her head. "She's always done that. Even with people around. It's embarrassing." She looked down at the bottle in Jason's hand.

"Cider." He raised it. "To celebrate." He kept his voice at a whisper.

In the background, Mother said, "Of course I'll win the Snapdragon Festival this year!"

Claire's eyes darted to the potting shed. She crossed her eyes and made a swirling motion at her temple.

"Well, at least she's having a good time." Jason grinned.

"I'm on my way to see my dad. Care to join me?"

He suddenly felt nervous.

Claire poked him in the ribs. "You're not anxious about meeting my father, are you?"

Jason shrugged. "Maybe a little."

"You're adorable. But don't worry. He'll love you. Come on." She took his free hand and they headed into the house.

Pink Roses and Ribbons

Fred Martin was a captive in his own body and had been since Carlene had been little more than a toddler. Since the accident had taken his legs all those years ago - such a foolish, ridiculous thing, falling off a ladder - he'd seen little but this room.

Carlene hadn't been easy around him once she saw the droop in his face and heard his garbled speech. Priscilla had told him he terrified their daughter, and wasn't going to make her visit him. The girl thought her own father was the bogeyman, Priscilla had said. He understood and wished he'd died in that accident.

And then yesterday, after years of silence, he thought he heard Carlene's voice - and that of a young man's. Just now, when he rolled onto the balcony and looked across the way and saw her, he thought she was a hallucination. Lord knew he'd had plenty of those over the last twenty-odd years. Carlene had smiled and waved, and he did the same. He hoped she was real.

***

Upstairs, Claire tried the door, but the knob turned uselessly. The deadbolt was locked. *Of course.* It wasn't a skeleton key lock like Mother had kept on her room and Tim's, and the bathroom they used, but a proper, modern lock. *I guess she doesn't feel the need to peek through the keyhole at him like she did us.* God, she'd hated living in Mother's house. *Dad must hate it even more,* she thought as she looked at the narrow side table where Mother kept medicines, towels, and a pitcher of water. A glass rested on a round white doily; she lifted it, felt under the doily and found the key.

"She keeps him locked in here?" Jason fingered the dried blue statice bouquet behind the pitcher. A dried-flower wreath hung on the door, all pink roses and ribbons. Every door had a wreath and there were small side tables of vases holding dried flowers lining the entire corridor.

"If he gets out, he could hurt himself on the stairs. After a near-miss, she began locking the door with *that*." She looked at the lock. "That's a double deadbolt - so he can't let himself out.

"It seems cruel to lock him away."

"It *is* cruel." Claire slid the key in, turned it, and the lock clicked. The door swung open. They stared into the room. The last dregs of sunlight shone through the slider, a thick swarm of dust-motes swirled lazily in the light.

Her father sat by the slider and, as they entered, he began turning his chair in a half-circle to face them.

"Dad?"

Her father's dark eyes, encircled in folds of gray flesh, turned watery. He raised his hands and they quivered in the air a moment; he was reaching out to her.

Claire approached and bent to embrace him. His weak arms circled her and he tried to say her name, but could only manage "Carrrr."

"Dad, I've missed you," she said when she finally broke the hug. His shoulders were so thin they creaked; she was afraid of breaking him. She had dim memories of a tall strong man holding her in his arms, though it might have been Timothy, not Dad. Her memories were blurred.

He studied her with his brown eyes. They were sharp, full of intelligence.

"Dad, I'm so sorry. I didn't realize …"

"Misss," he drawled slowly, painfully. "You." His eyes traveled to Jason.

"Dad, this is my husband, Jason Holbrook. Jason, this is my dad, Frederick Martin."

"Fredddd," he said.

Jason stepped forward and shook the old man's outstretched hand. "Good to meet you, sir."

Fred grimaced a smile and nodded.

"We're staying here for a little while," Claire said. "Jason is going to be teaching at the flight school at Snapdragon Airport. He's a pilot."

Fred nodded, his eyes bright and full. "Youu?"

"I'm a graphic artist now. I design websites for people. I own my own business."

Fred cocked his head.

"I'll explain later," Claire promised. "By the way, you're going to be a grandfather."

The old man beamed and looked from her abdomen to her face.

"In seven months," she said.

He made a sound of delight. Then his face changed and he looked at the door.

Claire followed his gaze. "She's coming?"

He nodded.

Mother rushed into the room in a wave of sickly-sweet perfume, a glass of water in her hand. Her gaze trapped Claire. "I'd rather you'd have let me know you were going to pay your father a visit. He has several nap times during the day and we don't want to interrupt his sleep. And as it happens," she said, reaching into her pocket, "it's time for his medication." She withdrew an amber prescription bottle and bustled toward him. Unscrewing the cap, she shook several white pills into her palm.

Something flashed in Fred's eyes.

"He hates taking his medication, but ..." She sighed. "Doctor's orders." She brought her hand to his mouth, pushed in the pills, then held the glass of water to his lips.

He raised a shaking hand and placed it on Mother's wrist.

"He likes to help," Mother said to Claire, who thought it looked more like he was trying to push her away. Finished, she stood back and gave her husband a sweet smile. "You always were so independent, Frankl-Frederick."

Claire wondered if she ever got anyone's name right. And if it bothered him that she'd almost called him by his brother's name after all these years.

"Now then," said Mother, facing Claire and Jason. "That's enough excitement for one day. Your father needs to nap." She looked at her husband and bellowed. "Are you ready for your nap?"

He winced and shook his head.

Mother fluttered her hand in the air. "Nonsense. It's nap time." She got behind his chair and wheeled him toward the bed. "Why don't you kids go downstairs? I have to check his didey."

Dad cringed, his face red with embarrassment. Then he looked at the bed and shook his head again. "Mother," Claire began, "I-"

"You two have plenty of time to play catch up, Claire. You can talk to your father later."

"Mother, Dad can talk. Why don't you let him?"

Priscilla shook her head. "I'm sorry, dear. He just makes sounds. Don't you remember? It's not just nerve damage, there's brain damage as well." She gave Claire a sweet, sad look. "I know you want your daddy, really I do. We all want him back. But he's gone."

"*Mother!* He's not gone and he knows exactly what you're saying. He's not deaf, either. If you'd pay attention, you'd know that."

"I've been the *only* one paying attention to him for years, and I've seen what I thought were moments of clarity, too. But Dr. Hopper has assured me that isn't the case, and I don't want you to get your hopes up the way I did. It's a very heartbreaking situation, Car-Claire."

"Carrrrl-"

Her dad's eyes were on her, pleading.

"Run along, now," said Mother. "Your father needs to maintain his self-respect and diaper-changing is a bit awkward, as you can imagine." She bent and hooked her arms under his.

"Do you need any help?" asked Jason.

Mother frowned. "I've been managing him all by myself for many years now, Jason, sweetheart. You do know I'm a registered nurse, don't you?" She glanced at Claire. "But I appreciate the offer."

Feast Your Eyes

"I think I'm really going to like this job," said Jason, taking a seat on the recliner Monday evening. "It already feels rewarding." He frowned at the TV. "I still need to get that thing set up. Maybe I should speak to your mother about getting the satellite people to take a look. Something's wrong. I can't figure it out."

Claire emptied the day's compartment of vitamins into her mouth, chased them with a glass of water, then replaced the pill organizer in the drawer before planting herself on the sofa. She hoped the vitamins would revive her - she'd woken up tired and it hadn't gotten any better. "No rush," she said. "So you enjoyed your first day?"

"I really did. It's not flying, but it's the next best thing. You know, when life gives you lemons …"

"Make lemonade," Claire finished. "So, you think you'll enjoy being an instructor?"

"I do. Seriously, I've got several really strong students I'm pretty excited about. I think two of them might even have commercial airline potential."

Claire watched her husband. She knew he was still heartbroken about giving up flying, but she admired his willingness to accept what life had handed him. You're so good for me."

Jason cocked a brow. "How do you mean?"

She shrugged. "You just have a great attitude. I adore that about you. I mean it."

Jason shifted in his seat. "Thank you."

She smiled. "Now tell me more about your job."

"Well, it's *almost* flying." His eyes brightened the way they always did when he talked about his passion. "We did some computer simulations that were a lot of fun - it's almost like being in the cockpit again." He grinned. "What about you? How was your day?"

"I did a lot of eating," she said. "Seriously. This pregnancy business is going to make me fat. Will you still love me if I get fat?"

"Of course, I'll still love you. I'll miss you, but I'll still love you." He laughed.

Claire threw a pillow at him. "Other than eating, I worked on the business - mostly trying to get things in order. I need to build my client list, do some advertising. It'll take time." She made a face. "I'm thinking of taking an ad out in the paper and drumming up some local business, too."

"Good idea." Jason stood and headed into the kitchen. "I'm glad you're back at it, but remember what Dr. Lightfoot said: Take it real easy, especially in the first trimester." He reappeared in the doorway, a diet soda in one hand and a piece of bread in the other. "Did you get a referral from him yet?"

"Not yet. There are only so many obstetricians in town, so I hope he finds me a good one."

Jason took a bite out of the bread. "Do you want anything to eat?"

"Absolutely not. I've had plenty. Don't tempt me."

"So, what about your mom's doctor? Hopper? Is he any good?"

Claire frowned. "I don't want the same doctor as my mother. She gets too close to people, and I wouldn't want them discussing my business." She heard Mother's car starting downstairs.

Jason moved to the window and stared out. "Speaking of your mother, where is she off to?"

Claire looked at the clock. "A Ladies Auxiliary Meeting. She'll be there until ten. She told me all about it. At length." She grimaced as Mother's BMW hummed away in the darkness. "Would you like to go see my dad with me? I want to pay him another visit."

"You've been waiting for her to leave to go see him, haven't you?"

"Guilty as charged. I'd like to spend some uninterrupted time with him."

"Maybe I should stay here, then."

"No," said Claire. "I'd really like you to come. It still feels kind of weird, you know? Actually talking to him?" She knew her father was far more alert than Mother claimed. It was eating at her; she needed to know more.

"All right," said Jason. "Do you want to head over now?"

"Let's go."

***

"The key's not here." Claire spoke softly so as not to disturb her father in case he was sleeping.

"Maybe your mother forgot to put it back."

"Mother never forgets. She removed the key on purpose. She doesn't want us going in unsupervised."

Jason touched her elbow and guided her away from the door. "Maybe, but we can't do anything about it now, so how about you give me a tour?"

She looked at the door, knowing Mother would have made sure she couldn't find the key. *Sorry, Dad.* "A tour? What do you want to see?"

"Everything." He grinned. "Let's start with your old room."

"Okay, but it's probably full of more of Mother's junk." She squared her shoulders, refusing to acknowledge the knots in her belly.

"Show me everything!"

"Follow me."

She led him halfway down the hall and as she paused in front of her old bedroom, a voice suddenly echoed in her mind. *"Touch them! Touch them, Carlene!"* It was the voice she'd heard in her dream when they'd been driving to Snapdragon. *"Touch them!"*

"Are you okay, sweetie?" Jason held her elbow. "What is it?"

"Nothing," she said. "I'm fine." As quickly as the disembodied voice had come, it vanished.

A wreath of dried lavender hung on the door in front of her. She glanced down the long hallway: Each door appeared to have a different kind of wreath, but all were dry, gaudy, and covered in a film of dust, as were the dried flower arrangements on the side tables dotting the hall. The very real smell of dust and dead flowers cloyed and mixed - for just an instant - with a ghost of Clorox. She knew the scent of bleach wasn't real - it never was - and had no idea why she'd smelled it. It had dogged her until she'd moved away, and now it was back. She shivered. "Chances are it's locked, but you never know." The knob turned. "It's your lucky day, Jason."

She gave the door a nudge, but something blocked it. After a harder shove, it opened about a foot and an avalanche of video and music cassettes clattered to the floor.

"Feast your eyes."

Gazing in, they saw plastic-covered clothes on racks, chairs stacked halfway to the ceiling, and several boxes of Corelle dinner sets that looked unopened. Poking her head inside, she spied a half dozen dust-covered three-foot stacks of *National Geographic*s, an upside down microwave, and what appeared to be a banged up wooden headboard leaning against a wall. There were lamps - lots and lots of lamps - some old, some relatively new, all ugly. Through small breaks in the jumble of videocassettes, LPs, and about a hundred dusty paperbacks, she could see the carpet - which had once been a shade of pale peach but was now a dirty beige. The smell of dust clogged her throat, but it was better than bleach.

"Jesus Christ!" Jason coughed. "What is all this stuff?"

Claire grinned. "It might be useful to someone, don't you know?" Her tone was mocking.

"But ..."

"And this is just *one* room. I guarantee you, they're all like this."

"But what does she *do* with it all?"

Claire chuckled. "She's going to have a yard sale." She made air quotes around the words. "She's been going to have it since I was in utero, but you know, one of these days, she'll get around to it." She laughed, forcing herself to see the humor, to keep her mind from conjuring up imaginary nightmares. *"Touch them!"*

"Won't she participate in the street's yard sale next weekend?"

"Oh, she'll be there, she always is, every year, but she only supervises. She's a pathological hoarder. I'd be amazed if she set out so much as a hanger."

Jason grinned. "We could steal our hangers back and sell them ourselves!"

Claire laughed. "Don't tempt me." She paused. "No, *do* tempt me! I want to watch her squirm!"

"I'm game. Where do you think she put them?"

"I haven't a clue, but if we can't find them, we'll find something. Something of ours to sell. Just wait until you see how she reacts!"

"Sounds good." Jason pulled the door closed and kissed Claire. "I'm sorry," he said.

"About what?"

He cocked his head toward the door. "All that."

"Why are you sorry? I told you what we'd find."

"I really thought she would have preserved your room."

"You're so sentimental. I love you. But that's Mother for you." She grinned and rubbed her hands together. "Let's try some other doors."

"Lead on!" They continued down the hall and made a random stop, found that door locked, then tried another. It was unlocked, and after a couple of shoves, they got the door open and Jason peered in. This room mostly contained heaping stacks of black garbage bags.

"Old clothes," Claire explained, rolling her eyes.

"And more lamps." Jason stared into the sea of dusty, abandoned light fixtures. "Why all the lamps?"

Claire shrugged. "Ironically, I'm afraid I can't shed any light on that."

Jason groaned then they moved to a third room, where they saw clothes racks, several old desks, all covered with an assortment of books, board games from the sixties and seventies, a few broken table fans, cookie tins, and several giant bags of empty soup cans. Embroidery craft sets were strewn among a clutter of *Reader's Digest*s, and several brightly-colored hula hoops were tossed haphazardly, like lifesavers, among the debris.

"Wait till you see what Mother refers to as 'the pantry.'" Claire shut the door and Jason followed her down to the basement. It was unfinished and smelled of dust, cement, and something dead. This, too, brimmed with outdated items, more clothes that appeared to be at least forty years old, and plastic tubs overflowing with records, cassettes, and yet more *National Geographic*s. A ceiling-high stack of lampshades teetered in a corner by the water heater.

"This," said Claire, pulling back a dusty curtain that concealed the area beneath the stairs, "is the pantry."

Wooden bookcases lined the walls and Jason stared in awe at row after row of canned soups, vegetables, and fruit. Other shelves held soaps, shampoos, laundry detergent, and cleaning supplies. There was even more here now than there used to be. *My mother, the hoarder.*

Claire plucked a bottle of ranch dressing off a shelf. "Expiration date, November, 2004." She took another. "June of 2001."

Jason was only half-listening. He'd fixated on several dozen packs of indeterminable dried fruit that had gone brown and black and looked like bags of dead cockroaches. She watched him gape at the rows of unopened laundry detergents, which sported images of women in white aprons, heels, and beehive hair-dos, smiling as they inspected the cleanliness of their linens. Others portrayed young hippie women with flowers in their hair, washing their tie-dyed garments with joy.

"Ooh," said Claire, shaking a bottle of A1 Steak Sauce. "This only expired three and a half years ago. Mother's really getting modern in her old age."

Jason blinked. "But ... why? It's not edible? Why keep it?"

Claire affected her mother's nasal voice and wagged a finger at him. "Waste not, want not, young man."

"Is she preparing for some kind of zombie apocalypse or something?"

Claire laughed. "No. She just refuses to throw anything out." Claire glanced at four black garbage bags in the corner. "Speaking of which ..." She dragged one into the light and untied it. "Yep. Just what I thought." She held it open for Jason to see.

Inside were the neatly stacked hangers they'd tried to throw out.

"We need to contribute something to the yard sale, Jason. After all, it was your suggestion." She grinned.

"You mean it?" He nodded at the hangers.

"Absolutely."

Jason laughed.

Claire retied the bag and set it aside. "So what do you think of all this?"

He looked around the vast basement at the heaping mountains of forgotten junk, then looked at Claire. "No wonder she drove you crazy."

Claire's smile disappeared. "Oh, you don't know the half of it, Jason. This is just the eccentric tip of the iceberg."

"So is this where your mom keeps all her diamonds and gold to make jewelry?"

Claire made a face. "That's what she calls it, but no, that's upstairs."

"Can we see her work room?"

"You're serious?"

"I said I wanted to see it all!"

Claire glanced at her watch. "We have at least an hour before she comes back, so, sure."

They trotted back up to the second floor, pausing only to deposit the bag of hangers by the kitchen door. Upstairs, Claire halted in front of the last room on the left and tried the knob. It moved freely. "If she hasn't moved it, this will be her workroom."

This door sported a nest of dried, dusty marigolds.

Father Andy Gets a Headache

Father Andy stood at the back of the meeting at Holy Sacramental and tried not to glance at his wristwatch. Priscilla Martin was on a roll, inspiring the Ladies Auxiliary to loftier goals in the fight to feed Snapdragon's poor and homeless. She was proposing the city make a homeless camp out by the airport. There, they could camp out and earn their meals - and even earn tents - by doing volunteer work for the city; picking up trash, beautifying the highway, gardening, and a myriad of other jobs Priscilla deemed them worthy to do.

Mary Bell raised her hand. "Prissy, I don't think the handicapped or even women or families with small children should be made to work so hard simply to qualify for a tent." There were murmurs of assent.

If looks could kill. Priscilla Martin fixed little Mary Bell, a woman in her forties who looked all of sixteen with her cute chestnut bob and rosy cheeks, in her sights. "Every human being, no matter what their station in life, deserves a chance to earn what they require. To take that away from them diminishes them."

In some ways, Father Andy admired Priscilla Martin, though he had to admit, he often disagreed with her ideas - she was too Old Testament for his tastes. He studied her; she was dressed in a soft lavender skirt and jacket and matching pumps that looked brand new but the padded shoulders screamed of the eighties.

"Father? Father Andrew?"

He looked up. Priscilla Martin was staring at him.

"I'm sorry?"

"Don't you agree, Father?"

He felt a vein in his temple start to throb. "I think everyone deserves shelter and food. These are basic human rights and the most Christian of tenets."

Priscilla's smile showed too many teeth. "And every human being has a right to earn these things, don't you agree, Father?"

The forehead vein did a boogie. "As it says in Deuteronomy 15:8, '*You shall freely open your hand to him, and shall generously lend him sufficient for his need in whatever he lacks.*' I think this means we must take into account the fact that some people need more help than others, and follow Christ's example."

He thought he saw a flash of anger in Priscilla's eyes. "I suppose, Father." She sighed. "Perhaps we can compensate for the handicapped and very young by holding contests among the homeless. You know, things that might entertain those of us more fortunate - things we would pay to see."

"Prissy wants bum fights," Lizzie Knudsen called out.

Father Andy cringed. A vein on his left temple bongoed along with the right one now. Lizzie was a brash woman, but fair and honest. And she loathed Priscilla Martin. Before Priscilla could speak, Andy forced himself to join her at the podium. "An amusing joke, Lizzie, but I'm afraid we're out of time for tonight, ladies. Before you go, I want to thank you for your wonderful report on our Winter Wonderland sales figures, Mrs. Dexter."

"My pleasure." Hannah beamed.

"And thank you, Priscilla, for starting plans for our St. Patrick's Day Social. We would be lost without you."

Priscilla's frown turned upside down, as he'd hoped. But still, his head ached more and more.

"Madame Secretary," he continued, before Priscilla could open her mouth, "please note that we were discussing sheltering the homeless and will continue on with that next week as our first order of business. Goodnight, ladies."

The twenty or so women rose, talking with one another as they filed out. Andy turned to leave.

"Father Andrew," called Priscilla Martin, "may I have a few words with you?"

He winced, wanting only some Excedrin and a bottle of dark beer to chase the pills. "Yes, Priscilla? What is it?"

"I thought perhaps we could sit down over a glass of wine and discuss this problem with the homeless." Her smile disturbed him.

Boom boom boom went his headache. He cleared his throat. "I'm sorry, I have other business I must attend to tonight. Perhaps you and Jane or Babs and some of the other ladies might relax and chat. I see Geneva-Marie hasn't left yet. I'm sure she'd love to talk."

Priscilla looked annoyed. "You're sure? I-"

"I really have to run," Andy said. "I'm sorry."

"Very well. Are you feeling all right, Father? You look a little pale. Do you have a fever?" She reached up to feel his forehead and he stepped out of reach.

Lying was a sin. "A bit of a headache," he admitted. "I need to get home before it gets any worse."

Priscilla tapped her folder of notes on the podium in time with the throbbing in his head, and passed him by on heels that clicked too loudly. The cloud of perfume she left behind tap danced in his skull. She walked quickly out, barely nodding goodbye to her friend, Babs Vandercooth.

Father Andy waited until the last knot of ladies left the room, then turned off the painfully bright lights, locked up in sweet darkness, and headed for the rectory next door. After letting himself in the white frame house, he headed upstairs for pain relievers, then back down to the kitchen, where he fetched a Guinness Black. He took it into the shadowed living room and sank into his easy chair without bothering to turn on the TV. When he had a headache, silence and darkness were the only entertainment he craved.

He finished the lager, closed his eyes, and just as he felt himself begin to doze, someone pounded on the door. Andy did not condone profanity, but it was with great discipline that he resisted the temptation to curse as he rose from the warmth of his easy chair and crossed to the door.

***

"Yep," said Claire. "This is Mother's workroom."

Jason followed her in. This was nothing like the other rooms; it was virtually spotless and everything seemed to have a place. A polished wooden worktable dominated the west wall under a large window with frilly stark-white curtains. Beneath a large task lamp, the desktop was home to neatly stacked plastic boxes full of beads of all colors and sizes, spindles of twines and wires, and small tools that Jason didn't recognize. There wasn't a speck of dust to be seen.

Claire held up one of the plastic boxes. "Want to see something really creepy?" She removed the lid and Jason peered inside.

"Hair?"

"Yep. That's what all of these are." She pointed to a stack next to the desk.

"Whose hair?"

"Some of it's hers. Some of it belongs to friends - after all, what's a better gift than a necklace or bracelet made out of your own hair? And most of it - like this - belonged to Tim."

Jason cringed. "Oh, my God. You're pulling my leg."

Claire shook her head.

"But how did she-"

"She had his hair cut short for the funeral. She said he looked like a hippie. He wasn't even safe from her criticism in death." She took a bracelet with turquoise stones off the desk and held it up. "Anyway, this is what she did with it." She handed him the accessory and he inspected it, shuddering when he realized the beads and stones were strung together with hair.

"She likes to keep him with her at all times. She always wears one of his hair necklaces. Always."

Bile rose in Jason's stomach as he recalled Prissy leaning over at dinner to pass him a dish and the necklace had dipped into the Alfredo. *"This necklace is very precious to me,"* she'd said. He remembered her sucking the cheese off the hair necklace. Queasy, he told himself that grief was a powerful emotion and had strange effects on people. *But the guy's been dead for years.* "You knew and you brought the Alfredo back to the apartment?"

Claire shrugged. "It went down the garbage disposal. Now, let me show you her bedroom."

***

"May I come in, Father Andrew?" Priscilla Martin smiled at him and he could've sworn she batted her eyelashes, but that was probably just the dregs of his headache, dull now, soothed with Guinness and Excedrin and a nap; a nap cut far too short.

"Uh, yes." He stepped back and she entered, her soft lavender skirt swirling gracefully around her knees. The matching jacket was unbuttoned now, and the ivory shell beneath it revealed her horrid hair necklace and more cleavage than he was comfortable with. It wasn't at all outrageous, though, and in fact, he was pretty sure his reaction was all about that Guinness and the headache. He felt groggy, a little stupid.

She turned to face him and held up a bottle of Merlot. "This vintage is guaranteed to cure headaches."

"That's very kind of you, Priscilla, but I'm afraid wine disagrees with me."

"This won't." With her free hand, she touched the hair necklace. Its golden beads shone in the lamplight. It held an amber pendant that matched her disturbingly pale eyes.

"Reds are particularly hard on my system," he told her. "I'm sorry. It's very thoughtful of you."

"Well then, I'll have a glass if you don't mind."

"Um, if you want."

"And I'll give you this." She brought a small plastic pill case out of her purse and opened one compartment. "This is a very mild painkiller - just a little acetaminophen with a teensy dash of codeine. It will fix you right up."

"That's a prescription drug."

She smiled. "And I'm here to prescribe it for you." She paused. "My dear boy, you do know I'm a nurse, don't you?"

"Uh, I thought you were retired."

She laughed. "I keep my license up to date because I'm my poor husband's full-time nurse. Now, you go ahead and take this."

"I just drank a beer, so I don't think I should."

"Nonsense. It's fine. You're a strapping young man. It'll make you feel better."

"No, really, it's okay. The headache is almost gone. Excedrin worked just fine."

"You know that has caffeine in it, don't you?" Priscilla lifted the amber pendant and let it drop inside her blouse, against skin.

"Yes, I do."

Her eyebrow arched. "That can make your heart race."

He forced a smile. "I rely on coffee to do that every morning." He saw annoyance flash in her eyes and he nearly accepted the pill, not to swallow, just to please her, but decided against it. "I'll get you your glass of wine."

"And I don't want to drink alone, Father." Priscilla practically purred. "I want you to have a beer with me, at least."

In the kitchen, he poured a modest glass of wine, then opened the fridge and started to take out a Guinness. *Wait a minute. I really don't want this.* He put it back and withdrew a can of Orange Crush instead.

Returning, he handed the wine glass to Priscilla Martin, who had perched on his sofa. He returned to his easy chair.

"Cheers," said Priscilla, saluting him with the Merlot.

"Cheers," he replied, hefting the orange soda.

She looked shocked and truly irritated when he popped the top. "Seriously, Father? Soda?"

"It's my favorite. I only allow myself one soda a day. This is my second, so it's a rare treat."

"Very well, Father." Priscilla Martin crossed her ankles and fingered the amber pendant through her blouse. "Now, let's talk about the homeless situation and how we can most painlessly deal with it."

Father Andy groaned.

Star-Spangled Angel

"Mother's bedroom," Claire said, opening a door directly across the hall from the craft room. This one sported a massive pink hydrangea wreath that matched the oversized bouquet on the side table. Unlike the other arrangements, these were dust-free. "Gentlemen first."

Jason walked in and stopped cold. "Holy crap! There are dogs on her bed! One's looking at me! I didn't know she had dogs." He hesitated. "Hey guys... girls, good dogs ..."

"Don't bother, Jason. They're dead." Claire walked to the foot of the bed. "That was Chopsticks," she said, pointing to a brown and white shih tzu nestled on the left-hand pillow. "The one looking at you was General Tso, and the black and white one on the right was Wonton."

Jason couldn't believe his eyes. He'd heard of people stuffing pets, but having them on her bed was the most morbid thing he'd ever seen. "They have names?"

"Of course. These were her beloved pets." Claire grinned. "Mother never lets go of anything."

"Tell me she doesn't sleep with them. Please."

Claire patted Wonton's head. "I don't know for sure, but probably. She did when I was a kid. But there were only two then. The third one was living and he wasn't allowed to sleep on the bed until after she had him freeze-dried."

"That's too creepy, Claire." He shuddered.

Her smile could fracture glass. "Tell me about it."

Jason made himself step closer and inspected the blank marble eyes and glazed noses.

"They gave me nightmares when I was little." By her tone, he wondered if the bad dreams had ever stopped.

"How old are they?"

"I only remember Wonton. I grew up with him. General Tso died right before I was born, and Chopsticks, his replacement, was hit by a car when I was only three."

"She must have really loved those dogs." He was trying hard to put a good spin on it.

"She still does, obviously." Claire looked at him. "You want to hear about the quilt? She made it herself."

The quilt had a lot of colors and appeared to be made of all kinds of materials, with a lot of blue denim stars sewn into it. It was well-made but odd, and old-looking. "Um, do I want to know?"

Claire barked a laugh. "It's her own design. She calls it 'Star-Spangled Angel.'"

"Okay... And ... What-"

"After my brother died, she cut up his clothes and made the quilt out of them."

"That's a little creepy-"

"Oh, there's more, Jason. There's more."

"I can't even guess ..."

"Most of the quilt squares and stars are made of the clothing he was wearing when he died. She added a few other things - some material from his childhood pajamas - see the blue flannel with the little rabbits and the yellow with red fire engines?"

Jason nodded.

"Mother likes lots of color. Now, most of the denim stars are from his death jeans, and the pale blue squares are from the shirt he was wearing - good thing it had long sleeves, huh? And see this white stretchy cloth? T-Shirt." She bent over and pointed at a square that had an odd overlaid stitching across it that looked vaguely familiar. "I kid you not, tighty-whities - nothing went to waste." Claire looked ill behind her hard expression.

Jason touched one of the white ribbed squares crossed by red stripes. "Socks?"

Claire nodded.

"And she told you all this?"

"I watched her make it. She treats it like it's a holy relic. I was never allowed to touch it."

"That is the creepiest thing I've ever heard."

"No it isn't. There's more."

He raised his brows.

"She made it without washing the clothes first. She never washes the quilt. That's why Wonton wasn't allowed on it until he died. She wanted to preserve - and I'm using her words, 'Timothy's essence.'"

"She wanted to be able to smell him?"

"I believe so. That's why it's a little yellowed, too. She only vacuums it. With a special vacuum." She moved toward the head of the bed and pointed out a discolored blue square. "Vomit," she said, her voice just short of shaking. "Enough of this. Come over here."

He followed her to a long desk that held a closed laptop and a small printer. Above it, the wall was filled with evenly spaced framed photographs, all surrounding a flat-screen TV. He looked them over: there was Tim Martin, about ten years old, in his baseball uniform. Another one showed him a few years later, grinning as a giraffe ate something from his palm at a zoo. Next to that, Timothy held a swaddled baby - Claire, he assumed - and Jason realized with a deep sadness for his wife that this was the only picture that included her. Scanning, hoping to see at least one more, he saw Tim as a young man, his golden hair flowing over his shoulders or in a ponytail, photos of Tim in a suit with Prissy on his arm dressed in her Easter finest, photos of him in shorts sunning himself in the back yard. Then Jason's eyes stopped. He gasped. The picture he stared at was centered in a thick gold frame edged with crosses. It was a close-up of Timothy's face, eyes closed, his features clearly painted to create a life-like appearance. "Oh, my God. Is he …"

"Dead. Yes." Claire pointed to a desk against another wall. "She has an entire album of his death portraits in there. She switches them out every so often. Or at least, she used to."

Jason's eyes returned to the picture of the dead man, his gaze riveted as he made out a small amount of flesh-colored dust that had flecked the short blond hair, the powdery over-pinkness of the cheeks and lips, and even some tiny pieces of glue at the corners of the straight, grim mouth. "I can't believe it," he said. "Why didn't you tell me about this before?"

Claire shrugged. "I don't like talking about it. I don't like talking about *her*. Do you want to see Tim's room?"

Jason hesitated.

"It's not as bad as this one, I promise."

He swallowed around the lump in his throat. Following her out, he noticed a framed five by seven atop the dresser in which a young man stood smiling in front of a shiny black classic Mustang. He looked a little like Timothy, but Jason was sure it wasn't him.

"That's our cousin, Justin," explained Claire. "From Madelyn. He died in that car just a few months after that photo was taken. He was street racing."

"Jesus Christ, Almighty." Jason's voice was a hoarse whisper. "I'm so sorry, Claire. Now I understand why you didn't want to come here."

She smiled, but it didn't reach her eyes. "Oh, there's more," she said.

The lump in Jason's throat swelled.

***

Father Andy's headache had made a comeback - a drum solo behind his eyelids that would have made Mick Fleetwood proud. It was strong enough he felt it in his teeth. Priscilla Martin was determined to sway him to her belief that every homeless person had to work in exchange for basic shelter. The longer she talked - she was finishing her third glass of wine - the more strident she became. It wasn't attractive. He understood clearly now that Priscilla Martin's main motive was to remove the homeless from view. That's why she insisted they be moved to a camp - she actually said "encampment" during the second glass of wine. Her unchristian belief was that they were an eyesore, and she simply wanted to tuck them neatly away where no "self-respecting citizen of Snapdragon" would ever have to be "subjected" to them.

He was very glad he'd skipped the second Guinness - he would have lost his temper and argued with her instead of trying politely to reason. But by her third glass, there was no reasoning at all. He stood up. "It's getting late and I have an early Mass. May I call you a taxi?"

She fluttered her eyelashes. "Oh, Father Andrew, I'm perfectly capable of driving myself home."

He almost argued, but held his tongue, telling himself it was pointless because no one ever won an argument with Priscilla Martin. But secretly, he questioned his motives - perhaps he was taking too much delight in the thought of her being arrested and hauled into jail for a DUI. *Priests are only human, after all ...*

She made no move to rise until he crossed to the door and held it open. "I'll see you at church Sunday morning," he said.

She stood and came to face him, her scent arousing his already-thudding headache. "Bright and early," she said, then her hand snaked, and she snatched at his face. "Got'cher nose!" She grinned at him, her Merlot breath competing with her perfume.

Andy cringed at her touch. She'd been fingering that hair necklace all night.

She giggled, then turned and walked briskly down the sidewalk to her car with no trace of a drunken stagger. Andy closed the door. Sighing, he returned to his easy chair and closed his eyes.

Priscilla was a good woman in many ways, and good for the church. She was industrious and indefatigable, a strong speaker, able to inspire the other ladies to greater heights. She was a powerful leader. Perhaps, Andy thought, a little too powerful. Her tendency to steamroll might get her thrown out of office as president of the Auxiliary someday soon, and he dreaded that day. Even if she was a bit of a tyrant, he was convinced nothing would go right without her. When Father Dave Flannigan had turned over the reins of Holy Sacramental to him, he'd said as much. Andy wondered what Flannigan really thought of Priscilla Martin.

He sipped the dregs of his Orange Crush. *Keep Prissy Martin happy, and your events will practically run themselves,* Flannigan had once told him. It seemed an innocent statement at the time, but now Andy couldn't help wondering exactly what he'd meant.

Dave Flannigan had said more on the night of his farewell party, but Andy couldn't remember much. *Keep her happy, don't cross her if you disagree, just turn the other cheek, and find another way around it. Keep her purring, Andy, but never get too close.*

He hadn't talked with Dave Flannigan in far too long. He glanced at the phone, but it was late and the old priest was probably asleep by now. *Time enough to talk later.* He rose and headed upstairs for a couple more Excedrin and a few hours of sleep.

***

This was not how Tim had kept his room. Her brother was twenty when he'd died and she'd never seen an American flag, baseball pennant, or football poster anywhere. This was the bedroom of a boy no older than ten - Claire assumed this was how it might have looked before she'd come along, and he'd been an only child - pushed by Mother to be an all-American little boy.

On the shelves of a wooden headboard were a series of books: *The Hardy Boys*, the scriptures, and a few installments of James Howe's *Bunnicula* series. Front and center atop the highest shelf was a bold golden crucifix, Jesus seeming to stare down at the pillow as he grimaced from the cross.

The bedspread was light blue, and a pillowcase sported grinning *Peanuts* characters.

Whether the chill came from within the room or from within herself, Claire didn't know, but she shuddered.

"This is a little boy's room," said Jason. "I thought Timothy was older when ..."

"He was. Clearly Mother has redecorated." Claire's eyes slid to the closet. She nodded toward it. "That's where he ..." She couldn't bring herself to say it.

Jason put an arm around her shoulder. "Do you want to leave?"

She shook her head and steeled herself, ignoring the tears that pricked her eyes. She broke from Jason's touch and moved toward the closet. Opening the door, her heart sank, and the beginnings of a dark rage threatened to overcome her. From hangers hung the clothes of a young boy, ranging from toddler-size and stopping before puberty. She recognized some of the shirts from photographs she'd seen over the years, and knew these were clothes from his boyhood. *She's sick. She's a sick, twisted woman.*

Jason stepped over but kept a distance, remaining silent as Claire slid the clothing on the rod. She looked down and saw masses of shoe boxes neatly stacked on the floor. Inside were Timothy's old shoes - dozens of pairs, beginning with baby booties and ending, again, just before his teenage years. Claire stood and stepped back. On a shelf above the clothing rod were six little green G.I. Joe action figures, weapons in hand, huddled together as if having a meeting. Beyond them was a stack of board games, all for the age group of six to twelve years old.

"This is her way of making sure he never grows up in her mind." Her voice shook.

"This is crazy, Claire. I think we need to leave." Jason's tone was solemn; she could tell he knew she was upset, and that bothered her. She cleared her throat and blinked away incipient tears before facing him.

"I'm okay, Jason. It's just hard to see. I never knew Tim when he was a boy. He was ten when I was born, so this isn't how I remember him. I never even knew he liked to play with toy soldiers."

Jason nodded, worry on his face. "I think we should go."

Claire opened her mouth to agree, but suddenly, from nowhere, a memory floated into her awareness. *The secret place. Tim's secret place.* He'd let her hide her favorite toy there when Mother had gone on a rampage. *Mr. Anton! How did I forget about Mr. Anton?* Claire had only been five or six and she'd talked back to Mother at the dinner table. Mother informed her that after the meal, she'd be holding Claire's toys for a month as punishment. Claire began to cry and while Mother lectured her, Timothy excused himself and sneaked into Claire's room, taking her stuffed golden bear, Mr. Anton. He stashed it away in his secret hiding place and let Claire come in and play with it when Mother wasn't looking.

Timothy used the hidey-hole for belongings he wanted to keep from Mother's prying eyes and hands: books she wouldn't approve of, drawings he knew she'd take away. Once, Claire even found a pack of cigarettes and some dirty magazines in there. That's when she'd stopped snooping. Curious as she'd been, there were certain things she hadn't needed to know about her brother.

She wondered now if Mother had ever found his hiding place.

"I just want to check one more thing." She crouched and reached under Timothy's bed and found the corner of loose carpet. She lifted a piece of the floor up and hesitated before reaching inside. She said a silent prayer that Mother hadn't discovered it and filled it with items of *her* choosing.

Her hand found something cool and smooth. She gripped it and lifted out a wireless notebook. A crude pencil drawing of a naked woman graced the front page. Flipping through, she noted the dates at the top of the entries. "It's a journal!" She felt around and discovered several more, excitement growing. "Tim's journals!"

There was a loud *thunk!* from outside and then headlights bobbed as they shot through the window.

Jason turned the light off then peered outside. "Shit! She's home!" He squinted past the baby-blue curtains. "And I think she hit the curb!"

Claire's heart raced. "Damn it!" They had to get out now. Mother would flip if she caught them in Tim's room. Unable to bring herself to invade what little was left of her brother's privacy, she let go of the journal, replaced the floor and carpet over the hole, and got to her feet, just as a car door slammed shut outside. A powerful jolt of dizziness threatened her balance. She took a deep breath and let it out slowly. "Come on!" Claire grabbed Jason's hand and they fled the room and raced down the hall. They made their way down the stairs and into the kitchen.

"Oh, shit. The hangers!" Jason grabbed the black bag and he and Claire slipped out the back door.

Only to see the front of Mother's BMW, its lights blazing against the garage door. The car door slammed. They could hear Mother muttering to herself, and then the click of her high heels. "Hide!" Claire pointed at the potting shed to their left. "Behind there. She won't see us."

They scurried to the far side of the shed and waited for Mother to go indoors. But she didn't. She unlocked the potting shed instead. Lights blazed.

Jason grimaced at Claire and she put her finger to her lips. They were stuck until Mother went in the house.

***

"She's drunk," Claire whispered, her voice giddy with amusement as Prissy muttered inside the potting shed.

Jason nodded and whispered in Claire's ear, "Maybe she's talking with her garden gnomes." He felt ten years old again, like when he eavesdropped on his parents after bedtime. It had always made him feel wonderful and wicked, and a little bit guilty, even though he'd never heard anything scandalous.

Claire stifled a giggle as the mumbling continued.

"Maybe she's got a bottle of the good stuff stashed in there." Jason spoke softly. He loved seeing Claire happy after all the depressing things they'd encountered upstairs.

"Stop it! She'll hear us!" Claire put one hand over her mouth, the other over his.

It didn't help; they were both shaking with pent-up laughter now. It felt really good. *And so what if she hears us? She's drunk. Who cares?*

Prissy's voice rose through the night. "Well, *there* you are!"

Jason wondered who on earth Prissy had on the phone at this hour. He could tell Claire was just as baffled.

"Well, I had quite an eventful day." Prissy's voice was loud, her words slurred.

"She's drunk-dialing!" whispered Jason. "Is she a heavy drinker?"

Claire shrugged. "She didn't used to be."

The one-sided conversation continued. "Father David Flannigan, you remember, silly. He was the priest you liked to talk to. Yes, Father Flannigan, right. Yes, he was nice to me - and you - for a time."

Claire leaned in close to Jason. "Father Flannigan was the head of Holy Sacramental when I was a kid."

"Well, young Father Andrew isn't nearly as agreeable." Prissy laughed, low and throaty. "No, I doubt he's a gay, he's just *so* earnest. I don't think he's ever been with a woman - let alone a man, Angelheart."

"Oh, my God." Claire's smile crashed and her eyes went wide. Amusement drained from her face. She looked stricken, unbelieving ... *stunned*.

"Claire?"

She ignored him.

Prissy laughed. "And he doesn't drink like a proper priest ... I know ... He didn't even touch the wine. He drank an orange soda, of all things - can you imagine? - and he wouldn't commit to any of our ideas."

Claire's eyes were fathomless. Jason moved closer to her. "Is something-"

"Shh!"

Prissy giggled. "So, what do you think, Angelheart? Will our snapdragons win the contest this year?" There was a pause. "Yes, I agree, they're still too small to be sure ... Don't you remember? They're pastels - baby blue like your eyes, pink like your lips." She giggled again. "Peach, lavender, white, pale green, and yellow. I have bright colors to define the faces and shapes ... What? You remember, I already told you - my theme is 'A Day at the Zoo' and there will be all *kinds* of flower animals." She laughed. "Yes, dragons, too. Snapdragons!" Another pause. "You're certainly right about that. Aida Portendorfer will be livid!" Her voice lowered to a confidential tone. "Phyllis Stine says Aida's planting an American flag motif. Isn't that the tackiest thing ever? We'll do much better than that! I don't think Geneva-Marie will even try - not with the trouble she's having at home." Prissy giggled. It was an ugly sound. "It's marvelous, isn't it?" A long pause. "No, Barbara isn't an issue. She knows better. I have no doubt we'll win the street *and* the city-wide contest again this year."

Claire's face was paper white. She raised a hand to her breast and Jason saw the tremble in her fingers. *She looks like she's going to throw up!*

"I think we should go," Jason whispered.

She shook her head.

"This Sunday, right after church," Prissy continued. "I'm bringing this pot of wild violets. They're frost resistant and will be nice until the snapdragons are ready ... Yes, I know you do. That's why I chose them, silly. You've always liked them." There was a long pause, then Prissy's voice went soft, sad almost. "My little Angelheart, let Mommy fix your shirt collar. It's all rucked up again ... There, that's better. Isn't that better, Timmy?"

Jason's heart froze in his throat. *Timmy? As in Timothy?*

Claire looked into his eyes and nodded.

***

"She doted on my brother," Claire said once they were safely in the apartment.

"Have you ever heard her, uh, talk to him before?"

"Not like that." Claire's gaze was far away. "'Angelheart' was her pet name for him. I haven't heard that term in years ..." She shook her head. "It's sick. The whole thing is just sick." She touched her belly protectively. "We need to get out of here, Jason."

He swallowed. "Let's start looking around right away and we'll move as soon as it's feasible."

"I've already looked online. It's surprising how cheap it is to live here compared to the city."

"Yes, but I'm making a lot less, so unfortunately, it evens out."

"I've been spending most of my time updating my website and getting clients lined up. I'm hoping to make enough money to help us move as soon as possible."

They sat together on the couch, their hands clasped. They'd hid behind the shed another ten minutes while Prissy finished talking to her dead son. It had been a long, cold wait. As soon as Claire and Jason got upstairs, they turned up the heat and lowered the blinds, cocooning themselves from the madness.

The silence hung, thick and loaded. Jason had believed Claire's stories about her mother but he'd never imagined ... *this.* It was unreal. "She probably just drank too much, Claire. We're overthinking things."

"This goes beyond a few too many drinks, Jason. She hates silence - I thought that's why she's always talked to herself. It was never a two-way conversation, even when she seemed to be talking to Tim." She shook her head. "She's gotten crazier since I left. After Tim died, I spent most of my time trying to avoid her. I remember wishing I could shut my door, but ..."

"But what?"

"I didn't have one."

"What? What do you mean, you didn't have a door?"

"She removed my bedroom door, just like she had Timothy's. We didn't have doors. We weren't allowed." Claire stared at him. "God, I'd forgotten all about that. At least she's put them back on."

"You probably needed to forget it, Claire."

"I wonder what else I've forgotten."

"Good question. I wonder what's in the potting shed."

"Why? Tim's certainly not in there."

"But maybe there's a reason she *thinks* he is."

"Unless ..." Claire gave him a peculiar smile. "Maybe she had him freeze-dried like the dogs and keeps him in the potting shed."

"Claire, you're not ser-"

She started laughing. "No, but I wouldn't put it past her. I mean, the evidence is all there - those poor dead dogs on her bed-"

Her laughter spiraled and her face turned red, tears streaming, her hand slapping the couch in glee. It was as if something inside of her had snapped. Jason had never seen her like this. He moved close and held her. Finally, the hysteria passed and the real tears came. He had rarely seen her cry before. Now there was a flood.

Next to God, Thy Parents

A week had passed; it was Monday again. Jason had left for work without waking her and, when Claire got up, the sun was high in the sky - it was after nine. It was the first morning she didn't feel a trace of dizziness. Aside from being very tired, she felt great.

Dressed in jeans and her favorite old T-shirt that said, *I stayed in the Dungeon Room at The Candle Bay Hotel*, she paused, standing before the wooden jewelry box on her dresser. She smoothed a hand over its polished surface, then opened it. The tinkling music began as the little ballerina, in arabesque position, began to whirl. "Tim said I could tell you anything I wanted," Claire whispered to the tiny dancer. It had been years since she'd confided in her, but she was surprised how naturally it came back. She didn't feel silly at all. "I think things are looking up," she said. "I think Jason and I are going to be very happy again soon." She saw herself reflected in the small mirror behind the ballerina, smiled, and closed the lid.

Padding into the kitchen in search of caffeine and sustenance, she smelled coffee and silently blessed Jason as she poured a cup. She took it to the kitchen table, opened her Mac, and perused the morning headlines, then Googled rentals in the vicinity. There were quite a few vacation homes that were pricey by the week, but might be reasonable by the month. Most of the year-round homes in town were on the expensive side, but not out of the question. Not if they saved.

We will *get out of here, and soon,* she promised as she checked her email. *A new client!* Actually an old client from her days at IMRU Designs, was asking if she might have time to design a new website for his bookkeeping chain. "Might have time?" she asked the air. "Might? I think I can squeeze you in!"

Finishing her coffee, she rose and grabbed the pill organizer from the drawer. She took it to the sink, drew a glass of water then opened a compartment and tilted her head back, letting the vitamins fall into her mouth.

Her phone rang. It was Dr. Lightfoot, back in Berkeley.

"Mrs. Holbrook," came her ob-gyn's deep, friendly voice. "How are you doing?"

"Pretty good."

He laughed. "Care to be a little more specific?"

Claire sighed. "All right, you win. I'm still having minor dizzy spells and a little queasiness. Nothing I can't handle. Oh, and I'm *very* tired. All the time. I mean, totally fatigued. It's ridiculous."

He chuckled. "Perfectly normal. But have you had any more fainting episodes?"

Claire's cheeks burned. She'd been humiliated when she'd told the doctor that one moment she was making the bed and the next, she was sprawled on the rug. She almost said no, but knew Lightfoot would see through her. "Yes," she admitted. "Once more, but it was a soft landing. I just stood up too fast."

"It's probably just the hypotension, then. But I don't want you to take chances." He cleared his throat. "Keep snacks around at all times. Healthy snacks. The dizziness and morning sickness should start diminishing as you enter the second trimester. Less than a month to go. I want you to tell your new doctor about the fainting. And the exhaustion."

"My new doctor? You've found someone for me?"

"Yes, an excellent obstetrician in Snapdragon. Her name is Lara Putnam, and she's a Stanford grad, over six years of experience in obstetrics."

"That's wonderful." Claire liked the idea of a female doctor.

"I took the liberty of contacting her. I hope that's all right."

"More than all right. Thank you!"

"You can call her office and make an appointment. I told her your pregnancy is higher risk than average and we don't want to take any chances. She'll see you right away." He gave her the number.

"I'll call now."

"It was great having you, Claire, and I hope your move proves to be a good one. I think you'll like Lara Putnam, but if not, call me and we'll find someone else."

Hanging up, she punched in Putnam's number and made an appointment for Thursday. After the call, she inspected herself in the bathroom mirror. Turning to the side, she saw no evidence of a bump, but her abdomen felt tighter, firmer. She smiled. Her petite breasts had grown fuller; she'd be shopping for a new bra soon.

She'd never wanted children - she'd just never been interested - but now that she was pregnant, she was excited. She patted her belly. "I'll be a good mother to you. I won't try to control everything you do or think. I won't remove your door, either." She wondered if the baby was a boy or a girl. She'd find out soon and they could start thinking about names. *And shopping for baby stuff.*

She thought of Mr. Anton, her favorite childhood toy. She wanted her own child to have the teddy bear. For the first time in her life, Claire was glad her mother never threw anything out. *But I wonder if she has any idea where he's stashed.* She had a feeling she would. Despite the utter chaos

Priscilla Martin lived in, there seemed to be some kind of order to things, if only in her own head. Claire made a mental note to ask about the bear.

Her stomach growled and she headed for the kitchen, smiling. Jason's job was going well, she'd acquired a new client - *that makes four!* - and she was growing more and more excited about becoming a mother. *Things really are turning around for us.*

Her smile collapsed when she opened the cupboard. On the shelves were canned items she knew they hadn't purchased. *It's the expired vegetables and soups we threw out!* She took one from the shelf and checked: Expiration date September, 2004. Yes, these were the same ones. *Mother's been in the apartment.* Angry heat flared. *She went through the garbage and brought the cans back!* The open bag of weevil-infested flour was back on the shelf, too. Claire looked around, wondering what else her mother had rummaged through. *It* is *her house,* said a voice in the back of Claire's mind, but she shoved it aside. *No! This is an invasion of our privacy. It's just like the old days.* She snagged two cans off the shelf, slammed the cupboard shut, and left the apartment, stalking toward the house.

***

"Phyllis, I want all the yard sale signs to match." Prissy Martin spoke in harsh nasal tones. "You need to use the same colors as the rest of us."

"Aida's doesn't match." Phyllis' plastic hoop earrings jittered like convulsing bluebirds as she stabbed a finger at Aida's sign.

"Of course it does. 'Yard' is in red, and 'Sale' is in blue. Those are the colors we decided on, Phyllis - red, white, and blue. You can use them in any order you choose, but you cannot use brown! It's vulgar! We want to *attract* people, not repel them."

Aida nodded agreement. "Brown is the color of poop."

Clucking her tongue, Prissy shot Aida a disgusted look.

Babs Vandercooth kept her mouth shut. She didn't care one way or another what color the signs were. It was simply easier to humor Prissy - or remain silent - than to argue.

"Fine," said Phyllis, clearly not fine at all.

Babs heard the back door open and slam shut, hard.

"Mother!" Claire's voice sliced through the air like a serrated blade.

Aida and Phyllis exchanged wide-eyed glances.

Prissy's false, twinkling smile faltered as she rose from her chair. "Excuse me, ladies." But she wasn't quick enough. Claire barged in, thrusting canned goods in Prissy's face. "What are these, Mother?" Her voice trembled with controlled rage.

Babs smiled to herself, glad to see Claire wasn't allowing Prissy to walk on her.

"Why, they're beets and corn, dear," said Prissy.

"No," said Claire. "What I mean is, what are they doing in the apartment? We threw them out." She turned the can over and pointed. "Do you see this? These expired more than a decade ago. We will *not* eat-"

"Keep your voice down, dear," said Prissy. "Let's go into the kitchen, shall we? As you can see, I have company."

Claire didn't acknowledge the women sitting around the table as she let Prissy herd her from the room.

"You went through our garbage ..." Claire's voice was clipped off as the door closed.

"Well," Phyllis gloated. "Apparently there's trouble in paradise."

Aida nodded. "Prissy says her children were always ungrateful."

Babs didn't say a word. She knew better. Neither Phyllis nor Aida were to be trusted with the truth. Prissy Martin's aversion to throwing things out was pathological. She cracked a smile, wondering what - if anything - Prissy would part with at this year's yard sale.

Phyllis, her spine ramrod straight, took a dainty sip of tea, her bangle bracelets chattering, as Aida helped herself to what must have been her fifth pumpkin cookie.

Babs smelled the *Opium* before Prissy re-entered the room. "Sorry about that, ladies." She took her seat, giving them a helpless look and shaking her head sadly. "Kids these days. They just don't understand how quickly things can change. Just like *that*," Prissy snapped her fingers, "the economy could collapse and we could *all* be back to plowing our own gardens for survival!"

Aida and Phyllis made sympathetic noises. Babs smiled gently at the nonsense and hoped she and Claire would be able to get together soon.

Prissy went on. "And considering the horse's ass we have in the White House now, I think that day may come sooner rather than later!" She paused. "I hope some day those kids will come to appreciate what I've done for them."

Phyllis and Aida nodded and continued coloring their signs as Pris stroked her hair necklace, a habit that betrayed anxiety.

Babs Vandercooth shuddered, then returned to her own sign. Claire and her husband had hit very hard times, indeed, to live under Prissy's totalitarian rule. She knew all too well what a toll that could take.

***

Jason Holbrook pulled into the driveway after work, a smile on his face, and a single red rose wrapped in white tissue lying on the passenger seat. While he would always miss flying, he took a good deal of satisfaction in teaching - more than he'd ever expected. In addition, the promise of a small raise on his first month's anniversary - with more to follow - and the fact that he honestly liked his boss, Paul Schuyler, made him feel pretty good about things.

Paul wasn't rated for the big jets, but often piloted private 24-seaters between Snapdragon and Reno or Las Vegas for wedding parties and other private events. He also owned a Stearman-PT17, a bright yellow biplane that he poured his heart and soul into. He flew it in the biannual Snapdragon Air Show, doing flips and turns and other aerobatics. As much as Jason loved flying, he couldn't imagine wanting to do loop-de-loops in the sky. But he admired Paul's enthusiasm.

He glanced at the main house, happy to see no sign of Prissy, then got out, grabbed the rose and a big brown sack from Wokamundo - Asian food Paul guaranteed to be delicious, despite the name. Claire was a fiend for Chinese food, and he'd chosen their favorites: kung pao chicken, chow mein, cream cheese wontons, and spicy broccoli beef. The bag smelled like heaven as he trotted up the stairs to the apartment.

The door was locked. "Lucy, I'm home!" he called, in his best Ricky Ricardo, which wasn't good at all. A moment passed then he heard the lock being turned and Claire opened the door. She was dressed in black sweats and looked tired and annoyed.

"Why's it locked?"

She ignored his question and stepped back to let him pass. "One remark about how I look and you're sleeping in the doghouse."

Deciding against teasing her about gestational mood swings, he set the bag on the dining table. Her chestnut hair was pulled back in a ponytail and her full lips and large green eyes looked even younger and prettier without makeup. Her skin looked fantastic - he wondered if this was the "glow" that pregnant women were supposed to have. Whatever it was, it suited her. "You look fine - and like you've had a very long day. Here." He presented the rose with a little bow.

Her smile turned her back into the girl he'd married. "You always know just what I need." She stood on tiptoe and kissed him quick. "I love you. How's Paul? It blows my mind that he's your boss now."

She had told him she remembered Paul as a kind, funny guy who always had his nose in a textbook. Claire'd had a little crush on him when she was about eight. "He's a great guy, and he remembers you - he says they used to call you 'Tag-Along' because your brother had you with him half the time."

Claire laughed. "I hope I get to see him soon."

"He wants to get together, too." Jason started gathering dishes while Claire put the rose in a glass of water and set it on the center of the table. "So, how was your day?"

Her tight, one-syllable laugh said it hadn't been a good one. "Well." She crossed her arms. "It seems Mother didn't agree with our decision to throw out the expired vegetables."

"What do you mean?" He pulled her chair out, then sat next to her.

From the sack, Claire lifted out white boxes with red Chinese writing on them. She opened and inspected them, sliding one toward Jason. "Apparently," she said, digging into white rice with her chopsticks, "she found the cans we tossed."

Jason, who could never manage chopsticks, used a fork on his broccoli beef. "What did she say about it?"

"She didn't say anything, Jason. Instead, she took it upon herself to retrieve them from the garbage and bring them back. I found them in the cupboard this morning." She nodded toward the door. "She's been letting herself in. That's why I locked it."

Jason paused, his fork hovering between his plate and his face. "You're kidding."

She shook her head. "It won't stop her though - she has keys. We need to get a chain-lock. At least."

Jason was disturbed by Prissy's invasion; he really hadn't expected that. At the same time, he realized this was her house, and they couldn't exactly tell her she couldn't come in. But he agreed with his wife on this one. "Yes. I'll pick one up at the hardware store tomorrow." He paused. "You know this means she found the clown portraits, too."

"I'm sure. Fuck her." Claire took another bite. "Needless to say, I've started looking at new places. There are definitely some possibilities." She paused to chew. "Most of them are on the outskirts of town."

"We'll start saving up. I think we can have the money in a couple of months."

Claire watched him a moment. "I wasn't going to tell you until it was final, but I'm ninety-nine percent sure I've acquired a new client. A big one."

"That's great, sweetheart! Who is it?"

She told him about her new customer as they devoured the Chinese food - which was every bit as good as Paul had said it would be.

"What about you?" Claire asked. "How was your day?"

He told her more about the job and Paul Schuyler and his Stearman. She listened in that way he loved - like she was *really* listening, not just being polite.

"That's great, Magic Man. You should ask him to take you flying sometime."

Paul was a great guy and they'd hit it off, but Jason wasn't fond of the idea of inviting himself along on sky-rides for tourists. Also, he wasn't sure how he'd feel about not being able to pilot the plane.

"I think it would be good for you." Claire seemed to have read his thoughts.

"Yeah," he said. "Maybe someday I'll ask him about it."

Claire smiled. "You can't stay out of the sky forever, Jason. It just wouldn't be you. Even if you can't pilot, I know you're itching to get back up there. Am I right or am I right?"

She was right.

There was a long silence before Claire spoke. "I want to go see Dad again. Maybe tomorrow."

Jason finished his dinner and pushed his plate aside. "Do you think your mother will allow it?"

"I don't know and I don't care." She reached into the sack and withdrew two fortune cookies. She slid one to Jason and cracked hers open. Pulling the strip of paper out, she frowned. "'*Next to God, Thy Parents,*'" she read. "What kind of Chinese place is this? When did *God* start making appearances in fortune cookies?"

Jason shrugged and read his own. "'*Family is Forever.*'"

Claire opened her eyes wide and spoke in a slow, mock-lunatic cadence. "And ever and ever and *ever* ..." The overall effect was indeed quite eerie.

He laughed then patted his belly. "I'm stuffed."

"Me, too." Claire started closing the white containers and Jason, groaning with satisfaction, took them to the fridge. "There's another entire dinner here." Jason rinsed his hands and returned to the dining room. "So, what did you do with the rotten cans?"

"In a garbage bag, awaiting proper disposal. Let's go for a ride."

"Hmm?"

"They'll just reappear if we throw them out here again, so let's take them to a public dumpster."

"But she's got lots more in the basement."

"Then we'll keep throwing them out until there aren't any left."

Jason nodded and grabbed the keys. He didn't want to fan the flames, but knowing Prissy had let herself into their apartment unannounced ate at him. "What about the hangers? Shouldn't we dump them, too?"

A mischievous grin brightened Claire's face. "The hangers? No way. Those are for the yard sale!"

Jason laughed. "You're serious about that, aren't you?"

She nodded. "I'm as serious as a Mormon on a mission. Mother will come *unglued!*"

He smiled, rather enjoying this vindictive side of her.

PART TWO
We're All Mad Here

"But I don't want to go among mad people," Alice remarked.
"Oh, you can't help that," said the Cat, "we're all mad here."

Late Night with Morning Glory Circle

Claire and Jason lay in a tangle of limbs and sheets, fast asleep, firmly in love, and very satisfied. Mother did not invade their sweet dreams, but Claire dreamed of the day her big brother, Tim, and his girlfriend, Steffie, had taken her to the carnival at the fairgrounds and pretended they were her parents. They rode the Ferris wheel and the Wild Mouse, had cotton candy and hot dogs and soda pop. It had been one of the best days of her life. In her sleep, Claire smiled.

The smile faltered when a coil of nylon rope entered the dream. Again she saw the looming shadow, heard the hissing whisper, and felt the pain blaze in her shoulder. She saw Timothy - a tear slipped from his blue eye … and then the rope became a noose around his neck.

"Touch them!"

She did as she was told.

"Now open your hand, Carlene …"

In her sleep, Claire whimpered.

"Now close your hand."

Claire closed her fist tight.

***

Clyde Stine, dutifully carrying out his weekly husbandly duties, grunted on top of his wife, Phyllis. It was a bony, clanky affair that required acrobatics to avoid ending up black and blue where her hipbones ground into him. Luckily, he had plenty of extra padding. He looked down at his wife of thirty years, her eyes rolled up behind brow-high blue shadow, her plastic earrings bouncing in time with his thrusts, as her gnarled hands squeezed his ample backside, urging him on. He picked up the pace, wondering if Aida Portendorfer was going to bake more of her delicious snickerdoodles for the sale this weekend.

"Oh, Clyde," groaned Phyllis. "Harder."

Clyde sighed and put a little more spirit into it. He thought of their neighbor, Candy Sachs, and her double-Ds. He envisioned her in those sweet little hot pink shorts and matching frilly crop-top she'd worn last summer - *I'd love to get into those, oh boy!*

He finished the job in record time.

***

Earl Dean waited until Earlene was sawing logs before he quietly left their bed and padded down the hall, past Daphene and Delphine's room, the bathroom, and into the kitchen, where he turned off the alarm and let himself out into their vast backyard. Looking up, he saw the Portendorfers' bedroom lights were still on. *But that just makes it more fun.* Earlene had seen Aida with those new binoculars of hers trying to see into their house just two days ago, and Earl was pretty damned pissed off about it. He neared the fence and pulled his cock out of his pajamas. "You wanna take a gander at this, Aida?"

He uncoiled his snake and hosed down the fence. He never understood why people preferred bathrooms to nature.

Without bothering to look up, he packed his dick away and returned to bed. In five minutes, he was asleep and dreaming his favorite dream: the one where he was Willy Wonka and everyone wanted a pack of his fudge.

***

Wide awake, Aida Portendorfer gasped and thrust the binoculars away from her face. *Of all the disgusting, putrid, unseemly things!* She brought the spyglasses back to her eyes and leaned closer to the window. There was no mistaking it: Earl Dean was urinating on the fence! She stole a glance at his manhood, which was substantially larger than Stan's, and again gasped at the filth of it all. Without so much as a glance around, Earl Dean shook it off, tucked it in, and headed inside. Disappointment flooded her. *Next time I'll have the camera ready!* She hefted herself from her swivel chair, eager to get to bed. She had a busy day ahead of her; by tomorrow afternoon, Morning Glory Circle would be abuzz, and Aida would be at the center of it all. She smiled, lay down next to Stan, and closed her eyes. In the dark, she reached down and touched her lady garden, just a little, giggling at the thought of telling her friends what she'd seen.

***

Ace Etheridge squirmed in his sleep. His daughter Iris had told him about her run-in with Priscilla Martin at the grocery store. *"Read any good books, lately?"* she'd said. *"I hear you're a fan of romance novels."* That was the part that hit him hard. It had troubled him even more than it had Iris. *Priscilla couldn't possibly know, could she?* All evening, it had worried him, and he dreamed that he had eaten too much at the yard and bake sale and was waddling toward the Martin house to confront Priscilla about upsetting Iris. Everybody thought Aida Portendorfer was the neighborhood snoop - and they were all wrong.

He sampled his neighbors' wares as he walked. *I must taste everything because I have to give an honest report in the newspaper. I can lose the weight again.* He had bought things from various yard sales, too. Roddy Crocker had put his badge and a billy club out on his sale table, along with some cat toys, comic books, and Bettyanne's underpants. After careful consideration, Ace bought the badge and the underpants and changed into them as he walked, because he'd gotten so fat from eating all the cookies and cakes, he'd outgrown his pants. The panties, sporting the badge, were stretchy and comfortable and people nodded politely as they passed him. *They respect the badge, just like Roddy said they would.*

At the end of the circle, he really had to take a leak, so he approached Priscilla Martin, who manned a table full of tribbles. She said William Shatner had given them to her, then offered Ace one, but he waved the tribble away. He meant to inquire if she had any romance novels for sale, but found himself instead asking if he might use her restroom. "Go on in," she told him with a winning smile, "But don't step on the tribbles!"

Ace woke up suddenly with a burning need to pee. *Damned middle-aged bladder!* He got up to relieve himself. He'd really wanted to see the inside of Priscilla Martin's home. He wanted to set fire to her collection of tribbles, once and for all.

***

Quinton Everett, dressed in flowing white lace, was trying to show little Jimmy Baxter how to hit the softball. Each time it came his way, however, Quinton missed. Over and over, he missed.

Suddenly, he lay on the red carpet in the vault at Snapdragon Bank & Trust, his nude body inexplicably tattooed with lipstick. He looked down at the craven images drawn on his skin, from the bottoms of his feet to his tender inner thighs. Now, in his dream, his taint was painted Cherry Blossom Pink and had been man-jazzled by Jennifer Love-Hewitt, who had entered his dream when he wasn't looking. But it was all good. She was trimming his pubes into a buzzy, musky dollar sign and was about to apply gold sequins and green glitter - *the color of money* - to Quinton Junior, who stood as tall and proud as the National Monument. "Next," she whispered as she turned Junior into a true Glitterati, "I'll paint Masonic eyes on your nipples."

***

Burke Collins was passed out on the sofa, an empty tumbler of Scotch on the floor beside him, the stink of alcoholic sweat wafting from his pores, fermenting the room. Geneva-Marie clicked the television off and stared at her unconscious husband with disdain, hoping he could feel the laser-like beams of hate she shot from her eyes.

Finally, she traipsed upstairs to the bedroom. *Another night alone.* At the edge of the bed, she pulled her red satin robe tight, and stared at her reflection in the mirror, wondering where she'd gone wrong. But she already knew and, in truth, had never regretted it and would never tell him. He'd never find out. Besides, Geneva-Marie wasn't a fool. Burke had plenty of indiscretions of his own. Her only regret was in marrying him in the first place.

He'd always been a drinker, but these past few months it had escalated. The furniture business was going under and, instead of fixing the problem, Burke was drinking it away. She didn't know how much longer he'd be able to function without making a spectacle of the entire family. *You'd better be sober for the yard and bake sale, Burke Collins.* It wouldn't do for the neighbors - Prissy Martin in particular - to know that Geneva-Marie's life was splitting at the seams. *Prissy'd enjoy every minute of it if she ever found out!* Geneva-Marie buried her face in her hands and wept.

***

Babs Vandercooth wished her Ambien would kick in. It was after midnight and Carl had been softly snoring beside her for ninety minutes now. *Not a care in the world.*

Babs was exhausted. She'd spent the evening baking some of the dozens and dozens of fruit and chocolate bars she'd promised for the yard and bake sale. After cooling the day's batches, she'd cut them in squares, wrapped each individual bar in plastic wrap, and placed them all in the freezer. *Prissy would have a fit if she knew I froze them.*

She was irritated with her friend tonight; her friend who dictated what everyone else on the street should bake while buying her cannoli at Bartoli's Deli and passing them off as homemade. *There are no secrets on Morning Glory Circle, Prissy. Everyone knows. Everyone. They're just too afraid of you to say anything.*

And that's why she was so disgusted - she had taken on far more baking than she wanted, just to make up for the neighbors who didn't want to participate - like the Crockers, who wouldn't be home, and the Deans, who never donated. She didn't do it for the neighbors, but she didn't do it out of guilt, either. She did it to stop Prissy's constant judgmental comments.

She glanced over at Carl. Priscilla was the reason she and Carl owned this house; she'd loaned them half the down payment and smoothed things at the bank so loan officer Quinton Everett - now the president - would okay the loan. Pris had even co-signed. When Carl developed his gambling addiction and lost their car, his job, and their savings, Prissy had stepped in and not only saved the house, but helped them buy another car - which she'd co-signed on, as well.

Carl had long since gotten help and hadn't gambled again - he was smart enough to understand his problem was immense - but Prissy had never stopped reminding him of it, even after fifteen years.

Thanks to Carl's problem, Prissy had not only remained a cosigner on their house but had guaranteed the loans on their next two cars. The cars had been paid off and were long gone and their newer ones had been free and clear of Priscilla Martin from day one, but Prissy never forgot. And she never quite let go of their house, either; every time they made a move to take her name off the loan, Prissy found a reason to remain. And when she'd run out of good reasons, Pris had gone behind Babs' back and talked to Quinton Everett. Babs was certain Pris had told Mr. Everett about Carl's gambling - and failed to mention he'd gotten help. Babs hadn't felt the same about Prissy since.

Babs had long ago forgiven her husband: forgiving and forgetting was how you got along in the world; it was the Christian thing to do. But Prissy Martin, who prided herself on being the best Christian at Holy Sacramental, neither forgave nor forgot anything. Instead, she kept Babs on a short leash, at her beck and call. It had gotten old. Very old.

The one good thing Prissy had given her was her daughter. From the time she was born, Priscilla was only too glad to accept her offers to babysit Claire and, later, to let her go to her house after school. Babs, childless herself, loved Claire like her own daughter. Claire had come over to have tea and cookies earlier this week, slipping out when Prissy wasn't around. It had been lovely.

But if Prissy had known that Claire'd been in contact with Babs from the time she'd left home, while refusing to have anything to do with her mother, she'd have been furious. *It's amazing Prissy's never found out. No secrets are safe on Morning Glory Circle.*

***

Budweiser in hand, Hank Lowell slid quietly into the kitchen from the backyard, hoping to hell Ben and Jerry wouldn't start barking. "Crys, where are you? You've gotta hear this!"

"Hear what?" Crystal poked her head through the living room doorway.

"Prissy Martin's at it again!" Hank grinned and scratched the poodles behind their ears.

"Talking to herself? I'm watching *CSI* ... It better be good."

"Oh, it's good, all right, it's good. She's got the garage door open, too."

"Can you see inside?" Crys grabbed a beer from the fridge and snapped it open. "Let's go!"

They could hear her the moment they stepped outside. She was chattering away and moving around in the garage. Cautiously, they crossed their driveway and approached the tall redwood fence that separated their backyard from Priscilla Martin's anal-retentive abode. *Proper Priscilla, everything in place, right down to the fake grass.* But recently, Hank had gotten a peek inside her three-car garage when she'd had everything moved out of the apartment above it.

Since they'd moved in four years ago, he and his family had endured a barrage of snide remarks from the woman about the color they painted their house, the condition of their lawn, and the fact that they had a few dandelions among the snapdragons. She complained when he had pool parties that lasted later than she liked, and she even called the poor cop, Roddy Crocker, who lived at the other end of the cul-de-sac, to complain about music being too loud a minute after the ten o'clock curfew. It was pretty funny, the way that backfired. Thanks to the call, he and Roddy became pals - Roddy had even bought a new Harley from him. *Thanks, Priscilla!*

On tiptoe, Hank led Crys to a knothole in the fence. He peered through and saw his neighbor stuff a black plastic sack into an open cranny in the overstuffed garage. A hanger popped out and she spoke. "Oh, Angelheart, what's the matter with kids these days? They just don't appreciate what God gives them." She put the hanger back in the bag. "There. Those won't be cluttering the basement anymore. But I would swear there was another bag. Did you see it anywhere, Timmy, or is your old mother just losing her marbles?"

"I'd say his mother lost her marbles a long time ago," Hank whispered in Crystal's ear.

"Oh, Hank, her son died. Have a heart."

"Roddy told me he died more than twenty years ago. She's nuttier than trail mix. He said she cleared out the apartment for her daughter and son-in-law. I heard they're going to have a baby."

Crys whispered, "Let me look!"

Hank stood back, letting Crys have a long turn at the knothole. He listened to Priscilla jabbering to her dead kid, while admiring Crystal's fine ass - still a great pair of cheeks after two kids and fifteen years of putting up with him. He wished she'd go back to being a blond, though - that fire engine red hair was getting old. She'd even wanted to get the carpet dyed to match the drapes, but thank God he'd been able to talk her into getting a Brazilian instead.

"Wow, she's got a really nice blue Tiffany lampshade in there," Crystal told him. "I wonder if she'll put it out for the yard sale."

Hank almost laughed. "Why don't you ask her?"

"I just might - ooh, listen."

Prissy's voice sounded concerned. "What do you mean, Timmy? You've always been my favorite. You know that, don't you, Angelheart?" She went silent, evidently listening to her deceased son. "Mm-hmm. Mm-hmm. I understand why it bothers you, but I promise you your sister won't snoop in your room again." A pause. "Yes, I know. She messed up your GI Joes and looked at all your shoes." Pause. "No, that wasn't nice, but she misses you, too, just like Mommy. I'm sure that's why she did it. Why, Angelheart, she looked in my room - and my jewelry room, too - but I didn't say a word." A longer pause. "Yes, if she goes in your room again, I'll have a talk with her." After a beat, Prissy sighed. "Phyllis told me Geneva-Marie is thinking of running for president of the Auxiliary. Against *me!* Can you imagine! The nerve!" She laughed. "Well, I think we can nip that in the bud, don't you?"

Hank heard the garage door close, then Priscilla Martin said, "Now, let's go have some nice hot chocolate, Angelheart. I have those itty bitty marshmallows you like so much!"

Hank and Crystal waited until their neighbor went inside her house, then Crystal took a long drink. "Okay, when you're right, you're right. Priscilla Martin is crazy on toast."

***

On the other side of town, Paul Schuyler stared up at the dark ceiling and wondered where Chastity McDonald was now; if she'd gotten married and had more kids, if she was having a happy life. It had been a long time since he'd thought about her, but his recent dealings with Priscilla Martin had roused a hornet's nest of painful memories he'd tried hard to forget. The passing years had done nothing to bridge the gap between himself and the pain.

After what had happened, Chastity's father, Palmer McDonald, had sent her away. Paul had never known what had become of her, but knew better than to ask questions. Palmer McDonald had been the mayor of Snapdragon then, just as he was now, and he could have made Paul's life hell. *He could still make my life hell.* They'd come to an agreement, though, and as long as Paul kept his end of the bargain, he knew there would be no trouble.

Priscilla, however, unnerved him. He hadn't seen the woman since the trouble with Chastity - when he and Tim Martin, his best friend, were seniors in high school. And now, after all these years, she'd contacted him, asking a favor - to hire her son-in-law without so much as an interview. Paul didn't really need another instructor, but the veiled threat lurking under Priscilla's words made it clear he had no choice. *She could make my life hell as easily as Palmer McDonald.*

Luckily, Paul had instantly taken a liking to Jason Holbrook. He realized now that this shouldn't have been such a surprise; Claire couldn't have turned out anything like her mother because she'd always been a chip off her big brother, and Paul might have guessed she would have married a decent man. And Jason Holbrook was decent.

Paul remembered Priscilla Martin. She'd always disliked him - and anyone else who came within five feet of her son. She'd done everything in her power to keep Tim to herself. It was a strange, twisted relationship that Paul had never understood. He knew Tim had had a mind of his own, that he'd wanted to put some distance between himself and his mother - that's why he'd moved to Arizona to be with Steffie Banks - but Tim had problems, too. He allowed his mother too much power over his life, and Paul had never understood why. He hadn't been gone more than a year before a hiking accident gave Priscilla an excuse to bring him home.

Tim had said he intended to go back to Brimstone after he'd healed - he'd told Paul he and Stephanie were going to be married - but his suicide said otherwise. It told Paul that Tim had resigned to a life controlled by his mother. He'd even given up on Claire; he'd wanted to get his little sister away from Priscilla, but ... *I guess he just couldn't take any more.* After all these years, Paul's eyes still welled at the loss of his best friend.

He wished there was something he could do to help Claire and Jason get away from her mother's clutches. He knew Tim would like him looking out for his baby sister.

Paul rolled over and closed his eyes. *I'll watch out for her, buddy.* As he drifted to sleep, he recalled the childhood he'd shared with Tim and Steffie. Those were the best times of his life.

***

Father David Flannigan couldn't sleep. Earlier, he'd had a chat with young Andy Pike, who'd taken over at Holy Sacramental when Dave retired. He'd hand-picked the boy who'd served as his assistant for five years before his retirement and he was a fine young man. There were none better. But now, Andy had called, asking for advice because Priscilla Martin was pushing him in a direction he didn't like.

Without giving details, Dave had advised him to handle the woman with the softest of kid gloves and warned him she was so strong in her righteousness, that she wasn't above ensuring her wishes were met. That was an understatement, but he didn't want to tell Andy what she'd done - or what he'd done. *It's a sin of pride not to confess. But I'll tell him if I must.* Still, he preferred to keep some secrets solely between himself and God.

***

Father Andrew Pike rolled over in his sleep, dreaming he was selling chocolate bars on Morning Glory Circle. He was dressed in an altar boy's surplice instead of his suit and collar, and so far, almost half the houses had bought at least one bar. *Priscilla Martin sure was right about dressing as an altar boy!* He would never have made so many sales dressed in his clericals.

He came to Priscilla Martin's door and, before he could knock, she was there, smiling, wearing a collar and a long black cassock. *My collar and cassock!* But that couldn't be.

"Priscilla, why are you dressed as a priest?"

She didn't answer him, only crooked her finger and motioned him inside.

Within, her house didn't look right - he remembered she decorated in pastels with lots of frilly lamps and paintings of snapdragons, and there was that big eagle clock over the fireplace. This wasn't her house at all, it was *his* house! *She's in my home! In my clothing! Why?*

Don't sit under the apple tree with anyone else but me ...

The music spun on an old record player in the corner. *Why are Priscilla's things in the rectory?*

Priscilla took his hand. "Dance with me," she commanded. "Dance with me, you little fool."

She whirled him around, this way and that, until he was so dizzy he could barely stand up. Then she pulled him close, clutching him to her chest as the song slowed to a crawl, the voice dragging over the syllables like a hearse grinding through mud. *Doooon't siiiiit uuundeeer theee aaaapple treeee* ... She moved him like a puppet, back and forth, putting his left leg in and right leg out, then commanded him to shake it all about.

"I'm tired," he said. "Please just buy a candy bar and go home."

"This *is* my home, Andrew," she murmured, and led him to the couch.

Helpless, paralyzed, he watched as she took off his cassock, whirling it overhead like a stripper before throwing it on the floor. She was naked now except for Birkenstocks, his collar and black dickey. She crooked her finger at him again. In her thrall, he approached. She reached out and undid his pants, pulling them down, leaving him naked except for the surplice.

Priscilla leaned back on the couch and opened her legs, showing a wet red gash that looked like an open wound.

"No," he said, then she snapped her fingers and a blinding pain shot through his head.

"You'll enjoy doing My will. I promise."

She spread her legs wider and a long purplish tongue snaked out of her opening, licking around, scenting him before pointing straight at him.

Despite himself, he took another step forward, his penis betraying him, betraying the Lord.

"I'm smiling for you," she said, spreading wider.

That's when he saw the teeth.

"Fuck me Father, for I am sin ..."

Father Andy woke up screaming.

Still Crazy After All These Years

Friday evening, Claire fluttered around the apartment, cleaning up, making dinner, barely able to contain her joy. She'd timed the lasagna - Jason's favorite - to be ready just as he'd be returning from work. When she heard his keys working the lock, she dashed to the door to greet him.

He entered, his shirt untucked, a smile lighting up his face when he saw her. He shut the door and bent to give her a kiss. "Mmm. Something smells good! Besides you. So ... how was your appointment?"

"It's a boy!" Claire exclaimed. "Congratulations, Dad!"

"That's wonderful!" He picked her up in a swooping hug and kissed her. "Congratulations, Mama!"

He'd said he didn't care about the baby's gender, though Claire had secretly wondered if he'd wanted a boy. But she could tell by the light in his eyes, the width of his smile, and the spattering of quick, noisy kisses he planted on her cheeks, lips, and neck, that he was genuinely happy.

The oven timer chimed as he let go. "I've made lasagna." She took his hand and led him into the dining table, where he sat while she donned mitts and removed the sizzling dish from the oven.

"What else did the doctor say? Did you like her?"

Doctor Putnam, a gentle, soft-spoken woman in her mid-forties, had been wonderful. She was everything she'd hoped for. "I liked her a lot." Claire placed the casserole on the stovetop. "She's much better than Dr. Hopper, for sure. Mother gave me the stink-eye again about not using him, but she let me borrow her car."

"She didn't try to go along?"

"Oh, she wanted to, but she had a meeting about the sale this weekend and couldn't get away. Thank God!"

"No kidding. I'm glad she was busy. Did you tell her about the baby?"

"Nope. I doubt she has any idea you can find out a baby's gender this early through a blood test, and I'm not about to tell her." She grinned.

"So, what about you?" Jason stood to retrieve plates and silverware. "Is everything tip-top?"

She frowned. "I'm still on the high risk side and have to take it easy - no heavy lifting, plenty of rest. That will go on for the duration of the pregnancy, I'm afraid, but nothing's wrong." She used a spatula to cut the lasagna into large squares.

"What about your fatigue?"

"It's normal, and Dr. Putnam prescribed Vitamin B shots for it."

"Injections?"

She nodded. "I start taking them immediately."

The lasagna squares became pools of steaming fragrant goo on the plates; she hadn't given it time to cool, but she didn't care. "It's still too soon to know many details, but the baby's developing at a healthy rate." She looked at the plate of goop. "Should we set these in the fridge for a minute?"

Jason shook his head. "Let's blow on them instead. I'm starving!"

"Me, too!"

They took their seats. Claire watched her husband beaming at her, his bright eyes full of life and love. She was certain their son would be beautiful. *I hope he has Jason's blue eyes.* "I want to tell Dad," Claire said.

"Why don't we visit after dinner?"

"Let's. I also want to ask Mother about Mr. Anton."

Jason cocked his head. "Mr. Anton?"

"The teddy bear my brother saved for me when Mother was on a rampage, remember?"

Jason scoffed. "Good luck finding anything in that house."

"Exactly. But I'd really like to find that bear." She smiled. "For our son."

Jason blew on his lasagna and pushed it around with his fork.

Claire looked at her plate, which was still too hot to bother with. "So …?" she asked. "Michael?"

Jason blinked at her, the emotion on his face betraying how touched he was. "As long as that's what you really like."

Michael. For Jason's father. Claire wanted Jason to have that. *It's the perfect name for him.* Michael Frederick Holbrook. Or maybe Michael Scott. Claire didn't care. As long as the baby was healthy, he could be named Egbert or Cecil. *But of course I wouldn't do that to our son,* she thought. *Our son.* Claire's eyes filled with tears of joy. She blinked them away.

***

Mother was at her Ladies Auxiliary meeting when Claire and Jason entered the house. Jason watched Claire rifle through a kitchen drawer and pull out a big set of keys. "Spares," she told him. "Come on."

Upstairs, Claire knocked on the door. "Dad? Are you awake?"

After a moment, he answered, though it was hard to understand him.

Claire tried likely keys and, miracle of miracles, the fifth one worked. The door opened and they entered.

The old man looked the same, crooked and frail, but his eyes were alert and he managed to say something that sounded like "Hello."

"Hi, Dad!" Claire went to him and kissed his cheek. "I've missed you. Mother seems to want to keep you all to herself."

His eyes sharpened. He nodded his head. "Yeaaah."

"Do you prefer just seeing Mother?"

"Noooo!" He shook his head vehemently.

"I'll talk to her about it."

Another strong shake. "No! No!"

"But-"

"No!"

Claire glanced at Jason. "I wonder what's going on."

"Good question. Your dad obviously doesn't want your mother to know we've been here."

"Yeaaah."

Jason nodded, looking at Fred Martin. "So tell him our good news. I'm going to snoop a little."

The old man understood and nodded. .

There was a writing desk on one wall and Jason opened the top drawer. It was completely empty except for a lone GI Joe action figure. Jason tried the other drawers; they held nothing but several Gideon bibles Prissy had probably filched from hotel rooms. He wondered how many bibles were in the house. *Hundreds, probably.*

The chest of drawers yielded nothing but clothing. Then he spotted a trashcan near the bed.

"You're going to have a grandson," he heard Claire say.

The old man made happy sounds.

Jason set the trashcan on the desk chair and dug through it, coming up with a couple of pill bottles, several hypodermics, and empty injection bottles. He didn't try to make out the labels, but he pocketed the several bottles and dumped everything else back in the trash. That's when he heard a car pull up.

"Your mother's home," he said.

"Go!" Frederick ordered.

Claire kissed him on the cheek then they fled, stopping only to lock the door. Downstairs, she dropped the keys in the drawer an instant before Prissy walked in, dressed in a pale peach pantsuit with a pastel yellow scarf threaded under the lapels. Her makeup was perfect and not a strand of her black hair dared move. Prissy's outfit, with its padded shoulders, looked dated.

"Well, Car-Claire! What are you doing here? Jason? You two look like you've been running."

"Actually," Jason said in his smoothest pilot's voice, "we just got back from a very brisk walk and decided to stop and see you before we went upstairs." *Now please fasten your seatbelts. It's going to be a bumpy ride.*

Claire looked at him and suppressed a smile. She always liked his pilot's voice. It was sexy, she said.

Priscilla looked suspicious. "Mm-hmm. But you could see that my car wasn't here."

"I had to pee," Claire said. "I couldn't wait, okay? The doctor said it's normal."

Prissy eyed them both, then nodded. "Sit." She indicated the kitchen table. "Would you like some juice? Or tea? Perhaps something stronger for you, Jason?"

"Sure," Jason said. "I'd love a cup of tea." *Something that will get the taste of that rancid perfume out of my mouth.*

"Me too," Claire said.

"Good. I'll just check on your father, and then we'll sit down and chat over some nice green tea. I want to hear all about this wonderful new doctor of yours." She spoke with a sneer as she put the kettle on. "Be right back."

As soon as he heard her on the stairs, Jason looked to Claire. "Will she know we were in there?"

"I doubt it. You didn't mess anything up, right?"

"Right. I found some drug bottles in the trash - I put a couple in my pocket. They were on the bottom under a lot of tissue, so she'd have to look hard to see that I took them."

"I don't think she will." Claire leaned closer to his ear. "What kind of drugs?"

"I don't know. I figured we could look at them up upstairs."

"Good idea. Find anything else?"

"Bibles in the desk. A little green army man. There's no paper or stationery or pens or pencils. He's unable to write?"

Claire glanced toward the stairs. "It might be difficult, but I think he can write. How else can he communicate?"

"I don't know. I didn't see anything to read, either. No magazines or books. Just that tiny ancient television and it wasn't even plugged in."

"I need to do something about it."

"How?" Jason asked. "You can't let your mother know."

"I know. I have to think about it, Jason, but I do know something's really wrong. He has to be in torment up there - it's so boring. It would drive me mad."

Jason looked at her. "It would drive anyone mad."

"We need to find out-" They heard Prissy starting down the stairs and waited while she was in the living room. Then Claire sighed as the turntable started and the Andrews Sisters melodiously warned against sitting under the apple tree with the wrong woman.

"Poor Frederick, such a dear, sweet man," Prissy said as she slipped into the kitchen and poured boiling water into pale pink china tea cups painted with tiny sprays of pastel snapdragons. She added a tea bag to each and carried them to the table. "Give it time to steep."

"How many years has Mr. Martin been incapacitated?" Jason asked as she sat down.

"Well, it just seems like forever. Ca-Claire was only three when he had his little accident."

Little? Jason's mind boggled. "It must have been very hard on you, Prissy."

Her look spoke of extended suffering. "It still is, but as long as the poor man fights, I'll be at his side, just as I've always been." She swirled the tea bag. "I don't know if my daughter told you or not, but I used to work as a nurse at Snapdragon General - the hospital where your baby will undoubtedly be born. It's a nice place."

"Yes, of course Claire told me. So have you." *More than once.*

"Well, it's a good thing nursing is my chosen profession. I might've retired from the hospital, but I've kept my license up so I can properly take care of Car-Claire's daddy." She brought her teacup to her lips, then paused, lost in thought, "I've prayed about it, and the Lord has assured me it was my destiny." She turned her washed-out amber eyes on Jason. "He only gives us as much as we can handle, you know."

"Uh, sure."

"It's my cross to bear," Prissy went on. "I sometimes wish the good Lord didn't have so much faith in me."

Claire narrowed her eyes. "Is that why you keep him locked up in his room all the time?"

"Hush, girl!" Prissy's eyes flashed. "You obviously don't know what you're talking about. He *prefers* to be there. It makes him feel safe."

Jason prayed Claire wouldn't let on they'd been in Frederick's room again. And she didn't.

"What does he do all day?" she asked as the Andrews Sisters continued their torment. "Does he have books? A TV?"

"Of course, dear. He loves his TV. I'm afraid he has trouble reading - his eyes don't maintain focus well-"

That's not true. At least short term, Jason had seen him focus just fine.

"-but I read to him for half an hour at least once a day. He watches television all the time. He has an oversized remote so he can change the channels himself."

"What are you reading now, Mother?" Claire's voice had that too-sweet edge that told Jason she was going in for the kill. He shot her a warning glance.

"Why, *Great Expectations*, dear. He loves that story so much that we reread it nearly every year."

Claire nodded. "Does he have any favorite television shows?"

"Oh, yes. He likes *Wheel of Fortune, Tomorrow's Singing Stars*, and *The Golden Girls*. He loves those old reruns, you know." Prissy cracked a smile. It looked painful. "He also enjoys *The God Club with Reverend Bobby Felcher*. I put it on for him Sunday mornings since it's too hard for him to go to church himself." She sighed. "He misses that, you know. At least when he remembers ..."

It looked like steam was about to shoot from Claire's ears. "Why can't he go to church with you? Why don't you install one of those stair-chairs so he can ride down easily? Maybe take him for walks, too, let him see something once in a while, take him out in the sun, for Christ's sake? Mother, you have plenty of money. You could even have an elevator installed. It's cruel to leave him up there all the time."

Prissy flashed Claire a look of contempt. "Perhaps if you'd been around these past ten years, you'd have a better understanding of your father's condition. As it is-"

Jason cleared his throat. "Claire? Weren't you going to ask your mom about your teddy bear, Mr. Anthon?"

Claire's jaw flexed and the ice in Prissy's eyes melted so quickly it was as if it had never been there. That rapid switch, Jason was sure, was borne of years of practice. "Oh, yes. Of course I remember your teddy." She laughed. "You carried that ragged old thing around with you everywhere."

"Is he still around somewhere?"

"Oh, yes!" said Prissy, rubbing the golden beads of her hair necklace. "I have a few ideas of where it might be, and as soon as I'm done with all of these projects I'm in the middle of, I'll start looking." Her red lips curled up in a smile that didn't reach her eyes.

"I can look for him."

"No, no, no. I'll find it. Now, tell me about the doctor visit."

"It was fine," Claire said between clenched teeth. "Everything's just fine, Mother."

Prissy nodded. "Good. Do you plan to find out the baby's gender?"

Claire had been right. Prissy wasn't aware of the new blood tests.

Claire opened her mouth, but Jason knew that whatever was about to come out wasn't going to be pleasant. "She's still a high risk," he interrupted. "We have to keep an eye on her blood pressure and it's probably a little high right now." He turned to Claire. "We should get back upstairs."

He saw the flush of anger in his wife's cheeks, but she didn't argue.

"Yes," said Prissy, fiddling with her scarf. "We mustn't upset our little girl." She blinked, no trace of enmity in her expression.

Claire's cheeks were crimson as Jason led her from the room. She sputtered, but allowed him to guide her out.

***

"That bitch," said Claire as they left the big white house.

"Just let it go, sweetheart."

She pulled away from Jason and turned to face him. "And you. How dare you tell her that I'm high risk?"

"But-"

"When she sees weakness, she pounces." Claire started up the stairs to the apartment. "She'll use it against me, Jason, mark my words. Is it too much to ask that you keep her out of our business?" A part of her knew she was overreacting, that she shouldn't be taking her frustrations out on her husband, but another part of her argued that she was right: Mother loved nothing more than seeing weakness. At the top of the stairs, she withdrew the key and opened the door.

"Look." Jason placed a hand on her shoulder. "I didn't mean-"

"Don't fucking *touch* me!" Claire jerked away from his hand and turned the key, letting herself in. He didn't follow and when she turned, she saw him standing outside the door, his mouth open, his eyes imploring. That's when it occurred to her. *This is what Mother wants: to turn us against each other. This is exactly what I warned Jason about and now I'm the one letting it happen.* Tears sprang. "Jason. I'm sorry." The tears slipped now and she wiped them away. "I'm sorry, I just get so upset lately."

Jason took a tentative step inside and approached, touching her as if she were a fragile piece of art in a museum.

"I'm so sorry, Jason." She'd rarely cried - *until recently* - and Jason's face betrayed his thoughts. *He thinks I'm a basket case.*

But to her relief, he pulled her close and let her cry.

Humiliated, she wept into his shoulder. *Yep. He thinks I'm losing my grip. And maybe I am.*

"It's just your hormones," he said into her hair. "Once the baby comes, you'll be your old self in no time."

She cried harder.

"Come on, let's get to bed. It's been a long day. We'll research later."

Ooh, Barracuda!

"I think we ought to write a very stern letter to Earl Dean and have everyone on the cul-de-sac sign it," Priscilla Martin announced as the yard and bake sale went on around them. "His disgusting actions will not be tolerated on Morning Glory Circle. I also believe that, as one of our own, it behooves Officer Crocker to deliver it to him personally. The nerve of that *filthy* Dean creature! He contributes nothing to this street's welfare in the first place - he neither participates in our events - including this one - nor does he have the courtesy to allow us to at least put a giant candy cane on his lawn. He actually ripped it out and set it in the trash when we tried last year, even though we put it up *for* him! And now he's urinating outside where everyone has to see him? I won't stand for it!" Prissy crossed her arms and stomped her foot. "None of us will!"

Aida Portendorfer had been enjoying spreading the news of Earl Dean's midnight indecency, but now she cringed under Prissy Martin's diatribe. "Pris, he urinated in his own backyard. Only I saw it. No one else did."

"I'm sorry you had to witness that, Aida, but remember, you're every bit as important as anyone else on this street. We must stop him! You have a right to look out your window without having to look at *that!*"

Feeling terrible, Aida refrained from mentioning that if she hadn't been looking through binoculars, she'd never have known.

"Aida," Prissy said, warily eyeing the baskets and tins of cookies on the Portendorfer table. "Why don't you write that letter up, since you were the victim in all this?"

Aida looked her straight in the eye for as long as she dared, then studied her own hands. "I'm a terrible, terrible, writer," she lied. "I barely passed English. I don't even like to read." *Did I overdo that?* "I'm not qualified." She glanced up, saw Prissy's sneer of disgust and looked away again. "We can't all be scholars, you know."

"I suppose not. I'll have Barbara do it. At least you're able to make good cookies, dear." Priscilla snatched one up, then glanced toward Stan's little table of yard sale goodies - mostly garden gnomes and undershirts - then continued her stroll down the street to see what all the other peasants had to offer.

Aida watched her go, unhappy with herself. She'd gotten straight As in English at UC Berkeley, and she loved to read. She should have known better than to bring up Earl Dean's late-night indiscretion.

Stan walked up, carrying his boom box. "What's your pleasure, today, Aida-honey? Acid? Rockabilly? Van Halen?"

Aida smiled at him. "You're so thoughtful. Let's have some metal, shall we? Prissy particularly hates Black Sabbath."

Stan bent and kissed her cheek. "I love you, Aida-honey."

***

"Have you heard the news, Bertha?"

Bertie Dunworth wished to God her sister Nelly hadn't chosen this moment to tour the cul-de-sac on her EZ Scooter, leaving her alone with Prissy. "News?" she asked in her smooth, sweet voice.

Priscilla sighed. "It seems *your* neighbor, Earl Dean, has been exposing himself."

"Aida told me he peed in his backyard. He's exposing himself, too?"

"Urinated," Prissy corrected.

"Whatever." *Jesus, everything offends her.* Bertie tried to squelch an incipient smile, but failed. "We've already sold nearly all our pies." *Good save.*

"Well, you should have made more. It's not even eleven yet." She paused. "Or is Eleanor inside baking now?"

"Who?"

"Your sister."

"Her name is Nelly, not Eleanor, and no, she's not baking. She's is touring the cul-de-sac, hoping to find a nice garden hose on the cheap."

"I see. Now, about Earl Dean. Have you witnessed any of his indiscretions?"

"No, why?"

"I need evidence to present to the proper authorities."

"Well, I'd rather not get involved if it's all the same to you. Honestly, I don't care if the man shits out there, as long as it's on his property." She laughed, enjoying Priscilla's pinched face.

"I believe the word you're looking for, Bertha, is *defecate.*"

Bertie shrugged. "As long as he does his business in *his* yard, I don't care if he shits *or* defecates."

Priscilla clucked her tongue and looked at the two remaining pies. "As chairman of the Morning Glory Circle Yard and Bake Sale, I appreciate your efforts, but this just isn't enough product to put you on the short list for an animatronic Santa this year." She glanced around, her face squinched up as if she were smelling dog shit.

Bertie smiled, buoyed by the tune the Portendorfers were rocking. Sabbath's *Children of the Grave.*

"To qualify," continued Priscilla, "you also need to get your yard properly landscaped."

"Not all of us can afford that kind of Astroturf."

Priscilla sniffed. "You use the Sachs boy to mow your lawn. Why not have him edge it, and plant some flowers for you?"

"If you want to pay him, we're happy to have him do those things. We spent all of our disposable income - and then some - buying ingredients for these damned pies. You can't have it both ways."

Prissy opened her mouth.

"And we don't want an animatronic Santa, thank you very much."

"You ought to consider your words more carefully. Words hurt, you know. Good day, Bertha." Throwing a sneer toward the low fence where Bertie and her sister had hung old shirts and skirts and pants as yard sale offerings, she glanced back. "You'll never make back the money you spent on those pies if you can't find something nicer to sell."

"Thank you, Priscilla. I'll go out to Nordstrom's and buy some new clothes right now."

Priscilla Martin kept going. Bertie stared at the two pies, then stuck a plump finger in one and sucked away the chocolate. "Mmm. You're not going anywhere but back into our fridge." And if the other pie lasted until Nelly returned, it was going to stay home, too. *Fuck you, Priscilla Martin.*

***

"How long have you been out here, Jason?"

"Not long. Just since your mother texted and asked me to watch her bake table while she checks on things around the cul-de-sac."

Claire stood on tiptoe and kissed her husband. "Thank you for letting me sleep in."

He laughed. "I was sleeping in, too, until she texted. Boy, when your mother wants something, she wants it *now!* I was in such a rush to get out here that I'm going commando."

Claire laughed and patted his butt. "Has she sold any cannoli yet?"

"She said she's sold six boxes of six for fifteen bucks a box. She told me, I can also sell singles for five dollars apiece."

"That's Mother. If she thought she could get twenty, she'd ask that." Claire reached out and took a single cannoli, unwrapped and munched it. "Mmm, yummy. You should have one, too."

"We can't afford these!"

"Who's going to tell her?"

"She'll know."

Claire stuffed half the cannoli in her mouth. "She won't know who, though."

"True enough ... and I haven't had breakfast."

"Right!"

Jason devoured a pastry, then handed both wrappers to Claire. "Here. Get rid of the evidence. Better take them to someone else's trash can!"

"I'll take them next door. Be right back." She headed toward the Pepto pink Sachs house.

Jason watched her chat with Candy and her son, Billy, then toss the refuse into a small trash can next to their table. Candy handed Claire two cupcakes.

"How much?" Jason asked when she returned and proffered a big chocolate frosted confection to him.

"Free. Candy is lots nicer than Mother." She bit into her cake, got frosting on her nose. "Yum. These are way better than cannoli."

Jason reached out, swiped the frosting off and licked his finger clean. "Simple pleasures are the best." He grinned.

"They are." Claire glanced at the little card table a couple of feet from the bake table. On it were several Mason jars, two yellowed boxes half-full of canning jar rings and lids, a yellow plastic flashlight without batteries, a Gideon bible, two trial-size tubes of toothpaste, and a cellophane-wrapped toothbrush, the kind given out in lieu of candy at the dentist's. There was also a trial-size box of dental floss, a pen that said *"Snapdragon Bank and Trust,"* and one that said *"Collins' Fine Furniture."* "That's quite a haul." Claire examined the final item, a can of fruit cocktail only seven years out of date.

"The way you talked, I'm surprised she put anything out."

"Me, too. So how long ago did she leave?"

"Nearly twenty minutes, now."

"Plenty of time." Claire scanned the street. "I'm going to go get the hangers."

"Really?"

"You don't want me to?"

"Go for it, but hurry. You don't want to still be setting up when she returns."

"Be right back!"

***

The knock at the door brought Bettyanne into the living room where Roddy was relaxing in his recliner, watching the game.

She peered cautiously out the curtains. "It's Priscilla Martin, Roddy," she whispered, eyes wide.

Roddy looked up at the clock over the fireplace. "Jesus Christ, it's not even eleven."

"What should we do?" asked Bettyanne, wringing her hands. "I have to leave for the airport in fifteen minutes."

"Open the door, I suppose." Roddy aimed the remote at the screen and muted the game.

"But what if she asks why we're not participating today?"

Roddy stood, groaning as he extracted himself from the warmth of his recliner. "I'll handle her." He pecked Bettyanne on the cheek. He loved his wife, but she was a timid little thing. It was a quality he'd generally found endearing, but at times, it was equally frustrating. *Times like this.* "We don't answer to her, Betty."

She nodded. "I know, but-"

Another hard knock sounded. "Helloooo," came Prissy's sugarcoated falsetto.

Roddy shook his head and opened the door. "Priscilla," he said. "What brings you here?"

She batted her lashes at him, her snaky smile splitting her face like a red gash. "I just thought I'd stop by and give you another invitation to the yard and bake sale. We certainly don't want you to feel left out." Tendrils of her cloying perfume reached through the doorway like ghostly hands going for his sinuses. Roddy had been blessed - or cursed - with a nearly superhuman sense of smell. He was known around the police station as The Bloodhound. His abnormally keen sense of smell often came in handy, but at times like this, he wished he had a head cold. It would be less painful.

"We're busy, Priscilla, but thank you for asking."

She peered around him into the living room. "Bettyanne?"

Roddy turned to his wife, who stood in the background, shaking her head.

"Would she like to-"

"I'm afraid she has a plane to catch, Priscilla." Roddy used his cop voice - but *good* cop, not bad. Yet. "Is there anything else I can help you with?"

Priscilla clearly caught his no-nonsense tone and the twinkle in her eyes almost went out. Almost. "Actually, there is." She frowned. "It seems we're having a little problem with one of our residents."

Jesus Christ. What's bothering her now? He raised his brows in question, already too exhausted by the woman to bother with words.

"It's Earl Dean." Prissy spoke low and she looked around conspiratorially. "He's been exposing himself to Aida Portendorfer."

Roddy started to laugh, but quickly disguised it as a cough. "Exposing himself?" The corners of his mouth twitched, threatening betrayal.

She nodded. "Mm-hmm. He was urinating out of doors, where anyone could have seen him. I'm preparing a formal letter of complaint right now-"

"Outside? Where?"

Priscilla Martin frowned. "In his backyard. Aida just happened to be looking out her window and caught him."

"She happened to be looking out her window, you say?" He knew Old Lady Portendorfer never just *happened* to see *anything* in this neighborhood; he'd seen her himself more than once, binoculars raised, nose pressed to the window.

"Yes, and she was scandalized - just *scandalized* - by what she saw!" Her jaw tightened. "As I said, I'm writing a formal complaint-"

Roddy held a hand up. "Don't trouble yourself, Mrs. Martin. I'll talk to him."

"You will? I hate to be a bother, Roderick, it's just that I don't think we should have to worry about seeing …"

Earl Dean's Tonsil Tickler, he wanted to finish for her.

"*That.*" She looked satisfied, having finally found just the right word.

"Indeed," said Roddy, his poker face intact. "First thing Monday morning, I'll have a chat with him." *Hey Earl, Aida watches you pee outside. Just so you know.* "Now, if there's nothing else, I'm afraid I have to get going. Bettyanne has a plane to catch, and I need to do some housework while she's gone." It was a lie. He needed to finish the game and drink a few more beers, but he had no problem lying to Priscilla Martin.

"Well, if you finish your chores and find yourself looking for something to do, we can always use your help at the sale." Her words were casual, but Roddy heard the direct order beneath them. And he didn't take orders.

"I'm afraid I'm going to have to pass, Mrs. Martin, but thank you for stopping by." He gave her a winning smile before shutting the door in her face.

Bettyanne hurried to the window. When Prissy was out of sight, she exhaled. "That woman," she said. "She's just so intrusive. And she calls you 'Roderick.'"

Roddy nodded, slipped back into his chair and turned up the volume.

"She has a lot of nerve."

"Indeed. You better hurry or you'll miss your flight." Roddy was eager for solitude.

Bettyanne looked at her watch and gasped. "Oh! I'd better go!"

"And Betty?"

"Yes, dear?"

"Don't bring back anything you didn't take with you." He gave her a pointed look.

"Of course not, Roddy."

As she headed toward the bedroom, Roddy called, "Open a window, would you, sweetie?" He didn't want Priscilla Martin's hideous perfume embedding itself into the furniture. He'd smell it for weeks.

A smile tugged at his lips as he thought of Aida Portendorfer - *just scandalized!* as Prissy had put it - by the sight of Earl's pork sword. *It's a sad world,* he thought as he sipped his beer, *when a man can't drain the tank in his own back yard.*

***

"Hey there! How're you doing?"

A tall, tattooed gentleman with blond hair and a prize-winning handlebar mustache walked over from the burnt orange house, where Johnny Mathis was crooning *Misty.*

"Hello." Jason put his hand out and the man shook it with admirable firmness.

"I'm Hank Lowell, from next door. That pretty lady with the red hair manning the bake table is my wife, Crystal, and those two boys playing in the tires are Harley and David, our sons."

"Jason Holbrook. I'm Mrs. Martin's son-in-law." Crystal, Hank's wife, appeared to be very busy with a long line of customers. There were people all over Hank's lawn, too, checking out a dozen motorcycle helmets, tires, rims, and all sorts of auto and bike paraphernalia. "You're doing a landslide business!"

Hank glanced back and grinned. "Nothing's stolen, either." His laugh was hearty. "I run the cycle shop in town. Do you ride?"

"My wife would kill me."

"Don't blame her." Another hearty laugh. "Mine says I have to get this stuff out of the garage." He chuckled. "I always mind the missus. She's right, too. She's making me sell off half of my helmet collection. I practically hoard the damned things. Love 'em dearly, but they've got to go."

Jason had heard Prissy grouse about the family next door, but he really liked Hank Lowell. "So, how are you attracting so many customers?"

His laugh could give Santa Claus competition in the jolly department. "Reasonable prices, just like at my business. It's the only way to clear out the garage, being reasonable. And Crys is selling pumpkin pies for five dollars a pop. Just like Costco." He grinned. "They're a little smaller of course, but we're making about two bucks a pie. Labor's free." He looked at the lonely cannoli. "Your mother-in-law isn't doing too well from the looks of things."

Jason told him what she was asking for the cannoli.

"Oh, hell, she's asking double what Giuseppe Bartoli sells them for. That's highway robbery." He paused. "Not so surprising, though."

"Not at all. Here comes my wife. Just a minute, I want to introduce you." Jason trotted back to Claire and took a folding tray and the black bag of hangers from her. "You're going to love the neighbors."

"Great."

"Hank, this is my wife, Claire Holbrook. Claire, Hank."

While they shook hands, Jason set up the tray and put a few dozen hangers on it - all that would fit. Claire had brought a roll of tape and a sign advertising "FREE HANGERS." Chuckling, Jason taped the sign to the tray.

"Hey, Crys," Hank called. "Do we need hangers?"

"Not today," Crystal called back. "But thanks."

"Sorry," Hank said.

"Why are you sorry?" Claire asked.

"I figured you'd want to get rid of them before your mother comes back. She won't take kindly to your giving them away."

"I know," Claire said, grinning. "I'm counting on it."

"Are they hers?" Hank returned the grin.

"No, they're ours. Though she fished them out of the trash can and put them in her house," Jason explained. "I thought she wanted them for the yard sale today, but I was wrong."

Claire laughed.

"I've noticed she has a little problem getting rid of things," Hank said, dimples showing next to the blond handlebar 'stache.

"You have?" Claire looked surprised.

"Yeah, when she was having that apartment you're living in cleared out, we - Crys and I - saw inside that garage. No offense, but I don't know how they got all that stuff in there - it was already packed full." He chuckled. "Good thing it's a three-car garage, right?"

"Right. We'd like to see in there, too," Jason said. "She won't open it for us."

"Well, you can come on over here and spy on her any time you want." Another happy guffaw. "In fact, I actually came over to tell you two what we overheard the other night. Might be important."

"Please tell us," Claire said.

"Well, she had the garage open and was jabbering up a blue streak so Crys and I went out to listen."

"And?" Jason prompted.

"And that ... um ... *invisible friend* of hers is evidently upset."

"My deceased brother."

"Yes ma'am. I was trying to be delicate."

"You're fine, go ahead."

"Okay, well, she acted like he was talking to her - that's nothing new, we've heard it before - but she was telling him she knew you two went into his bedroom."

Jason's stomach clenched. "She knows we were in there?"

"Apparently, your brother told her ..." said Hank in a sheepish tone.

"It's fine," Claire said. "Go on."

"Well ... the way she tells it, you went into her bedroom and some other rooms, and, um ... she said she would 'have a talk with you two' if she hears you did it again." His cheeks flushed. "I'm quoting. I didn't mean to pry. Just thought you should know."

"Thanks, Hank," said Claire. She and Jason exchanged glances. "I should have known she'd notice. That woman sees everything."

"But how?" Jason's panic burgeoned, making him feel slightly dizzy. They'd sneaked around like children. They had no right to go through Priscilla's house. She must be furious. *And she may be eccentric, but she* is *trying to help us.* Jason felt ashamed of himself.

But Claire was unrepentant. "I'll bet she noticed we took the pill bottles from Dad's trash can."

Hank cocked his head. "Dad? Your old man lives there?"

Claire nodded.

"I've never even seen him."

"He's confined upstairs. He's handicapped," Claire said.

Jason, still feeling guilty, opened his mouth to suggest they take the hangers back inside, but his words were cut short.

The guitar riff of *Barracuda* rent the air.

"No, no, no, no ..." Priscilla Martin bustled toward them and their folding tray full of evidence.

Jason's throat went dry. Claire's back stiffened. Hank chuckled.

Prissy snatched up the stack of hangers and clutched them like homeless puppies. "I didn't mean for *these* to be sold, or -" she glanced at the FREE HANGERS sign, "-*given* away."

Claire made a grab for them. "They're *our* hangers, Mother, and we decided we wanted to give them away." She turned to Jason. "Isn't that so?"

Jason nodded as Prissy hugged the hangers closer.

Hank's face was a mask of fascination as Claire jerked the hangers from Prissy's clutches.

Prissy turned to Hank, all smiles. "Run along, Mr. Lowell. Certainly, you have your own matters to attend to. And please, turn that horrible music down."

"I'm outta here." Hank returned to his own house, but didn't turn down the music.

Huffing, Prissy pulled at the hangers, but Claire held them tight.

There they stood, each clutching opposite sides of the hangers, staring each other down like rabid dogs. Jason cleared his throat and was about to speak up, when Prissy cut him off.

"As it happens, I've decided I can make use of these after all." Her practiced smile was warm, non-threatening.

"How's that, Mother? To take up more space in your house? You have more bags, and they belong to us, anyway. I just might decide to sell *them* this afternoon, too."

Jason glanced toward the Lowells, who were openly staring. *Just kill me now.*

Prissy sighed, the earlier blaze in her eyes dimming to a tired spark. "We mustn't be wasteful, Carlene. Someone can use these."

"It's *Claire,* Mother, and I agree. Someone *can* use them and that's why we put them out here. You don't need them. I think we *all* know they'll just sit in their trash bags until Kingdom Come, collecting dust in a room already stuffed with shit you don't need."

"Carlene! Watch your language. You owe the swear jar a dollar!"

"These. Hangers. Belong. To. Us." Claire's mouth was a hard line and her eyes could have cut glass. "Fuck. The. Swear. Jar."

Jason wanted to leave, but forced himself to face the horrible music. "A compromise," he said.

Both women cut glances at him.

He cleared his throat. "We have one bag here to give away, and you can keep the others and use them however you wish, Prissy. Fair?"

Priscilla's eyes lit and Claire's smoldered.

"See?" said Prissy to Claire. "A compromise. I think it's a wonderful idea, Jason."

"Claire?" Jason's tone was cautious. "Does that work for you?"

"Fine," she said through gritted teeth.

He breathed a great sigh of relief. This wasn't about the hangers, he knew that. This was a lifelong power struggle between the two women ... and he'd stepped right into its festering core.

Slowly, Claire's rigid stance relaxed and Jason's relief grew. He'd never seen his wife like this before - so hell bent, so angry, so ... *petty.* It unsettled him.

Prissy brushed her mint green polyester pantsuit off, ridding it of invisible dust. "Very well, then," she said. "Everyone's happy." She smiled, then continued, "Be sure to buy a cannoli or two, kids. It's for a very good cause."

"We will, Prissy," said Jason. "It smells wonderful." In truth, the only thing he smelled was something citrusy behind the stink of his mother-in-law's perfume. He didn't recall seeing any lemon pies or orange cakes, but it made him hungry for dessert.

***

"Here she comes," Duane Pruitt said to his partner, Jerry.

"I think I need to go check on Waldo." Jerry Park made to rise from the table loaded with brownies and blondies.

Duane touched Jerry's wrist. "Oh no, you don't. You're not going to desert me during Prissy Martin's inspection."

"Well, she's got to be in a bad mood, now." Jerry reseated himself. "That was quite a show. I wish we could have heard what they were saying."

"Fighting over hangers." He frowned. "It's just so ... *Mommie Dearest.*" Duane chuckled. "I wish we'd filmed it - we could have dubbed in the conversation and put it on YouTube!" He switched on the Bluetooth speaker, hit KNDL and stopped - Lenny Kravitz was singing *American Woman.* Duane sang along: *"Stay away from mee-hee."*

Jerry laughed his giggly laugh and Duane kept singing, not noticing Prissy Martin's arrival until she stepped under their big striped umbrella.

"Well, how are you boys doing today?"

Jerry stared at her like a schoolboy trapped in an angry nun's gaze.

"We're fine, Mrs. Martin," Duane said. "And how are you?"

"Absolutely perfect," she said. "And please, call me Prissy. All my friends do."

"My," Duane said, beginning his performance, "that's a lovely pantsuit you're wearing, Prissy. Is it vintage?" *Vintage, as in J.C. Penney, 1984.* Out of the corner of his eye, he saw Jerry fighting down more giggles.

"Why yes, it is. Thank you for noticing. Not everyone does, you know."

"I love the padding in the shoulders. It does something for you."

She batted her eyelashes at him. Simultaneously, Jerry began shaking with laughter. Duane kicked him under the table. They couldn't risk Priscilla Martin catching on that they were making fun. He knew she could make their lives a living hell and they already had one mark against them: She didn't condone their *questionable* lifestyle. Fortunately, she was enough of a sucker for flattery that it overrode her conservative sensibilities. "You look wonderfully elegant," he added.

"Why, thank you, Duane." Her eyes glittered. "How are your brownies selling, may I ask?"

"Like hotcakes." Duane fed her ego with a shit-filled smile. "Would you care for one?"

"I would indeed."

"Brownie or blondie?"

"Brownie, please." There went the eyelashes again. "A girl needs her chocolate."

Duane handed her a wax paper-wrapped square.

"Here," Jerry said as he picked up two more brownies and tried to give them to her. "I bet your daughter and her husband would each like one."

She looked down her nose at him. "I keep them quite well-fed, thank you."

Jerry shrank at her condescending tone.

Duane was certain Priscilla Martin blamed Jerry for his "sudden" homosexuality, and she made no effort to disguise her disapproval.

Duane cleared his throat. "Well, let them know we have plenty, if they get the urge."

Priscilla continued glaring at Jerry, so Duane pulled out the big guns. "That perfume," he said. "It's absolutely breathtaking." *I can hardly breathe!* "I was telling Jerry just this morning how wonderful you always smell. What is it called, and where can I get some? I have a sister who would just adore it."

Priscilla Martin's eyes twinkled. "It's called *Opium*. It's a special blend. I believe you can get it at Nordstrom's." She paused. "I thought you people would know that."

Jerry gaped. "*You* people?"

Duane stiffened. "*Opium*, you say?"

Prissy ignored him. "I don't mean *you*, silly boy," she said to Jerry. "I'm not prejudiced against the Orientals. They make the absolute best chop suey. " She leaned forward, as if sharing a secret. "I was referring to people like you both who have non-traditional ... *values.*"

Jerry's eyes almost bugged out of his head, but Duane retained his rictus grin. "Well, we people can't be everywhere. And I understand why you heteros keep that *Opium* scent to yourselves." He winked at her and she blushed.

"I just can't believe you're a *real* gay, Duane, not with that look in your eye." She paused and Duane felt Jerry cringe at his side.

Priscilla smiled. "You fellows keep up the good sales. I'd love to see you earn the animatronic Santa Claus this year."

"Thank you, Mrs. Martin - er, Prissy." Duane widened his patented fake smile.

She nodded, waggled her fingers goodbye at them, and turned toward the Collins home.

"What a bitch," Jerry said when she was out of earshot.

"Bitch Supreme - with extra cheese," Duane agreed. His mouth hurt from smiling.

"I don't like what she implied. You don't think she knows something, do you?"

Duane shook his head. "I don't know how she could." He squeezed Jerry's hand. But he wondered, too.

Around the Sac

It was so humiliating, the scene Carlene had made over the hangers. After her daughter stomped upstairs, Prissy had asked her long-suffering son-in-law to continue minding her table of cannoli. She could tell he really wanted to run after his wife and apologize, but that wouldn't have been a good idea. It would just spoil the girl even more.

And all the music was giving her a headache. *The cacophony of it all!* They would have to raise funds for a street-wide sound system that would give her jurisdiction over the music. All this rock and roll undoubtedly drove people away. They needed a uniform playing of the classics - Frank Sinatra, Dean Martin, perhaps a selection of Lawrence Welk's orchestrations. Wholesome music that people would enjoy.

Prissy slowed in front of the Collins house. She had to think of something to dissuade Geneva-Marie from running against her for president of the Ladies Auxiliary; she was Prissy's only real competition and had to be stopped. *For the good of Holy Sacramental. We can't have that scarlet harlot in power!*

Prissy sighed - Carlene had sucked her dry and she didn't have the strength to deal with Geneva-Marie right now. She *tsked* to herself as she passed the gaudy Spanish-style monstrosity and headed to the Vandercooth home, eager to sample Barbara's fruit bars. She was also eager to see if Barbara had made as many as she'd promised - last year, she'd barely lifted a finger, using pneumonia as an excuse. *Utter nonsense.* Considering what a great friend she claimed to be, Barbara wasn't terribly reliable. On top of that, she'd become mouthy. *And after* all *the things I've done for her.* Priscilla *tsked.*

***

Well, hello Carl, how are you?"

Carl Vandercooth cringed at the sound of Prissy Martin's voice. "Excuse me," he said to Quinton Everett. "Hello, Prissy. I'm afraid you've just missed Babs. She's taking a stroll around the sac - I believe I see her talking with Aida, if you want to catch up with her."

"That's all right, Carl, I'll talk to her later. I just wanted to check out your wares. And please, don't call Morning Glory Circle 'the sac.' That's vulgar. Now, give me your sales figures."

Quinton turned to look at her, and Carl watched her demeanor instantly change. She batted her eyelashes with syrupy coyness. It seemed very strange, considering ...

"Why, what are you doing here, Quinton? Surely Carl has paid his mortgage this month." She chuckled as if the old joke were funny. It never had been. It never would be.

"Of course," said Quinton. He wore gray running pants and a charcoal IZOD jacket that matched his hair. "I was just stopping by to purchase fruit bars for my Little League players."

Carl Vandercooth was no fool. His skin crawled, remembering what Babs had confided. He saw young Billy Sachs headed toward the table - the Sachs family always bought a couple dozen of Babs' fruit bars - and Carl wanted to warn him off.

Billy arrived, out of breath. "Hi, Mr. V! Hi-" He recognized Prissy and looked away quickly. Pulling a twenty and a ten out of his pocket, he laid them on the table. "I'd like an assortment of whatever this will buy." He grinned. "Heavy on the raspberry, okay?"

"You've got it, Billy," Carl said. "You sure did a nice wax job on Mrs. V's car last week. Will you do my SUV tomorrow? You can make all this money back!"

Billy's face lit up. "I sure will, Mr. V! Thanks! I'll do a great job!"

"I know you will." Carl smiled at Billy as he placed an extra half dozen raspberry bars in the bag along with the rest of the cookies.

"You wax cars, young man?" Quinton Everett smiled his slick smile at the boy and licked his lips.

"Sure."

"How would you like to wax my Jaguar?"

"Wow! I sure would!"

"Billy," Carl said quickly. "I need to show you something. Come up to the house a minute?" He turned to the banker and Prissy. "Excuse us, won't you?"

He led Billy up the driveway and to the other side of the SUV, where they couldn't be seen. "Billy, don't ever - and I mean *ever* - have anything to do with that man."

"But-"

"Listen, it's just hearsay, so I can't tell you why, but don't talk to him, don't look at him, and don't let him look at you. Now, take your goodies and run home. Wave to me and yell, "Thanks, Mr. V, I'll ask my dad!" real loud, so the man hears you."

"Ask my dad what?"

"Nothing. It's just a means to get you away from him. I'll see you tomorrow, anytime you want, for that wax job."

"Okay." They returned to the sidewalk and Billy trotted off, yelling back that he'd ask his dad.

"Well, what was that about?" Prissy asked. She looked annoyed that he'd ignore her in favor of a mere child.

"Man stuff," Carl said, looking Quinton right in the eye.

Prissy sighed, and Quinton Everett looked wistful.

"Carl, if you and Babs took the time to decorate these packages of cookies - add a festive ribbon or some glitter or even stickers to attract little kids - you might sell more."

Carl hid his annoyance. "It's only noon and we've already sold half. Babs worked very hard to make these, and frankly, I worked very hard cutting and wrapping them. I think they look great, don't you, Quinton?"

"Indeed. They look as good as they taste."

Prissy's lips puckered like the drawstring of a coin purse. "Well, I think you would really benefit from a little repackaging, Carl. It's important that your products appeal to the customers."

"We'll be out by three o'clock."

"Well, then you should have made more."

"We're looking forward to closing up early, Prissy." Carl had just about had it with the old windbag.

"Then, can you just imagine how fast they'd be flying off the table with some improvements? You could make twice as many and sell them all!"

Quinton Everett's head swiveled back and forth between them.

Carl sighed. "Maybe next year, Prissy."

"Very well. I'll be sure and let Babs know you've committed to it." She eyed the table. "You might consider a new table. This one doesn't seem to be holding up too well. It's scratched. At least add a nice tablecloth."

Carl felt his blood pressure rising. "I'm not putting any more time - or money - into these events of yours. As it is-" he clipped the sentence off, shocked by his outburst, but it was too late.

Prissy watched him, fire in her eyes. "A penny saved is a penny earned, Carl. We've learned *that* lesson, haven't we?"

Carl was on his feet. "Just who do you think you are?"

Prissy's jaw was tight, her mouth a firm, hard line. Despite her soft tone the force of her words brought the cords in her neck to the surface. "I'm the person who cosigned on your house when you nearly lost it, Carl." Her gaze softened and that loathsome smile returned to her lips. "As I'm sure you well remember."

Carl had never hit a woman in his life, but he was certain the only thing stopping him now was Quinton Everett, who surprised everyone by drawing himself up and rounding on Prissy.

"I think that's enough, Priscilla. We all know what happened, and we're all sick to death of hearing about it. It was a long time ago. All Mr. Vandercooth owes you is a thank you, and I believe he's given you that, many times over."

Prissy gaped at Quinton. Carl realized she was at a loss for words. It was wonderful. Unprecedented and wonderful.

Quinton, cool as a cucumber on a cold day, said, "Now, please, Priscilla. Go bother someone else."

If Prissy had been speechless before, she was utterly stricken now. She raised a hand to her throat, clutching that dreadful hair necklace of hers. "What did you just say to me, Quinton?" Her dry whisper cracked.

Quinton didn't miss a beat. "You heard me, Priscilla."

Her gaze flicked from Carl to Quinton.

Carl just stared. *If she expects me to come to her rescue, she's in for a disappointment.*

She dropped her hands. "Well!" There was nothing more to say. She turned and stalked off, head high, shoulders back.

Quinton sighed. "I hope I didn't make you uncomfortable, Carl. I'm just tired of seeing you pushed around by her. She doesn't own you *or* your home, and if I'd known she was going to hold it over your head for the rest of your life, I'd have advised you to get a different cosigner."

Now it was Carl who didn't know what to say.

"We can get her off that loan, you know," Quinton said. "It's been more than enough time."

"We could?"

Quinton nodded. "Come and see me next week."

Carl had never wanted to hug another man so desperately in his life, even "Creepy Quinton," as the neighbors called him. He handed the banker a few dozen extra fruit bars. "Here," he said. "For the Little League team."

***

Ace Etheridge had watched the exchange between Prissy, his neighbor Carl, and Quinton Everett, with interest. It was obvious something had happened to upset Priscilla Martin, and now she was barreling toward him. He glanced around, but Iris was nowhere in sight.

As she neared, her angry frown softened and was replaced by a false smile. "Why, Lance, you baked!" She looked at the three chocolate cakes on his tiny table. "Or did your daughter bake for you?"

Lance. God, he hated his given name - no one used it except for Prissy, who refused to call him Ace.

"You must have sold lots of cakes this morning already, you've so few left." She bent toward him, getting in his face. "Isn't that right, Lance?"

"No, there were just six."

"Oh, you bachelors. I hope you and Iris had fun making them - it's such a great bonding experience for a father and daughter."

"Neither of us bakes. Babs was kind enough to bring these over for us to sell."

Prissy's eyes narrowed to angry slits. "Barbara made these, you say?"

Ace knew he'd fucked up, but wasn't sure how to fix it so Pris Martin wouldn't come down on Babs. "Um, yes."

"I see." Prissy stepped back.

"It was very kind of her, don't you think? She's always been such a nice lady. Very charitable."

The smile didn't slip but Prissy's eyes were hard chips of pale stone. "Very charitable, indeed. I only wish she'd put her efforts into her fruit bars and allowed you and Iris to do your *own* work." She looked him up and down. "Or were you too busy writing?"

Ace examined her, tried to see what knowledge was in those eyes. *How much could she know? And how?* He sat a little straighter. "I own the newspaper. It's my job, Prissy."

"Of course, it is," she said. "But we all need to pull our own weight around here."

"Duly noted." He smiled and resisted the urge to give her a Nazi salute.

"Well, then, I suppose I'd better find Barbara."

"Tell her thank you again, from Iris and *Ace.*"

"Duly noted, *Lance.*" And she was off.

All in all, Ace figured he'd gotten off pretty easily. But he cringed at the thought of what Babs Vandercooth had coming to her.

***

"Why, hello, Priscilla." Aida Portendorfer spoke an instant before Prissy Martin's finger poked Babs' shoulder. "You don't look very happy, Prissy," she continued. "I thought the sale was going very well."

Babs jerked away from the finger and turned to look at Prissy. *Oh, crap. What's up her butt now?* "Hello, Pris," she said, putting on her best oblivious look, the one that usually fooled Priscilla Martin. "Isn't it a lovely day? It feels like spring is coming early this year."

"Hello, girls!" Phyllis Stine approached in white go-go boots and too much makeup. "How's everything going? Aida, Clyde just came back to take over the gingerbread table and he's sitting there stuffing his face with your snickerdoodles. You *must* give me the recipe." Phyllis barely paused for a breath. "I swear. I went from trying to sell my sister's New Age books to offering one free with every gingerbread purchase, but I can't give them away. I don't know how Constance ever sold a single one." She rolled her eyes. "Babs, I was just going to head over to your table for some of your apricot bars."

"I told Carl to hold some for you," Babs said. For once, she was glad to see Phyllis, since her presence would distract Prissy, but the aging cage dancer always annoyed her. She hadn't seen her in days and it appeared she'd had a bit of an eye tuck - her skin was tight enough to split, just a thin layer stretched over sharp bones. *Maybe it's just too much Botox.*

Babs had decided natural aging was the best thing for herself, and it was obvious Aida agreed with her - Aida had stopped keeping the gray away and was now adding to it, seeming to relish her jolly grandmotherly appearance. But then, she had grandchildren. Babs herself had always been a blond and now she used a little tint to keep it that way - her hair was turning white. She exercised, did yoga, and wore a modest amount of makeup, but that was all. And Priscilla - well, she and Botox were obviously old pals, and had been for a while, but she dyed her hair shoe-polish black - it had been dark brown when she was young. *Maybe it's a tribute to Ronald Reagan. After all, he's still her favorite president.* Babs suspected Pris had had an occasional nip and tuck, too - her neck was too smooth for her age - but she'd never dare ask her and hell would freeze over before Prissy volunteered such information.

"Babs?" Pris said. "Are you listening?"

"Why no, I wasn't." She gave Pris a sheepish smile.

"Aida? Are you listening?" Prissy crossed her arms.

"Oh, sorry. I was trying to eavesdrop on Geneva-Marie and Burke." She lowered her voice. "I think he's tipping the bottle."

"Shame on you, Aida, for condoning gossip," Prissy said. "As it says in Proverbs, '*For lack of wood the fire goes out, and where there is no whisperer, quarreling ceases.*'"

"Oh, Miss Pris, lighten up." Phyllis laughed. "Without gossip, the sac would be a very dull place." She stared across the street at the Collins house where Burke tilted a beer, wobbling a bit, while Geneva-Marie glared at him from her table. "I believe you're right, Aida. I think he's two sheets to the wind and working on the third."

"Listen up, ladies," Priscilla said, her eyes drilling into them. "I'm seeing a lot of problems out here today. People aren't adhering to our rules. And one of the rules is we don't call it 'the sac.'"

Phyllis rolled her eyes again and Prissy glared daggers at her.

"Why, whatever do you mean?" Aida asked. "What other rules are being broken?"

"Well, I'm not going to name names but a certain unmarried man on this block got someone else to bake cakes for him instead of doing it himself."

Babs gasped. "No!"

Prissy's look could have left a polar bear shivering.

"What's so awful about that?" Phyllis asked. "I didn't even know there was a rule."

"Why, Phyllis Welling Stine!" Prissy exclaimed. "It's in our Morning Glory Circle bylaws, and I pass out a new edition every January. You mean you haven't reviewed your copy yet?"

"I didn't know I had one."

"What about you, Aida?" Prissy asked. "You've read them, haven't you?"

"I … Guess I missed that."

"Barbara?"

Babs shook her head.

"My Good Lord!" Prissy blew out a load of hot air. "I gave a whole stack of those to Daphene and Delphine Dean to pass out. Why I pay those little good-for-nothings a dime apiece if they didn't even deliver them! I'll have to speak to their parents."

"Be nice," Aida said. "Those little girls aren't too bright, you know. You'd be better off paying Billy Sachs. He's a very reliable young man."

Prissy made a disgusted sound. "That boy wanted five dollars to do it. That's highway robbery!"

"No, it's not." Phyllis shook her head. "That's pretty good, actually. I'm surprised he didn't ask for ten."

"Obscene. I'll see that everyone gets a fresh copy myself. And there will be an update. A new rule. No more of this raucous blaring music. It drives away customers."

Phyllis rolled her eyes yet again. "All I hear is *Candle in the Wind.* Elton John is *hardly* offensive, Prissy."

"Elton John, not offensive?" Prissy glared. "I don't think I need to get into the dirty specifics of that fancy Nancy's lifestyle choices. From now on, there will be no more of this racket. If we *must* have music, it will be family-friendly, and it will be uniform. I don't want to hear a different song at every house, and neither does anyone else!" Prissy glanced across the street and stared for several moments. "Barbara, Aida, come along with me while I speak with Geneva-Marie about the Ladies Auxiliary."

Babs followed her gaze. Burke Collins had disappeared; Geneva-Marie was alone, ready to be pounced upon. With a frown for Phyllis, Babs followed Prissy across the street to the Collins house, Aida close behind.

Given that Geneva-Marie was the only woman on the circle who wouldn't roll over for her, she was Priscilla's only real rival, and Babs knew Geneva-Marie was going to challenge Pris for president of the Ladies Auxiliary. As they approached, Babs felt her stomach tightening. She looked at Aida, who seemed eager for the drama.

"Geneva-Marie Collins," said Prissy as they approached the woman's table of fragrant cinnamon-pecan rolls. "How are you today?"

Geneva-Marie wore a red felt jacket that complemented her glossy dark hair and dark red lipstick. *She looks like a scarlet harlot,* is what Pris always said, but Babs didn't think so. Next to Candy Sachs, Geneva-Marie was the prettiest woman on the block - and that was just the beginning of Pris' problems with her.

Geneva-Marie stood. "Priscilla." She nodded at the women. "Babs. Aida."

"Hello, Geneva-Marie," said Babs.

"Good day," said Aida.

"And how are sales?" asked Prissy, craning her neck to examine Geneva-Marie's product.

"Oh, not too bad. We're running a little behind and weren't able to get set up as early as we wanted, but-"

"Yes, I noticed that." Prissy's voice frosted the air. "And where is Burke? I thought I saw him a moment ago." She gave her the snake smile.

Geneva-Marie looked at her well-manicured hands. "He wasn't feeling well and decided to go inside."

The poor woman, thought Babs. *It must be so difficult living with an alcoholic.*

Prissy made a sympathetic noise. "Is there anything we can do for him? Perhaps he'd like some of my special chicken noodle soup."

"No, Prissy, it's fine-"

Pris plowed on. "Aida. Go to the door and ask Burke if he prefers chicken noodle or cream of mushroom." Geneva-Marie's eyes shifted nervously. Pris continued. "Both are very good for the stomach, you know." Prissy turned to Aida and glared. "Aida? Are you listening?"

Aida was staring at the cinnamon rolls, her mouth practically watering. She didn't respond and Pris repeated the request.

"Oh, of course!" Aida bustled toward the Collins home.

Geneva-Marie stood. "I'd really rather you didn't bother him."

"Nonsense," said Prissy. "Burke will just love my soup. I assure you, it will fix him right up."

Defeated, nervous as a call girl in church, Geneva-Marie sat.

The Dean twins, Daphi and Delphi, came to a stop several yards away, hands clasped. Upon seeing Priscilla, they obviously changed their minds about buying a cinnamon-pecan roll. Babs smiled at them but they stared on with pale blank eyes, then turned and ran, still holding hands. It was probably a good thing. Prissy would surely lay into them for not delivering her bylaws. *Such strange little girls.* Their parents, Earl and Earlene, were odd themselves, very clannish, but the twins were … well, it almost seemed like there was something wrong with them. *Maybe something genetic, a little syndrome of some sort.*

"So, Geneva-Marie," said Prissy, all smiles. "Is there any truth to the rumors I've been hearing?"

Geneva-Marie's eyes darted. "Rumors?"

Prissy was silent just long enough - Babs knew - to make the woman sweat. Babs glanced at the Collins house. Aida was rapping on the front door.

"I hear you're running for president of the Ladies' Auxiliary." Pris' voice was buttery.

"Yes," said Geneva-Marie. "I haven't made the announcement yet, but-"

"I do hope Burke is giving you his full support."

Something flashed in Geneva-Marie's eyes. "Of course he is, Priscilla. Why wouldn't he?"

Prissy laughed. "Well, just seeing you out here by yourself … most of the couples on the circle work *together* on these events. I'd hate to think there was any trouble at home."

Babs felt sick. She'd expected this to be awkward, but Pris wasn't even trying to be pleasant.

Geneva-Marie challenged Prissy with an unwavering gaze. "I wouldn't worry about it, Priscilla. Things are just fine."

"That's wonderful, dear," said Prissy. "Now then, if you *do* win, I certainly hope you'll have the homeless shelter moved out by the airport."

She wagged a finger at her. "I've put a *lot* of work into bringing it this far along, and I'd hate to see my efforts go to the wayside."

"I'm going to have to respectfully disagree with you on that topic, Priscilla. I don't feel that-"

"*Feel*? This is a matter for the mind, Geneva-Marie, not the heart." She tapped her temple then turned to Babs. "Wouldn't you agree?"

Babs was stricken, staring at the house. Aida gave the door another hard rap.

Geneva-Marie smiled. "Well, in order for the-"

There was a sudden *Bang!* as the Collins' front door slammed open. Burke stumbled down the steps toward them, beer in hand. Aida trailed behind him, her face a stark mask of worry as *Candle in the Wind* extinguished, and Billy Joel's *Big Shot* blasted.

Prissy raised a hand to her throat and gasped.

Geneva-Marie was on her feet, trying to head him off.

But Burke plowed past her. "You ladies tried the pecan cookie things?" His words were slurred. "Pretty goddamn fucking good, if you don't mind my saying so!"

"Burke ..." Geneva-Marie tried to corral him, which earned her a hard slap on the ass. "My little lady's been hard at it all morning and all last afternoon." He pointed at Prissy with his beer hand. "I hope you 'preciate all the work she does for you and these goddamn causes of yours, Pris!" He laughed. "Ever goddamn week, it's something, and ever goddamn week, I say to Genever-Mree, I say, goddamn it, honey, quit participle-tatin' in these goddamn time-wastin', money-suckin' events!" He roared with laughter and gave Geneva-Marie another ass slap. "But she don't listen, do you honey?"

Geneva-Marie's cheeks went red with humiliation. "Burke!"

Burke turned to Prissy. "What's this that Aida here is asking me about *soup*? She says you're making soup or somethin'?" He took a pull on his beer, teetering a little. "Instead of makin' me soup, why don't you stop by the store and buy a new sofa? I'll give you a helluva deal!"

Prissy cleared her throat. "I heard you weren't feeling well and thought you'd enjoy some chicken noodle soup. Or perhaps-"

Burke guffawed. "Not feeling well, huh?" He eyed his wife, then leaned in conspiratorially. "That's her gentle way of saying I've got myself shit-faced too early in the day!" Another hearty laugh.

"Burke! That is enough!" Geneva-Marie was mad now, and it wasn't lost on her husband. "Go. Inside. Right. Now." She spoke through gritted teeth.

Prissy was rubbing her hair necklace, eyes wide.

"Fine," said Burke in a drunken slur. "Fuck you, too!" He laughed, turned and staggered into the house.

"Well," said Prissy. "I didn't realize-"

"Just go." Geneva-Marie stared Prissy down. "Just go." She turned and power-walked into the house, slamming the door behind her.

Babs' heart broke for the poor woman.

Prissy clucked her tongue sadly and picked up a pecan roll. "I hope this doesn't affect her election plans. It certainly reflects poorly on her stability. The poor, poor dear."

Aida's eyes were wide with excitement. "I've never *seen* a man so drunk!"

"Mmm. Delicious." Prissy turned to Aida and Babs. "Remember, ladies, we mustn't gossip." She gave Aida a meaningful look.

Babs looked at Aida and could already see the secret burning a hole in her tongue. Something told her things had transpired exactly as Priscilla had wanted them to. They usually did.

***

Claire felt terrible for being so angry at Jason. After going upstairs, she'd had a good cry. She was glad she'd spoken to Dr. Putnam about her emotional swings and had been reassured that they were totally normal and expected. Still, she hated being controlled by her emotions. And control her they had.

She came downstairs with an icy Pepsi for Jason. "I'm sorry," she said as she placed the cold can in his hand. "Stupid hormones. Forgive me?"

He turned in his chair and studied her face a long moment before smiling. "Forgiven," he said.

She rubbed his neck. "Normally, she wouldn't get under my skin like this. I've always prided myself on being impervious to her."

"I know, sweetheart. Don't worry about it." She thought she heard something unpleasant in his voice but decided to ignore it. *It's probably just my damned hormones again.* "Have you sold any cannoli?"

"Half a dozen each to her friends Babs, Aida, and Phyllis." He grinned. "I think they're afraid *not* to buy."

"I saw Phyllis fluttering around here. I don't think it's the cannoli she's eyeballing." Claire gave his shoulder a playful squeeze. "I think you have a fan." She watched a little girl in a green Girl Scout uniform talking to the Lowells next door. She handed over two cookie boxes and took some cash from Crystal then began walking toward them. "There's a kid who's going into marketing some day."

"Hi!" said the little girl. She had long dark braids, dimples, a big smile, and a huge backpack on her back. "My name's Tracey. Would you like to buy some Girl Scout cookies?"

"Is it that time of year already?" Jason dug out his wallet.

"Well, next week, but my mom bought some extra that I could sell myself."

"Do you have any Do-si-dos?" Claire asked.

"Lemonades?" Jason chimed in. "I've been fantasizing about citrus all morning. I must have sensed you coming."

"Yes!" The girl slipped off her pack and opened it. She put a box of each on the table. "Anything else?"

"That's all for now, Tracey," Claire said as Jason forked over the money. "But come back soon." She pointed at the garage apartment. "We live up there."

"Okay!"

"Don't forget us."

"I won't!"

The girl slipped on her backpack and was ready to leave when Mother appeared out of nowhere. Fury blazing in her eyes, she commanded, "Get those cookies off my cannoli table. Right. This. Instant!" Her face was purple with rage, her eyes bulged, her neck pulsed. "And turn down that bull-honking music right now!" she yelled in the Lowell's direction.

Claire scooped the cookies up and held them close, not willing to get into another tug-of-war with Mother.

Mother turned on the little girl.

"What's your name?"

"Tracey Weathers," she squeaked.

"Where do you live?"

"884 Hollyhock Lane."

Mother rounded on her, hands on hips. "Well, little Miss Hollyhock Lane, you have rudely crashed Morning Glory Circle's bi-annual *charity* yard and bake sale. Were you born in a barn?"

Jason stood up. "She's just a little girl, Prissy. And she's allowed to sell cookies."

"Not today, she isn't," Mother intoned. "Not on *my* street!" She glared at the child. "Get out of here! Go home! How dare you interfere with our charity event! I will speak with your parents later."

Tracey threw Claire a terrified glance, then ran down the center of the street, braids flying behind her. Halfway, she tripped, skinned her knees, but brushed them off and kept going, like a trooper.

"Mother enjoys terrifying children," Claire said. "Don't you, Mother?" She glanced around and saw the Lowells pretending not to watch, along with Candy Sachs, Phyllis, and the Portendorfers. "Uh-oh. All your friends are watching, too." She turned on her heel.

"Carlene!" Mother called, barely below a yell. Then she took a deep breath - Claire could hear it. "You come back here and apologize this minute!"

"Let her be, Prissy," Claire heard Jason say. "She's pregnant and I don't want her upset."

Claire turned and looked daggers at her husband, then took the cookies and went upstairs. "Fuck you, Jason," she muttered as she slammed the door. The man was so busy making peace that he put his own wife down to shut up a woman who had just bullied a Girl Scout. She touched her abdomen. "You will never have to deal with Priscilla Martin. I promise!"

***

"Would you mind staying on a bit, Jason?" Prissy asked as he stood up.

Jason felt bad about his choice of words and wanted to apologize to his wife. "I-"

"I know," Prissy said, taking his hand and patting it. "I know. But it's best if you let her cool off; she's always had a hot temper, you know."

Even though it was a cool day, the strong sunlight was making his headache worse. Jason knew Claire had a temper, but he'd rarely seen it before the pregnancy. And honestly, she had every reason to be mad at him right now: he did owe her that apology for sounding condescending. "I think I should go talk to her."

"Jason, sweetie, Mother knows best." She squeezed his hand when he started to pull away. "It will be better for both of you if you just give her a few minutes to cool off. I really need you here to help me." She fluttered her eyelashes at him.

He glanced back at the apartment. "Okay. Ten minutes."

"Ten minutes, it is. You'll thank me later."

He doubted it. "What do you need me to do?"

"I need to run in and powder my nose-"

"Excuse me." It was Crystal Lowell, her hair the color of a fire engine, her little nose stud reflecting the sun.

Prissy Martin, shorter than Crystal by several inches, still managed to stare down at her. "Mrs. Lowell. Do you need something?"

Crys Lowell smiled, unintimidated. "Well, when you had your garage door open the other day, I saw a blue Tiffany lampshade and wondered if you might be interested in selling it. I collect Art Nouveau pieces and-"

"No." Prissy's voice was flat. "And how could you have possibly seen in my garage unless you picked the lock?"

"It was when you were moving things out of the upstairs apartment." Crys' smile appeared oblivious. "I was pulling into my driveway and saw it. It looked like a real Tiffany, but even if it isn't, I'm willing to pay you well for it."

"You were pulling into *your* driveway and you could see it was a genuine Tiffany? You must have the eyes of a hawk, Mrs. Lowell. Or binoculars. It *is* a real Tiffany-"

"And you just stack it in your garage with all that other junk?" Crystal looked horrified. "It deserves better than that."

Jason cringed as Prissy's face turned as red as Crystal's hair. But at that moment, Candy Sachs strolled up. She was well over six feet tall in her shiny black stilettos, her stunning figure sheathed in form-hugging pink capris, a matching sweater with marabou feathers framing her jaw-dropping cleavage, and a wide shiny black belt around her tiny waist. She held a glittery gift bag. Crystal stared, Jason stared, Hank and his boys stared from next door; no one, male or female, could take their eyes off the statuesque blonde. She belonged on the cover of *Cosmopolitan*. She belonged in an art museum. She was sublime. She was unreal.

But Prissy had no trouble ignoring her; her eyes remained on Crys Lowell.

"A real Tiffany lampshade?" asked Candy. She sounded like Kathleen Turner in her smoky-voiced prime. "You have one?" Her big green eyes flicked to Crystal. "Are you buying it? If you're not, I'd love to see it. If you are, congratulations!"

Her eyes were warm and friendly as they fell on Jason. His heart skipped a beat - it couldn't help it. This woman looked like a Hollywood confection. *Marilyn would be jealous.*

"No one is buying my lampshade," Prissy announced. She eyed Candy, unimpressed. "It's not for sale." Clearing her throat, she demanded, "What do you want, Candy Sachs?"

"I brought you some cupcakes." She proffered the gift bag but Prissy only nodded at the card table.

Jason, embarrassed, reached out and took it. "Thank you, Candy. My wife brought me one earlier - they're fantastic!"

"Hello everybody!" Babs Vandercooth approached the table, carrying several bags.

"Barbara," said Prissy. "I thought you were going back to your table to put ribbons on your packages."

"Oh, Prissy, be nice," Babs said. "Carl's there and I'm still buying goodies from our neighbors' tables." She held up a brown bag. "Phyllis' gingerbread isn't half bad this year. You should buy some." She dug in the bag. "I even took one of her sister's books. She insisted." She held up a small blue tome titled *Crystal Consciousness* then smiled at Jason and thrust it at him. "This might help you pass the time."

"You don't want it?"

"No. It's all yours."

"Thanks."

"Barbara?" Prissy said. "What's that you've got there?" She pointed at a pink baker's box tied with brown string.

"Oh, it's one of Crystal's pumpkin mousse pies. She's giving away samples. Have you been over there yet? I've never tasted anything so wonderful in my life. You should be a chef, Crys."

"Why thank you," Crystal said. "That's very kind of you. Hank and I've been making them for days. Even the boys helped."

"Well, they're just superb," Babs cooed. "If you have leftovers, I'd like to buy another one. This one I'm going to serve Monday night when Carl and I play bridge with the Portendorfers."

"I'll save you one back," Crys said, smiling.

"Thank you! Do you and Hank play bridge?"

Prissy huffed. "If none of you are going to buy my cannoli, then I must ask you to back away from the table so others can." She glared at Babs. She looked rabid.

"I'll buy some," Candy said in her breathy voice.

"How many?"

"How about a dozen? They look so yummy!"

Without even bothering to smile, Prissy motioned to Jason to hand over the cannoli, then took her money before turning back to Babs. "You should go back to your table, Barbara."

"And you should stop marking up Giuseppe Bartoli's cannoli to three times what he charges and passing them off as homemade." Little red spots glowing on her cheeks, Babs looked to Candy. "You've just been royally screwed, dear."

"Oh, well ..." Candy said, looking uncomfortable. "It's for a good cause."

"It is," Crystal said gamely. "And not everyone can bake, so we shouldn't judge. I'll take a half dozen myself. It's for a worthy cause." She handed a twenty to Jason who reluctantly took it and passed a box to her.

Prissy opened her mouth, but Babs was already accompanying Candy back to her cupcake table, talking animatedly with the beautiful woman, whose low sultry laughter made Jason's toes curl. "She's a force of nature," he said softly.

"No kidding," Crys Lowell said, taking her leave.

Prissy eyed Jason. "Candy Sachs is a *farce* of nature."

He could see Prissy's envy as she glared after the woman. "I should get upstairs …"

"No, not yet, I haven't powdered my nose- oh, wait, look there's dear Father Andrew coming our way! You go on upstairs, Jason. But be firm."

Firm? About what? Realizing he really didn't care, Jason made for the apartment.

Just a Little Chill

"Father Andrew!" Priscilla called. "How good of you to come to our little charity event!"

Andy Pike, clutching a small bag of the Vandercooths' lemon bars and a box of brownies, reluctantly passed a table of magnificent cupcakes to greet Priscilla Martin, who stood alone at a half-full table of cannoli. A stunning woman several inches taller than he, dressed in pink, smiled as she passed and he realized the sight of her had made him square his shoulders like a man on the prowl. *I'm a priest, but I'm not dead!* He smiled to himself.

"Hello, Priscilla," he said. "It's wonderful that your entire street participates in your charity event."

"Oh, well, I have to threaten them sometimes, but it's worth it." Priscilla smiled.

He knew she wasn't kidding. "And what is the charity you're doing all this fine work for this afternoon?"

"It's for Morning Glory Circle's Christmas decorations, Father. Our neighbors are all out trying to sell enough baked goods to be the next to get the honor of having an animatronic Santa grace their yard."

Charity begins at home, he reminded himself. "Charming."

"So, Father Andrew, how many of my homemade cannoli would you like to buy?"

"They're a little too pricey for my pocketbook, I'm afraid."

"Nonsense. I'll give you half price on anything you buy."

"That's very generous of you, Priscilla, but I'm afraid I've already over-spent."

She cocked her head and clucked her tongue. "I see. Then you'd better come on inside and have a free cup of tea." She glanced around, picked up two cannoli, and gave him a conspiratorial wink. "Let's just sneak these inside."

"Very well."

Following the woman up the walk, Father Andy remembered his nightmare about Priscilla taking over his house. Jung called the house a metaphor for the self and Andy
believed that. Obviously, he was worried about her interfering in his life - even taking it over. His dream, he thought as she stepped back and waited for him to open the door for her, was a warning.

"Thank you, Father," Priscilla said, brushing by him in her cloud of noxious perfume. "You're a gentleman." Once inside, she turned. "Now come in and make yourself at home while

I powder my nose and start the tea. Would you like some music?" Before he could say no, she was at her relic of a record player and an instant later, the Andrews Sisters began singing *Don't Sit Under the Apple Tree,* their voices full of the scratches and pops of old vinyl.

"Isn't it a lovely tune?" Priscilla called over her shoulder as she headed out of the room. "I never get tired of it. Never."

Cringing, Andy sat down on the edge of a pale yellow chair. Its flat square cushions, like those of the low-armed sofa, looked like they belonged in a woman's magazine, circa 1970. It astounded him there were no plastic covers. Everything looked the same as it had on his last visit nearly a year ago. Perfect and pastel, the walls were covered with framed snapdragon prints and needlepoint; the smell of fresh paint was nearly palpable. *She must have this place painted every year.* He wondered what the upstairs of this large house was like, if all the rooms were as pastel and oddly pristine as this one.

Perched on the chair, Andy wondered what he was doing here. It had seemed like a nice idea, coming by for this event, since Priscilla, along with several other of his flock - the Vandercooths, the Stines, and Geneva-Marie Collins - had all worked so hard on the Winter Wonderland event. He'd only paid his respects to Carl and Priscilla so far. It was nearing four o'clock; he needed to get out there and see the others before the sale ended.

Father Dave Flannigan had told him to let Priscilla Martin have her way, but he really couldn't this time. Just as he made to stand up, he saw a young woman tiptoeing down the stairs. He stared. She was a beautiful girl in jeans and a Slipknot T-shirt, her dark hair pulled back in a bouncy ponytail. She reached the bottom of the stairs, stopped cold when she saw him, then put her finger to her lips. He nodded and she turned toward the back of the house.

"Carlene!" came Priscilla Martin's voice. "I was just about to call you to come meet Father Pike from Holy Sacramental. What are you doing here?"

The daughter's eyes flashed to her mother, back to Andy, and toward the back door. Then she said, "Looking for Mr. Anton."

"Mr. Anton?"

"My old teddy bear, Mother. Remember?" She approached and shook Andy's hand. "Nice to meet you, Father. My name is Claire." Her eyes, full of reproach, slid briefly toward her mother. "I had it legally changed many years ago. Mother seems to have a problem remembering that."

Andy kept his most serene smile in place, but the tension between the women was suffocating. "Andy Pike. Glad to meet you, too." He decided to avoid saying Claire, not wanting to rile Priscilla.

"Carlene," Priscilla began. "Or rather, *Claire,* would you be a good girl and go watch Mother's cannoli table for a few minutes? I'll help you find your teddy bear later, after Father Andrew leaves."

"I really should be going now-" Andy began.

"Nonsense. Sit down. We have things to discuss over tea." She turned her gaze on Claire. "Please dear, go watch Mother's table. I promise we won't be more than fifteen or twenty minutes."

"Less than that," Andy said. "I have more calls to make."

"Whatever. Go, Car-laire. Be a good girl."

Claire nodded and let herself out the front door, looking none too happy.

Priscilla turned to Andy. "Please excuse Carlene's manners. She's going to have a baby and you know how that plays with the emotions."

He didn't know, nor did he think Claire was irritable because of her pregnancy. Priscilla had a way of making everybody irritable. Even priests. "Let's forgo the tea, Priscilla. I'd like to pay my respects to a few of your neighbors. I just couldn't get here any earlier. I'm sorry."

"I can guess who you're going to visit. You needn't bother with Barbara. She has a lot of work to do and shouldn't be disturbed; she's been in quite a mood today and, trust me, you want no part of that. As for Phyllis, she'll still be out there after dark - she's not very good at putting things away, you know. So you have plenty of time to see her." She sighed. "And poor Geneva-Marie, I suppose you intend to see her as well? I'm afraid she's had to stop work early today due to her husband's indiscretion." She lowered her voice. "As I'm sure you know, Burke drinks quite a bit."

Andy didn't know, and it wasn't Priscilla's place to tell him. He wanted to say so, but held his tongue. "I'm sorry to hear that. I trust Geneva-Marie is safe and sound?"

"She can take care of herself." Priscilla paused, her face darkening. "It's difficult when you've been humiliated in public, you know. Very difficult. I should know."

Apple Tree ended and immediately restarted, reminding Andy Pike once again of the invasive nightmare. He shuddered.

"Is something wrong, Father?"

"Just a little chill."

"Well, let me get us our tea. We'll be naughty and have cannoli with it." She fished the necklace out of her blouse and rubbed the amber pendant it held. He cringed, seeing the golden hair of her dead son strung between the beads and resolved to call Dave Flannigan when he got home. He would buy his old mentor a steak and a beer and find out what he could about Priscilla Martin.

He waited while Priscilla bustled around in the kitchen. Five minutes passed then she came out with a silver tray holding a steaming white teapot, cannoli, and all the accoutrements. Placing it on the coffee table, she sat down and patted a spot by her on the sofa. "Do join me, Father." She smiled with her lips but not her eyes. In the background, the Andrews Sisters kept telling him with whom he was allowed to sit under the apple tree.

Reluctantly, feeling pushed around, he moved to the pastel sofa. Priscilla handed him a cannoli on a silver doily on a bone china plate. *Straight from Bartoli's.*

"Sugar?"

"Yes, please."

She picked up tiny silver tongs. "One lump or two, Father?"

Her hairy necklace drooped as she bent forward, brushing over the sugar cubes. "You know, I think I'll stick with black, today."

"I guess you're just sweet enough on your own, aren't you Father?" She batted her lashes.

He tried to smile, but couldn't take his eyes off the corpse-hair necklace. He wished she'd slip it back inside her blouse.

"I wanted to talk to you about moving the homeless shelter-"

"I'm sorry, I'm not comfortable talking about it without the rest of the Auxiliary present. Especially since it looks like we're going to have an actual election this year." With very little difficulty, he met Priscilla's gaze and held it. "Do you have campaign plans?"

Priscilla didn't miss a beat. "Of course I do. Don't I always campaign?"

"Surely you do, but in the time I've been here, you've never had an opponent. Will that influence your campaign?"

Priscilla affected a little "O" with her lips. "I see you've heard the rumors as well." She smiled and sipped her tea. "I can assure you, Father, that after today's scandal, there will be no opponent. Geneva-Marie will be in no mood to run." Her eyes twinkled. "And even if she did, the earlier spectacle will certainly sway the voters' opinions. This church relies on the strength and stability of its leaders and I trust the ladies to make the right choice." She took another dainty sip of tea, pinkie erect, her eyes fixed on Andy.

He lifted his cup and sipped. The tea was acrid and unpleasant, but he didn't show his distaste.

"Well, how is it?" she asked.

Andy made a noncommittal noise. "Well, Priscilla, may the best woman win-"

From outside, there came a scream. A terrible, blood-chilling, frantic scream that brought Andy to his feet.

Priscilla gasped and set her tea down.

Andy was already out the door.

***

Claire froze as Phyllis Stine's scream rent the air. Registering the panic, she leapt from her chair and gasped when she saw Jason - he lay in a heap on the lawn, his head bent hard to one side. Claire ran to him.

"One minute we were talking and the next -" Phyllis' fingers tap-danced around her mouth. "He just … collapsed!" Blue eye shadow streamed down her face, making her look like an extra from *Braveheart*.

"He's had a seizure!" Claire reached for him, feeling for breath. She gasped when Jason blinked at her. He struggled to sit up. Claire helped.

A crowd had gathered. Phyllis wept into Babs Vandercooth's shoulder as the priest rounded the corner, out of breath. Mother stalked out behind him.

"Call 911!" Babs ordered, steadying Phyllis, who flailed and teetered and bawled.

Jason held up his hand. "No. Don't." His voice was clear and firm.

"But-" Claire began.

"No. I'm fine." He got to his feet, his movements steady.

The priest, Father Andy, made a move to help him, but Jason waved him off.

"I'm okay, everyone. Please, I'm fine."

Claire wrapped an arm around his torso. "I know you hate a scene, Jason," she said under her breath, "but we need to get you to the hospital. You need to be checked out."

"Fine," he said.

Mother stepped forward. "Oh! Jason honey, are you sure I shouldn't call an ambulance? I really think you need medical atten-"

"No." Jason's tone left no room for argument. "No ambulance."

Mother worried her necklace. "Well, at least let me drive you to the hosp-"

"Claire's taking me, thank you."

Claire caught the look Mother flashed her. She hated not having the spotlight.

Father Andy cleared his throat. "I'll follow you there. It's on my way-"

Mother stepped forward. "I'm sure that's not necessary, Fath"

"Thank you, Father," said Claire. "We appreciate it."

Mother let go of her necklace, her eyes hard and cold.

They made their way to the car, the entire neighborhood staring after them in silence, except Phyllis, who still wept as if it were her tragedy. Mother stood stock-still, hands on hips, glaring as Father Andy got into his little blue Honda.

New Disgusting Things

"Botox," Claire said. "This vial had Botox in it." She glanced at Jason who was resting in his recliner after the blessedly uneventful hospital trip. They'd been home for hours, and keeping Jason still had been difficult - he was fine, but the doctor had prescribed rest for the evening. The TV still wasn't connected to the satellite dish, so they had the radio on. Classic rock and the crazy DJ named Coastal Eddie poured in from KNDL Radio across the state. As always, the music was good and Jason kept chuckling over the DJ's dire pronouncements about various apocalypses and alien invasions - and vampires of all things - but Claire felt like punching the jock in the neck. *People are such fools sometimes. I bet a lot of listeners actually buy that horseshit he's selling.* She glanced at Jason. He had his hands behind his head and a relaxed smile on his face. The doctor had given him a Xanax.

Coastal Eddie's voice startled Claire. "That was Gracie Slick and Jefferson Airplane performing *White Rabbit.* One pill makes you larger, and one makes you small. But remember, kiddies, the ones that Mother gives you don't do anything at all. But the ones Uncle Harold has are killer."

Claire glanced at the radio and rolled her eyes. "Jase?"

"Um hmm?"

"Why would a Botox vial be in Dad's trash can?"

Jason sat up. "Your mother uses Botox, that's pretty obvious by that smooth forehead of hers. Maybe she shoots herself up in there?"

"Do people give themselves Botox injections?" Claire asked.

"I don't know, but she's a nurse, right?"

"Right." Claire turned back to the computer and read a moment. "Apparently, medical types giving themselves injections is common enough." She paused. "But why does she do it in Dad's room?"

"Well, he has that big magnifying lamp in there by the mirror. She probably uses it for accuracy."

Claire nodded. "Makes sense. I've heard a badly placed injection can really screw up your face." She stifled her amusement. "You know, she's so vain that I'm surprised she would do it herself."

Jason padded into the kitchen. "Maybe she doesn't even want the doctor to see her wrinkles. Do you want hot cocoa?"

"Sure, with whipped cream on top. And sprinkles. If we don't have any sprinkles we need to get some. Oh! And get those cupcakes out that Candy gave us, too. I can't stop thinking about them!"

"You're not eating for two or anything, are you?" Jason brought the gift bag of cupcakes to the table and kissed the top of Claire's head. She looked up and kissed his chin. "I feel like I'm eating for three." Or four, if she were completely honest.

She'd saved the cupcakes for last. Since getting home from the hospital three hours earlier, they'd had tomato soup and grilled cheese sandwiches, put away an entire half gallon of milk - well, Jason only had one big glass - then eaten almost a full dozen of Babs' fruit and chocolate bars. Well, Jason had eaten three; she'd had seven. *I'm going to have to watch what I eat.* She smiled to herself. *I'll start tomorrow.*

Jason brought the hot chocolate and asked, "So, the empty pill bottle - what was it for?"

Claire's thoughts returned to her father. "Blood pressure pills, nothing too interesting. Mild dose." She sipped hot chocolate. "Mmm. You know, now I can't stop seeing Mother sitting in that room under the lamp shooting her forehead up. That's a creepy image, isn't it?"

Jason laughed. "You're thinking about this way too much." He smiled. "To be honest, I don't really care what she does to herself up there."

"I *do* care about what happens to Dad, though."

"He's survived this long alone with her."

Her husband was right. She snuggled close to him, successfully fighting the urge to argue. "I'm so glad you're okay, Jason."

"Me, too." He kissed her cheek.

"I wonder where your seizure pills went?"

"They're probably in plain sight. When your mother called this morning, I rushed downstairs. I didn't even think about taking one." He grinned. "Of course I forgot my underwear, too."

"Well, never miss a dose again, okay?" She looked at him. "Promise me."

"You think I *like* having seizures?" He laughed. "I won't forget."

After getting home, they'd searched for his pills but couldn't find them. Claire didn't say it - she had the feeling Jason was tiring of the topic - but it occurred to her that perhaps Mother had taken the pills. They had yet to change the door locks, so she could let herself in if no one was home. *But why? ... Then again, why does Mother do anything?*

***

Geneva-Marie Collins rolled over. It was too hot, and Burke was snoring too loud. It might not have been so disruptive if the man could saw logs with any kind of consistency, but instead he oinked, breathed steadily for a few seconds, and then oinked again. At times, he even stopped breathing altogether. Geneva-Marie realized with a deep sadness that, while this used to worry her, Burke's sleep apnea no longer concerned her at all. Because she didn't love him, not even with the generic love you felt for someone you'd known for so many years. She had no feelings left for him, and if it happened that he stopped breathing permanently, her only concern would be the creepy-crawly feeling of waking next to a cold corpse. *And it will be his own fault if that happens anyway.* Sleep apnea and alcoholism weren't pals.

But Burke's guttural noises weren't the only thing keeping Geneva-Marie awake. Every time she closed her eyes, she saw Priscilla Martin's face - *that pinched, superior mouth; those cold, piercing, soulless eyes; that ridiculously perfect ball of tar-colored hair* - and it wouldn't allow her to relax.

The woman had gotten under Geneva-Marie's skin. With the failing business, the crumbling marriage, and two sons growing further away from her with each passing day, Geneva-Marie had drawn the conclusion that her only option was simply to stop caring. About anything. This new philosophy was part of why she was running for President of the Auxiliary. Whereas her fear of losing had always prevented her from taking such chances in the past, the Geneva-Marie of today would refuse to care.

Oh, you care plenty. She thought of the humiliation Burke had rained down on her - and the boys - this afternoon. She'd been mortified. Humiliated down to her toes. She closed her eyes against the memory and shuddered at the thought of what Priscilla Martin must have seen. *And heard. And what has she told people?* The burn of the earlier embarrassment warmed her cheeks even now.

Geneva-Marie was certain of one thing. She was going to stop Priscilla Martin from moving that damned homeless shelter out to the fields by the airport. It was crass to treat the homeless as if they were eyesores, cluttering Prissy's perfect town. It was heartless, and it wasn't right. Homeless people weren't usually homeless by choice, and if the shelter was so far out of town, it would only make finding employment that much more difficult for them. There was nothing noble about Prissy's idea; it was, as usual, all about Prissy. Though, thanks to Burke, she might not win the presidential campaign, she resolved to stop Priscilla Martin from taking control of even more territory. *She's already got the whole goddamn neighborhood dancing on puppet strings. I'll be damned if she's going to start dictating what happens throughout the* rest *of the town.*

Burke coughed, snorted, and exhaled a stream of boozy sour breath into her face. The stink of yeast, bacteria, and alcohol wafting from his mouth and pores turned her stomach. She jabbed him hard in the sternum with her elbow. Not because he was invading her space but because she could. Burke gurgled, groaned, and mumbled, then resumed snoring.

That was the next thing on Geneva-Marie's agenda. To leave Burke Collins. She just had to get her finances in order - and that was going to take a while. But it would happen. She solemnly vowed: It would happen.

***

Claire took a final bite of her peanut butter, jelly, and Parmesan cheese sandwich. She'd drawn the line at buying a can of aerosol EZ Cheese during the last trip to the supermarket she and Jason had taken - sans Mother, of course. Even though she'd really wanted it, she just couldn't respect herself if she had canned cheese in the house. Jason had looked disgusted enough when she'd first begun sprinkling Parmesan on her PB & Js - *He'd probably vomit if he knew what I was thinking now* - and for that reason, she'd waited until he was in bed to make it. She sucked a glob of peanut butter off her thumb and went to the fridge for a sweet dill pickle and maraschino cherries - which she ate together. It was delectable. This pregnancy business was crazy and she'd had just about enough if it. But it was a great excuse to try new, disgusting things.

She could *not* stop thinking of EZ Cheese. She sighed, disgusted with herself. It occurred to her she'd seen a can of it in Mother's kitchen cupboard. She took her moral temperature: *Will I be able to live with myself?* It didn't take long to decide that, yes, she would. Since she was starting her diet tomorrow anyway, she figured she'd better live it up tonight. She stood and checked on Jason - he was sleeping soundly - before slipping out of the apartment.

The lights were on, so she knew her mother was still up. She'd been hoping that wouldn't be the case. She was in no mood for Mother - *Am I ever?* - but it would be worth it. The promise of EZ Cheese urged her on.

Through the window, she saw Mother in the kitchen. She wore a light blue nightdress with a lacy collar and sleeves with delicate pearls sewn into them. Her makeup had been washed off, minimizing the size of her eyes - of all of her features.

Claire rapped on the door.

"Car-Claire," said Mother. "Is everything okay?" She stepped out of the way and allowed Claire inside. The absence of her perfume was a nice reprieve. "It's not Jason, is it?"

"No, Mother. He's fine. He's sleeping like a baby. I just wondered if you had any …" she couldn't bring herself to say it.

"Any what, dear?"

"EZ Cheese. I've been having the strangest cravings."

Mother laughed. It was a hearty, warm sound. She placed a hand on Claire's shoulder and gave it a little squeeze. "When I was pregnant, I couldn't get enough fish. Have you had that craving yet?"

Claire considered as Mother opened a cupboard and reached inside. *Fish?* It sounded damned good, actually. She wondered what frozen fish sticks would taste like slathered in a thick coat of EZ Cheese. Or peanut butter. Or both.

Mother proffered the can of cheese and Claire took it, her mouth watering as her hand closed around the cool cylinder.

"Would you care to sit down?" Mother placed several kinds of munchies - sweet and salty - on the table.

Claire eyed the ranch-flavored corn chips and wondered how they'd go with the EZ Cheese. Probably great, but not as good as with chocolate chip cookies. Or Oreos.

"Don't worry," said Mother with a wry smile. "No judgment here. Do what you have to do."

Claire sat down and stared at the buffet of junk food. Her stomach growled.

"It will be our secret, I promise." Mother sat.

"I don't know where to start!" Claire laughed.

Mother reached into a bag of Oreos and placed several of them in front of Claire. She didn't bat an eye when Claire squirted a cheese flower on top of one and popped it in her mouth.

"Would you like some milk?" Mother stood.

Claire nodded, her mouth too full of bliss to speak. It was everything she'd dreamed it would be.

Mother poured them each a glass and sat down next to Claire. She ate one cookie - if you could call it eating. She dissected the Oreo with surgical precision, removing the white filling with a look of distaste, and nibbled the edges of the black wafers. "How is your morning sickness?"

Claire nodded and swallowed. "Better. But the hardest part has been the fatigue. I've been terribly sleepy."

"Well, you know you should see a doc-"

"I know, Mother. I did. And she prescribed me vitamin B injections. I don't much care for giving myself shots, but it really helps my exhaustion." She stuffed an Oreo into her mouth. "Eliminates it, actually."

Mother nodded. "It isn't uncommon for pregnant women to have vitamin deficiencies. So much nutrition goes to the baby. I was very deficient during my pregnancies."

"Both of them?"

Mother went still. "I've been pregnant *three* times, as a matter of fact."

Claire tipped her head. "Three? But ..."

"I had a miscarriage," said Mother. "After you were born."

Mother stared down at her hands and Claire could see the pain in her eyes. "I had no idea," said Claire. "How come you never told me?"

Mother sighed. "It never came up. And it isn't a pleasant memory. It was a very difficult time for me."

Claire wanted to ask more questions - *when had this happened exactly? It must have been before Dad had his accident, right? And what caused the miscarriage? Was there a reason it had happened?* - but when she opened her mouth to ask, Mother made it clear that the subject was closed.

"The point is, if you're craving something, it's probably just what you need." Mother placed her hand over Claire's.

Claire stuffed another cheese-covered Oreo in her mouth. As she ate, her mother told her about her own pregnancy cravings, and Claire found herself almost enjoying the woman's company. It was like talking to a different person, as if the removal of her perfume and makeup had washed away her other bad qualities as well.

On a private, long-hidden level, it moved her that Mother had confided in her. The miscarriage was obviously a tender topic, and that she'd exposed something so painful seemed a show of trust - a wave of the white flag, perhaps - and for the first time, Claire saw her mother as more than just her mother. She saw her as a woman. And that she'd never even heard of her mother's miscarriage before made her feel like a terrible daughter.

"Oh!" said Mother. "I almost forgot. I've found Mr. Anton!"

"You did?" She felt a surge of joy.

"He was in Timothy's room, of all places. I left him on the bed for you. I thought you'd like that." Her smile was warm.

Claire's emotions were unstable indeed, because she had an urge to hug her. But she didn't. "And speaking of your brother, I'm taking a trip to the cemetery tomorrow to visit him. You're welcome to join me if you'd like."

"I'm afraid I can't. The doctor wants Jason to rest tomorrow and I'd like to keep a close eye on him. Plus, I'll be busy with some work projects. I've acquired several new clients."

"That's wonderful, dear." There was an unpleasant edge in her tone.

Claire ignored it. "Thank you, Mother ... for finding Mr. Anton."

Mother's eyes warmed. "Of course, Claire. You can go up and get him whenever you please. He's waiting for you."

Claire was pleased to hear Mother use her chosen name; she wasn't even stumbling over the word. "I'll get him now. I'd better get back soon and get some sleep."

Mother stood and put the milk away. She smiled at the junk food. "Take whatever you want with you. And you're sure you won't join me tomorrow to visit your brother's grave?"

"I'm sure. Maybe next time."

"Very well. I'll tell Timothy you said hello."

It was an odd comment. Odd and sad. Claire made no reply.

"You mentioned that you don't like giving yourself the vitamin shots," Mother said. "Remember, I *am* a registered nurse with vast experience - you won't feel a thing."

Claire found that an unpleasant idea. "Thank you, Mother, but I can manage."

Mother smiled. "I need to get some sleep myself. Lock the door on your way out, will you, Claire?"

"I will." Again, Claire almost hugged her mother. It was natural that during her pregnancy she would have unfamiliar maternal feelings. She thought this was just part of that. *Or maybe it's because she's using my name and acting like a human being.* Whatever it was, it was nice.

Mother smiled then turned and left the room.

Claire ate another cheesy Oreo, listening as Mother headed upstairs. She could hear the stairs creak, then the hall, under her footsteps. Almost directly overhead, Mother unlocked Dad's door, went in, spoke briefly, then moved on down the hall, her footfalls loud in the utter silence of the house. Finally, Claire heard the door to Mother's room at the far end of the hall open and close, then water running and the flush of the toilet. Still, she waited. Finally, she heard the creak of footsteps and what had to be the bed settling as Mother climbed in with her freeze-dried pets.

Claire killed a few minutes nibbling another desecrated cookie, then headed upstairs and padded down the hall to her big brother's room. Her stomach knotted around the junk food as she laid her hand on the knob; part of her expected to see Tim look up at her and grin. *How you doin', Little Sister?* And then he'd sing a line of Billy Idol's *White Wedding*. How Mother hated that. She said Billy Idol - and all of his contemporaries - made devil music.

Smiling to herself, Claire opened the door and stepped inside, closing it behind her. Only a slit of light from the streetlamp shone between the curtains. She put her hand on the light switch but waited, soaking up atmosphere. She recognized the faint scent of her brother within the room.

It's all the old clothing and shoes Mother stuck in here. She wondered if Tim's scent was on the bed pillow. *If it is, I'd like to take it.*

Or would that make me as weird as Mother? "Timmy, I miss you so much," she murmured. Then she turned on the light.

Mr. Anton, his gold fur a little scruffy, his big green bow freshly retied, sat in the middle of her brother's bed, staring at her with his big black button eyes. She picked him up and hugged him. "You're going to make a new baby very happy." She turned, caught her reflection in the mirror, then saw the little green GI Joe soldiers. They were lined up on the dresser, weapons pointed directly at her.

"What the-"

Were they there the other day? She couldn't remember. *That's just weird.* Hugging the bear to her, she walked over to the closet and opened it. The little soldiers who had huddled together on the shelf above the clothing rod were no longer there.

Why did Mother move them? She shook her head. *Why does Mother do anything?*

She glanced at the spot under the bed where Timothy's hidey-hole was located and wished she dared get into it, but knew Mother would hear her. She glanced at the soldiers again. *Why did she move them?* She glanced at the hidey-hole again.

She decided to come back tomorrow, while Mother was at church. The first time she'd been in here she hadn't taken anything, because she'd felt like she was invading her brother's privacy, but the more she'd thought about it, the more she felt he would want her to look. *There may even be something he'd want me to find.*

As she stole back down the stairs, she heard her mother's bedroom door click open, but she didn't look back.

***

"I miss you so much," Prissy Martin said.

Jason, unable to sleep, had tiptoed out to the Prius to see if his missing seizure meds had rolled under the seat. They hadn't, but when he heard Prissy open the back door, he'd ducked and waited, listening as she unlocked the potting shed. She left its door ajar, so he didn't dare move, and when she'd begun speaking, he froze.

"Oh, my little boy, my heart breaks every time I visit your grave. I hope you like your violets."

Jason wished he could walk away, knowing this was a private moment that ought to be respected, but the woman's words - and her pain - transfixed him.

"Timothy ... Oh, Timothy. Why did you leave me? *Why?*" She began to cry, horrible wracking sobs that sounded a little too theatrical.

In spite of himself, Jason strained to hear the jagged breaths, the soft keening between her words.

"Was I a good mother, Timothy? Tell me what I did wrong. What made you leave me? What was so bad that you couldn't go on?" She sobbed for several moments - a heartbreaking sound. "My baby," she mewled. "My sweet, sweet baby. My boy ..."

Jason's heart sank and churned. He thought of his own unborn son, tried to imagine the worst, but shied away, his parental instincts forcing distance between himself and the painful thought. *I can't even bring myself to imagine losing a child. And this woman is living it.*

Prissy took a shuddering breath. "I always thought time would heal my heart. That's what they say, Timothy - that time heals all." She keened. "But it isn't true! It's a lie! My heart will stay broken until we're reunited in heaven."

Jason felt like an intruder. And an asshole, to boot. *We shouldn't have made fun of her.* His vision blurred and he realized he was tearing up. *She's pushy and eccentric, but we've demonized her, made her into a monster ... laughed at her.*

"Timothy," Prissy whispered. "Come back to me."

A tear slipped from his eye and Jason stepped away, unwilling to eavesdrop any longer. It was a private moment, and he would respect that. Glancing at the doorway, he saw no sign of his mother-in-law, so he went upstairs, vowing to keep her private moment to himself. It was the least he could do.

Another Snapdragon Sunday

The eight o'clock service had been ... okay.

Phyllis Stine generally preferred going to the later mass, but she was eager to see Prissy Martin, who always went early. In fact, most of the churchgoers from Morning Glory Circle were there: The Portendorfers sat in the front row, and Geneva-Marie Collins and her two sons fidgeted near the confessionals. Phyllis was not at all surprised to see that Burke Collins didn't attend. *Sleeping off the hangover.*

As Father Andy read a verse from the bible, Phyllis regretted sitting directly behind Prissy Martin. With each enthusiastic bob of the woman's head, Phyllis was struck by a nauseating wave of perfume - *Does she spritz it in her hair?* - and Prissy Martin bobbed her head a lot in church, no doubt to show Father Andy her rabid agreement with the Word of God. *Ass kisser.*

Next to Phyllis, Clyde was relaxed, his eyes heavy-lidded as if it were dawn instead of nearly nine in morning. He, too, preferred the later service, but Phyllis had insisted. A tiny snore escaped and she gave his love handle a hard pinch.

He jumped and slapped her hand away. "Goddamn it, woman!"

Prissy gasped, craned her head, and shot Clyde an icy look.

Bertie and Nelly Dunworth - whom Phyllis hadn't noticed before - swiveled their heads to stare.

Aida Portendorfer giggled.

If Father Andy had heard her husband's blasphemous outburst, he showed no sign of it.

Phyllis ignored them all and fished around in her purse for another mint, tilting the bag slightly so Clyde wouldn't see the pack of cigarettes. Swishing her hand around, she found a roll of sugar-free peppermint Lifesavers buried beneath the assortment of other diabetic candies. Phyllis wasn't a diabetic, and she had no intention of becoming one.

Father Andrew raised his fist. "'Why hast thou forsaken me!'" he quoted.

Prissy Martin bobbed her head with great vehemence. "Amen," she called.

Phyllis rolled her eyes and sucked her mint. As the minutes droned past, it occurred to her that after the service, Clyde would have time to change the oil in her car.

She quietly spun her plastic bangle bracelets - white in honor of Sunday- keeping her eyes on the altar and trying to follow along, until finally, right on the hour, Father Andy ended the service with a prayer.

Phyllis had to give Clyde another nudge, and together they knelt. Phyllis didn't pray, though. She waited for Prissy, who was obviously adding to the priest's prayer, and after a long interval during which she undoubtedly talked the Lord's Celestial ears off, Priscilla snapped her head up. She turned and smiled at Phyllis, but didn't give Clyde the same courtesy. She glowered at him. Clyde yawned.

"How is your son-in-law, Prissy?" Phyllis had been eager to hear about Jason Holbrook's recovery. After all, *she* had been at his side when it happened, but she couldn't bring herself to call or stop by. Once Prissy started talking, it never ended - Phyllis couldn't get a word in edgewise - so she figured church would be the perfect place to ask. Prissy was a lot less talkative in public.

"Oh, he's just fine," said Prissy. "The doctor told him to rest today, but he'll be well enough to return to work tomorrow, and-"

"Is he epileptic?"

Prissy nodded, a sad expression on her face. As she blathered on about the details of the young man's malady, Phyllis became annoyed. Priscilla made absolutely *no* mention of Phyllis' pivotal role in the young man's ordeal. *Why, I practically saved his life!* She found herself inspecting the hideous pink and black suit Prissy wore. She even had a red rose pinned to her bosom. Overall, the effect was ridiculous, offensive, and somehow familiar.

"-so as long as he takes his medication every day he shouldn't have any more episodes, but-"

"My nephew has epilepsy, you know. He almost died in a hot tub when he had a fit! Did you know there's something about hot water that instigates epileptic fits?"

Prissy ignored Phyllis and continued on and on about her son-in-law's very *minor* condition. It was much less interesting than Phyllis had hoped. Not that she'd wanted to hear Jason Holbrook had endured any permanent damage, but she'd hoped he'd at least have been hospitalized. She doubted even Aida could squeeze any juice out of this dull narrative. Since it was clear she wasn't going to get any gratitude from Priscilla, she looked at her watch.

"Jason was a pilot. Thank God he didn't seize in the air. He misplaced his medication, you see. The doctor gave him a new prescription, of course."

When she could bear no more, Phyllis broke in. "That's wonderful. Clyde and I ought to get home. He's promised to change the oil in the car. It's needed it for some time now, you know. My oil is as dirty as a politician in a mud wrestling competition. Clyde? Are you ready?" At the sound of his name, Clyde grunted. "I just wanted to be sure Jason was okay," Phyllis said, offering Prissy one more chance to thank her.

Prissy smiled. "He's recovering just fine." She placed a hand on Phyllis' shoulder. "Thank God you were there, Phyllis."

There it was. *Finally!* Phyllis waved away the compliment but soaked up the spotlight just the same.

"I don't know *what* might have happened if he'd been somewhere else," said Prissy. "Somewhere where no one was watching." She sighed. "Thank God for you, Phyllis."

Phyllis smiled. She only wished Prissy would speak a little louder so the rest of the congregation could overhear.

***

It was a crisp and beautiful morning, the sky clear blue with big puffy clouds, as Prissy drove out of the church parking lot. The lovely little violet plant sat happy and healthy on the passenger seat. It would be perfect on Timothy's grave until the snapdragons began blooming. *Oh, how you love your snapdragons, Angelheart!* But first, she had another errand to run; she needed to take care of something she should have dealt with a long time ago. It had been eating at her a lot lately, and after yesterday's yard and bake sale, Earl Dean's behavior positively rankled her - *How dare that man urinate outdoors?* She might have to wait for Officer Roderick Crocker to handle *that* vulgar issue, but she would deal with the rest of Earl's neighborhood negligence herself. Never had she met a man more disrespectful and it was high time someone did something about it. *My work is never done!*

She drove into downtown, found a parking spot on Main, and began walking. Across the street was the Snapdragon Hotel and Daffodil Grill where Carlene and Jason had gone to spoil their dinner the day they'd arrived.

She'd hoped church would settle her nerves - she didn't want a trace of irritation left in her body when she drove out to Briar Rose. She'd nearly had Timothy interred in Holy Sacramental's memorial park, but opted instead for Briar Rose because he would hate being talked about; suicide was frowned upon so heavily by certain judgmental Catholics, and she knew he'd be uncomfortable there. *Oh my little Angelheart, your love will sustain me until the day I join you.*

Main Street was fairly empty this early in the morning. She passed Collins' Fine Furniture. It was closed of course, but would open at noon, according to the sign in the window. She wondered if Burke would be recovered enough to do it himself, or if he'd have an employee do it for him.

She'd always detested the man, but at the moment, his behavior was her delight - it would help keep his scarlet harlot wife, Geneva-Marie, out of her territory. She paused, inspecting the store's interior - rather barren and somewhat unkempt, judging by the dust on the windowsills - then examined her own reflection. Today she wore a pale pink suit, discreetly trimmed in black, designed in the manner of Jackie Kennedy's famous outfit. She even wore a red rose on the lapel in honor of the blood spilled that horrible day. She smiled. Everyone at church had looked at her - it had been an excellent choice.

"Onward," she said softly. She passed two small storefronts: Wholly Cheeses and Penelope's Pet Shoppe, neither of which would open for another hour or two. Right next to the pet shop was The Fudge Depot, the store owned by Earl and Earlene Dean. Decadently rich odors of chocolate and caramel assaulted her nostrils before she even entered. The Deans opened early Sundays, beating everyone else by two hours. Earl and Earlene loved money more than anything else - including the welfare of Morning Glory Circle.

Old-fashioned bells jangled as Prissy entered; looking up she saw no bells, only an electronic device that aped the sound of real bells. *That thing must have cost them a fortune, but they can't even donate to Morning Glory Circle's events!*

"Hello!" called a male voice. "We'll be out to help you in just a moment."

"Very well." She didn't recognize the friendly tone.

"Hello, lady," two childish voices said in unison.

Prissy jumped, then whirled to face Daphene and Delphine Dean, who stood behind her, holding hands, in matching green-and-red plaid pinafore dresses emblazoned with "Get Your Piece at THE FUDGE DEPOT."

"Where did you come from?" Prissy demanded. "It's not polite to sneak up on people!"

The pinch-faced girls' oversized heads swiveled on skinny necks to consult one another. Something wordless passed between them, then the one on the right looked back at Priscilla. "We were just standing in the corner is all." The one on the left pointed to a dark nook with wallpaper similar to their pinafores, then raised her hand to her mouth and licked brown goo off it. "Mmm."

"Are you standing in the corner because you're being punished?"

Another swivel, then, simultaneously, "No."

"Girlsss," called a female voice from the kitchen. "Don't play with the customerssss!" Earlene Dean came out from behind the bat-wing kitchen doors to stare at her children. Her dull dark red hair hung in two braids, just like those of her daughters. She wore a dress in the same plaid underneath a green apron. It was hideous.

"I'm sssorry," she said, "they do like to have fun, my girlsss do." She turned to face Prissy. "How may I help yo-- What are you doing here?"

"Is that how you treat a paying customer?" Prissy asked. The woman, whom she rarely laid eyes on, had the same whey-faced complexion as her daughters and her eyes were pinched so close together that rats were surely envious.

"You're here to buy sssomething?" She hesitated, staring at her daughters. "Jusst a moment. I'll be right back." With that, Earlene darted into the kitchen. The twins, however, stood at attention, staring up at Prissy with dull eyes that wandered independently every now and then.

"You live in the White House," one intoned. "My daddy says you are the president of the street but we didn't vote for you."

"You have plastic grass," said the other. "And flags."

Prissy gazed out the window and pretended the girls didn't exist.

"My daddy says you have a stick up your butt," said one.

"Is it fun?" asked the other.

"We wanted to try it, but our mommy said not to because it would hurt and make us bleed from our butts." This was spoken with great solemnity.

"And leave splinters," supplied the other, in a tone suited to Wednesday Addams.

Prissy could stand it no longer. "What is the matter with you children? Were you born in a barn?"

"Mrs. Martin!" Earl Dean came through the swinging doors so fast they slapped his rear end. An instant later, Earlene peered over one batwing, her buckteeth biting her lower lip. "What can I do for you?" Earl Dean asked.

"Daddy, we can't see the stick. You said there's a stick."

Earl, his close-set eyes magnified behind Coke-bottle lenses, swiveled his gigantic head the same way his daughters did. Prissy wondered how those toothpick necks could hold those pumpkin-noggins up.

"Earlene, take the girls for a walk."

Earlene nodded but hesitated.

"Come on out, honeycomb, she won't bite." He looked at Prissy. "Promise not to bite Earlene?"

Beyond words, Prissy raised an eyebrow.

Earlene dashed past her and tried to get between her daughters, but they wouldn't unclasp their hands, so she got behind them and pushed them out the door. She reminded Prissy of a farmer herding lazy cattle.

"I'm sorry about all that," Earl Dean said. "My girls are a little special, you know?"

"A *little* special? They're about as *special* as they come, Mr. Dean."

His magnified eyes goggled at her and a fleshy orange mole on the side of his nose did a little dance. "Best watch your mouth, missy," he drawled. "Those are my ladies. I'm going to take that as a compliment."

"What the bejabbers is the matter with you?" Prissy glared at the man, thinking maybe it was a good thing they didn't participate in the neighborhood events after all. Still, she needed to resolve the situation.

"I haven't a clue what you mean, Mrs. Martin, but I'll thank you to keep a polite tongue, if you don't want to be banished from The Fudge Depot."

"I congratulate you on the success of your business."

"Thank you." He nodded and she thought he might lose his balance, but the head successfully came back up. "Would you like a salty chocolate nut ball?"

"How dare you!"

He nodded at a big glass candy jar full of fudge balls. "I was only being polite. We do offer samples."

"You should think more carefully about what you call your candy."

"I don't understand." His head bobbled. "Perhaps you're looking for caramel or penuche? We also have some fine divinity. The recipe was passed down from Earlene's mother. Or perhaps it was her older sister. We don't quite recall."

"I'm sure it's quite a mystery," Prissy said, nearing the counter, squaring her shoulders.

Half his mouth grinned. "Yes. One never knows exactly who-"

Prissy stepped closer and sighed. "I am not interested in your family history or your candy, Mr. Dean. I've come by to inform you that we of Morning Glory Circle have taken a vote and it's been decided that we don't appreciate your refusal to participate in the neighborhood events."

He blinked his rat eyes at her. "You voted about not appreciating it?"

Prissy raised her chin. "That's correct."

He watched her a long moment, then sighed. "Well, Mrs. Martin, I wish I could say that I'm sorry, but quite frankly, I'm not. I don't have the time or the inclin-"

"Mr. Dean," interrupted Prissy, "your failure to fulfill your neighborhood obligations is not to be taken lightly. You *have* to take part. You *must*. You listen to me, Mr. Dean, as President of-"

Earl closed the distance between them with one long stride, his buggy-whip body towering over her. "No, you listen to me, missy. I will not have you ordering me and my family around." His voice was powerful, commanding, and Prissy couldn't help shrinking under the finger he jabbed at her nose. "Furthermore, I don't give a good goddamn how you or anyone else in the neighborhood thinks my family should be spending our time. To be honest, Mrs. Martin, we don't like you either, not one single bit, and while you may be able to get away with bullying everyone else on the block, you will not come into *my* place of business, throwing your political propaganda around, and making demands of me or anyone in my family." He took a slow, deep breath and straightened. "Am I understood?"

Prissy's mouth moved, struggling for words.

"Mrs. Martin? Am I *perfectly* understood, or do I need to take this harassment of yours to the next level?"

"I ... I ..." Prissy's cheeks flared, the humiliation burning like a rapid fire under her skin. A cold sweat broke out above her lip but did nothing to cool the flames. She fingered her hair necklace with rapid, nervous rubs. "I ..."

Earl Dean smiled. It was superior, self-satisfied, and both sides of his mouth participated this time. "There now. I think we've reached an agreement." The smile collapsed as his eyes went grave, his voice lowering to a near growl. "Now get the hell out of my store before I call the authorities to escort you out. And don't come back. Don't you *ever* come back."

Threatened by Earl Dean! The neighborhood pervert! It was more than Prissy could take. She spun on her heel and stalked toward the door. She paused, raised a fist. "You'll get your comeuppance, Mr. Dean!" She slammed the door behind her.

Yes. Earl Dean would pay for this, and she knew exactly how to make that happen. She had everything she needed, and had for years. It was a simple matter of timing ... and delivery.

***

"Well, what do you think?" Claire asked as she handed her laptop to Jason.

"It looks terrific! You're going to become a Fortune 500 company if you keep turning out this quality of work. Your client is going to love his new website."

"Thank you. If he likes it half as much as you do, we'll probably have a check next week. A pretty nice one. Maybe even enough for a deposit and first and last month's rent on our own place." She beamed up at him.

"That would be nice," Jason agreed.

"I have three more jobs due this month, too. And I've been getting more inquiries. Things are looking up. I'm sure if I do good work, we'll be able to move out in March. At the latest. Before I start showing. That's when the snapdragon wars really get going. I'd like to miss that."

"Snapdragon wars? What's that? A reenactment?"

Claire laughed, "No, Jase. Nothing so exciting. You've seen all those flower beds they're getting ready along the cul-de-sac?"

"There does seem to be an awful lot of garden prep going on, considering February starts tomorrow."

"Yep. The neighbors compete to win that flag Mother flies. Well, not that one. There's a little pennant flag for each street and Mother doesn't bother to fly it because the one she flies is for the town-wide competition. Which she *always* wins."

"That sounds like fun."

"Not at all. It's brutal. Sometimes fights break out. Flowerbeds are vandalized. You've heard of the War of the Roses, right?"

"Yeah ..."

"That's nothing compared to the War of the Snapdragons."

"Charming." He chuckled.

Claire saved her work and shut the computer. "Mother should be headed out to the cemetery by now. Let's go see Dad and get the stuff out of Timothy's hidey-hole."

"You're sure she won't come home?"

"Yes. Once a month, she always goes out there. She won't be back for hours. It'll be safe."

"Okay, let's do it."

***

Aida Portendorfer stood on the sidewalk in front of Phyllis and Clyde Stine's two-story home, staring at the neatly trimmed hedges as Phyllis continued rehashing the morning gossip. "She said he's recovering just fine." Phyllis dug into her bag. "Apparently, he misplaced his seizure medication or something. That's pretty much all she said."

Aida gasped as Phyllis pulled out a pack of Benson & Hedges and corked one into her mouth. "Phyllis! I thought you quit!"

Phyllis' bangle bracelets jangled as she raised a match to the cigarette, her mouth puckering around it like a chapped anus. She inhaled and blew out a stream of smoke, then looked around self-consciously. "I did quit, but ever since my sister Constance's tragic death, I just can't seem to put them down. My nerves are shot." She took another long pull and Aida stepped away from the thick blue cloud of smoke. "Did you *see* what Prissy was wearing this morning?"

Aida nodded.

"It looked like Jacqueline Kennedy's suit on the day of her husband's assassination. Why I thought that rose Prissy wore was a chunk of JFK's brains!" Her girly laugh quickly turned to a barking cough. Aida examined Phyllis' scoop-neck blouse, denim skirt, and scuffed white Nancy Sinatra go-go boots, and thought that people who live in the 1960s shouldn't throw stones at each other.

"It *was* pretty ghastly," agreed Aida. "Tasteless."

"Well, I don't think *pink* is appropriate for church at all. Or for Prissy's age." Phyllis pulled hard on her cigarette, the cords in her throat straining against the thin, withered skin of her neck. From this viewpoint, it was apparent how much work Phyllis had had done on her face. *She really ought to do something about her neck, too. It doesn't match.*

Aida waved away a cloud of smoke. "So what are you planting for the Snapdragon Festival?"

"I just fill them in a little between the roses. Why bother trying? You know who'll win, of course."

Aida nodded. It was true. Prissy had never lost the competition - not once; but still, Aida couldn't help thinking it might not be so easy a win if people tried a little harder. "I'm doing an American flag," she said proudly. "It'll take up the lawn, all red, white and blue snapdragons. It will take Prissy's breath away. I think I might even win this year."

Phyllis snorted. "Not likely." She eyed Aida's binoculars. "So what are those for?"

Aida looked down. The field glasses rode so comfortably on her bosom she'd forgotten she was wearing them. But she didn't miss a beat. "I was looking down at my lawn so I could get an idea about how to do the spacing of the stars and stripes." It wasn't true. She'd been looking in Priscilla Martin's windows for some hint of what Prissy planned to do for the festival this year. When Aida had seen Phyllis step out - for a smoke, she now realized - she'd been eager to hear about Jason Holbrook's seizure and bustled outside, her binoculars forgotten.

"Well," said Phyllis. "I wouldn't get my hopes up. Prissy will never let you, or anyone else, win." She pointed her fingers at Aida, the cigarette clenched between them. "That woman refuses to lose. At anything." She drew in another lungful of nicotine then dropped the cigarette, crushing it beneath her boots-made-for-walking, then dug into her purse for a mint, a surefire sign Clyde wasn't aware she'd picked up her old smoking habit again.

As if a mint could kill that stench.

Phyllis pointed at Priscilla Martin's house. "I thought Prissy was at the cemetery."

Aida saw movement in one of the upstairs rooms. "She is."

Phyllis gave a self-righteous snort. "Seems her kids have gone snooping around. While the cat's away ..."

"Prissy would be *very* upset if she knew they were poking around up there," said Aida. "Unless they have permission - the girl *is* her daughter, after all."

Phyllis considered. "Have you ever been allowed upstairs? I've lived here for thirty years and she's never let *me* up there. Why, I haven't seen hide nor hair of Frederick since his accident!"

Aida nodded. She hadn't seen Frederick either, nor had she seen beyond Prissy's first floor. She watched the curtains move in a second-story window. "I wonder what they're doing up there."

Phyllis' gaze lit on Aida's binoculars. "There's only one way to find out. Come on, let's go inside." She tilted her head toward her own front door.

Aida considered arguing - for appearance's sake - but didn't bother. She was just as eager to see what Claire and Jason Holbrook were doing. *Plus, this close, I might finally be able to see inside some of those rooms!*

***

"I hope Dad's okay," Claire said, as she peered out the curtains in Timothy's room. She saw Phyllis and Aida walking into the blue-and-white Stine house. "He was sleeping so heavily it seemed like he was drugged."

"Maybe he was - after all, your mother has gone out for quite a while today."

"It's not right. She shouldn't drug him."

"If she did, I agree," Jason said.

"She should have asked me to look in on him."

"She's been doing it alone all this time; I don't think it's something she'd think of. Remember sweetheart, we're not going to be here much longer."

"True. It really bothers me though." She dropped the curtains. "Not a car in sight. Let's clean out the hidey-hole."

"I'm on it." Jason uncovered the secret compartment and began moving the contents - mostly composition notebooks with black and white splotched covers - into a plastic bag. The compartment was almost a foot deep and about half full. It only took a moment before he completed the task and stood up.

"Good." Claire lifted the curtains again. "All clear. Let's get out of here."

***

At one-thirty, Father Andrew arrived at the Daffodil Grill and found Dave Flannigan waiting. Andy had been unable to keep his mind on the sermons at either mass, but during the eleven-thirty, he'd been completely unfocused.

Father Dave waved Andy over. He sat in a corner booth beneath a wisteria and daisy stained glass hanging lamp, a tall glass of beer before him. Andy noted the second glass Dave had ordered for him, and he'd never been happier to see an alcoholic beverage in his life.

"Good to see you, Andy."

Andy took a seat in the tall oak booth and sipped his beer. It was crisp, cold, satisfying. "Good to see you, too, Dave."

Before he could say more, a waitress appeared. Andy ordered a bacon cheeseburger and Father Dave asked for a Caesar salad. "I don't digest the way I used to," he told Andy after the waitress left. "Enjoy it while you can."

Andy took a gulp of beer in hopes the alcohol might work its magic quickly.

Dave sat forward, clasping his hands in front of him. A candle in a small red hurricane glass lit a little smile on his face. "You're nervous." It wasn't a question.

Andy gave him a weak smile. "I wanted to ask you about something. I'm not quite sure how to approach the subject."

Dave Flannigan watched him a long moment.

"It's about Priscilla Martin, Dave."

"What about her, Andy?"

Soft music played overhead - something classical and comfortable, but it did nothing to ease Andy's nerves. "Well, she's been really putting the heat on me about moving the homeless shelter out by the airport. I believe her only motive is vanity and I can't agree with her. I paid a visit to the bake sale she ran yesterday and she managed to get me alone." He cleared his throat. "She invited me into her house for tea. Her neighbor, Geneva-Marie Collins, is running against her for president of the Auxiliary this year and I think that's gotten Priscilla more ambitious than ever to have full control of the group." He cleared his throat again - something seemed to be lodged there, but aside from pending words, there was nothing. "I managed to pacify her. For now. But this is going to come to a head and I see no way to divert her - and there is no compromising on this." He paused. "How can one woman wield so much power? No one seems able to cross her, though Geneva-Marie is evidently going to try. Dave, you've told me not to stand up to her. What's going on?"

Dave Flannigan raised a brow. "And what was her response to having the issue of the homeless shelter put off?"

"She wasn't happy about it, but she backed off. Though I doubt that will last long." He took another gulp of beer; it fizzed deliciously down his throat and warmed his belly, but his nerves were still taut. He looked around the dining room.

"I trust you handled her with care."

"Oh, of course. I simply told her I wasn't comfortable having the discussion in the absence of the other Auxiliary members. She appeared to understand and was quite polite about it, if a little condescending. I do believe she thought me weak."

"Then what's bothering you?"

There was no delicate way of saying it. "It's her behavior, Dave."

The old priest narrowed his eyes.

"Toward me, I mean. It's ... well, it's subtle, but it's ... *inappropriate.*"

Dave leaned forward. "Inappropriate in what way?"

Andy cleared his throat. He felt like a child confessing a terrible deed to his parent. *But I didn't do anything wrong.* "Well, I can't help getting the impression she's trying to-"

The waitress startled Andy. She gave the men a bright smile and moved to top off their beers. Andy placed a hand over his glass and said, "No, thank you," but Dave allowed her to fill his, watching the amber liquid with hungry eyes. *Now he's the one who seems nervous.*

When the waitress was out of sight, Dave leaned in close. "Listen to me, Andrew. You need to stay away from Priscilla Martin. I don't want you to do anything that might upset her, but you need to keep a wide distance. I don't care what you have to tell her: tell her you're busy, tell her you're ill, but don't ever go into her home again. Ever. Nothing good can come of it."

"But how do I avoid her at church?"

"Simply don't let her separate you from a crowd at any time. I don't care how you do it, just make it so."

"What about the confessional?"

"Let your assistant, Father Phillip, take her confessions. I don't even want you alone with her in that capacity." His eyes were grave. "This is a serious matter, Andy."

Andy's next words tumbled from his lips of their own accord. "Tell me what she did to you, Dave."

Fear or anger - Andy couldn't be sure which - flashed in the old man's eyes. "This is not a discussion I'm willing to have with you, Andrew."

"But you *must* tell me. You say I need to be cautious of Priscilla Martin, that I need to avoid her at all costs, yet you won't tell me why." The beer had loosened his nerves. Now, the frustrations he'd been feeling for weeks came pouring out. "Take me into your confidence, Father. I think I deserve-"

"Absolutely not." The tone left no room for argument and again, Andy felt like a naughty child under his father's glowering gaze. "Nothing good can come from rehashing the past, Andrew. Some things do not need to be said. Sometimes, you just have to have faith."

"But how can I have faith when I don't know what's going on?"

Dave smiled. "This, coming from a priest?"

Despite himself, Andy felt his lips twitch a little.

Dave went serious. "Have faith, Andy, that the less you know the better. Have faith when I tell you that you must not have any personal association with Priscilla Martin. Trust that I'm telling you this with good reason, and more importantly, trust that what I'm *not* telling you is with good reason as well."

The men watched each other a moment. "All right," Andy said. "I'll take you at your word."

"You'll steer clear of Priscilla Martin?"

Would he ever. He was now certain of one thing that had been haunting him: Dave Flannigan had retired early because of Priscilla Martin. "Yes. I'll stay away from her. I give you my word. But I have one question for you, Dave, and I want an answer."

Dave eyed him.

"It won't leave this table, Dave."

Dave sat back and sighed.

"Did you have an affair with Priscilla Martin?"

Dave was silent a long moment, his eyes downcast. He took a sip of beer, then looked up at Andy. "I did."

Even though he'd thought as much, hearing the words was like a punch in the gut.

"But that isn't why I resigned. My affair with Priscilla is only one drop of water in an ocean of trouble."

The Telltale Neighbor

The trip to Briar Rose Cemetery had been exhausting, and Priscilla Martin breathed a sigh of sadness and relief as she let herself into her house. She unloaded a single grocery sack into the refrigerator - some Greek yogurts for the kids, and her own dinner, a pre-made Cobb Salad - then headed into the living room where she turned on the record player. As soon as the Andrews Sisters began, she felt better and headed upstairs.

She changed out of her church clothes and slipped into a pink velour top printed with snapdragons and a pair of matching pants then blew wistful kisses to her shih tzus. "Such good little boys," she murmured before heading down the hall to Frederick's room.

As she unlocked the door, she sighed. The Lord had given her a burden, but she never shirked it, no matter how much she wanted to. Frederick had been a good man in his time, even if he wasn't a hero like her first husband, his twin Franklin. But oh, Frederick's time had been short, only a few years, and then he had the accident that changed her life. She'd had to go back to work at the hospital for a while, but only part-time, since Frederick couldn't fend for himself and tended to get into trouble because of his independent streak.

"Frederick, are you awake yet?" She entered the room. He was propped up on his pillows in bed, eyes half-shut. "No, you're not very awake, are you, dear?"

He didn't answer. He was easier to take care of now that his independent streak wasn't as wide as when he was a younger man. He'd obviously been awake - he'd put an extra pillow behind himself - but thankfully he rarely tried to get in his wheelchair and go exploring on his own these days. Still, she locked his door religiously, just in case, and whenever she left for more than an hour, she gave him a sedative.

She approached him. "Frederick? I'm home from visiting Timothy." Slipping her hand under the covers, she checked his diaper. It was slightly damp. That was a side effect of the sedative; an annoyance, but well worth it to keep him safely in bed. She fetched a fresh diaper from his nightstand and quickly and efficiently changed him. He watched her, not attempting to say a word. He hadn't been vocal around her for two years now, but she knew it was an act; she'd heard him talking to himself - and to Carlene. She didn't let on, though.

She crossed to the mini-fridge, extracted a can of Ensure, and offered it to him. He didn't take it, so she set it on the nightstand. "It's strawberry. Your favorite. Drink it when you're ready, but don't wait too long. I'll bring you your dinner in just a few hours. You're having creamed corn and crackers and a slice of chicken, all blended into a nice shake so it's easy to eat. You'll love it." She patted his head. "But first, your little Prissy has some work to do."

She went to the door, then turned and fixed him in her gaze. "Frederick, has Carlene come to see you today?"

His stony eyes gave no answers. "It's fine if she does, dear Frederick. You can tell me."

He didn't respond, but turned his gaze toward the blank TV screen.

"Okay, be that way," she said sweetly, then headed downstairs, where she turned up the volume on the record player and hummed along as she began tidying up.

She wondered if Carlene had snooped again while she was gone. She set her dust rag down and headed back upstairs. Though Carlene had no idea, Prissy knew she and Jason had slinked through the rooms upstairs on two separate occasions. Oh, they thought they were so clever, but the first time, they'd made a mess, toppling her movie and music cassettes in one of the rooms. Prissy spent over an hour restacking them properly. *It was quite a project!* After that, she'd checked the other rooms, and while she'd found nothing else so telling, it was easy to see they'd snooped in her workroom and her bedroom, among others. Poor Timothy's was the worst.

A brief flash of anger took her, but she fought it down. *The nerve!* She'd immediately set traps in case they did it again, and they had, during the yard and bake sale. *Kids these days!* She'd said nothing, but if they'd done it again while she was out today, she was going to give them a stern talking to. The Lord didn't abide by sneaks, and neither did Priscilla Martin.

Just as she was about to go check on the nearly invisible threads she'd placed in the drawers and on knobs in Timothy's room, the doorbell chimed out *The Star-Spangled Banner.*

She sighed. *No rest for the righteous.* Trotting downstairs, she smoothed her hair and clothing. The bells began their patriotic chime again as she opened the door.

Phyllis Stine, reeking of tobacco and bad taste, smiled at her and held out a plate of gingerbread. "Leftovers from the bake sale," she said.

"Thank you." Prissy accepted the plate. "It's very kind of you."

Phyllis stepped inside. "Do you have time for coffee?"

Prissy wrinkled her nose. "If you're going to insist on smoking, please take a shower before coming. You know I'm allergic."

"Sorry, I forgot."

"And put on fresh clothes. Let's go in the kitchen where I can open the window and have you sit on a wooden chair so you won't leave residue on my upholstery."

Under her makeup, Phyllis reddened. "My goodness, you sure are sensitive!"

Prissy lifted her chin. "I have very delicate sinuses."

"And that perfume of yours doesn't bother them?"

Anger shot through Prissy. "*Opium* is one of the few my system can tolerate. As I'm sure I've mentioned before."

Sometimes Phyllis made her so mad that she wanted to let her know she wasn't fooling anyone with all that plastic surgery - that Prissy knew exactly how old Phyllis *really* was. *And maybe I'll ask her how she likes living with a cross-dresser for good measure.* Clyde Stine's late night exploits had been one of Prissy's more interesting finds in the deep neighborhood closet.

Phyllis sat at the kitchen table and stared up at the kids' apartment while Prissy made coffee and brought dessert plates, knives, and forks. "How is your son-in-law this afternoon?" she asked. "I hope he's feeling better."

"I'm sure he is. I haven't seen him or Claire today."

"That's too bad. I thought they might come to church with you this morning."

"So did I," Priscilla grumbled. "Or at least drive with me out to Briar Rose to see Timothy. But no, they refused both and have been holed up all day as far as I know." She watched Phyllis' reaction and saw that there was something the woman wanted to say. Prissy had an idea what it might be.

"That's too bad," she said. "Children must be so trying."

Prissy brought mugs of coffee and sat down. "They certainly are."

Phyllis tried her coffee and swallowed with an unseemly gulp that set Prissy's nerves aflame. "So, I talked to Aida earlier." She feigned a sad look. "I'm afraid she's been running her mouth again."

Prissy sighed. "What is it now?"

"Well." Phyllis leaned in close, her eyes excited. "She was discussing the suit you wore to church today."

"Oh? And what did she have to say about it?"

Phyllis looked around. "Well, you didn't hear it from me, but she's been telling everyone your suit's in bad taste. She says it looks like the one Jackie Kennedy wore on the day of the assassination. She says she thinks it's morbid. I, of course, think the suit is lovely. I just thought you should know what's been going on behind your back."

Prissy sipped her coffee, certain that Phyllis had agreed - and added her own two cents - to the conversation with Aida.

"I didn't say a word, of course," said Phyllis. "I was so ... *shocked* by the whole thing, I was speechless." Another slurp of coffee.

Prissy's hands tightened around her cup. "I'm sure you didn't, Phyllis, and I appreciate that." She offered her a smile but let her eyes go dark. "You've always been *such* a good friend to me."

Phyllis blinked. "I do try."

"Well, we'll just let Aida think whatever she wishes, and go on dressing ourselves in the ways we see fit, won't we?" Her gaze slid down Phyllis, taking in the low-cut, too-tight, flared-sleeved peasant blouse that exposed her bony shoulders, the skirt that showed too much stick-like thigh, and, of course, the outdated go-go boots.

Phyllis nodded. "You know what I always say." She inhaled more coffee. "People ought to mind their own damn business."

"I couldn't agree with you more, but please don't swear in this house."

"Oh!" said Phyllis. "I almost forgot to tell you: I saw something earlier, while you were gone, that I thought you might like to know about. I just happened to glance over at your house and-"

The national anthem cut her off.

"Oh, good heavens, who might that be?" Prissy dabbed the corners of her mouth and rose. "Hold that thought, Phyllis." She bustled into the living room. "Coming," she called.

It was Aida Portendorfer, no doubt here to tattle on Phyllis for smoking. She held out a plate of snickerdoodles. "I thought you might enjoy these, Prissy."

Prissy stood back. "Come in, dear. I just made some coffee."

"Lovely." Aida trundled toward the kitchen, her wide buttocks fighting it out beneath a flower-print skirt.

Prissy followed her, a few steps behind, and smiled when she heard Aida and Phyllis say each other's names. Both sounded surprised, neither happy.

Prissy entered, her very best smile gleaming. "Sit down, Aida," she ordered as she brought a third mug to the table. "How lovely to have a coffee break with you both this afternoon."

***

Claire had gone back to work on her client's new website after rifling quickly through one of Timothy's composition books. It had made her smile; it was filled with drawings of junior high classmates. Tim had been a good caricaturist, and some of the faces looked familiar. There was a boy with twinkling eyes and a happy smile that was labeled "Paul S." She marked the page to show Jase when he finished his phone call. She'd always liked Paul Schuyler - he'd listened to her when she was a kid. The next page featured a girl simply labeled "Steffie." Even with the large head, too-wide mouth, and tiny body, Claire recognized Stephanie Banks. She'd been a tall, skinny girl, with curly auburn hair, big green eyes, glasses, and full lips. Her caricature was beautiful, despite the exaggerated features.

Claire recalled all the times Tim and Steffie had taken her along on dates. The fair, of course, but there were so many others - picnics, horseback riding, the cavern tour. When the cavern guide turned out the lights for sixty seconds, the darkness had been so thick that she was terrified and had pushed between Tim and Steffie, practically pulling their fingers out of their sockets with her grip. Both had bent to pick her up and had bumped heads in the dark. They'd giggled, breaking the silence, breaking the fear.

Jason entered the dining room, phone in hand. "That was Paul. He was telling me about some work that needs to be done next week." His eyes twinkled. "What do you say we get out of the house for a while?"

"And go where?"

He shrugged.

"What are you so happy about?"

"Nothing. I just thought a ride out in the country would be nice."

She stood. "I think that sounds like a wonderful idea." She stood on tiptoes and kissed the edge of his jaw. "Now tell me what's really going on."

"Nothing, I swear!" He laughed.

"Whatever you say, Magic Man."

***

"I was just about to tell Prissy what we saw earlier," said Phyllis.

"All right," said Prissy. "Let's hear it."

"Well." Phyllis leaned closer. Her cleavage - if you could call it that - twitched like wrinkled prunes. "As I said, we just *happened* to be outside-"

"Because Phyllis was *smoking*," interrupted Aida, unable to contain herself.

Phyllis shot her a hateful look.

"Well, I hate to ruin your fun, Aida," said Prissy, "but I'm well aware of Phyllis' decision to take up smoking again." She gave Phyllis a disapproving look. "I can smell it a mile away."

"*Anyway*," said Phyllis. "We thought we saw movement in your upstairs window-"

"I had my binoculars because I was looking at my yard," said Aida, nodding.

Phyllis sighed. "Would you like to tell the story, Aida?"

"I just wanted to make it clear why I had the binoculars."

Prissy knew full well why Aida carried those binoculars around. Everyone did.

"*Anyway,*" said Phyllis. "We looked into your window-"

"With the binocul-"

"And we saw Claire and Jason in one of the rooms upstairs."

Prissy sighed. "I see."

Aida sat forward, waiting for a reaction.

"We aren't trying to pry or anything, of course," said Phyllis. "We just thought you should know."

Aida nodded.

Prissy heard a car starting outside. Jason and Carlene were going somewhere.

"Anyway," said Phyllis, "you didn't hear it from us, but you might consider putting some locks on the doors or something. They spent an *awful* lot of time up there." She paused. "I wonder what they were looking for."

Indeed. "I appreciate your letting me know. I'll have a talk with them."

"You didn't hear it from us, though," said Phyllis.

Aida nodded.

"Of course not." Prissy stood. "I'm getting a headache." She gave Phyllis a pointed look and the woman reddened. "I'm going to have to go lie down, ladies."

She ushered them out of the house, noting the Prius' absence. *And they didn't even bother to tell me where they're going.*

Prissy smoothed her clothes and hair and headed up the stairs.

***

"Well," said Phyllis, as she and Aida walked home. "You'd think she could have at least offered some leftover treats we brought her."

"It's your cigarette smell, Phyllis," said Aida. "She's allergic."

"Oh, bullshit," said Phyllis, digging into her purse. She lit another smoke and pulled on it. "Why is it that everyone is allergic to smoke these days? I don't buy it."

"Some people really are, Phyllis."

Phyllis wasn't listening. She paused and looked back at Prissy Martin's house. *I know when I'm being lied to.* She didn't know what Prissy was up to, but it sure as shitting wasn't a headache that had made her usher them away so quickly.

**

Prissy shoved the key in a third time and jiggled it. Nothing. They'd changed the lock on the apartment.

Rage trembled in her fingertips. Locked out of my own home! How dare they? Just to be sure, she tried one more time.

Nothing. "Well. I see. So it's okay for them to enter my home without my knowledge and rummage through my rooms, but apparently, I'm not allowed access on my own property!" It wasn't acceptable, and Prissy intended to do something about it.

New Digs

"I'm hungry," Claire said. "You've driven us all the way around Snapdragon. It's pretty, but I need sustenance."

"Your wish is my command." Jason turned right onto a narrow street dotted with well-kept little houses.

"Are we lost?"

"Nope."

"Where are we going?"

"It's a surprise. And, it's a picnic."

"I don't see any delis. Or parks."

"Be patient."

Claire sat back, her stomach growling. "Our baby is very demanding, Magic Man. He needs me to eat something, now."

Jason turned onto another street then into a driveway behind a black Toyota pickup. The house was white with dark green trim.

"Who lives here?"

"Paul Schuyler."

"We're seeing him?"

"That's who I was talking to - he's invited us over for a barbecue."

"You could've told me."

"He wanted it to be a surprise."

"Why?"

"I dunno." He killed the engine and grinned. "He's my boss. It would have been rude to ask."

Claire opened the Prius' door, then looked at her husband. His eyes were twinkling like Christmas lights. "You're still keeping something from me."

"Who, me?" He got out, taking her arm and guiding her up the walk to the front door.

She could smell charcoal burning. "I wish I'd worn something decent."

"You look great."

Jason rang the doorbell.

"In ratty jeans?"

"Yep. You're glowing." He grinned.

The door opened and Paul Schuyler appeared. "Jason, thanks for coming." He turned his baby blues on Claire. "Jason showed me your picture - but it didn't do you justice. You look beautiful, all grown up."

"And you look as handsome as ever."

"Except for the extra twenty pounds." He laughed and pulled Claire into a bear hug. "We have some catching up to do, but my coals are perfect right now, so let's get our burgers grilled before we start talking."

Claire felt dizzy. "That's a good idea."

They followed Paul into the house, through a neat but rather bare living room, into a sunny kitchen with white cabinets. Paul opened the back door for her but she pulled a chair from the kitchen table and sat. "You boys go do the grilling. I'll wait here."

"Are you all right, Claire?" Jason asked.

"Just a little dizzy."

Paul looked concerned. "Can I get you some water?"

"Yes, please." Her forehead broke into a light sweat as nausea threatened.

Paul drew a glass and grabbed a chip bag off the counter. She drank while he opened it and put it in front of her. "They're just plain chips. I didn't know what you guys would like."

"Perfect." Claire drained the water. While Paul drew another, she began on the chips.

Paul handed her a refill. "If you want to lie down … "

"I'm fine."

"You sure?" Jason asked. He glanced at Paul. "She's passed out before. The doctor put her on vitamin B shots." He turned back to Claire. "Did you take your shot this morning, sweetheart?

"I did, and I'm fine. This is more about low blood sugar than anything else. Dr. Putnam said it will pass soon." She went at the chips with gusto, already feeling better. "Go grill those burgers. Medium-rare for me, please."

"Yes, ma'am!" Paul headed out, leaving the back door open.

"You're sure you're all right, sweetheart?"

"Yes, Jason, I'm fine. I'll sit here and rest. Don't worry." Outside, Paul was whistling the Andy Griffith theme. "He's such a big doofus. I love him."

Jason chuckled. "As well you should."

"What do you mean?"

"Nothing." He kissed the top of her head and went outside.

He's not telling me something. She ate another chip and then noticed what lay on the table, half hidden behind condiments and plates of sliced tomatoes and onions. The Snapdragon High School yearbook from Tim's and Paul's junior year. She wiped her hands on her jeans and picked it up.

Paul's yearbook was signed by the entire student body, from the looks of it. Seeing a few bookmarks, she turned to the first one and found the junior class student photos. She flipped to the M pages and found her brother's solemn face. He was boyish, his golden blond hair combed back, his shirt and tie immaculate. But it was his eyes that gave Claire pause. They looked distant, tortured. *What were you thinking when they took your picture?* Her own eyes tried to well up. *Damned hormones!* It wouldn't do to have the guys come in and find her blubbering. She flipped quickly to S and found Paul Schuyler. He wore a great big grin and had freckles over his nose that wouldn't fade for another year. His cheeks were a little round, but he was adorable. Someone had kissed the photo, leaving hot pink lipstick behind. It was signed, *"Love you, Paul! Chastity."* Claire didn't remember anyone named Chastity.

Turning to B, she found Tim's girlfriend, Stephanie Banks. She wasn't as pretty as Tim's caricature made her, but that was love for you. She was a gawky girl with thick glasses and braces on her smile. Her dark auburn hair was permed into a frizzy mass of curls that would have been right at home on a poodle. Claire wondered what Stephanie was doing these days … and if she ever thought of Tim.

Jason entered and set a paper plate in front of her. She looked at the big toasted sesame seed bun and the huge patty on it. "This is a work of art."

"Yep," Paul said, bringing in two more plates. "I am an artist and meat is my medium."

Laughing, Claire began loading the burger with mayo, ketchup, onions, cheese, pickles, and tomatoes.

"She never used to eat like this," Jason said as he and Paul sat down.

"I'm eating for an army." She examined the burger. "Um, you don't have any peanut butter, do you?"

Paul stopped squirting mustard to stare at her. "Peanut butter? Seriously?"

"She's pregnant," Jason said. "And she's got a thing for peanut butter right now that you wouldn't believe."

"Well, no, I don't have any. I could run to the market-"

"No, no, that's not necessary." Claire brought the burger to her lips. "It was silly. Eat, both of you. I hope you have enough meat for seconds."

Paul laughed. "That I do."

***

"Something's going on with Prissy, and I don't like it." Aida Portendorfer studied her husband.

Stan, who'd been absently petting Pookie Bear while reading a John Grisham novel, looked up. "What do you mean?"

"She's up to something, Stan. And I don't like it. I don't like it one bit."

"You're going to have to be a little more specific, Aida-honey."

Pookie Bear whimpered and pawed at Stan's hand, urging him to continue petting.

"She seems edgier than usual. Nastier. I almost thought she was going to threaten me."

Stan's brow shot up. "She couldn't possibly know-"

"Of course not," said Aida quietly. She didn't even want to mention *that* subject. She'd given it a lot of thought and had drawn the conclusion that the secret was safe, but there was something about Prissy's eyes, some hidden knowledge that gave Aida doubts. It was a look that said, *I know* all *about you, Aida Portendorfer. Don't press me.* It had chilled her.

Stan set his book down. "There isn't anything you're not telling me, is there, Aida-honey?"

"No. I'm probably just being paranoid. Prissy's been on edge and I'm reading too much into it."

Stan relaxed, watching her a moment. "You need to let it go, Aida."

She nodded.

"It's time to let it go. I wouldn't care if the world knew what we did, but since you do, we're going to make sure no one ever finds out."

***

"You *bitch!*"

Geneva-Marie ducked just as the crystal vase her mother had given them as a wedding gift flew past her head. It exploded against the wall behind her. "Burke, please." She cowered behind the chair, tears flooding her face.

"How dare you question me, you stupid whore!" Burke clamored toward her on unsteady feet and grabbed her by the hair, pulled her upright. He shook her hard. "This is *my* house and I'll come and go as I please, you fucking bitch!" His breath, thick and rancid with whisky, washed over her.

He slapped her and the force sent her flying, toppling over the chair. She crumpled to the floor like a rag doll. "Please, stop!"

But Burke Collins did not stop, would not stop. He ambled toward her like a gorilla, and just as she got to her hands and knees and tried to crawl away, he kicked her in the ribs. Her wind knocked out, pain shooting through her, she fell face-first into the carpet.

"You bitch! You *fucking* bitch!" He kicked and kicked. "Why the *fuck* do you care when I get home? Are you hiding your boyfriend in here?" Another kick to the stomach. "Is that it, you cocksucking whore?"

He stopped and looked around, teetering. "Where is the fucking sumbitch, huh?"

"Burke." Geneva-Marie's voice was just above a whisper. "No one's here but me and the boys." He'd come home early from the furniture store, reeking of liquor, and had continued drinking for the last hour. Geneva-Marie had made the mistake of asking him why he'd left work, and it had set him off. In the past, he'd thrown things, slammed doors, and punched walls, but he'd never hit her. Until now.

"Calm down? Calm *down?* Is that what you say to the man who's taken care of you your whole goddamn good-for-nothing life? Calm down?" He issued another hard kick, knocking her down before she could gain ground.

"*Mommy!*" The voice of her youngest son, Chris, barely registered.

Through a blur of tears, Geneva-Marie watched as the little boy's face fell into a tortured mask of shock.

"Son," said Burke. "I ..."

Chris' older brother, Barry, appeared in the doorway and stared. "You bastard!" Barry charged Burke. They landed with a hard thump. Glass broke, and Barry was screaming - wild savage screams of incoherent rage.

Geneva-Marie struggled to her feet. "Barry, *stop!*" She ran toward him but it was too late. The sixteen-year-old was big enough now to overpower Burke ... and that's exactly what he did. Barry straddled his father, fists flying, pummeling Burke's face. Burke warbled and made impotent attempts to dodge the wild beating, but Barry didn't miss, not once. "Don't touch my mother!" he screamed.

Geneva-Marie rose, stumbling back, staring in horror as blood spurted from Burke's mouth and nose.

Chris was screaming, flapping his arms wildly as he wept, the front of his Angry Birds T-shirt wet with tears and snot. "Chris!" Geneva-Marie scooped the eight-year-old up and held him tight.

"You fucking bastard!" Barry's blows went on. "You fucking drunk son of a bitch! Don't you ever, *ever,* touch my mother again!"

"Barry, please *stop!*" Geneva-Marie held Chris' head to her bosom, covering his ears. His body shook with wracking sobs.

"Do you hear me? Do you *hear* me?" Barry plowed on.

Burke's arm shot up and he smacked his son.

Barry toppled to the floor.

Burke was on his feet, his body heaving with strangled, ragged breaths. He wiped away a string of bloody saliva dangling from his lip and looked at Geneva-Marie with pleading eyes. As if emerging from a trance, he stared around the room, shocked. His swollen battered eyes returned to his wife. "Oh, honey," he burbled past his split lip. "I'm so sorry."

He made a move toward her but Geneva-Marie dodged him, holding Chris close. "Don't touch me! Don't come anywhere near me or my boys!"

He froze, stunned.

"Barry! Come on!" She used the voice her children knew not to argue with. Barry, who appeared as stunned as his father, ran to Geneva-Marie. "Get my keys and purse and wait by the front door."

He hesitated.

"Right now. Go, both of you." She let go of Chris and the boys ran down the stairs.

"Geneva-Marie," said Burke. "Honey. I'm so sorry." His face crumpled and he raised a hand to his eyes, weeping. "I didn't mean to-"

The fear was gone. She didn't know where her courage had been ten minutes ago, but it was here now. She stepped closer to him as he fell to his knees and wept in his hands. "You listen to me, Burke Collins, and you listen good." Her voice was steady, steel, and calm. "You'd better get yourself a damned good lawyer-"

"But, hon-"

"I'm taking the kids away from here, away from you." She raised her finger and jabbed it in his direction. "First thing tomorrow, I'm calling a lawyer and I'm beginning divorce proceedings." She turned and headed for the door.

"No honey, please! It was an accident! I didn't mean-"

She paused at the top of the stairs and faced her husband. "And I'd start packing now, Burke, because you're not getting the house."

Burke wailed. "It won't happen again!" He got to his feet and started toward her and she held up her hand, stopping him.

"You're right, Burke. It won't happen again." She took in the stained shirt, the extra thirty pounds, the greasy graying skin of his face, the sagging beard-stubbled jowls. It was suddenly unfathomable that she'd ever had doubts about leaving this man. "You're weak, Burke. And you're a coward."

He gaped at her, then wiped more blood from his face.

Geneva-Marie Collins turned and left the house.

***

In a foul mood, Prissy pushed one of her trash bins to the curb and stared at the way Burke Collins had parked his silver Lincoln - half on the lawn - just as Geneva-Marie and both her boys came out the front door. The older one, Barry, was supporting her - she was limping badly. Both of them were bloody - she could see it from three houses away. The little boy was beside them, crying and sniffling, but untouched. Barry looked up and saw her staring, then turned away. Leaving Geneva-Marie with Chris, he ran past Burke's car. An engine roared to life and the pearl white Escalade backed down the wide driveway, barely missing Burke's Lincoln. Barry pulled into the center of the street, then got out and hurried his mother and brother into the SUV, then they tore down the street, like the proverbial bat out of Satan's lair, screeching, burning rubber.

Prissy saw Candy Sachs on the sidewalk. Then Duane Pruitt came out of his house, as did his houseboy. The Oriental remained on the porch, but Duane joined Candy. They whispered together, then the two of them approached her.

"What happened?" Duane asked. "Did you see?"

Nosy idiots. Mother wiped the grin off her face and put on her most concerned voice. "Oh, I think Geneva-Marie and Burke had a little tussle."

"That's too bad," Candy said.

Duane stared at the Collins house. "I hope Geneva and the boys are okay."

I'll just bet you do. "I think I saw some blood," Prissy said softly.

"On Geneva? The boys?" Duane sounded very alarmed. Candy gasped.

"Yes." Prissy said after waiting a beat.

"Where were they going?"

"I have no idea."

"The hospital," Candy said, turning to go home. "If there's blood ..."

"Excuse me." Duane trotted back to his house. A moment later, he and Jerry pulled out in his F-250.

Prissy stood in the fading light, warm despite the chilly air, and smiled to herself, knowing her position as president of the Ladies' Auxiliary was secure.

She watched Duane Pruitt's brake lights disappear around the corner and couldn't help wondering if Burke had found out what Prissy had known for many, many years. She doubted it; Geneva-Marie knew better than to confess, and no one else had any way of knowing. Maybe it was time to let the cat out of the bag.

***

"Why did you make me a second burger?" Claire wanted to unbutton her jeans and take a nap.

"You asked me to." Paul grinned at her from across the table.

"Guilty." She snatched another potato chip.

"More soda?" Jason asked.

"Yes - no. Maybe later."

"Can I interest you guys in a tour?" Paul asked.

Claire nodded. "Yes. I need the exercise." She looked around the neat square kitchen. "It's really nice. How long have you lived here?"

"I bought it about fifteen years ago." Paul stood and collected the paper plates, then tossed them into a sack by a refrigerated chest in the corner. "Come with me. I'm proud of this little place. I like showing it off."

Jason and Claire followed him into the living room. There were no chairs, just a couch and end tables with nothing adorning the freshly painted walls. "You like the spartan look," Jason said.

"He just painted, Jase. He hasn't put everything back yet." Claire looked around. "A few prints, some flowers, and this room will be perfect. It gets great light. I love the front window."

Paul chuckled. "Truth be told, Claire, Jason's guess is closer. I've never gotten around to putting anything up." He grabbed a remote off the end table and aimed it at the opposite wall. "Except this" A TV came to brilliant life. Claire hadn't even noticed it before. "Follow me."

He led them into a hall that contained a small bathroom, then paused to open another door. "The master bedroom suite. What do you think?" Paul beamed at them.

It was a simple bedroom with walls the pale color of bamboo shoots, a bed with an ivy print comforter, and a dresser. Claire smiled, amused at how proud Paul seemed to be. "It's very pretty," she said.

Jason grinned and nodded.

Paul went further into the room and opened what she'd thought was a closet door - but it was a master bath with two sinks.

"That's really nice," Claire said.

"She's always wanted two sinks." Jason chuckled.

Paul led them into another room, a small second bedroom with a desk against one wall and a closet. "It's so cozy," said Claire.

But Paul was already back in the hall, leading them past a laundry room and to another door. "And *this* is the third bedroom. I've just had it redecorated."

Claire was even more amused. Paul's idea of decoration was very limited.

"Come here, Claire," Paul said. "I want you to see it first."

"Sure." She stepped forward, opened the door, and gasped. "What- I mean, I didn't even know you were married, Paul, and you're going to have a baby?"

Paul took her hand and patted it. "No, I'm not married. *You're* having a baby."

"I- I don't understand."

"This was my first home. I paid it off last year."

Claire stared at him.

"I rent it out. It's empty - the tenant was transferred very suddenly. I'm hoping you and Jason will move in and take care of it for me. Believe me, you won't find lower rent anywhere." He paused. "Except maybe at your mother's."

Claire glanced at Jason, whose grin nearly split his face in two. "You knew!" She gave him a playful punch.

He grabbed her wrists, laughing. "I knew, sweetheart, but I haven't known for long."

"My tenant was transferred and gave notice a week ago and vacated three days later," Paul explained. "He left the furniture, if you can use it."

Claire's stupid pregnancy hormones made her cry, and she threw her arms around Paul and hugged him for all she was worth. Then she did the same to Jason.

"You think she likes it?" Paul asked.

"I'm not sure," Jason said.

"You guys, knock it off!" Claire was laughing *and* crying now.

"Let's go back in the kitchen and have some coffee," Paul said.

Within five minutes, they were warming their hands around fragrant paper cups of instant coffee as Paul went over the details. Claire was stunned at the miniscule rent - they were going to pay little more than taxes and utilities for now. Plus, they'd be about as far away from Mother's as possible while remaining in Snapdragon. She felt dizzy again, but with joy. "I can't believe it," she said. "I just can't believe it."

"Believe it," Paul said. "You're the little sister of the best friend I ever had. You deserve it."

She fought back tears. "Thank you." She looked at her husband, then back at Paul. "I guess my guy impressed you, huh?"

"He's the best thing that's happened to Schuyler Flight School in its entire history, and I want to keep him - and you - around." He twinkled. "When you two are a little more on your feet, maybe we can discuss your buying the place. Would you be interested?"

She almost blurted *yes* then thought of Mother and looked at Jason. "What do you think?"

"I think it's the best thing since jet engines." He grinned.

She looked to Paul. "I absolutely love it, Paul, but I really wanted to go back to the city as soon as possible. I mean, I'd be hugging you to pieces over the offer right now except for-"

"Your mother?" Paul asked.

Claire's jaw nearly dropped. "Did Jason tell you about our ... problems?" She glanced at her husband.

"No. No, no, no. Don't even think that. Jason doesn't tell tales. Tim did."

"What?"

"I've known what your mother is like since the very first time I came over to play with Tim - long before you were born. She was always watching him, always in his face. And she didn't like me; she didn't like any of his friends." He paused to sip coffee. "She didn't say so, but it was easy to sense."

Claire's interest was piqued. "And what did Tim tell you about my mother?"

Paul stared.

"Don't worry," said Claire. "I have no loyalty to her and won't rush to her defense."

He seemed reluctant. "Tim didn't talk about her much. He told me by the way he acted around her. He didn't really like to bring friends over, but she insisted we play there as much as at my parents' house. We'd watch TV and she'd come in and tell us we should be watching something else. Usually religious shows. It was pretty freaky. Tim would pull faces when she wasn't looking. Or he'd shrug in this funny way he had."

"I remember that shrug," Claire said. "It was his way of saying he couldn't do anything so he'd roll with the punches."

Paul nodded. "He wouldn't talk about guy-stuff - or her - especially at his house. He told me she was always listening through the vents and I believed him, because we could hear her in the living room through the same vents. God, she was always playing an old record-"

"*Don't Sit Under the Apple Tree*?" Jason asked.

"She still plays it?" Paul's eyes went wide.

Claire nodded, though a quiet memory, something deep and long buried, tried to nudge into her awareness. *Mother played another song, too ... one that scared me.* But she couldn't recall the melody. "She does love the Andrews Sisters, yes."

"It probably helped keep you from hearing her talk to herself," Jason said.

Paul laughed. "I remember that."

"She still does it too," Claire said.

Paul nodded. "So, anyway, I got to thinking about you guys living there and figured it couldn't be too much fun, so I asked Jason if he thought you'd like to live here, where you'd have more privacy. He said yes."

"I did," Jason added.

"You don't need to think of living here beyond however long you need to save up to go back to the city, but if you want to consider it, the offer will stand as long as you're here." Paul looked at Jason. "I have to admit, I don't want to lose this guy. And your mother may well leave you alone out here."

Claire nodded. "Good point. If something isn't about her, she doesn't bother with it. And my life - our lives - are *not* about her." The stupid tears welled again. "Paul, this is wonderful of you. You're so kind."

"You're Tim's sister - and that makes you my honorary family. It's not always about blood, you know."

She blew her nose. "First you gave Jason a job and now you're letting us live in your house. You're the best Santa in the world."

"Paul, why did you offer me that job?" Jason sat forward. "You're a businessman and you hadn't even seen my resume. How did Prissy convince you?"

Paul's laugh was awkward. "Let's just say that she pushed me into it. I was very hesitant, but I remembered Claire - she's a chip off Timothy and her dad - not her mother. I figured that if you were good enough for her, you were probably the right man for me." His cell rang. "Excuse me a minute." Standing up, he walked out of the room, talking business.

A moment later, he returned. "I was just asked to replace a pilot for a wedding party flying to Reno tonight, so I have to get going."

He handed a key to Claire. "I'll get a couple more of these made. Meanwhile you two can move in whenever you want. We'll work out shifting the utilities over and all that fun stuff next week."

Claire hugged him again then Jason shook his hand. "Need any help?"

"None at all. I'll see you bright and early, Jason."

"Yes, sir!"

Jason and Claire exited their new house and had just pulled out of the driveway when Paul came out and put the cooler and trash bag in his truck. He waved and grinned as he climbed in.

Claire tried to remember all the turns they took as they left the pristine little neighborhood and thought Mother would never find her way there.

Once on the main highway heading back to the cul-de-sac, she spoke. "I can't believe this is happening."

"Me neither. Paul's not only my boss, he's our fairy godfather."

She laughed. "He is. I love him ... but I wonder what Mother had on him that made him offer you the job in the first place."

"So do I, schweetheart," he said in his best Bogey. "So do I."

***

As they got out of the Prius, the back porch light shot on. They paused as Prissy appeared in her kitchen doorway. "Kids," she said.

Claire and Jason exchanged glances. "Yes?" said Claire.

"Could you come in here a moment? I'd like to speak with you." Something about her tone made Jason nervous. He stifled a groan and they headed into Prissy's kitchen.

She stood at the sink, rinsing dishes that didn't need to be washed.

"Yes, Mother?"

"Sit down, sit down." Prissy gestured at the kitchen table.

Claire and Jason sat, looking at each other. Prissy didn't stop washing, but spoke over her shoulder. "It was inevitable, of course, that living together, we would need to set up some ground rules." She sighed.

"What are you talking about, Mother?" Claire's eyes narrowed.

"Well," said Prissy, "I've been meaning to discuss something with you for a while now, but I've just been so busy with all these projects that I haven't had a chance."

Jason wondered what projects she was referring to. Aside from the bake sale, which was a done deal, and worrying about what everyone else was doing, he hadn't seen any of these projects she always spoke about. One thing was certain; she hadn't taken on cleaning out the rooms upstairs. He tried not to smile.

"Get to the point, Mother." Claire's tone was cold but Prissy's stare was even icier as she turned to face them.

"Very well." She dried her hands on a dishtowel. "It's come to my attention that the two of you have been letting yourselves into my home without my knowledge, and going into the rooms upstairs, which, I might add, are private, and not to be rummaged through. The items in those rooms belong to me and-" She stared hard at Claire. "Don't even try to deny it, young lady. I've known about this for some time."

"I don't think she was going to deny it, Prissy," said Jason. "I believe we owe you an apology. We went in there looking-"

Claire cut him off. "I was looking for Mr. Anton, and-"

Prissy crossed her arms. "I told you that *I* would locate him for you and I did, so you had no reason to-"

Claire stood and Jason hoped like hell there wouldn't be another scene. "I figured you'd never get around to it. You never get around to anything."

Prissy sighed. "Well, I found the teddy bear, now, didn't I?"

Claire couldn't argue that.

They stared at each other, neither backing down. Jason could practically smell the fury mounting in the room.

"It won't happen again, Mother. Now, if you'll excuse us, Jason and I need to get to bed."

Prissy stomped her foot. "That's it!" she said. "I am putting my foot down!" Another hard stomp.

Jason was on his feet, staring as Prissy's face, formerly a mask of contained tolerance, now distorted into the frenzied face of a madwoman.

Claire stepped back. "Are you serious, Mother?"

"I didn't say anything the first time this happened," Prissy's voice rose an octave, "or the second - but the third is where I draw the line. You will *not* come into my house unannounced, and you will *not* lock me out of my own gosh darned bull honking home!" A vein throbbed above her eyebrow.

"Lock you out of your own home?" asked Claire, her voice deadly calm. "What in the unholy *fuck* are you talking about now, Mother?"

Prissy gasped and clutched her disgusting hair necklace. "Don't you *dare* use that word with me, young lady!" Her eyes were wild, her mouth pulled down in a ghastly grimace that showed her age. "Don't think for one moment I don't know you've changed the locks on my apartment door!" She stomped her foot again. "And you owe the swear jar!"

"Of course you knew that, Mother." Claire stepped close to Prissy and held up a hand to stop Jason from interfering. "You must have figured it out after going through our garbage and trying to put all those expired cans of soups and vegetables back in our cupboards."

Prissy stared at her.

"That's right, Mother. While we're on the topic of privacy and ground rules, we'd appreciate you not letting yourself into *our* rooms, as well."

"This is *my* house!"

"True. But that gives you no right-"

"I am *trying* to help you, young lady!"

"Well, we don't need any more of *your* help."

Prissy gasped. "I never-"

Jason put his hand on Claire's waist and tried urging her to the door, but she stood rooted.

"You don't need my help?" Prissy exclaimed. "You need to *open* your eyes, young lady!" She brought her hands to the sides of her face and splayed her fingers on the word *"open,"* to demonstrate. "*Open* your eyes!" she shrilled. "*Open* your eyes!"

"Okay, that's enough." Claire looked at Jason. "I'm ready to go."

He guided her out the kitchen door, but Prissy was close behind them, still not finished shrieking and stamping her feet.

"If you don't need *my* help, then would you mind telling me why you're here? And another thing," she went on, following them outside. "I will not have you disturbing your father without my knowledge."

Jason and Claire kept walking. He'd wanted to say something, but the truth was, he was stunned. He'd never seen a grown woman throw a tantrum.

"You have both been nothing but ungrateful since the day I let you-"

Claire stopped at the foot of the apartment stairs. "Well, you don't need to worry about it anymore, Mother, because we won't be here much longer."

Prissy stopped cold. "You have nowhere to go. Don't give me your empty threats. "

"It's not a threat, Mother, it's a promise." Claire squeezed Jason's hand. "Isn't that right, Jase?"

"Yes," he said. "That's right."

Claire turned and he followed her up the stairs, leaving Prissy staring after them, mouth open and eyes wide.

Desperately Seeking Dominance

"How's your sundae?" Jason smiled, his blue eyes crinkling in that way Claire loved.

"Everything I dreamed it would be." She glanced up at the stained glass lamp above their table at the Daffodil Grill. It was a replica of the Tiffany wisteria lamps she loved. Claire hadn't wanted to let Mother's tantrum ruin the good mood, and after the coast was clear, she'd suggested they go, pleading a need for ice cream. "When I said I was craving a sundae, I didn't expect you to go all out. I would have been happy with Dairy Queen."

"Not for my girl. Tonight, we celebrate." He eyed the remains of her dessert as she spooned up a melting mix of pistachio, chocolate mint, and peanut butter ice cream. "That's quite a flavor bomb you've got there."

"I wish I'd gotten some banana and marshmallow, too."

"We can do that."

"No, I'm stuffed. I'm just being a pig." She put her spoon down. "I'm really sorry about tonight. I didn't mean to get in a fight with my mother."

Jason reached across the table and took her hand. "You weren't the one who lost her cool." He chuckled. "I'll bet Hank and Crystal next door sure got an earful of Prissy tonight."

"No kidding. It's so embarrassing."

"No, sweetheart, your mother only embarrassed herself. And the Lowells are good guys. I think they're probably the only people on this block besides Babs who don't see gossip as a way of life."

Claire nodded. "True. But I still wish she hadn't gone ballistic. If Phyllis Stine was outside, she no doubt got an earful too." She couldn't help smiling at the thought.

"Who cares?" He squeezed her hand. "We're moving! This week!"

Claire squeezed back. "We are! I'll start packing tomorrow and we can even take a few boxes over tomorrow night."

"Remember, the doctor told you to take it easy, so don't do too much. Pack some clothes. Let me do all the heavy lifting."

"There's not much to lift, so I bet we can be sleeping there in two nights and be completely out of Mother's lair by the weekend! We'll even put her old locks back on." She grinned.

"I love seeing you so happy. You're glowing like a Chinese lantern." He paused. "I want to ask you a question - and it's serious, so don't laugh."

"What is it?"

"Do you think she'd care if we take the recliner?"

"Seriously?"

"That's what I said."

"Don't take it. She'll see that as a debt to her. She may even use it as an excuse to come over and nose around."

"You really think so?"

"I know so. Trust me on this. We'll buy you a new one. We aren't taking anything but what we brought with us. Not one fork, not one hanger. Not one can of fourteen-year-old peas." She grinned.

"Oh, heck, let's just splurge and buy new ones!"

"You're on. Now take me home, Magic Man, and show me what you can do with those magic hands."

His eyes twinkled and he waggled an eyebrow, then put money on the table. "You got it, schweetheart." They went into the chilly night.

"I'm going to save for a second car," Claire said, buckling her seat belt. "I had another inquiry about my services in my email today. Pretty soon, I'll be able to afford *something* drivable."

Jason pulled onto the dark, quiet street. "Now that we're living near my work, I could give you the Prius and buy a bicycle. You could just take me when it rains. You'll need the car more than I do when the baby comes."

Claire nodded. Snapdragon was sleepy at ten o'clock on a Sunday night, and after they turned off Main Street they saw virtually no traffic. *Which is kind of nice*, Claire thought. She liked it here, except for her mother's presence. *It wouldn't be a bad place to live if I can Mother-proof the house.* She almost said as much to Jason, but figured he was sick of the subject. "Jason, that's so kind about the car. I *will* take you up on it, so I hope you're serious."

"Absolutely. And when I do need a ride home, Paul lives less than a mile away - I probably wouldn't even have to get you to pick me up."

"Aw, I never mind picking *you* up." She placed a hand on his knee and squeezed. "Jason?"

"Hmm?"

"Can we afford to buy some curtains and dishes and things for the new house?"

"Yes, just as long as you don't want to buy at Crate & Barrel."

She laughed. "Target will do nicely. Can we go this week? I can't wait to get out of there."

"Absolutely. After we take the boxes over we'll do a little shopping tomorrow night."

"Great." She hesitated. "Jase, seriously, it's important we do this quickly because I don't think Mother has really even begun to explode yet. She's liable to become impossible and it makes me a little nervous."

"Well, at least she doesn't have a key." He pulled onto Morning Glory Circle. "Are you sure you're not being a little paranoid?"

"I don't think I am. Mother loves a good scene and she'll find a way to make one. You can bank on it."

"Well, in all fairness, we *were* snooping through her house." He pulled into the driveway. "You can't blame her for being upset."

"True." She could see Mother's point. Still, she wanted to get out of Dodge, and fast.

As they made their way toward the apartment, they heard Mother's voice from the potting shed. Claire took Jason's hand as she brought a finger to her lips.

He shook his head. "I don't think it's a good idea."

But Claire pulled him closer and they crouched near the window. Jason sighed and Claire strained to hear.

"I handled it all wrong, Angelheart." Mother's voice was stuffy as if she'd been crying. "I wish I could take it back."

Claire felt a stab of guilt.

"They're just children, after all."

The guilt dissolved.

"I think she just misses you terribly, Timmy." A pause. "We all do."

Jason squeezed Claire's hand and nodded toward the apartment. He wanted to leave. But Claire wasn't done listening.

"I'll apologize to them, of course," said Mother. "I only hope they'll accept. I certainly can't blame them if they don't." She sniffed. "I just keep failing." Her words came out in a high mewl. She was weeping. "All I want is to be a good mother."

Claire was struck. She'd never heard her mother weep like this before. She looked at Jason, but his eyes were far away, disinterested.

Mother sobbed - great, heartfelt-sounding sobs. *She must know we're listening.* Mother had missed her calling as an actress. Claire looked at Jason. He wasn't amused.

"Come on," he whispered, tugging her hand. "That's enough."

"You're not *actually* buying any of this, are you?"

The look in his eyes said it all.

"Boy, she's got you fooled, doesn't she?"

He glared at her and she realized that not only was he buying it, but he thought Claire was being an utter bitch. He stared at her a moment, incredulous, then straightened and headed to the apartment, shoulders stiff.

Shit! Claire went after him. She heard Mother's hitching sobs from the shed as she caught up to her husband. "I'm sorry, Jase," she said, taking his hand. "I was being a bitch."

He kissed her perfunctorily on the cheek, but he didn't argue with her.

He sighed and unlocked the door. "I'm just glad we're getting out of this place. I don't think it's good for either of us."

And *that*, Claire knew, was the truth. "She pushes my buttons. She's the only one who's ever been able to get under my skin."

"Well, I think you need to stop letting her."

She sighed. "I'm trying. I really am."

"I know. But now there's light at the end of the tunnel. That ought to help, right? "

"Right."

Jason leaned in for a kiss. A real one.

***

"Franklin, darling, I'm so worried about our little girl."

Fred Martin, a prisoner of his own body, did not respond. He never did now; it just resulted in condescension and tranquilizers. He didn't even look at his wife; she'd often called him Franklin, the name of his long-dead twin, her first husband. He'd died in Vietnam, a war hero, mere months before his son, Timothy, was born.

"Carlene has dizzy spells, you know, but she won't talk about them to me, her own mother. And I'm a nurse! What do you think of that?"

He thought their daughter had a good head on her shoulders and knew what she was doing. He was proud of her and her choice of a new name. 'Claire' suited her well. He'd hated 'Carlene,' but it was Priscilla's middle name and she'd insisted on it, paying no attention to his suggestions. She never had.

Fred stared at the blank TV screen as Priscilla went on about how the girl wouldn't share anything with her, and how she and her husband were so ungrateful that they intended to move out, but wouldn't give her any details. Priscilla was beside herself. She was always beside herself.

When his brother Frank had died, Priscilla had mourned him - and his heroic status - so long and loudly that Fred and his parents had been a little embarrassed. Then she had begun coming over to Violet Street, where he and his bride, Shelly, lived, looking for companionship and help around the house. She'd tried to befriend Shelly, but from the first, Shelly'd known what she really wanted: another husband. She'd been polite to her sister-in-law, but unforthcoming as Priscilla asked Fred - or Frederick, as she always called him - to come to Morning Glory Circle and fix a gutter, move furniture, or help her paint Timothy's bedroom.

That had gone on for years, and Fred had always been aware that what she really wanted to do was seduce him; he'd listened to Shelly when she told him that and, before long, could see it himself. He had remained impervious and life had gone on. He and Shelly had a good marriage; he was a well-paid structural engineer and Shelly had taken over as manager of her dad's accounting firm when he retired. She was good at it, too. Good with numbers, and with people. He'd loved his wife. They'd been happy.

"I do wish Carlene would take my advice and go see Dr. Hopper," Priscilla was saying. "I don't trust this obstetrician of hers. She's too young and inexperienced, don't you think?"

He didn't reply, of course, and she prattled on. After being widowed, Priscilla had gone back to working full-time at the hospital - she'd been Dr. Hopper's nurse back then. Fred had always thought the two might get together, but it hadn't happened; Eugene Hopper was as married then as he was now. The doc was about the only person who ever came to see him - not that he really liked the man; he was a wimp, always caving to Priscilla's wishes.

Six years passed and then Shelly had died in an auto accident. Priscilla came to comfort him. He didn't want comfort; he only wanted Shelly back. Priscilla brought him food; she even came on Saturdays, her small son in tow, and cleaned his house.

Poor little Tim. The boy was the reason he finally married her. He needed a father, that had been clear; Priscilla was turning him into a momma's boy and Tim deserved better. He needed to know all about Frank - and he needed his uncle Fred to help raise him, to see to it that he was prepared to have a good life.

And so they married and he'd sold his own home and moved into the one on Morning Glory Circle because Priscilla said it was a nicer house and Timothy's friends all lived nearby. That was fine by him. As quickly as he bonded with Tim, Priscilla had become pregnant again. While he'd never enjoyed his new wife's company, he loved Tim - and Carlene - with all his heart and would have given his life for either of them. *Perhaps I did.*

Then, when Claire was three and Timothy almost twelve, his own accident had taken everything from him. He'd been Priscilla's prisoner ever since, stuck in this room with only a balcony for fresh air. There was plenty of money, but she never even put in a damned chairlift so he could ride downstairs and get out in the world. He'd never leave the house again.

"Do you have a sour stomach, dear?" Priscilla asked. "You look like you do."

He barely shook his head, not wanting her to pour some god-awful medicine down his throat.

"Good. Well, then, let's get a diaper on you and give you something to help you sleep all night."

For years, he'd wished for death, and only since his daughter had come back and sneaked in to see him, had he sometimes been glad he was still alive. She gave him hope. But at this moment, he would prefer moldering in the grave.

***

Priscilla looked at the alarm clock. It was past three and she had yet to get a wink of sleep. *Oh, Lord, Please hear me. It's Your unworthy servant, Priscilla. Thank You for all the blessings You've bestowed upon me, but could You please see fit to help me sleep? Dawn is only hours away and I must care for my husband, my home, and Your church as well as figure out how to make Carlene see the error of her ways. I do try very hard to please You, oh, Lord, but I'm not certain I can uphold my obligations to You without proper rest.* She sighed heavily, hoping the Lord would see her exhaustion and appreciate her efforts.

Oh, Lord, help me show my wayward daughter the Light and help me guide her unto Your waiting fold. She's going to be a mother and she must grow up now. Please see that she gets past her contrary nature so that I, her mother, might give her the guidance she needs. Please urge her to listen to me. Yours in Christ. Sincerely, Amen.

She sighed and stared at the ceiling, knowing the Lord heard her, but unsure whether or not He'd do anything to help her. *The Lord only helps those who help themselves.* She continued staring, listening. Slowly, as softly as the whisper of leaves on a gentle wind, the Lord advised her.

Getting a Leg Up

Jason had left the coffee on for her when he left for work Tuesday morning and now Claire sat at the table in her bathrobe and sipped, hoping it would energize her. *Maybe I overdid it yesterday.* It was hard to believe, but possible. She'd packed up nearly all their clothes, spent a few hours working on her clients' websites, then she and Jason had dropped off the suitcases and a couple of small boxes at their new house and gone on a little shopping spree at Target before treating themselves to dinner at Hamburger Heaven.

She'd slept like a rock, but getting herself moving this morning had been difficult. Even the vitamin B shot, which had quickly perked her up every morning, had no effect. She set the cup down. The coffee wasn't helping either - she felt sleepier than ever. She thought about going back to bed, but decided not to give in to her exhaustion. *What I need is a good hot shower!*

Within five minutes, she stood under the pulsing jets, enjoying the feeling as the water hit her neck and shoulders. But she still felt sleepy and when she bent to pick up the bar of soap, her head swam. Dizzy, she decided it was time to get out.

***

Paul Schuyler sat on the edge of Jason's desk, a grin on his face. "So," he said. "Are you all packed up and ready to go?"

Jason had been grading tests, but his mind hadn't been in the game. All morning, his thoughts were on the move. "Claire's doing most of the packing. We didn't bring much with us from home, so it should be a quick task. We bought some new things for the house last night - Claire's really on the nest - and we'll do it again tonight." He paused. "She's hoping to be sleeping there by tomorrow night and be totally moved out of her mother's place by the weekend."

Paul nodded. "Great."

"I'm really grateful for this, Paul. Things have gotten pretty tense at Prissy's, and I'm not sure how much longer we could have taken it."

"Living with people rarely works out. Even parents."

"No kidding!"

"Well, I'm happy to have you. As soon as things have settled down, I'll take you guys out for a celebratory dinner. Anywhere you want, my treat."

"You don't have to do that, Paul."

"Oh, I insist. Independence should always be celebrated."

Jason got the feeling Paul wanted them away from Priscilla Martin as much as they did. It made sense, he supposed; Paul knew how unpleasant Prissy could be.

His intercom beeped and he held up a finger to Paul. "Yes?"

"Mr. Holbrook," said Bridget, the school's secretary.

"Yes?"

"I'm afraid you have an emergency at home."

His heart leapt. "What? What kind of emergency?"

"Your wife," said Bridget. "She's had an accident and is at Snapdragon General. Your mother-in-law called. She doesn't have your direct ext-"

"What kind of accident?" Jason was on his feet and Paul's face showed concern.

"I'm not sure, Mr. Holbrook. She just said you needed to come right away."

"On my way." Jason slammed the phone down and grabbed his jacket off his chair.

"Is everything okay?" asked Paul.

"I don't know, I've got to run. I'm sor-"

"Don't worry about it," said Paul. "Just go."

"Thanks." Jason hurried, breaking into a run when he reached the parking lot.

***

Claire opened her eyes.

The room was all white, and bright morning sunlight streamed through a large window. She stared at a stainless steel sink. *Where the hell am I?* From the corner of her eye, she saw movement. She turned her head, her entire body aching with the effort.

Mother, face buried in a tissue, sat on a green chair. When she saw Claire, she jumped to her feet. "Oh, Claire," she said through the wadded tissue. Her eyes streamed with tears. "Oh, Claire, my baby."

Claire looked down at herself. She lay on white sheets in a hospital bed. Tubes ran from her arms into an IV stand. *I'm in a hospital!* She tried to sit up and that's when she noticed the pain. It shot up her hip and down her leg.

Mother dithered over her. "No, you just rest." She fluffed a pillow.

"Where's Jason?" Claire's voice was sluggish, dry. *Painkillers.*

"He'll be right back. He just went to get coffee."

"What happened?"

"You had an accident in the shower." Mother pressed her face to the tissue as new tears sprang. "I heard you scream. I knocked, but there was no answer. And the shower was running." More tears. "I found you on the bathroom floor."

Claire tried to remember. Yes, she recalled the shower. And feeling dizzy.

"You broke your leg, honey."

Claire stared down at herself. Even through the haze of painkillers, she knew it was the truth. It hurt like hell.

"Where's Dr. Putnam?" She had to know if her baby was okay.

Prissy straightened and wrapped her fingers around her hair necklace. "She's not on duty today. Of course *she* wasn't there when you needed her." She sounded disgusted. "You're under Dr. *Hopper's* care now. I'll fetch him."

The door opened and Jason entered, smiling when he saw her. "Here's the coffee you asked for, Prissy."

Claire winced as she tried to sit up.

"She's awake." Mother moved to Jason's side and clung to his arm, speaking to him in funereal tones. "I'll go get the doctor," she said, and left the room.

Jason stooped and kissed her on the cheek.

"How is the-"

"The baby is fine, sweetie."

Relief crashed over her.

Jason took her hand and squeezed it. "I wish you'd told me you were still having bouts of fainting, Claire." He looked at her. "When I went for coffee, I bumped into Dr. Hopper. He said, according to your records, you've fainted multiple times. Why didn't you tell me?"

"Multiple? What are you talking about?" Her cheeks reddened and fury shot through her. "What the hell ... He had no right ... I'm not his patient." She couldn't think.

"I know how stoic you are, but you really could have been hurt, sweetheart."

"He had no right to look at Dr. Putnam's records."

Jason sighed. "The point is, you can't keep these things to yourself. You could have died, Claire! What if you'd been standing at the top of the stairs?"

"I hate Dr. Hopper." She did not want to acknowledge Jason's statements, mainly because she knew he was right.

"Well, he's all you've got right now. Apparently, Dr. Putnam is on administrative leave."

"What does that even mean?"

"I don't know what it means. All I know is that she's been suspended."

Claire blinked. "Why?"

Jason shrugged and smiled at her. "How do you feel?"

Claire struggled to imagine Dr. Putnam under investigation. *For what?*

Just then, the door opened, and Mother returned with Dr. Hopper.

Eugene Hopper had aged badly. Claire hadn't seen him in a dozen years, and the watery-eyed GP had developed puffy bags that hung beneath his wire-rimmed glasses like sagging breasts. He looked like a frowning clown. He always had. It was supposed to be his serious face, she figured, but he just looked like a tired bloodhound, droopy and dragged-down.

"Well, young lady," he began.

"Did Dr. Putnam discuss me with you?"

"No-"

"Then why do you have my records? I want Dr. Putnam."

"Claire!" Mother said between slugs of coffee. "Be respectful!"

"A broken leg is not in Dr. Putnam's venue," Hopper said.

"My baby is."

"Your son is fine. Happy and healthy."

Mother smirked. "Your secret's out, dear. It'll be so nice to have a little boy around the house again."

Claire ignored her mother. "I want Dr. Putnam. Why is she suspended?"

"Just an administrative matter. She'll be back soon."

"I want to talk to her."

"Honey, please! Calm down." Mother spoke as if Claire were yelling, even though she had carefully kept her voice soft and low.

"I am calm, Mother."

"Since Dr. Putnam isn't available right now, won't I do?" Hopper pulled his long face up into the semblance of a smile. "After all, I brought you into the world and saw you through your appendicitis, influenza, and all those accidents." He shook his head. "My, you were a terror on your skates and bicycle. Why, I'm amazed you survived those monkey bars." Claire remembered the appendicitis and the flu that had turned into pneumonia. She even had dim memories of wearing a cast on her arm one summer after a fall she couldn't quite recall. She knew the scar on her upper arm was from running into a glass door at home, but she couldn't remember any details. *It's normal to forget things that weren't any fun.*

"You broke your arm, Claire?" Jason sat on the edge of the bed and gently pushed a stray hair from her cheek. "You never told me."

"I was a tomboy," she said lightly. "I was always getting into scrapes."

"She certainly was," Mother said. "Evidently you never grew out of it, did you, dear?"

Feeling sleepy again, Claire gave her a weak smile.

"I remember that arm. Compound fracture. Nasty," said Hopper.

"Well," said Mother. "I hope you'll be more forthcoming about your health issues in the future, Claire. You could have really been-"

"I *know,* Mother. I already heard it from Jason."

"What's done is done," said Dr. Hopper. "The important thing is that you're okay. You're lucky. The breaks were clean, but you fractured both your tibia and fibula." He looked her over. "I'm not anticipating any problems, but since your pregnancy is already high-risk, I'm putting you on bed rest for the next six weeks."

"But-"

"Your leg needs to heal," said Dr. Hopper. "And we don't want to add any extra stress to the baby." He nodded at Mother. "You're lucky to have a live-in nurse. She'll take good care of you and her new grandson."

Mother beamed. "I'll get your old room all ready for you!"

"I'll stay in the apartment. We're moving in two days! I don't want-"

"You can't get up and down those outdoor stairs, Claire. And it would be dangerous for Jason to try to carry you. Why, he could fall and break his neck, and yours." Mother looked to Dr. Hopper for support.

"There are no stairs at our new house," said Claire.

Hopper looked from Mother to Claire and nodded. "Your mother is right. You need to take it easy for a while, stairs or not."

Claire looked at Jason. He read the question in her eyes: *What about the move?*

"It's just six weeks," he said. "After that, we'll resume as usual. I'll let Paul know."

A great sinking feeling overcame Claire, but she nodded. There was nothing to argue about. Getting out of Mother's house wasn't worth risking the baby's health. *It's just six weeks. Just six weeks. Maybe less after I talk with Dr. Putnam.* Her eyelids started to droop.

"Now, then," said Hopper. "I believe our patient needs some rest."

Smut and Blue-Gray Bruises

The days that passed were a haze - a blur of fragmented moments between long bouts of drug-induced sleep.

Mother had returned Claire's old bedroom to a semblance of its former self - her childhood nightstand stood beside a comfortable bed with a new mattress. Even some of her old posters hung on the walls and her beloved teddy bear, Mr. Anton, watched her with button eyes from the dresser. The drab peach carpet had been vacuumed, but it was stained and pockmarked from years of sitting under Mother's junk.

In fleeting moments of clarity, Claire glimpsed Mother fluffing her pillow, giving her water to take with her pills, and dithering about in attempts to make her comfortable.

In the evenings, Jason brought Claire dinner and they ate together, watched some television, and then - despite Claire's protests that the bed in the apartment would be more comfortable for him - Jason slept with her, ignoring Mother's disapproval. She was grateful he stayed with her during the nights.

The light streaming through the curtains was dim and gray and fading. She struggled to sit up, her head feeling heavy; the drug fog was getting old. She glanced at the clock and saw it was just after four. Jason wouldn't be much longer now.

The pain in her leg was little more than an ache, though that might have been because of the drugs. Of other discomforts, however, there were plenty. Her shoulder, which had always been given to aches, was in agony from oversleeping. Her back ached and the skin under her cast itched furiously. She reached for the chopstick Jason had brought her and pulled the sheets down. Her thigh, knee, and hip were still bruised, though the purple had faded to an ugly blue-gray, and the swelling appeared to have gone down substantially. She slipped the chopstick inside the cast and wiggled it around. A moan of ecstasy escaped as she found the right spot and the chopstick did its work.

There was a tap at the door and, instinctively, she withdrew the stick and hid it under her leg. Mother had warned her about the dangers of scratching herself with stories of everything from rashes to staph infections.

She opened the door without waiting for Claire to reply and, beaming, held out a silver tray. "Oh! You're up!" Her voice was far too chipper for Claire's taste. "I brought you some toast and tea."

"I'm not hungry." She hadn't been hungry since the accident.

Mother frowned. "Well, you need to eat just the same, young lady." She bustled over to the bedside, withdrew a TV tray and began arranging the teapot and cups, a plate of toast, butter, a butter knife, a small glass of orange juice, and an assortment of jam and jelly packets - the kind restaurants provided.

But, Claire had to admit it smelled good. She sighed and sat up straighter and Mother hurried to position the pillows behind her for support. As she fluffed and batted at them, a heavy hit of that dreadful perfume ruined what little appetite Claire had. "It's fine, Mother."

Mother drew back and smiled. "I just want to be sure you're comfortable." She looked tired. Her hair, which Claire had never seen out of place in her life, had a few renegade strands poking out. She looked frailer somehow, as if she'd lost some weight, and Claire wondered if perhaps caring for her husband all day, and now her daughter as well, was taking a toll.

She decided to be pleasant. "Thank you, Mother. I appreciate it. All of it, I mean." She saw the flash of surprise at her kindness.

"Of course, dear. That's what mothers are for."

Claire glanced at the jellies and jams. They didn't appear to be too old - they weren't even dusty.

"I know you like strawberry, apricot, and grape, so I brought you all three." Mother carefully placed a bed tray over Claire's lap. "The tea is green, which is good for clearing out toxins and speeding the healing process."

Claire hated the taste of green tea but refrained from saying so.

"Oh-" Mother reached into the pocket of her flower-print apron. "And I brought you some sugar." She placed several packets - probably filched from some unsuspecting restaurant - near the tea.

Claire looked down at the golden toast, the jellies and jams, the packets of sugar. Her mouth watered for the first time in days.

Mother brought something else from another apron pocket. "And we mustn't forget these, of course." She placed two large pain pills on the tray. "I also wanted to tell you I'm taking a trip to the library tomorrow. Is there anything you'd like me to pick up for you? One of those mystery novels you used to like so much, perhaps?"

"You don't have to do that."

Mother waved the comment away. "I'm going anyway."

No doubt to collect more books you'll never read. Mother probably had late fees with the library that would make American Express envious. When Claire was younger, she remembered her mother checking out books, skimming them, returning the ones that didn't interest her, and claiming to have lost the ones that did. The keepers went straight into a box where they undoubtedly sat, untouched, to this day. Eventually, the library stopped asking questions and just sent a monthly bill.

"That might be a good idea," said Claire. "I haven't done any reading in a long time. It might be nice."

"Of course it will. Are there any titles you want me to get, or should I just use my best judgement?"

Claire, not willing to be bombarded by books on religion and politics, wracked her still-foggy brain. She'd loved Sue Grafton's Kinsey Millhone books, but had no idea where she'd left off in the series. "Get me anything by Agatha Christie." She'd only read a handful of Christie's books but couldn't remember the titles. It was a pretty safe bet Mother would return with something she hadn't read.

"Oh," said Mother. "I'm certain I have several of her books already." She beamed.

Of course you do.

"I can make a quick trip to the basement and get one for you."

Claire had no idea how the woman kept track of the things she owned, but she had no doubt Mother knew exactly where to find it. "Okay," she said. "Whatever's easiest for you." Her leg began to itch but she resisted scratching. Her eyes watered with the urge.

"I'll be right back, then." Mother slipped from the room and Claire took a small bite of her toast. It was warm, buttery, and blissful. She opened the tub of grape jelly and slathered the whole thing on a single piece.

As she spread, she heard Mother's footsteps disappear down the hall, then, when she heard the sound of the basement door opening, she grabbed the chopstick and began digging under the cast. It was better than sex.

The itch was as satisfied as it was going to get, which wasn't enough, but Claire still marveled at the lack of pain. She glanced at the pills, wondering if she might be fine without them. It would be nice to be lucid enough to go back to work.

When Mother's footsteps approached, Claire slipped the pills under her hip next to the chopstick and drained some orange juice. Mother entered, brandishing an old war-torn book. "I found it!" Plunking the book down next to Claire, Mother scanned the tray and said, "I brought your pills, didn't I?"

"Yes. I took them already."

Mother's eyes lit on the juice glass. Satisfied, she said, "Well, be sure to eat all your toast! You shouldn't take them on an empty stomach."

Claire took a big bite of toast and the worry in her mother's eyes dissolved.

"Good girl," said Mother.

Claire cringed, but smiled. "Thank you for the book."

"Of course."

Claire looked at the novel. Stamped across the edge was, "Snapdragon Public Library" just as she'd suspected. It looked to be about as old as Agatha Christie herself, and the back cover was stained by something dark and questionable. She considered asking Mother if she knew where any of her own old Kathryn McLeod romances were, but Mother had never approved of those books. *Smut,* she'd called them.

"If you need anything else, just yell or send me a text."

"I will, thank you."

Mother gave her a warm smile and smoothed Claire's hair with a gentle hand. "I'm so sorry about your accident, Claire. I know this puts your plans on hold."

Claire, startled by the rare show of affection, almost choked on her toast. "It's okay. Really."

Mother's eyes welled with tears, and for a moment, Claire felt very sorry for the tired woman. "I'm just glad you're okay, sweetie."

"I really am."

Mother smiled. "I know. You've always been so strong." She kissed Claire on the top of the head, and turned to leave. At the door, she said, "If you need anything, I'm just downstairs." She paused. "Do you want me to help you to the bathroom?"

"No." Claire glanced at the crutches beside her. "I'm not an invalid."

"Of course you aren't." Mother left the room, closing the door carefully behind her.

For a long moment, Claire stared at the door, then she returned to her toast. As she chewed, she picked up the book. *A Cat Among the Pigeons.* It was, of course, one of the few she *had* read. *Probably this very copy.* She decided to have Jason pick her up some new Kathryn McLeod books. She could easily hide them along with the pain pills and chopstick.

***

Claire didn't realize she'd dozed off while reading the Agatha Christie novel until she heard Jason's shave-and-a-haircut knock. "Two bits" she called, glancing at the clock. It was nearly six p.m.

"Sorry I'm late," Jason said. "I stopped at Wokamundo. It was packed."

"Mmm. It smells like it was worth the wait." Claire smiled. Her leg wasn't any sorer than it had been a couple of hours before and that told her she was right - she didn't need the pain pills anymore. "What's in your other hand?"

He held out a white box of See's Candy. "Chocolates from Paul. He says they'll help your bones knit."

"He's such a sweet guy," she said, as Jason handed her the box. While he dished orange chicken, chow mein, and rice onto paper plates, Clair opened the candy. "Mmm. Nuts and chews." Stomach growling, she snagged up an almond cluster and popped it in her mouth.

Jason brought her a plate, pulled up a chair, and grabbed his own laden dish. "Good thing your mother didn't come up and catch you ruining your dinner with candy."

Claire snorted. "Screw that. Did you remember the chopsticks?"

"You're eating in bed." Jason pulled plastic utensils from his shirt pocket. "You're stuck with a fork."

"You're such an amateur, Magic Man." She grinned and grabbed the fork. "Soy sauce?"

"I didn't bring any. You're pregnant. That's too much salt - it'd make your ankles swell."

"Spoilsport." She smiled. "Thank you for thinking of that. I sure didn't."

As he ate, Jason looked around the room. "Do you want me to bring anything over from the apartment? Things that might make you feel more at home?"

She shook her head.

"Not even your music box?"

"Especially not that. I don't want Mother snooping through it. Besides, it's already packed."

"Have you heard from Dr. Putnam yet?" Jason asked around a mouthful of fried rice.

"I was going to call her office but I slept too long. Stupid pain pills. I'll call tomorrow. No more pain pills for me." She dug under her hip and drew out the two she'd stashed. "Would you dispose of these?"

He dropped them in his shirt pocket. "You're sure you don't need them?"

"Nope. Got a dull ache, same as I did when I was taking them - but the difference is, my brain is working."

"What did your mother say?"

"Jason, Jason, Jason. If I told her, I wouldn't be asking you to ditch them, would I?"

"Don't you think you should? I mean-"

"She's a nurse, yada yada yada. No. She'd just dither. It's going to be our little secret." She forked up chow mein and chewed. "I need you to bring me my laptop before you go to work in the morning. And something to stash pills in."

"Sure. Or just throw them in the toilet."

She grinned. "If I do that, we can't sell them on the black market."

Jason laughed. "You *are* back, my little smart-ass. I'm glad you don't need those pills anymore. I missed you and your big mouth."

She threw a noodle at him.

It stuck to his forehead and he calmly picked it off and put it in his mouth. "Two can play that game." He lobbed a nugget of orange chicken at her. It landed on her chest and fell into her cleavage.

She giggled.

Jason set his plate on the nightstand and bent toward her. "Let me get that out for you." His hand snaked into her nightgown.

"What in the world?"

Claire and Jason froze.

Mother stood in the doorway. Claire had never seen her with a dropped jaw before. She giggled again, loving her clear mind and Mother's expression. "Jason dropped his orange chicken, Mother. He's just retrieving it."

Jason's eyes were wide, the color drained from his face. He shifted, hand still cupping a breast, and said, "Umm ..."

Then, the unthinkable happened. Mother *smiled.* "Oh, you kids," she said, waving a hand. "Just make sure the curtain's closed. You know how Aida likes to spy." She chuckled, then turned and disappeared, closing the door gently behind her.

Claire stared. Jason gaped.

"Holy shit," he said. "I thought we were going to get a major lecture."

"Maybe she's been taking some of my pain pills." Claire was as stunned as Jason by Mother's easygoing response. "That is *not* the woman who raised me."

"Maybe aliens stole her."

"We can only hope."

Three Little Words

Burke Collins had been out of jail for several days, and found himself alone in a studio apartment overlooking Pink Blossom Park where, despite its cheery name, hookers roamed, junkies shot up, and boozers drank from brown paper sacks. Burke watched as a ragged homeless man tipped a bottle to his lips and wiped his mouth with the back of a ratty flannel sleeve. "There but for the grace of God go I," he whispered. It was just one of the many soul-soothing colloquialisms he'd recently picked up.

Geneva-Marie, quite rightly, had filed a restraining order and filed for divorce. He didn't blame her, but he wasn't giving up either. In the days since his brawl with Geneva-Marie and the kids, he'd dedicated himself to sobriety, attended several AA meetings, and was prepared to start the anger management and substance abuse courses required by the court. When his wife next saw him, she'd lay eyes upon a changed man. But whether or not she forgave him, he reminded himself, was not his business. *I will make amends because it's the right thing to do, not because I expect it to wipe my slate clean.*

He felt good about his new life, his rediscovered self, and was looking forward to getting the furniture business back on track. *But nothing before sobriety.* That was his motto now, and he was going to live by it.

He looked around the tiny apartment, envisioning what it might look like with some new drapes. *And maybe I'll get the new Xbox for the boys.* He liked the idea of them coming over to visit once the restraining order was lifted and Geneva-Marie was comfortable with them having contact. He sighed, hoping that day would come sooner rather than later. *But I'm not in control of that. I can only control my own reactions, one day at a time.*

He took a seat in his small chair and cracked open the Alcoholics Anonymous book he'd received at his first meeting - the "Big Book" as the recovering drunks all liked to call it. He was on chapter five, *How it Works,* and so far, it *was* working.

A knock startled him. It was after eight p.m., and he knew nothing of his neighbors; he couldn't imagine who might be out there, and he stared for a long moment at the door, confused. Another rap sounded, and he sprang up.

A ratty-haired woman in a dirty wool jacket over several stained sweaters looked at him.

"Can I help you?" Clearly, she belonged in Pink Blossom Park.

"You Mr. Collins?"

"Collins, yes. That's me."

"This is for you." She held out a wrapped gift box with a light blue bow that seemed very out of place in the woman's dirty hands.

"What? What is it?"

The woman shrugged. "I don't have a damned clue. I'm only delivering it because I got paid fifty bucks."

He took the box from her. "Who's this from? Who paid you?"

"Can't say. It's part of the deal." She turned and sauntered down the hall.

Burke closed the door, and stared at the package. *It must be from Geneva-Marie.* Hope swelled his heart. Maybe it was a peace offering, and since she couldn't violate the restraining order either, she'd paid that woman to deliver it. Yes, that made sense. He smiled as he began unwrapping the box. Geneva-Marie had always been so rigid about following the laws. That kind of nobility had been part of the reason he'd fallen in love with her so many years ago.

He frowned, pulling out a tall bottle of scotch. "What the hell?" There was a card attached to the neck. He opened it and read the three typed words, but they weren't the three words he'd been hoping to see. And this, he was certain, was not from his wife. "You'll need this," said the delicate white card.

Resting on a cloud of fluffy purple gift paper at the bottom of the box was an envelope. He opened it and read the words, typed in Times New Roman.

As he read, his entire world collapsed.

The Christian Thing to Do

The following day, Father Andy arrived at Priscilla's house against his better judgement. He'd meant it when he promised Dave Flannigan he wouldn't go to the Martin home under any circumstances, but he hadn't anticipated Claire's injury. When Priscilla said a visit from him would lift her daughter's spirits and show that the community and the church cared, it seemed like the decent thing to do.

Priscilla ushered him upstairs and into Claire's bedroom without any eyelash batting, then returned with tea and cookies. She did nothing to make him feel uncomfortable, and for that - and for her quick departure - he was grateful. He hoped his leaving would go as smoothly.

"You look very well for someone who's stuck in bed." He sipped tea.

"Thank you." Claire favored him with a smile. "Would you do me a favor?"

"Certainly."

She picked up her phone and turned on Pandora. She turned the volume up and Fleetwood Mac's *Silver Springs* played. "Would you take this to the other side of the bed and set it by the vent?"

An odd request, but Andy honored it.

"It will keep Mother from eavesdropping."

He nodded. "How are you feeling?"

"I'm able to get around. I'm just being careful because of the baby. I'll be off bed rest and into our new home soon."

"New home?" Priscilla hadn't mentioned that.

"Yes. Jason's boss is renting a house to us way out on the other side of town, not far from the airport." She lowered her voice. "I can't wait to get out of here!"

He couldn't help asking. "Why is that?"

She hesitated. "I prefer to fend for myself. My mother means well, but I'm not the patient type."

He laughed. "She must take very good care of you."

"Too good." There was a desperate look in her eye and she lowered her tone to a near whisper. "You're a priest. You won't repeat anything I say, right?"

"Of course I won't."

She studied him. "Ordinarily, I wouldn't talk to a stranger, but ..."

"Sometimes it's good to talk to someone who isn't involved."

Claire nodded. "That's exactly right. My mother is being kinder than I ever thought possible. I mean, I'm seeing a side of her I've never seen before. But ..."

He waited.

"But she had me taking pain pills and the first few days were a total haze. I stopped taking them over a week ago and should have stopped sooner. Even the first time I skipped them, there wasn't even enough pain to warrant an aspirin."

"That's a good thing."

"Yes, it is. But she still thinks I'm taking them. A couple times, I've suggested that I should cut back, and she says no, that I need them, that she's a nurse and knows best. She won't discuss it. I don't need them, Father Andy. I don't like them; they make me drowsy. She wants me to take them, so I pretend to."

Alarm bells sounded inside his head. "You're doing the right thing. I'd advise you to consult your doctor, but I can't imagine it's good to take medicine you don't need at *any* time, let alone when you're expecting." He paused. "But don't you think you should simply tell her?"

"No."

"Why not?"

"Because then she might put them in my food."

"Okay ..." At first thought, that seemed unlikely, yet after the things Father Dave had told him about Priscilla Martin, he wasn't so sure.

Claire cleared her throat. "There's something else."

He waited.

"Have you ever met my father?"

"No, I haven't."

"Did you know he's just down the hall?"

"So I've heard, but your mother has never asked me to visit him."

"Remember, this is between us."

"Of course." More alarm bells.

"She doesn't even like Jason and me to visit him. She says we upset him - but we've seen him and I think he's afraid of her." She hesitated. "Father, I'm only guessing, but I think she keeps him tranquilized. Does that sound crazy?"

Andy flashed on Priscilla trying to give him prescription pills for his headache during her recent surprise visit. He didn't know how to answer, so he spoke the truth. "I don't know. Can you tell me anything else?"

"When we've sneaked in to see him and he's awake, he's happy to see us. He has a hard time talking, but he tries, and we can understand him. But Mother claims he doesn't communicate at all." She shook her head. "The first night I was here, I looked out my window from the apartment and saw him, so I waved. He waved back. Jason and I went to see him after that - she keeps him locked in but we found the key; he *can* speak. He's done so repeatedly since we've been here."

"Why does she lock him in?"

"She says it's for his own protection," Claire said. "She always did, even before I left home. She said he almost tumbled down the stairs once."

"Why not put a gate at the landing?"

Claire stared at him. "I'm guessing that would be too easy."

Andy nodded. "How many times have you seen him since you've been back?"

"Very few. She caught us that first day and hid the key." Claire's gaze was direct. "We found another one, but have had few opportunities to use it. And most of the time, he's asleep. I'm not an expert or anything, but I think she gives him tranquilizers - he won't wake up. It's not normal."

"Why would she drug him?"

Claire shrugged and winced. "He's less trouble?" She rubbed her shoulder.

"True, but why doesn't she just hire someone to spend a few hours with him every day - or at least a couple days a week - so she can have some time to herself?"

Claire shook her head. "It sounds nuts, but it's like she's hiding him from the world - I don't think he's as incapacitated as she makes out." She paused. "She never lets anyone come upstairs. I'm amazed she invited you up here."

"Why would she want to hide your father?"

"She doesn't like anyone touching her property. And he *is* her property - I think she's trying to make me her property, too." She paused. "She's a hoarder. You should see all the junk in the other rooms."

He almost laughed. "You're kidding, right?"

"They're all full of junk except for my father's room, her bedroom, her workroom, and now my bedroom. It was so full of stuff a few weeks ago you couldn't even walk in here." She hesitated. "And Timothy's room is spotless. It's like … a shrine."

"You're not joking."

"No, I'm not. Swear to God."

"I believe you. It's just so - well, your mother is so neat and orderly. The way she dresses and behaves; she's a very precise woman. She single-handedly keeps the Ladies Auxiliary organized. It's hard to imagine she's a hoarder."

"Look in a room or two, Father. Just look. They're so full that I keep wondering how and where she stowed all the things from *this* room - it was stuffed to the rafters. She must have carried all of it down to the basement."

Andy looked around at all the childhood memorabilia - from boy-band posters on the walls to a Monopoly box, to a large Victorian dollhouse on a child's table in the corner. "Someone must have helped her with all this."

"It would seem like it, but no, I don't think so. Like I said, she doesn't allow people up here."

Andy gasped when his gaze snagged on an old teddy bear sitting in a child's rocking chair in the far corner. "That bear." The worn stuffed animal had dark red circles painted around its eyes and mouth, giving it the gruesome appearance of a bleeding thing. On the chair next to it was a tube of lipstick.

"What in the world?" The color drained from Claire's face. "Who did that to Mr. Anton?"

There was something else in her expression, something he couldn't read.

She turned her gaze on him. "It's her."

"Excuse me?"

"Mother." The fiery glint in her eyes set Andy on edge.

"You're saying your mother did this?"

Claire nodded. "She must have."

"But ... but why?"

"She's crazy."

Glancing at the defaced bear, he forced an uneasy smile. "I'm sure there's a logical explanation." Suddenly eager to leave, he looked at his watch. "I'm terribly sorry, but I've got to run. I'm late for an appointment."

Claire's face was flushed, her jaw firm. "I understand. Thank you for stopping by."

"Any time." He patted her hand as she stared at the teddy, a spark of disconnection in her eye. The skin crawled on the back of his neck. He'd seen that glassy look during his visits to patients at the Snapdragon Gardens Mental Health Facility.

"I'll see you again soon." As he turned to open the door, an explosion of sound rent the air and shook the windows, as if someone had set off a firecracker - or a bomb.

"What on earth ..." Claire gathered her crutches and struggled to the window.

Andy was at her side. "What was that?" He saw nothing unusual below.

"A gunshot," she said without glancing back.

"It couldn't be."

"We lived in a bad part of Oakland for a while. Trust me. That was a gunshot."

"I believe you." Still, he saw nothing.

Another blast cracked the air and Claire gasped. "It's coming from the Collins house!"

Andy looked in time to see the front door explode open. Geneva-Marie raced into the street. She ran hard, arms flailing, her screams high and shrill. Red splattered the front of her white shirt and streaked her face. A figure emerged from the doorway. Andy gasped as Burke Collins raised a shotgun and aimed it at his wife.

Claire screamed, "Call 911!"

Another boom blasted the air.

Geneva-Marie's hair shot out at all angles and a halo of red mist burst around her head. She flew forward, then crashed onto the asphalt of Morning Glory Circle, a shattered heap. Andy's cell phone dropped to the floor as he stared at the bloody stump where Geneva-Marie's head had been. Gray gobbets of brain, splinters of bone, and hanks of blood-soaked hair surrounded her.

Claire screamed.

Burke Collins stalked down the steps, breaking into a clumsy run toward the house next door, ignoring the big dog barking behind the fence.

"I have to go downstairs." Andy grabbed his phone, punching in 911.

She turned to look at him with stricken eyes. " Be careful. Promise me."

"I promise."

She turned back to the window, and Andy barreled down the stairs. He found Priscilla Martin in the living room, staring at the carnage from her picture window.

"Priscilla?" She didn't turn. *"Priscilla?"*

He stopped cold when he saw the smile on her face.

"Priscilla!" He grabbed her wrist and pulled. "Get away from the window. It's not safe."

Her head swiveled like a viper about to strike. Her eyes were vacant but the smile was gone so fast he wondered if it had been there at all. "Did you see that?" Her voice was hollow. "They're going to have a terrible time getting those bloodstains out." She blinked. "They'll be scrubbing for weeks."

Andy's stomach dropped. "You're in shock, Priscilla. Come away from the window."

But she wouldn't move.

"I've called the police," he said. "You need to go upstairs and comfort your daughter." He pulled Priscilla's arm, forcing her. He hardened his voice. "Your daughter needs you. Now!"

She glared at him, resisting.

"Mrs. Martin! In the name of God, go to your daughter! It's the Christian thing to do!"

Priscilla nodded then headed upstairs. From the vents, Fleetwood Mac played on.

At the window, Andy watched Burke Collins stalk toward the pale green house next door to the Collins residence. Shotgun in hand, Collins stared at the hysterically barking dog, but didn't threaten it.

Andy retreated to the safety of the kitchen and prayed for Geneva-Marie's soul, for her husband's, and for the safety of their two boys.

***

Burke Collins pounded on Duane Pruitt's front door. "Get out here, you sumabitch!" He beat the door until the meaty edge of his hand split, leaving scarlet streaks on the pristine white paint. "You coward! You motherfucking queer!" Through the rush of pumping blood and the sludge of his alcohol-soaked brain, he heard distant sirens. "Fucker!" He kicked the door again and again, spears of pain shooting up his leg, the nails of his toes splintering inside his boots with each bone-crunching blow.

As the sirens neared, thick nets of fog cleared and his actions came back to him in blurred and bloody fragments.

"Sumabitch!" He slammed his shoulder into the door and tears streamed down his cheeks. "You dirty, double-crossing cocksucker!"

He cocked the shotgun and aimed it at the lock, pulled the trigger. It clicked with empty impotence. "Motherfucker!" He turned, staring at the world behind him. It had tilted, slipped on its axis. He made his way down the steps, his legs bowing like rubber beneath him. He staggered toward the shattered figure in the street, weeping, his shotgun at his side. "Geneva! Oh, God, Geneva! What have I done?"

His wife lay on the asphalt, her once pretty face now a raw, mangled mass of blood and gore. Clots of bloody hair and bone surrounded her. Burke keened in horror and grief. "Geneva!" He threw his head back and shrieked at the sky. "No!" Unleashing primal screams, he dropped to his knees in the street beside Geneva's scattered remains. Hunched over, he buried his face in his hands, pleading with God to turn back time.

Red and blue lights flashed as a clutch of police cars screeched onto Morning Glory Circle, skidding to a stop just feet from where he knelt.

Officers opened their doors, using them as shields as they pointed guns at him.

"No, no!" He staggered to his feet, held his free hand up. "My wife," he cried. "She's hurt! And my kids. Oh, *God*, my kids!"

"Lay down your weapon, sir, right now!" a voice boomed from a loudspeaker. "Lay down your weapon and raise your hands above your head!"

The world was blurry with tears and booze, but he saw that he was surrounded. He looked down at his shotgun. He'd used his last shell on Geneva-Marie. His face crumpled and tears spilled. But there was still a way out. "Geneva, I'm coming." He raised his empty shotgun and aimed it at the officers.

"Fire!"

His body shook, quaked, and jerked as the blasts of guns deafened him, but there was no pain. There wasn't anything.

In Status Symbol Land

Aida Portendorfer squeezed Stan's hand as they stood on their front walk staring at the havoc. Police photographers snapped pictures of the bodies, which remained in full view, though more than an hour had passed since Burke had been shot down. At the opening of the cul-de-sac, a barricade kept a barrage of reporters and TV vans at bay on Daisy Drive. Overhead, a news helicopter hovered like a vulture, in small, tight circles.

A cop approached Father Andy and drew him from the sidelines, toward the bodies. The priest knelt over poor Geneva-Marie, giving her last rites a little too late.

Stan put his arm around Aida and hugged her close. "On our street ..."

Aida's eyes drifted to the big white house presiding over the circle. She could see Prissy Martin standing in a second-floor window, watching.

***

"Go back to bed," Mother had said when she arrived in Claire's room. She fetched the phone from its place near the vent. "I imagine you're looking for this." She dropped it on the desk. "Watching that will only raise your blood pressure, and that can harm the baby."

Reluctantly, Claire sat in her desk chair, still stunned.

Mother stared down at the street.

"I'd like to talk to Jason now, then take a little nap, Mother."

Mother didn't move.

"Where's Father Andy?"

"He appears to be giving last rites to Burke." She turned. "I can't imagine why Andrew thinks Burke deserves last rites, but I guess that's what priests get paid to do. Are you going to call Jason, dear?"

Claire stared at her phone. "Yes. As soon as you leave."

***

"Mom!" Billy Sachs said for the hundredth time, "I want to see!"

"No, Billy." Candy spoke with uncharacteristic firmness. "No." She'd called Milton, but he was stuck in a meeting and couldn't get home early.

She looked at all the closed drapes and drawn blinds and prayed Billy wouldn't find a way to look outside - he'd come home just before the shootings, thank heaven. *He could have been killed!* She wondered if Burke

Collins would kill a child and shuddered. "Billy, the popcorn's ready. Let's go watch *X-Men*!"

"I want-"

"I know, but this is better." Taking the bag of popcorn, she pushed Billy toward the TV room in the back of the house. "Put the movie on. I'll be right in."

The boy sighed, but did as he was told. When he was gone, Candy lifted a drape and pushed her fingers between the blinds. Cops surrounded the bodies, but she recoiled, seeing all the blood in the street. The Collins house was wide open, with police officers and detectives, photographers and videographers going in and out between the squad cars and ambulances. *I hope their boys weren't home when this happened.*

***

"You like that, big boy?" said Nellie Dunworth in a breathy tone. She sat in her electric scooter wearing her headset, as she polished a piece of china.

Her sister, Bertie, gaped out the window at the drama beyond. The gunshots and sirens had put a real damper on the mood, but the man on the other end of the line who called himself Mr. Xtra Big, was nearing the ten minute mark, and at four ninety-nine per minute, Nellie and Bertie Dunworth could not afford to lose the call.

"Oh, yeah, baby," said Mr. Xtra Big. "And then I'd pull your hair and slap your ass while I did it."

Nellie rolled her eyes. So, he was a spanker. While he went on, she turned to face her sister, and mouthed, "What's happening?"

Bertie shook her head. "Nothing new," she whispered. "Lots of cops and photographers."

"Oh, oh, ohhhh …" said Nellie in the throes of faux-orgasm. "Keep talking to me, baby. You're making me so hot."

"Are you touching it?" asked Mr. Xtra Big.

Nellie looked down at the china teacup. "Oh, yes. I'm rubbing it so good. I'm making it glisten for you, baby."

Mr. Xtra Big groaned as he very clearly finished himself off, losing her several valuable minutes. *Damn it!*

She wondered what the residents of Morning Glory Circle would do if they knew what she and Bertie did for a living. *At least it's an honest living.*

***

Phyllis Stine sat at the dining table, weeping into her hands as Clyde wrapped a second shawl around her quaking, bony shoulders. She'd already called anyone who'd been willing to listen, from her cousin in Pennsylvania to her former pharmacist who'd retired to Santa Fe. When Clyde had warned her about going over their minutes, the tears had come in a torrent and hadn't stopped since.

"I just can't believe it," she wailed. "Right here on Morning Glory Circle! Is nowhere safe?"

"Shh-shh-shh. It's over and done, now."

Phyllis could sustain herself on this kind of drama for months, years even, and Clyde dreaded the story's countless retellings and Phyllis' embellishments before the topic finally grew stale.

"Such a good woman. So kind." Phyllis bawled and pressed a wadded tissue to her face as camera flashes flared in the early evening dusk.

Clyde didn't point out that only this morning, Phyllis had been on the blower with Aida Portendorfer, saying she was glad Burke had come to his senses and finally left the dreadful Geneva-Marie. Burke could do so much better than that trollop, she'd said. It was probably Geneva-Marie's fault Burke had turned to booze, she'd said. And who could blame the man for *that?* she'd asked.

"Now, now, dear." Clyde rubbed his wife's shoulders. "Is the Valium working yet? Would you like to take a nap?" He cast a longing glance toward the living room where, on ESPN, the crowd went wild as a sportscaster announced another win for Clyde's team.

"There were so many things I should have said to her." Phyllis honked her nose and looked at the tissue, her fingers trembling with exaggerated effort. "And now, I'll never have the chance!"

"Perhaps another Valium, dear?"

She shot him a look, twisted from his touch, and said, "No. It doesn't work. Go next door and get some fresh from Prissy." Prissy always had the best drugs. "And bring me the phone. I need to call Gladiola."

"Who?"

Phyllis sighed. "Gladiola Gelding, in Crimson Cove! I went to school with her. I've told you all about her. We were in drama together!"

And apparently, you still are. Clyde was almost certain he'd never heard the name before in his life, but nodded and tried to appear in the know.

"She just isn't going to believe this." Her face crumpled. "I think I'm in shock, Clyde."

"Now, now, dear." Clyde handed her the phone.

***

"No, Prissy, I'm sorry, but I'm not going to come over." Babs Vandercooth's heart pounded at the very thought of walking past the bodies of Geneva-Marie and Burke Collins. She'd lived her entire life without seeing a dead body and she wasn't about to change that now. Prissy's earlier call, detailing the horrible death of the couple, had not been welcome.

"I *need* you to come over, Babs. I *need* to talk to you."

In the past, Babs would have gritted her teeth and gone, but lately, she'd found great satisfaction in standing up to Prissy; today, of all days, she wouldn't knuckle under. She glanced at the drawn drapes and blinds. She hadn't even peeped out, had no desire to, and couldn't understand why anyone would. Yet, she could imagine most of the neighbors doing just that, especially Prissy, Aida, and Phyllis. They were the eyes and ears of the neighborhood.

"If you need to talk, Pris, you are welcome to come over. Carl is on a business trip, so I'm alone."

Prissy huffed. "Claire is upstairs. And Frederick. I can't leave them."

Bullshit. When has that ever stopped you? Overhead, a helicopter swooped over the cul-de-sac and brilliant white light briefly glowed against the covered windows. "I'm sorry, Prissy, but I'm not coming over tonight. Not until all the … all the horrible things out there are gone. In the morning, I would be happy to come and visit with Claire, though. If you want, you could even go shopping while I'm there. I'll keep her company."

"I thought you were a real friend, Barbara. A real friend would come here tonight, when *I* need you. You can just turn your head away when you pass. You won't see a thing."

Babs heard Pris's doorbell start chiming out the national anthem. Prissy ordered her to hang on, and an instant later, she heard Prissy greet Clyde Stine. She couldn't understand what he said, but Prissy was loud and clear: He was looking for Valium for Phyllis and Pris was happy to oblige.

"Babs? I have to help Clyde with Phyllis. She's terribly upset; we all are. I hope you'll take that to heart and come see me now." She heard Pris tell Clyde to wait, then the connection ended. Babs shook her head. While she didn't approve of Pris' role as the Morning Glory Circle pharmacist, she knew she was only trying to help. *Maybe I can get past the horrors by now - it's been hours - and what about Claire?*

She went to get her coat.

***

Ace Etheridge sat in his office, staring at the wall. His daughter, Iris, had called a couple of hours ago, telling him what had happened, but he already knew via the newspapers' police scanner. He'd told Iris not to wait up and had been sitting here since, not bothering to leave work on time and fight the crowd of emergency vehicles and reporters that Iris had told him were blocking the street. Instead he sent a reporter to cover it.

He shifted his gaze to the window and thought about going to get something to eat, but his appetite was MIA, his guts too tight with anxiety.

Right on Morning Glory Circle. He couldn't wrap his mind around it. *Morning Glory Circle, where the sun always shines, and everyone knows who their neighbors are.* Though apparently, no one really knew Burke Collins.

Everyone has two faces. The one we see, and the one that's hidden from view. It astonished him how different these two faces could be. He couldn't help wondering how well he knew his other neighbors - what dark secrets lurked beneath the surface of Morning Glory Circle.

What kind of face it hid from the world.

***

Roddy Crocker stood guard at the barricade that kept the TV vans and reporters off Morning Glory Circle. The police line was right beside his own house, and Bettyanne had come out twice now with paper cups of coffee for him and the other two cops assigned to guard the street. That had been sweet, but he'd noticed a new gold bracelet around her wrist that he'd never seen before and hoped to God she wasn't slipping back into her old ways. Last week, she'd shown off a pair of earrings she claimed her sister had sent her, and Roddy hadn't had the heart to check out the story.

He wanted to trust his wife. He wanted her to be happy and well. He wanted her never to steal another thing in her life. When they met a dozen years ago, he'd been called to pick her up for shoplifting at Dudley's Department Store. She'd been caught lifting an inexpensive piece of jewelry and, after chatting with her a few minutes, he'd gone in and talked the manager out of pressing charges. She willingly went into therapy for her kleptomania and they'd married six months later. She'd only had a few slips over the years, a few clusters of minor thefts, but he always kept his eye on her. It wouldn't do for a police officer's wife to be arrested for shoplifting.

"Roddy?"

Roddy looked up and saw Duane Pruitt and his partner Jerry Park approaching him from the sea of reporters and gawkers. The captain had told him to keep an eye out for Pruitt. Roddy motioned the pair through the police line.

"What's going on?" Duane asked, his handsome face concerned, Jerry's frightened.

Roddy walked them out of earshot. "Burke Collins went on a rampage. He killed his wife-"

Duane turned white. "Geneva? Geneva is dead?"

Roddy nodded. The horror on Duane's face verified Roddy's suspicions that Burke had intended to kill Duane, too. But Roddy didn't know why.

Duane was craning his neck, trying to see the crime scene, but it was impossible now. Roddy didn't know if the bodies were bagged yet, but there was a three-sided canopy set up around the scene. Duane turned to Roddy. "She's dead? Are you sure?"

"Yes. So is Burke."

Duane paled even more. "What about the boys?"

"I don't know yet." It was a lie. "But Burke tried to break into your house and we need to talk to you about that." He palmed his walkie-talkie. I'm going to tell them you're on your way. Detective Logan will meet you in front of your house - unless you'd rather talk at the station."

"My dog-"

"He's fine."

"Thank heaven." He looked at Jerry, then back at Roddy. "Let's go talk to the detective. We've got nothing to hide." He squeezed Jerry's hand and fought back tears as they began walking toward their house.

***

It was cold out. Babs kept her eyes forward as she crossed Morning Glory Circle. There was no way she was going to stay on her own side of the street. The Collins house, next door to hers, was wide open with police cars, a coroner's van, and ambulances lined up. There was a tent in the middle of the street and it was open, facing the Collins house. Police were everywhere, like ants, crawling over the crime scene.

Nellie Dunworth was on her scooter, heading toward the Portendorfers, who stood on the sidewalk behind the tent. Bertie walked behind her. The Dean twins - those creepy little girls with skin so white that their faces glowed in the dark - stepped out in front of the scooter and Nellie laid on the horn and yelled something Babs couldn't hear over the din of the helicopter and radio noise. The girls stepped back and, after Nellie and Bertie passed them, both solemnly gave the Dunworths the finger.

Then Babs' attention was back on Aida, who waved to her. A man in black joined them and she recognized Father Andrew from church. Babs approached and Aida took her in a warm embrace. "I wondered if you were home."

"I was. I haven't been out until now" Babs nodded at Father Andy. "Prissy called and told me what happened hours ago. Then she called again - she wants me to come over." She locked eyes with the priest. "I didn't want to, but decided to, for Claire's sake."

He cocked an eyebrow and gave a bare nod.

Babs glanced toward the tent and was relieved to see it hid everything from view. Well, almost everything. The helicopter's spotlight passed over and she saw blood drying on the ground. She looked away. "I'd better get to Prissy's."

"Give her our best," Aida said, then turned to talk with the Dunworth sisters.

As Babs approached Prissy's door, she paused, unable to look away as several men exited the Collins house, pushing a gurney holding a black body bag.

"Oh, Holy God, no." The whisper slid from her lips without any effort. It had to be Barry, the Collin's oldest son, wrapped in there. When she saw more men exit with a much smaller bag, her throat tightened and her eyes blurred with hot tears as she thought of Chris Collins, who was little more than a baby.

A tear slipped down her cheek. *How could he? How could he have murdered his own children?*

Her fingers trembled as she reached for Priscilla's doorbell.

The anthem rang out and when Prissy answered, all smiles, Babs had a moment of sensory confusion - as if she'd dreamed the whole thing and it was just another day on Morning Glory Circle.

"Come in." Prissy, still beaming, stepped aside.

Babs had a feeling of unreality, as if the whole scene were something she was witnessing in a theater. Her feet carried her into Prissy's living room, but Babs was unaware of walking - the earth seemed simply to be moving her, pulling her after Prissy, into the kitchen. The Andrews Sisters were singing *Don't Sit Under the Apple Tree.* It was surreal.

"The children," said Babs, taking an unsteady seat at the table. "He shot the children."

Prissy brought a hand to her throat.

"I saw them. The body bags." She stared at the white tablecloth, embroidered with American flags and soaring eagles, barely aware of the steaming cup Prissy placed in front of her.

"If you ask me."

Babs looked at Prissy, who now sat across from her. She'd been speaking. "I'm sorry, what?"

Prissy sighed. "I said Geneva-Marie should have gotten herself and those children away from Burke Collins a long time ago, if you ask me."

Babs nodded.

"Drink your tea, Babs. You look like you're pretty shaken up."

Babs sipped the hot sweet tea. "Yes. I am." And it was Priscilla's fault. *If she hadn't coerced me into coming, I wouldn't have seen that ...* Anger flared, but Babs bit it down. *No. It's not Prissy's fault. None of this is anyone's fault.*

Prissy sighed. "Apparently, Phyllis is having a meltdown over the whole thing." She looked at Babs and sipped her tea. "You know what a drama monger she can be."

Babs blinked. "What did you want to see me about, Pris? You said you needed to speak to me."

"Oh," said Prissy. "Of course." She leaned close. "I wanted to talk to you about the Ladies' Auxiliary campaign. With Geneva-Marie no longer in the running, there's no question I'll be retaining my presidency, and I think we still have a long way to go to convince the other members to see the wisdom in moving the homeless shelter. Can you believe that Lizzie Knudsen had the nerve to go behind my back and tell several of the other ladies I'm trying to move the shelter so we can use the old one for more sales and events? We really need that space. This is all such nonsense."

Her words were a barrage of sound - the rumbling of a train on its tracks. Babs had stopped listening at the mention of Geneva-Marie's no longer being in the running. "People are dead, Prissy."

Prissy blinked, then patted Babs' hand. "I know. And it's such a terrible, terrible tragedy. I've just been beside myself with worry over those kids."

Babs was stunned. Despite Prissy's words, her eyes gleamed with the spark of victory. She'd remain president of the Ladies' Auxiliary and that, Babs could plainly see, was all she cared about. She wanted to spit fire at Prissy Martin, to ask her how she lived with herself. But like a raindrop on a hot sidewalk, her words dried up. There was nothing she could say. She sipped her tea and listened as Prissy regaled her with the plans for the next term of her presidency.

***

Despite herself, Claire had fallen asleep; now she awoke, and took a moment to get her bearings. Through the vent, she could hear Mother talking with another woman and quickly recognized Aunt Babs' voice. She wanted to see Babs.

Claire sat up and carefully moved her injured leg over the edge of the bed, then slipped on her robe. She situated the crutches under her arms so she could go to the bathroom. *And then, I'm going to call downstairs and ask Babs to come up and visit me.*

Claire was getting good with the crutches, even though her arms were sore. She hobbled to the bathroom and opened the door. *At this rate, I'll be able to stay home alone in my own house in a week or two!* The thought made her giddy with joy.

Inside the bathroom, she stopped cold. Her brother's little green soldiers were lined up on the edge of the sink, all facing her, weapons raised and aimed at her.

How? How could they be there?

She nearly fell in her haste to get to them. She grabbed the soldiers and swept them into the pocket of her robe. Ever since that first time she'd seen them in Tim's room, they'd haunted her.

She relieved herself then went straight back to her room instead of calling for Babs. She'd stuffed the defaced teddy bear in a Wokamundo bag and put it in her trash as soon as Father Andy had left the room. She had no explanation for that, any more than she had for the toy soldiers. *Because Mother did it.* She couldn't envision it - it was too crazy, even for Mother - but there was no other explanation.

She looked in the trash where she'd hidden the bear, Mr. Anton; that wasn't a good spot - Mother loved to go through the refuse. Her thoughts raced, collided, and tangled. She had a hard time breathing, as if her lungs simply wouldn't expand. She paused, closed her eyes, and took a deep breath, clearing her mind.

She couldn't ask Jason for help with this. *He'll think I'm nuts.* Given her recent emotional outbursts, she couldn't blame him.

She withdrew Mr. Anton from the trash and toed the bear out of sight behind the bed skirt, then moved to the window and pushed the curtains halfway open. Morning Glory Circle was still lit up, but a canopy hid the bodies. There were fewer cops now. Two ambulances were just pulling away from the Collins house and Duane Pruitt and Jerry Park were talking with a couple of men in front of their house. She remembered Burke trying to break in, pounding and kicking at Duane's door, shouting obscenities. She wondered what Duane had to do with the Collins family ... and why Burke had lost his mind.

***

"It's almost midnight," Jerry Park said. "We both have to work tomorrow."

"I can't sleep." Duane sat in his leather easy chair, as he had since the police left just after nine, staring into space at times, head in hands at others. Now he looked at his partner with bloodshot, teary eyes. "I really wish I could sleep."

"Would you like warm milk with a shot of bourbon? A big shot?"

"I guess that might help. I'm willing to choke it down."

"Coming right up." Jerry went to the kitchen and took his time, heating the milk slowly in a saucepan because he was worn out and needed a few minutes to himself. He loved Duane dearly and understood - and shared - his grief, but he felt wrung out after the hours with the police, the hours talking and answering too-personal questions, the hours watching Duane try to control his pain. The knowledge that, if they'd been home, Duane - and Jerry himself - might be dead, too, weighed heavily.

He poured the milk into a mug and dug the bottle of bourbon from a low cabinet. Neither he nor Duane were drinkers, and this bottle had waited three years to be opened. He rinsed the dust off. It had been a Christmas gift from one of Duane's employees and they'd nearly regifted it. Now, as he poured some into the steaming milk, he was glad they hadn't.

He squeezed some honey into the drink, and added a cinnamon stick stirrer. Finally, he shook a little nutmeg on top, then considered adding lemon peel, but knew it was time to stop finding ways to kill time. He was Duane's partner and he would help him through this grief.

Duane looked up when he entered and smiled as he took the drink. "Thank you, Jerry," he said, stirring the stick, then taking a sip. "You managed to make this palatable."

Jerry sat down on the edge of the couch and watched him. "I'm glad you told me everything when we first got serious."

"Would've been quite a shock if I hadn't."

With a soft chuckle, Jerry nodded. "Indeed."

***

Claire and Jason were asleep upstairs; Priscilla had looked in on them, enjoying the innocent, childlike expressions on their faces. Claire had been curled up against Jason and his arm was over her, protective, as a man should be. It was such a lovely sight that Prissy pulled her smartphone from her pocket and snapped a photo.

And had nearly woken them - she'd forgotten to turn the sound off and the flash lit the entire room. She saw Jason grimace and she quickly stepped out of the doorway and pulled the door shut. Jason might understand, but then again … *Well, there's just no sense courting trouble, is there?*

Priscilla checked on Frederick; he was sleeping like a baby. A snoring baby. With no desire to snap that photo, she closed the door, relocked it, then headed downstairs. After making herself a cup of chamomile tea - *Lord knows I need it* - and spiking it with a big dollop of whiskey, she took it to the living room, turned on the record player, and sat down in a rocker in the shadows by the picture window.

She had a good view of the street. The emergency vehicles were long gone, as were the bodies. The bloodstains remained - despite Aida and Stan spending half an hour trying to hose them away, she could still see them in the white glow of the streetlamps.

What a mess.

As the Andrews Sisters sang, Prissy stared out into the night. Duane Pruitt's house was dark and shuttered up tight, as was every other house she could see except for a single light that shone in one of the Portendorfers' second-floor windows. She wondered what Stan and Aida were talking about tonight - what kind of secrets they shared that they'd managed to keep from her. There was something, she was sure of it, something deeply hidden in the dusty recesses of their past. She wondered what the Portendorfers would think - what *all* of her neighbors would think - if they realized how much she knew about their little lives.

The Andrews Sisters sang on and on.

Copulating with Company

Tins of cookies, courtesy of Aida Portendorfer (homemade chocolate chip) and Phyllis Stine (Oreos in a repurposed Christmas tin) annoyed Claire as she sat up in bed. She was going to be as big as a house before she was off bed rest if people kept plying her with desserts. She settled in with the Dean Koontz hardback in her lap - an old favorite titled *Intensity*. Hidden inside was one of Timothy's journals - a slender one she hoped would entertain her as much as the first four had. There'd been nothing shocking in any of them: some off-color poems and lots of drawings of dinosaurs (a sixth-grade journal), cars and more off-color poems (eighth grade), and then one nearly full of drawings and half-finished poems - not dirty, but romantic. They were about Stephanie Banks. She remembered liking Steffie and that she was always around - before she was his girlfriend, she'd been part of the gang of kids he'd hung out with. But until reading the journals, Claire'd had no idea how hard he'd fallen for her.

This new journal, a pale blue spiral-bound notebook, dated back to Tim's junior year at SHS. There were no drawings, but page after page of cramped writing, the pressure of the pen embossing the backs of the pages, making it impossible to write on both sides.

Sept. 21. Coach Zellner said I should try out for track. He thinks I'd make Varsity. He gave me the permission forms and I should have faked them because Mother said no. Of course. She's afraid I'm too "delicate" and will get hurt. God, I hate her sometimes. I told the coach today and he said he'd talk to her. I said don't bother.

Tim had never struck Claire as delicate. Was she remembering wrong? *Maybe.* She'd been a little kid of six or seven at that time. Shrugging it off, she read on, rifling through pages until she came across an entry written in angry letters, so sharp there were holes in the paper.

Mother caught Steffie and me kissing at the Four-Plex. We were a couple rows from the back and she followed us. We didn't know she was there until after the movie when the lights came up. And there she was, in the back row, just staring at us. It was so embarrassing! She yelled that we were "sneaking around" behind her back because I didn't ask her permission. I didn't ask because I knew she'd say no. I'm sixteen. I can go to the movies with my girlfriend if I want to! But Mother doesn't think so.

So, she walks up to us in front of everyone and says, "I saw what you were doing." Then she says to Steffie, "Do your parents know where you are? And do they know what you do with strange boys, like a little tawdry Audrey, when you're not home?" Steffie said that yes, they knew, and that I wasn't a "strange" boy, that we'd been going steady for months. Then Mother went red and slammed her fist down on one of the seats. People stared and Mother started yelling. She called Steffie a slut, a whore, and said she was corrupting me. A man with tattoos and a walrus mustache stopped to ask if everything was okay and Mother jabbed her finger in his chest and told him to stay out of it. I've never been so humiliated in my life.

Mother dug her nails into my arm and dragged me out of the theater. She screamed at me the whole way home, and when we got there she gave me the "Bad Punishment." The worst of them all. I still feel sick from it.

I feel dirty. I want to stop her from doing that and the other things, but I can't. When she gets mad, she goes crazy, and I never dare argue with her. I grew six inches this summer. I'm taller than Mother, bigger and stronger, but I didn't stop her.

Am I a coward?

Maybe I am. All I know is that as I write this, I am so angry I want to sneak into that bitch's room and cut her throat!

The words shocked Claire. She'd never seen such raw hate in her brother, and wondered what on earth Mother did to punish him that had gotten him so upset. She wanted to put the journal down, to stop reading and let Tim retain the dignity and kindheartedness he possessed in her memories, but she couldn't put it down, couldn't stop reading.

I hate her. I wish she were dead. Maybe then she'd realize what a horrible mother she is. She never acts like this with Carlene. She just ignores her. Carlene's a lot younger, but I remember Mother being a lot harder on me even when I was young.

Now I have to face Steffie tomorrow at school. Mother won't let me call her and says if I ever speak to her again she'll call her parents and tell them to "put their harlot of a daughter on a leash." If that happens, I might as well just die.

After this, I'm going to write to Steffie and say I'm sorry and I hope she still wants to be my girlfriend. I wouldn't blame her if she didn't, though.

I don't know what to do. There's no way out. I want to leave, but where would I go? And what would happen to Carlene?

Claire turned down the corner on the journal page and closed it. She was stunned. Sure, Mother was a nosy pain in the ass and always had been, but what could Tim be talking about when he spoke of a punishment that made him feel dirty? Maybe he'd say later in the journal, or maybe Paul would know. Or, more likely, Steffie Banks. Claire pulled the journal out of the book, stood on her good leg, grabbed one crutch, and balanced so she could hide the notebook under the mattress. It was overkill; she could probably leave it in the novel right on the nightstand, but she couldn't risk Mother finding this one.

Claire maneuvered to the writing desk and sat down. She really wanted to read more of the journal, but refused because she could practically feel it raising her blood pressure. She opened her laptop and began working on one of her client's web designs. Not wanting interruptions, she turned her phone to silent.

It was a web page for a farmer's market in Santo Verde, California and she became engrossed in designing the colorful logo, weaving squash and corn and tomatoes with peaches and berries and herbs around the company name. She took one bathroom break about an hour in, then got back on the job. She was in the zone and when Mother rapped on the door it startled her. The sun was lower in the sky - she must have been at it for at least another hour, but it felt like only minutes. She loved being in the zone. Sometimes she wished she never had to leave it.

"Claire? Are you still awake?"

"Yes, come in, Mother." She was pleased that her mother had stopped opening the door without permission. *And she's calling me Claire.*

Mother appeared, holding a big glass of tomato juice and a few packets of Saltines. "I thought I'd give you some crackers, too."

"What?"

"Crackers." Mother held them up. "To go with the V8. You used to hate it! Is it a craving?"

"It's not a craving. I still hate it. Why did you bring this?"

Mother hesitated. "You asked me to."

"What? When?"

Mother blinked at her, then a little smile crept to her lips. "Less than an hour ago, Claire. Are you toying with me?" She paused. "I'm sorry it took so long to get it to you. I was on the phone with Barbara and you know how that is."

Mother's sincerity confused Claire. Was it possible the woman was losing her wits? "I didn't ask for that, Mother. Like you said, I hate tomato juice. I don't know what to tell you."

Mother's brow creased, concern in her eyes. She reached into her pocket and withdrew her phone. She held it out to Claire. "So, you mean to tell me you didn't send this?"

Reading the message, Claire's stomach dropped, and her throat tightened. Right there, right in front of her, was a text to "Priscilla Martin" from "Claire Holbrook:" *Will you bring me some V8, please?"*

Speechless, Claire gaped at her mother, then cleared a spot on the desk for the glass. "Oh, yes," she said. "Of course. I was working so hard I guess I forgot about it."

Mother stared a moment, but didn't say anything, just set the glass down.

"The doctor says I should drink it," explained Claire. "It's good for the baby." She offered a smile but it twitched and didn't feel real.

"Well, if you don't like it, I'm sure we can find another flavor. Maybe some nice Clamato." She looked at Claire another endless moment, then smiled, turned, and left the room.

As soon as the door *snicked* closed, Claire bustled on her crutches to the nightstand and found her phone. She checked the sent texts and felt the blood drain from her face. She froze, cold to her bones as she stared at the irrefutable truth: fifty-three minutes ago, Claire had texted asking for V8.

And she had no memory of it.

***

Claire's fingers played over the toy soldiers in her pocket as she thought about the V8 incident. She wanted to tell Jason, but was afraid to, for the same reason she wouldn't mention the toy soldiers.

Am I losing my mind?

She'd thought she could talk to the young priest, Father Andy, but the look he'd given her when she'd denied having defaced the teddy bear made it obvious he didn't believe her.

Maybe Paul ... She wanted to ask him about Steffie Banks anyway. *And he's known me since I was a child. Maybe he'd listen ... But would he agree not to tell Jason?*

She glanced at the clock; Jason would be home in half an hour. Claire grabbed her cell and pushed Paul's number.

He picked up on the second ring. "Paul Schuyler."

"Paul, it's Claire. Holbrook." She spoke softly, her back to the vent in case Mother was listening.

"Hello there, Claire. You just missed Jason. He's on his way home."

"I know. I wanted to speak with you."

Paul's warm chuckle put her at ease - at least a little bit. "I'm honored. How are you feeling? Jason says he thinks you'll be able to move in soon!"

"I'm fine, and yes, I'm going to ask my doctor about it - I think I'm ready. I'd move tonight if I could. But that's not why I called."

"What can I do for you?"

"Well, I wanted to ask you some questions about my brother… and I'd like to get in touch with Steffie Banks. Remember her?"

"Of course. If it hadn't been for Tim, I would have courted her like bees court flowers."

"Really? That's so sweet! Are you still in touch with her?"

"It's been a while. She's a psychiatrist now, in a little burg in Arizona."

She lowered her voice. "I've been reading Tim's journals and … I'd love to talk to her about Tim. Maybe she can tell me some stories."

"I'm happy to answer questions and contact Stephanie. I'll bet she's got some good stories. I'll see if I can hunt her down this evening."

"I'd really appreciate it." Claire gave him her email address to pass on to Steffie. "Paul, this may sound weird, but please don't mention this to Jason."

"Sure, but why? I can't imagine he'd disapprove."

"I can't either, but he worries that I'm living in the past, trying to find out more about Tim. It's a little weird because I have to keep the journals hidden from Mother and he thinks that's excessive."

"Of course you must hide them. She'll take them otherwise. I can explain that to him."

Relief swept over her - Paul was the right person to talk to. "I might take you up on that later, but for now, I'd rather you kept mum."

"Your wish is my command. If you want, I can pay a lunchtime visit any day this week. I'll bring burgers. We can talk."

"Paul, I think you'll understand this. Mother is likely to get interested if you come to visit me. Maybe we should wait till I'm out of the house to actually get together in person."

"Good idea. Can I try and answer anything for you now? One burning question?"

Claire lowered her voice to a near-whisper. "Did Tim truly hate our mother?"

"With bells on," Paul told her. "I don't remember a time when he said anything good about her, not even in grade school. Even when we were only eight or nine, I had the feeling he was terrified of her. He never said much about her, but by high school, he openly admitted to hating her. He couldn't wait to get away. His only concern was you. He didn't want to leave you alone with her. The night before he followed Steffie to Arizona, he told me they were going to work, save money, get a place together and bring you to live with them."

Claire's eyes filled with tears. "He was going to do that?"

"He was. He said your mother ignored you."

"She did ignore me. I was like a piece of property - or one of her stuffed dogs."

"What?"

"Remember her shih tzus?"

"I do."

"They're stuffed now. She keeps them on her bed - I hear her talking to them at night."

"That's creepy. Tim and I mostly hung out at my house, but sometimes she'd insist he bring his friends over to play. Those dogs yipped non-stop and tried to hump everything that moved. Once, she yelled at me because I had the nerve to shake one off my leg!"

Claire laughed. "She yelled at me, too. They were allowed to do whatever they wanted. Including copulating with the company." A memory tumbled into her mind - mother watching the dog hump her leg. Smiling and encouraging it. She pushed it out of her head.

Now Paul laughed. "Well, I'll let you know as soon as I get hold of Steffie. Sound good?"

"That would be great. Thank you, Paul. After we've moved in, I hope you'll let me cook you dinner at least once a week."

"You know it. You couldn't keep me away."

Flash Funeral

On Saturday morning, Father Andy peered out from the sacristy at the crowded pews of Holy Sacramental. "It's standing room only out there," he told Dave Flannigan, who was still adjusting his cassock. "There's not a seat anywhere, even in the balcony, and people are lined up several deep along the walls. There must be another hundred standing in the rear."

"Just so the fire marshal doesn't find out." Dave smoothed his silver hair. "I'm glad I'm only assisting – a crowd this big would give me stage fright."

Andy checked his watch; five more minutes before he could start the funeral mass. "It's a shame this scandal is what made people flock to the church."

"It is. But it's to be expected. I'd imagine there'll be plenty of gawkers out there very disappointed that it's not an open casket." Dave shook his head. "I remember back in 1968, when I was still wet behind the ears, a husband shot the milkman and his wife while she was, uh, milking him. Killed them, then went on the lam. The funeral was nothing like this, but the pews were packed. Reporters kept taking flash pictures for the paper. It was a zoo."

"Hmm. I hadn't thought about that. There are probably plenty of news people out there today."

"Yes, but don't worry about it. Can't do a thing to control it anyway."

Mabel Thompson, the church organist, played the first chords of the processional. The congregation quieted, all eyes on the three caskets in front of the chancel. The adult-sized ones hugged the smaller one and all were covered with masses of red and white flowers – they looked like bloodstained snow. Andy crossed himself, nodded at Dave, and walked to the podium. As the music played he looked out upon the congregation. People stared, some dry-eyed and fascinated, some with horror on their faces, many weeping. Silently, Andy said a prayer, asking for strength to get through the service.

When the music ended, he led a prayer, then the choir sang *Ave Maria* a cappella, a song that always made him want to weep for its sheer beauty and grace. Today, he barely held himself together. He'd witnessed these tragedies, given last rites to all four, though only Burke Collins had been alive for his. Burke's body wasn't here – he'd been cremated and his ashes sent out to sea days before. Only Geneva-Marie's side was represented, older, stern-faced men and women occupying half the front pew. It was hard to imagine sweet Geneva-Marie being related to the stony group; only one elderly woman dabbed her eyes now and then.

When he'd met with the relatives – two aunts and uncles – Andy knew there would be no forgiveness for Burke Collins from them; indeed, they seemed almost as unimpressed with Geneva-Marie. *She had it coming for marrying below her station,* whispered the most severe aunt. She looked like she had sucked the sour off a barrel of pickles. Bart Underhill, the mortician, confided that the relatives had sprung for the most expensive coffins and ordered the finest flowers. This made Andy sad as well – these things were for show, not for Geneva-Marie and her sons.

The song ended; Mabel struck the first chords of *How Great Thou Art* and the choir joined in. It was beautiful. Andy looked out at the faces. In the second and third rows, most of Morning Glory Circle gathered together, though Priscilla Martin, in her pink-and-black JFK assassination suit, sat with Claire's husband Jason in the front pew, directly before the podium. Claire was still on bed rest, and Andy was glad she didn't have to be here. He wished Priscilla had worn black, this suit of hers always caused chatter, but at a funeral it would cause a minor scandal. He wondered what she had up her sleeve to turn the scandal in her favor – or if she was simply so self-involved it didn't occur to her this was an inappropriate outfit.

Andy felt sorry for Jason, who looked ill at ease.

***

Jason Holbrook tugged at the stiff collar of his starched white shirt. The church was hot and Priscilla's extra helping of perfume nauseated him. He hadn't wanted to attend the funeral – it wasn't as if he'd known the deceased – but when Prissy practically begged him, to escort her, he couldn't refuse.

Father Andy took a long solemn look around the room, cleared his throat, opened a bible, and began to read from Psalms 23:4: "Yea, though I walk through the valley of the shadow of death …" As the priest went on, Jason stole glances around the church.

He was worried about Claire. Though her leg was healing well, she remained on bed rest, and Jason felt a guilty relief to be out of the house – and away from her. As time passed at Prissy's, his wife was becoming dangerously stir-crazy. *Or something.* Her edginess wore on him. She wasn't herself.

Jason hoped like hell they could get into their own place quickly … and without incident. Claire was convinced her mother would make it difficult to leave – she was convinced of a lot odd things lately. Jason couldn't foresee any trouble from Prissy, but he harbored a secret worry that something might go wrong. Perhaps Paul would get tired of his house sitting empty. And what if Claire's pregnancy became more precarious? He'd been plagued by fears since the day of Claire's accident.

Meanwhile, Claire was obsessing over every move her mother made, every word she uttered, and Prissy herself spoke in a way that made it clear she hadn't yet accepted that he and Claire were going anywhere at all. This made him nervous. Not because she could stop them, but because a small superstitious part of him couldn't help seeing Prissy's attitude as an omen of some kind.

From somewhere behind him, a mewling moan came, followed by a clutch of breathy sobs. He glanced back to see Phyllis Stine, her makeup-streaked face buried in her husband's chest as her body shook with grief. Clyde patted her shoulder and stifled a yawn.

***

Clyde Stine wished he hadn't worn the red thong and matching demi-bra. They were a little tight and after leaving the house, he realized the crimson bra was visible through his white shirt, so he had to keep his jacket on even though it was stifling in the church.

Clyde never dressed in full female uniform in public, of course, but he liked the way most feminine garments felt next to his skin. And he liked knowing that he - and Phyllis - were the only ones who had any clue what he wore beneath his undeniably masculine clothing. He chuckled to himself and disguised it as a cough.

Phyllis, who had always been competitive, took this as a challenge and sobbed louder. "There, there," he whispered, patting her bony shoulder, and wishing like hell he'd married Tonya Watson, his high school sweetheart. She was a quiet gal; she never would have caused the kinds of scenes Phyllis did. But Phyllis, older and more experienced, had been good in the sack and that had gone a long way with Clyde. At the time, anyway. These days, his only interest in sex was the little thrill he got when he slipped into a silky pair of tiny panties. And despite her histrionics and addiction to plastic surgery, Phyllis was tops about that, bringing him new undergarments and enthusiastically taking the role of photographer while he modeled. Doubting Tonya Watson would have been so supportive, he hugged Phyllis closer. He still loved the old girl. She'd turned out to be a pretty good wife for a woman he'd picked up dancing in a cage at the Whisky a Go Go all those decades ago.

As Father Andrew read another bible passage, Clyde Stine's manhood stirred, twitched. Another wail from Phyllis withered it right up, though. He sneaked a glance at his watch and suppressed a sigh. It was going to be a long day. He wondered if anyone else shared his sentiments. He looked at the back of Babs Vandercooth's head - which nodded in agreement with Father Andy's words - and felt utterly alone in his misery.

***

Between Phyllis' non-stop sobbing behind her and Prissy's horrible pink suit in front of her, Babs wasn't sure if she was sad or angry. Both women were so caught up in themselves that they didn't care what kind of impression they made. The funeral was about Geneva-Marie, Barry, and poor little Chris. It was not about drawing attention to oneself.

Babs dabbed away fresh tears. *Those poor children, poor Geneva-Marie.* She even felt sorry for Burke. *What demons must have chased him to cause him to commit such a terrible act?* Things had been looking up for the family. Geneva-Marie had told her Burke was living in an apartment and going to AA meetings once, sometimes twice, a day. He was determined to turn himself around, and was already talking with a business advisor, aiming to get the furniture store back in the black. It had all been good - and then this happened. *Why?* she wondered. *Why?*

Beside her, Carl sniffed and wiped his nose. He and Burke had been friends once, fishing on the lake, hosting barbecues, even managing a kids' soccer team together. But that was all in the past, before Burke got lost in the bottle. Babs wiped away fresh tears.

Those poor boys. Cut down so young. It wasn't fair. Her gaze drifted back to Prissy in her obscene pink suit. Prissy's son, Timothy, hadn't had much of a chance either. *But Claire's boy - he's going to make it - he has a fine mother and father, both.*

She was determined to visit Claire soon - while Prissy was away. They had things to talk about. She looked daggers at the back of Prissy's head. Prissy didn't care that Geneva-Marie and her sons were dead. Pris turned around and glanced at her, an odd look on her face. *Maybe she felt the daggers.*

How have I remained friends with her all these years? I was her lapdog, her toady. I allowed her to use me. How could I have been so stupid? But she knew the answer.

Blackmail was a powerful thing. Thank God Quinton Everett had gotten their home out of Prissy's name and she had no leverage over them now ... and that was a game changer.

Realizing the room had gone silent, Babs looked up.

***

The words dried up on Father Andy's tongue as his gaze settled on Priscilla Martin - and he realized what he was looking at. He wished he hadn't left the podium to stand in front of the caskets because he now found himself dumbstruck. In the shadowed depths between Priscilla Martin's thighs, he plainly saw the cleft of her sex. She wore no panties, no hose ... no *nothing*. And her knees were spread just enough to give Andy - and only Andy - a perfect view. He heard the congregation stir in the sudden silence.

Priscilla smiled at him.

Father Andy cleared his throat and headed back to the safety of the podium. He continued the sermon and avoided looking at her, pushing away the terrible memory of the recent *vagina dentata* nightmare.

***

Quinton Everett sat with his nephew, Greg, and half the little league team, as he listened to Father Andy's words. Greg had been close to young Chris Collins and had begged Quinton to bring him to the mass. When his sister, the boy's mother, said she thought it would help Greg find closure, he agreed; and after that, parents of the other Little Leaguers called and asked if he might take their sons to pay their respects as well. As a result, Quinton had walked in like Father Goose with a trail of goslings. He'd intended to sit closer to the front, but spotted Priscilla Martin and quickly ushered the boys into a pew halfway back. He knew what kind of rumors she liked to spread and, while he didn't fear her, he saw no reason to provide her with any ammunition.

He'd closed the loans - the mortgage, and the second for the remodel - on the Collins home himself and had gotten to know the family. He didn't care for Burke, who seemed a little arrogant, but Geneva-Marie was a sweetheart, always ready to send treats along for the team or help chaperone a night at the pizza parlor.

Barry Collins had been in Little League a few years ago and had been a good athlete and quite a scholar. He would have been accepted at any Ivy League college if he'd lived. But little Chris was why Quinton had to keep wiping his eyes. A sweet-natured big-eyed boy, he wasn't a great athlete like his brother, but his heart was big enough to hold an entire baseball stadium. How his own father could have shot him down - the very thought made Quinton's old war injury throb.

***

Officer Roddy Crocker wasn't listening to the sermon. His mind had been hovering around one thing since Burke Collins' suicide: the note one of his men had found on the dresser in the hotel room.

It was addressed to Burke, typed, and unsigned. It stated that not only was Geneva-Marie having an affair with her neighbor, Duane Pruitt, but that Barry and Chris were not, in fact, Burke's children. The note promised proof, should Burke doubt these claims, adding that only since Jerry Park's arrival had Duane and Geneva-Marie called off the affair.

It hadn't been released to the public, of course, but the detectives - and the rest of SPD - believed this letter was the cause of Burke's rampage. And Roddy knew it. Not just because it was the only practical explanation, but because - on an instinctive level - it felt true. And after twenty years on the force, Roddy had learned never to disregard his instincts.

Had the note been handwritten, it would have been easier to identify the sender, but people were rarely that careless. There'd been no envelope, and it had been printed on generic paper. But the list of suspects wasn't long. It had to be someone close, someone who knew Geneva-Marie - or Duane - on an intimate level. Usually, that meant family; but in this case, Roddy didn't think so. He suspected the perp was someone closer - maybe even someone who lived on the sac. Again, his instincts leaned heavily this direction. However, it might also have been someone out to ruin Burke Collins himself. A jilted lover - so far there was no sign Collins had strayed - or a business associate or a customer who got screwed over.

Roddy saw Bettyanne wipe her eyes with an embroidered lace handkerchief he didn't recognize. Whoever "C.J." was, his wife had evidently lifted her best kerchief. *Probably someone from the baby shower.* Thanks to his ultra-powerful sense of smell, he scented the sweet perfume that wafted from the new handkerchief. *Lilac, with a hint of jasmine.* He was thankful for the little piece of cloth - it helped mask the smells of hairspray, sweat, cigarettes, aftershave, and Prissy Martin's dominating perfume.

Ignoring the clusterfuck of smells, his mind returned to the note. He had a few ideas who the sender might be, but unfortunately, those finely honed instincts of his couldn't single any one person out, and there were no fingerprints.

As Father Andy wrapped up the first reading, Roddy couldn't help stealing a few glances around the room; though there were plenty of gawkers, he saw no signs of guilt. That came as no surprise. Whoever was responsible had ice in his veins. The note was not an angry one. It was deliberate, well-worded, perfectly calm. Only a sociopath could be so cold - and feel no guilt.

Father Andy began another long bible passage. Roddy sighed.

Boy Stains

I hate my mother. Hate her! Tonight at dinner, right in front of Carlene, she told me she found "boy stains" on my sheets. I wanted to die.

Claire's eyebrow rose. "Boy stains?" Yes, it sounded just like something Mother would say. She continued reading Tim's ninth grade journal.

But then, she started lecturing me about abstinence, and I got so mad I talked back and told her that in Sex Ed they said wet dreams are normal. All guys have them. She got in my face and screamed at me for telling lies in front of my sister. Then she sent me to my room without dessert. Like I give a fuck about dessert! I've got everything I need in my room. I'm glad she sent me here.

Disturbed, Claire set the journal aside. *I'll never embarrass my son like that! What a horrible thing to do to a child!*

After Jason and Mother had left for the funeral, Claire spent time reading at the desk. Mother nagged her to stay on the bed, which was ridiculous. She was taking it easy and that's what mattered. This journal hadn't been too interesting until this entry: Tim had filled the previous pages with drawings of racecars and little poems about Steffie. It intrigued her, but before she read any more, she wanted to go visit with her father.

She didn't need to change; she was dressed in a sweatshirt and shorts, and that felt good. Mother seemed to think she should stay in the flannel nightgown she'd bought for her.

Using her crutches, she hurried down the hall to her father's room and knocked. She wasn't sure if she heard a reply or not, so she called out that she was coming in to visit as soon as she found a key.

She first looked through the items on the little table beside the door, not really expecting to find it - but there it was, stuck between two medicine bottles. "I'm coming in," she called as she turned the lock.

"How are you, Dad? I'm sorry I haven't come to see you - I broke my leg and-"

He raised his head and her heart iced over. It was as if he were wearing a mask - his face was too smooth, like skin stretched over bone. She drew closer, trying to comprehend. This was not her father. Taking an involuntary step back, her thoughts raced and her heart hammered. The man's lips were too red, his cheeks too pink. His eyes were rimmed with thick, black, uneven lines, and a crescent of false eyelashes had slipped and stuck to his cheek. Scarlet lipstick was smudged, making it look more like a wound than a mouth.

"Dad?" It was a croaking whisper.

Something lit in the man's eyes - something familiar.

"What has she done to you?" Her voice splintered.

There was no reply from her father. He seemed unable to move his lips - or any part of his face, except his eyes.

"Are you okay, Dad?"

His eyes closed and his head drooped toward his chest. With great effort, he raised his arm to his face. The half-circle of false lashes slipped from his cheek and stuck on his sleeve.

Uncontrolled rage blazed through her. *Mother did this*. But why? Hot tears stalled in Claire's eyes, blurring the room.

She stepped closer, her heart pounding with revulsion, terror, and confusion. A thick sickness roiled in her belly. She plucked the false lashes from his sleeve - as if this would somehow restore his dignity. "Who did this to you, Dad?"

He said nothing. His mouth hung open and a line of drool spilled. He was clearly drugged.

Claire was unable to tear her gaze off the broken, humiliated man in the bed. As she turned on her crutches, something on the desktop caught her eye, and she gasped. Her teddy bear, Mr. Anton, was spread-eagled on his back, staring at her with eyes rimmed with even more red lipstick than when she'd first seen him in her room. His mouth had been defaced, too. A lipstick-red smile had been painted, clown-like, over the stitching, making the bear appear as if he were in the throes of a lunatic passion. The hideous thing was surrounded by an army of green plastic soldiers, each aiming his weapon at him, and Claire suppressed a scream as her gaze lit between his legs. A slit had been cut into his crotch and edged in the same red lipstick. But worse than that, another green soldier had its gun shoved halfway into the hole. "Oh, my God." Claire's hand moved to her roiling stomach and tears felt cold as they streamed down her cheeks.

She's mad. She's gone completely mad! There was no way her father could have - or *would* have - done this. Any of it.

A wave of dizziness overtook her and Claire steadied herself against the wall, afraid she might pass out. She touched her abdomen. *I have to get out of here. I have to get help.* She hurried from the room and shut the door, her hands quaking, her mind reeling.

What kind of monster is she? Why? Why would she do this?

Back in her room, she searched frantically for her cell phone, but it wasn't where it was supposed to be. *I could swear I left it on the nightstand!* She threw open drawers, searched beneath pillows, checked the bathroom, and even managed to look under the bed.

I just had it! She tried to recall the last time she'd used it, but wasn't sure. She double-checked the bed, under the sheets.

It's gone. I left it right on the nightstand, and it's gone!

Communion

Father Dave Flannigan finished helping Andy with the Eucharist. It had been a long ceremony, with perhaps two hundred people taking Communion. When Andy had asked him to assist he couldn't find it in his heart to turn him down. Dave was done with the church - he'd been done many years before he'd left - but he loved Andy like a son and could never bring himself to disillusion the young man. Andy was a believer, and Dave hoped he would never lose his faith. Life was so much easier that way.

Dave stood back now, just in front of the caskets, and surveyed the congregation; his eyes landed on Priscilla Martin, sitting there so regally in her dated finery that didn't suit a funeral. That deviation from convention was how she had put him off his guard a dozen years ago. He had received her into the rectory for a visit, not realizing what she wanted. Everything had gone downhill after that. It wasn't even the sex, though that certainly was something he regretted. It was a sin far worse.

Priscilla Martin was staring holes through him. He stared back, daring her to continue. Her eyes never leaving him, she adjusted the sweater draped over her lap and sank a little further into the pew so he could see she'd rucked up her skirt. Gaze unfaltering, she lifted the sweater slightly and smiled at him.

He was staring at her naked pudenda.

He gasped and Andy glanced back. Meanwhile, Priscilla covered herself up.

It made him glad he had retired, glad he had groomed Andy to take over, and glad the church had agreed with his selection. Andy would not make the mistakes he had. Sins of the flesh were not so tempting to him. More importantly, he lived by an inner morality that would resist the blandishments of evil better than the fear of God alone. Dave Flannigan had not resisted evil and he would never stop paying for it.

The Numbest Ass in the West

"That was a lovely service," said Prissy as she pulled her silver BMW onto Morning Glory Circle.

Jason didn't know how a funeral could be considered lovely. Personally, he found the whole thing morbid, but as far as public mourning went, yes, he supposed it had been nice. He made a noncommittal sound and stared up at the second story of Priscilla's big white house as they pulled in. The curtains were open in the bedroom and he imagined Claire was probably still reading. "Well," said Prissy. "That's what I thought."

"Huh?"

"It seems my alignment is off. I thought it was pulling to the left, and just now I let go of the wheel to test it. Just as I suspected, it's pulling."

"Maybe you need some air in your tires." Jason tugged at his collar and wriggled in his seat. He was eager to get out. His ass had fallen asleep during the funeral and had yet to come to.

Prissy sighed. "I suppose you're right." She stared, pinning him with the black pinpoints of her pupils in those eerily pale amber eyes. "You wouldn't mind running down to the gas station and filling the tires would you?"

Jason resisted an urge to groan. "Of course not." His tone flat as toast.

Prissy smiled and leaned over, reaching into the glove box. She pulled out the owner's manual. "Let's see," she said, flipping pages. "Oh, here we are." She thrust the manual at Jason. He took it and she pointed. "This is the section about the tires. It will tell you what the pressure should be at."

"It's pretty standard, I'm sure."

Prissy's smile fell. She took the manual back and began reading aloud, her finger moving along the page. She spoke slowly, too clearly, as if he wouldn't understand her otherwise.

The tire pressure was indeed standard.

"Got it," he said. "But you know that the pressure is listed right on the tires, don't you?"

She stared at him with crazy eyes. "I don't trust them. No doubt the tire company wants you to buy tires more often, so they change the numbers to make them wear out faster."

"Okay." Jason stifled a groan and concentrated on flexing his numbed glutes instead.

"I'd also like you to read the section about the gears before you take it out."

Is she fucking kidding me? "Um, I'm sure that's not necessary, Prissy. It's a standard automatic transmission."

"Yes, but I think it's important to understand how a machine maneuvers before you take it on the road. It's a very different machine than an airplane, you know." She began flipping pages. "Here we are." And she read aloud.

It occurred to Jason that Prissy could have taken the car and filled the tires herself in the time it had taken her to give him a course on the car. His ass was twitching with pins and needles now. He flexed some more, dry-humping empty air with as much discretion as he could muster.

When she finally finished reading, she asked, "Does that make sense, Jason?"

He hadn't been listening. "Crystal clear."

"You're a darling, Jason."

He nodded, got out - *Ah, blessed relief!* - and walked around to the driver's side and opened the door.

"You're such a gentleman." Prissy got out of the car then watched as he slipped into the driver's seat. "Oh, do be careful," she said as he slid the chair back to the furthest point. "Don't hurt my Beamer!"

Prissy fiddled nervously with her hair necklace as he adjusted her rearview mirror and side mirrors. "Just move everything back where it belongs when you're done, okay?"

Jesus Christ. If it's this much trouble, do it your damned self! "I will, Prissy."

"And don't go to Chevron. Go to the Shell on Honeysuckle and Hyacinth. I *always* take it to that one." She hesitated. "You know where it is, don't you? You should be filling your car there, too."

He nodded but Prissy began giving him directions nonetheless. *Of course she goes to that one. It's a million miles further away than any of the others.*

"And tell Johnnie V. I said hello, will you? I've told him all about you. I know he'd love to meet you."

Well, shit. There went his plan to fill the tires at the Chevron right up the street. She'd know if he didn't go straight to the Shell across town. Jason sighed and, under Prissy's watchful eye, put the car in reverse.

She stared until he could no longer see her. *Sorry, Claire, I'll be back soon.*

***

Sitting at the desk by the bedroom window, Claire looked up when the BMW pulled into the driveway and was happy Jason was back. But ten minutes later, it pulled out again. *Oh, hell. They're probably going to the store. Poor Jason.* She tried to distract herself by thinking about the horrors of shopping with Mother, but it didn't help.

Claire wished she could pace to work off the nervous energy dogging her since she left her father's room. The image of his made-up face haunted her and she'd set to looking for her phone again, wanting to call someone about Dad.

As soon as the BMW turned off Morning Glory Circle, she'd returned her gaze to the journal from Tim's junior year. Looking for more, she flipped further into the notebook and stopped when she saw hard, cramped writing. *Don't read it,* she told herself, knowing the pen pressure meant Tim had been upset. But she read anyway.

I've never been so humiliated. After school, I finished my homework, ate dinner with Mother and Carlene, and then went upstairs to shower like I always do. While I was washing, I heard a noise and thought Carlene must have wandered in. Mother never allows our bathroom door to be locked, even though Carlene is getting old enough to start snooping around. When I peeked out of the shower though, it wasn't Carlene who'd come in. It was Mother!

I yelled at her to get out, but she wouldn't. She said she'd noticed I smelled bad sometimes and wanted to tell me about proper hygiene. I told her I was learning about it in Health and Fitness class, but she didn't care. She said they obviously weren't teaching us the right way to wash. I slammed the shower door and told her to get out again, but she just started telling me things no boy should ever hear his mother say.

She explained I needed to pull back my foreskin and wash it really good. She said I had to pay extra special attention to the area under my testicles and my armpits, and my butt crack. Then she started explaining how I should wash my butthole really well with my finger. I was so humiliated but I didn't say anything because, once she starts, she doesn't stop. I even plugged my ears when she started talking about my penis. I didn't think it could get any worse until she said she could show me how to do it right if I needed help! I told her OF COURSE I don't need her help. She laughed and said she was a nurse and that it wasn't weird at all.

Not weird? NOT WEIRD?!?!

She sat outside the shower door and waited for me to finish, but I wouldn't come out until she left. When she finally did, I dried off, and ran to my bedroom and got dressed in my closet. I will never forgive her for invading my privacy like that. And I will never use the bathroom again without putting a rubber wedge under the door. She'll come unglued when she realizes she can't get in, but I don't care. I am almost grown now, and I can't handle these invasions anymore.

"Oh my God!" Claire shut the journal and resisted the urge to throw it across the room. It wasn't what Tim had written here, as horrific as it was, that shocked her - it was a lost memory of her own that tumbled, full blown, out of some secret vault in her mind.

She was barely eleven the day she got her first period, but she thought she was bleeding to death because Mother hadn't bothered to tell her about it and it would still be months before they'd show the girls-only movie in sixth grade.

First had come the blood, then the cramps. She'd even vomited a few times, it made her so sick. It was September, just before Labor Day, and she'd been reading in her bedroom when it hit. *Thank heaven I wasn't at school!*

She couldn't bring herself to tell her mother, because the woman would demand she strip and let her examine her privates. She couldn't, she just couldn't. She thought she was going to die, but even that was better than confiding in Mother.

She got out a medical encyclopedia and looked up vaginal bleeding and was shocked at what was going to happen to her over and over for the rest of her life. But she was also relieved to know she was normal.

She shoved wads of toilet paper or Kleenex in her stained cotton panties and each time they leaked through, she wadded the underwear up and shoved them in her desk drawer, way far back where Mother wouldn't see them. She used her allowance to buy boxes of Kleenex each month because she was too embarrassed to buy the real thing, let alone talk about it with anyone. *Why did I have body shame like that? What did that woman do to me to make me feel so humiliated over a normal bodily function?*

She didn't know the answer, but realized she must have had some sort of hygiene run-ins with Mother similar to what Tim recounted. *Something.* To this day, talking about menstruation embarrassed her to no end. She avoided the subject or changed it when her adult female friends brought it up.

Back then, by October, she was running out of underwear and had to do something because she didn't get enough allowance to buy Kleenex *and* new underwear. She couldn't go to the school nurse because Mother would find out. She had nowhere to turn.

Then, one day, when she was staying at Aunt Babs' house while Mother was out of town, Babs asked her if Mother had bought her a bra yet. Claire had turned a hundred shades of red, and sweet Aunt Babs set her down and told her how embarrassed she herself had been about asking for a bra the first time. Then she talked about periods and how embarrassed she was about hers at first - and asked Claire if she felt that way.

Claire burst into tears and ended up in Aunt Babs' arms for half an hour. Babs asked a few questions, then gave her a soda, waited for her to wash her face, and then took her shopping for new underwear and bras and Kotex. After that, Babs bought her another box every month that she carried home in her backpack so Mother wouldn't know. And Babs never asked why she didn't want to tell Mother.

God love Babs Vandercooth. I would have run away before high school without her.

Tears threatened, and overflowed when her memory skipped to the day she'd come home from school and found all the stained underwear - now white and reeking of Clorox - draped throughout the living room, dining room, and kitchen, for all the world to see.

She'd been a fool to leave them hidden in her room - she knew Mother snooped through everything. And she hated the woman for it. She hated her then, and hated her now.

That day, cheeks burning, heart in her mouth, she had gathered the underwear up and taken them to her room as fast as she could. She was afraid Tim would see. *Too bad he didn't; he would have understood.* She'd slammed the underwear into her drawer and not ten minutes later, Mother had appeared in her doorway.

And she hadn't said a word. Not a single word. No yelling, no understanding, no explanations, nothing about periods. Claire had been relieved. But the look in Mother's eyes came back to her now. Ugly, triumphant, mean, like it had all been a joke. She'd smiled at her daughter like a dragon smiles at gold. Then she'd turned and left the room.

Claire wiped her eyes as sadness gave way to fury. Aunt Babs had kept her in feminine hygiene products for years, until Claire could buy her own. Babs had hugged her and said never to hesitate to talk to her if she ever had another problem.

I need to see Aunt Babs.

***

"Where the hell have you been?" Claire was on her feet, crutches in place, when Jason entered the room. "I wanted to call you but I can't find my phone. She took it! I know she did!"

Jason's heart sank. He was in no mood for this. He tried to sound chipper. "Your mom asked me to go put some air in her tires. I'm sorry. You lost your phone?"

Her face was a mask of rage, her eyes burning coals. She was pale and her hands were shaking. *The baby!* He placed a hand on her shoulder. "What happened? Is everything okay?"

She shrugged from his touch. "No," she said. "It's not okay!" Tears brimmed, then spilled from her eyes. "Do you know what she's done to my father?"

Jason blinked, confused. "Your ... father? What?"

She wiped tears away with brusque swipes. "Go look at him, Jason. Just go look and see for yourself! The door is unlocked."

Jason narrowed his eyes and flexed his jaw. "Jesus Christ, Claire. I thought something happened to the baby! We can buy you a new phone. And if this is about your mother again, I don't give a damn! Enough is enou-"

Claire pounded the end of her crutch on the floor, cutting him off. "She's nuts! Completely fucking nuts!" Spittle flew from her lips and her eyes were wild.

"Claire. Please, just calm down. You need to take it eas-"

"Go look! Go *look* at him, Jason! Go see what she's done, then I'll tell you what she did to Tim, and to me!" Her cry was shrill, unexpected, and undoubtedly heard throughout the entire house. She was panicked, perhaps in a full-blown anxiety attack, and Jason wasn't sure what to do for her.

"Why don't you just sit down and tell me what happened? Maybe you imagined something. In your condition-"

Her eyes narrowed to cruel slits. "No. I will not tell you a fucking thing, Jason. I don't want to hear about how I'm being paranoid, or how I need to just take more vitamins and rest. I need you to see this for yourself."

Jason's heart hammered in his chest and his tongue was sandpaper dry. He raised his hands in surrender and spoke in gentle, soothing tones. "Okay, honey. I'll go look."

Claire's jaw hardened to match her eyes. "And when you come back, you tell me she isn't completely insane, Jason. You tell me we don't need to leave this house right *now*." She grimaced - her lips curving into a disturbing humorless smile, and then her face crumpled and she was overcome by wracking sobs.

Jason's instinct was to go to her, to hold her, but he knew that would prove disastrous. She was like an angry cat, hissing, spitting, ready to attack.

"You're scaring me, Claire. I've never seen you like this. Please, just-"

Claire's head snapped up and she jabbed a finger in his face. "Go look, Jason. Right. Now."

He spoke carefully. "I'll go look. Right now."

Brimstone

Stephanie Banks looked out the window of her office on Main Street in Brimstone, Arizona. Tourists strolled the historic town and the faint music of Brimstone Joe, the resident street corner violinist - fiddle player, she corrected - rode in on the chilly breeze. He'd put a Western twist on a movement from Mozart's *Jupiter Symphony* and it sounded great. She smiled to herself. She'd moved to Brimstone twenty years ago, yet it seemed like yesterday and forever.

White clouds puffed in the brilliant blue of the high desert sky. She'd never regretted coming to this tiny historical monument of a town, or giving up her hippie dreams and going to medical school. *What would Tim think of me now? Stephanie Banks, doctor of psychiatry.* He'd be pleased, she knew. Sadness began to tinge her thoughts, so she made herself think of other things.

Her last patient had been Nick Johnson, an employee up at the Brimstone Grand. He was worried about voices he thought he was hearing in the hotel, and she'd already ascertained he had no schizophrenic tendencies. A lot of people heard voices at the Grand, probably due to acoustics and all the ghost stories attached to the former mining company hospital. Nick's problems were minor, really more for a psychologist or just a therapist, but Stephanie was the only game in town. She didn't mind; she liked being in a small place, and her reputation had grown enough that people from nearby towns were calling for appointments. She took those she could, but the citizens of Brimstone always came first.

She closed Joe's file and opened her email, scanning for anything interesting. There were charities begging for money, a couple of psychiatric journal newsletters, some notifications from Facebook - then she saw an email from Paul Schuyler and her stomach did an excited little flip. Her memories of Snapdragon were overwhelmingly sad because of Tim Martin, her lost love, but Paul was a bright spot; she'd known him as long as she'd known Tim.

Paul had been such a sweet guy, Tim's best friend, and they'd all hung around together from second grade until high school graduation. If not for Tim, she might have gone with Paul. But Tim Martin had needed her to listen, to tell his secrets to, to understand his problems, all the way to the end. Tim was the reason, she knew in her heart of hearts, that she'd taken up psychiatry. She had tried to help him and ultimately failed. Though she knew his death hadn't been her fault, she never wanted to face that kind of failure again. Between that and a driving need to be helpful, she had taken to psychiatry, studying hard, and working harder. She loved her job.

Unlike herself and most of the gang she'd grown up with, Paul Schuyler had always had direction. He was smart, too, and he'd gone off to get a business degree when she'd moved to Brimstone with no real aspirations but to get away from Snapdragon and be a free spirit. Paul, who'd had a pilot's license before a driver's license, had been a straight-A student who made it seem effortless. He'd been destined for big things. She liked that. She liked him.

But then there was Timothy Martin. A gentle soul, Tim loved music and art and could have made a living here in Brimstone. He'd planned on it. He was talented and was learning jewelry technique from one of the best artisans in town. He was especially good with copper, marcasite, and azurite, the minerals that put Brimstone on the map - he was a natural.

But then he'd had the accident and his mother had come and torn him away. She'd never seen him again. Not alive, at least. Priscilla had seen to that. Stephanie recalled the day she'd returned from work to find the apartment empty - and knew Priscilla Martin had made true on her many promises to keep Tim away from her. All Steffie had was a printed note from Tim - which she was certain Priscilla had written - saying he was going home with his mother, that things weren't working out. And that if anything changed, he'd be in touch. But he'd never called or written. Her eyes welled at the memory.

Stop with the dark thoughts! she told herself. *Enough already!* She opened Paul's email and began reading.

Dear Steffie,

How have you been? I realize it's been some time since we've talked, even on Facebook - so sorry you couldn't make it to the high school reunion. Believe me when I say you didn't miss a thing. Mark Cox is still a dick, though now he has a drinking problem to enhance his douchebaggery. Valerie Swenson, whose Facebook picture is at least a decade old, has been married and divorced four times since she and Tyler Rogers eloped - and no one's heard a word from him since he ran off with a stripper several years back. And that's as exciting as life has gotten for anyone from our graduating class. But I do have some interesting news, and that's the real reason I'm writing.

I'm sure you remember Tim's little sister, Carlene. We called her Tag Along - at least I did. She was kind of our mascot? Well, she goes by Claire now - had it legally changed - and she and her husband, Jason, have temporarily moved back to Snapdragon to live with Priscilla until they can get back on their feet. Claire came across some of Tim's old journals and has asked me to contact you. She's been tight-lipped about the contents, but there are some things she says she would like to ask you about. She wasn't comfortable contacting you herself, for fear you might not want any involvement (my contacting you is her way of giving you an easy out, I suspect). When I told her you and I still spoke (though not nearly often enough these days!) she asked me to have you contact her - but only if you're interested.

All that aside, it's been too long since we had a chat. I've expanded Schuyler Flight School and it's doing very well. (At the urging of Priscilla Martin, I gave Claire's husband a job and he's one of the best I've had. They're pregnant, by the way.) I'm still single, still eating TV dinners that are way too high in cholesterol, and still pretty happy.

What about you? When you get the chance, I'd love to hear all about what's going on in your world. How is the psychiatric business treating you? Are you married? Kids? Do tell!

Write back when you can, and let's have a real-life phone conversation one of these days. If you're interested in contacting Claire, I've included her email below, along with my phone number, and my Skype address, if you're into that.

Stephanie stared at the screen and blinked. She hadn't thought of little Carlene - *Claire now* - in a while, and as she remembered her, she found herself smiling. Of course, she'd email her. She was dying to know what kind of woman she'd grown up to be. Changing her name gave her hope that Priscilla Martin hadn't broken her spirit. It concerned her a bit that Claire and her husband were staying with the woman, but she was glad to hear Tim's little sister had married a good guy and was expecting a child. Little Carlene was pregnant. *God, that makes me feel old!* She was also happy to hear from Paul Schuyler. He was right: It had been too long since they'd spoken. She'd always had a soft spot for Paul, probably because he was the only person she'd ever known who could make her smile - no matter what misery might be going on around her.

Who's Crazy Now?

Claire flushed the toilet, washed her hands, then stared at her reflection in the mirror. Despite the vitamins, her face was the color of wet ash and dark purple crescents hung below her eyes. She didn't look like herself. *I need some sun.* She also needed to put on a little more weight - what she had gained before the accident had dropped off, and then some.

When she heard Jason reenter the bedroom, she grabbed her crutches and stumped from the bathroom, then sat on the bed.

The stricken look on his face said it all. Claire felt a surge of relief. "Well, did I tell you she was crazy, or did I tell you she was crazy?"

His eyes searched her face, and he gave a small, uncertain shrug. "Claire," he said. "I don't know what I was supposed to be looking for, but nothing was out of the ordinary."

An anvil dropped into the pit of her stomach, cold and steely. "Did you look at my father?"

"He was sleeping like a baby."

"But did you *look* at him?" Rage bubbled within her.

Jason's jaw flexed and his eyes went hard. "Yes. I looked right at him. Up close. Like I said, he was sleeping."

Hot tears pricked Claire's eyes but she held them back. "You didn't see anything out of the ordinary? *Nothing?*"

Jason's gaze bored into her, his concern apparent. *His concern for* me. "Not a thing, sweetie." He sat on the bed carefully, as if any sudden movement might trigger a bomb.

She stared at him, then to her own surprise, laughed. And laughed. "Of course, you didn't!" she said. "Of course!" She realized that Mother would have had plenty of time to clean up while Jason was on the wild goose chase.

Jason moved toward her. "Tell me what you saw, Claire. Talk to me."

She'd heard the hysterical edge in her laughter and knew Jason heard it, too. She waved his question away. "Nothing. I didn't see a thing. Don't worry about it. Just pretend it never happened." Her breath hitched as she suppressed a sob.

"Damn it, Claire." Jason's voice was hard. "Talk to me. What the hell is going *on* with you? Tell me how I can *help* you!" He moved to touch her and she turned away.

"Just don't worry about it, Jason. I must have had ... some sort of reaction to the vitamins or something." She wasn't about to explain what she'd seen - not the defiled teddy bear, not her father - not when her husband was already looking at her like she'd lost her grip. "I'm okay, Jase. I really am."

"Do you want me to make an appointment with Dr. Hopper-"

"No. Dr. Putnam's back and she already said it's just hormones and I need to rest."

"I'll leave you to it, then. If you need me, just holler. I'm going to take a shower." He looked at her a long moment. "What would you like for dinner?"

She stared at her hands. "I don't care. Pizza maybe? Take-out?"

He paused. "Claire?"

"Yes?"

"I don't think you should read any more of those journals. They're upsetting you."

Claire knew there was some truth to his words, but was unwilling to agree. "I can handle it."

Jason sighed. "All right. I'll call for pizza when I get out of the shower. Decide what kind you want."

"Sounds great."

"You said your phone was missing?" Jason's eyes flickered toward the nightstand.

At her phone.

There it sat, right where she'd left it.

She opened her mouth to say it hadn't been there before - she *knew* it hadn't, she'd checked - but what was the point? It would only make her look crazier. Instead, she shrugged. "I'd lose my own head if it weren't attached."

Jason frowned.

"Pregnancy hormones. Dr. Putnam says there's nothing to worry about, remember? Sorry for upsetting you."

He didn't look satisfied, but managed a weak smile.

Claire wasn't satisfied either. *I'm not losing my mind. I am not!* She glanced at her phone, knowing it hadn't been there before.

Under Mother's Thumb

Stan and Aida Portendorfer had stayed up late watching *Casablanca* Saturday night, so they skipped mass, and when Aida went straight to work on the flower beds - it was time to plant the seedlings - the sun was high.

Meanwhile, Stan took Pookie Bear for his morning constitutional, saying hello to the neighbors. Many were doing the same as Aida. Phyllis Stine was just finishing up sowing snapdragon seedlings among her white rose bushes and Hank and Crystal Lowell were planting snaps in the flowerbed bordering the sidewalk. Stan shot the breeze with them for a few minutes before moving on. *Nice people, those Lowells.*

Priscilla Martin, as usual, had beaten everyone else and already had her seedlings planted. She must've gotten up at the crack of dawn to do it - they weren't there yesterday. Duane and Jerry hadn't planted, and likely wouldn't this year, and of course the Collins house stood dark and flowerless. It made him sad, so he moved on. Carl Vandercooth was planting, as were Ace and Iris Etheridge, and Bettyanne Crocker. Even the Dunworth Sisters had joined in by filling a big flowerpot with young snapdragons. The Deans never participated. As he returned to the house, he saw his Aida putting in her mass of seedlings. She was going at it like a soldier headed into battle.

"Looks great, Aida-honey!"

She looked up. "Did he poop?"

Stan sighed. "Yep. Everything was perfectly normal."

She eyed him, probably trying to see if he was holding anything back, then smiled. "You ready to help?"

Damn. "Yes. I'll be right back out, Aida-honey." She never let him off the hook when it came to the annual Snapdragon Festival. Honestly, he was surprised Prissy Martin always took the flag because Aida's plantings - and Geneva-Marie's, *rest her soul* - were spectacular. But Prissy always won and he admired Aida for never giving up.

"Did you check the mailbox yesterday?" he called.

"No," she replied.

"Hold it a moment, Pookie," he told the dog, who was straining to go inside. He put his hand in the mailbox and came out with an electric bill, a postcard from his optometrist telling him it was time for a checkup, and a white envelope.

He took the mail inside, set Pookie Bear free - he went straight for Stan's chair and made himself comfortable - then opened the white envelope addressed to himself and Aida. It was typed:

Stanley and Aida Portendorfer: You think no one knows what you did, but I do. I know every detail about you. Do not underestimate me.

It wasn't signed. "Jesus Christ. Again?"

"What's keeping you, Stan?" Aida came up behind him.

"This." He handed her the paper.

She read it aloud. "It has to be some kind of joke. It's been decades since we've done anything worth talking about."

"It's probably just some kid who thinks he's funny. Something random."

"Probably. But I'd hate for anyone on the sac to know about ..." She laid her hand over his.

He turned and hugged her. She hugged back, and they stayed that way for long minutes without saying a word.

***

"As I live and breathe! Steffie Banks, it's good to hear your voice!" Paul Schuyler tilted his La-Z-Boy back, muted the football game, and settled in for a chat. "How are you?"

"I'm fine, Paulie! I read your e-mail but didn't have a chance to call until now. That's so wonderful about Carlene becoming Claire. I'm glad she did that."

"It suits her." Paul reached for a bag of chips, then stopped himself. Even though she couldn't see him, he always liked to look his best around Steffie.

"Would you rather Skype?" she asked.

"Sure."

"Let's do it."

"Okay. Skype me." He hung up and pulled his laptop from the end table. A moment later, they were connected and there was Stephanie Banks, looking like a million bucks. Her auburn hair curled softly over her shoulders and her green eyes glinted with pleasure. Her lips looked soft and full, her smile generous.

"Wow, you haven't changed a bit, except to get even more good-looking, Steffie."

"Thanks. Now turn *your* camera on."

He quickly ran his fingers through his hair and brushed away any crumbs that might have been clinging to his face or shirt - *damn, I wish I had a nicer shirt on!* - then clicked the camera. "Like I said in my email, I pretty much eat what I want - you know, no wife to keep me in line - so I'm a little porky."

Stephanie's laugh was like the tinkle of bells. "You're not porky, you look great. You've hardly changed a bit."

"There's a little more of me to love, and a little less hair to comb."

She laughed. "Thank heaven you didn't take after your father - you'd be a cue ball by now."

He'd relaxed under Steffie's old spell, as always. "I'm so glad you called - I wasn't expecting you to."

"I almost answered by email but it just didn't sound as fun as actually catching up. So you said Priscilla Martin got you to hire Claire's husband-"

"Jason."

"Jason, thanks. How'd she get you to do that?"

"Jason's a great guy. He doesn't know it yet, but he's about to get a promotion to assistant manager."

"That's wonderful," said Steffie, "but you know full well that's not what I'm asking about."

He sighed. "I hired him because Priscilla Martin told me to."

"God, I'm glad I left Snapdragon. That woman. She's still holding that high school drama over you?"

"Yep. She hasn't forgotten a thing."

"Mayor McDonald must be out of office by now."

"Nope, he's pretty much the King of Snapdragon to this day."

"And Priscilla Martin fancies herself the queen."

"She does, indeed." Paul cleared his throat and told Steffie about the house and Claire's accident. "Claire's on bed rest, but Jason says they're hoping to move in about two weeks - if everything goes according to plan and the doctor gives the okay. Jason says Claire is really chafing under her mother's thumb."

"I'll bet. I would have shot her by now." Steffie laughed. "I'd like to come visit. Maybe I can help move things along, or at least offer Claire some moral support."

"You're not thinking of talking to Priscilla, are you?"

"You're joking, right? If I'm lucky, she'll never even see me. Is Claire able to leave the house?"

"I don't think so - she really doesn't want to take any unnecessary risks with her baby. Priscilla goes out frequently - maybe we can take you to see Claire then."

"That'll work. Hang on, I'm checking my calendar. Most of my patients are vacationing over the next few weeks - my schedule's fairly clear toward the end of next week. Maybe I can catch a flight to Snapdragon, come see you and Claire for a few days. Would you be up for that?"

"Are you kidding? I'll fly down and pick you up myself."

"You're serious?"

"As a heart attack."

"That's an invitation I'd be a fool to refuse. Brimstone even has a nice little airport now."

"Door to door service, then."

They talked on, reliving their shared childhoods, remembering Tim, and catching each other up on all the changes in their lives. Like Paul, Stephanie had married badly and briefly years ago; they both loved to travel, and liked the same books and movies.

Long after sunset, they finally hung up; Paul sat smiling awhile before rising to make himself some sort of healthy dinner. After that, he'd take a walk. Steffie always loved to walk and he needed to get in shape in case she wanted to go hiking.

Cookies and Mayhem

Claire had barely heard the alarm at six a.m., had barely heard Jason tell her goodbye as he left for work Thursday morning. Now, noises coming from down in the hall woke her up. It sounded like Mother was moving stuff around just a few doors away. Drowsy, she thought she heard a child's voice as she drifted back to sleep.

When she awoke again, it was nearly ten. She'd been dreaming about Winchester Mystery House, about Sarah Winchester, who always had carpenters enlarging her home because she so feared death. Now, hearing taps and knocks on a wall a few doors down, she knew the dream was rooted in reality. *What's Mother up to now?*

She sat up and grabbed her crutches, then crossed to the door and tried the knob. Once, twice. It wasn't moving. *The door's locked! What am I supposed to do, pee in the trashcan?* "Mother!" she called. "Open the door!"

The tapping continued.

"Mother! Open the damned door!" She hammered on it. "Let me out!"

The tapping stopped then, smooth as you please, the door opened and Mother, wearing a flowered pinafore apron, opened it. "What's the matter?"

"Why was my door locked?"

"It wasn't, darling."

"Yes, it was."

"Perhaps it just stuck. We had a little rain last night. Sometimes that makes it grumpy. It used to happen sometimes when you were little, remember?"

"No, I don't remember that, and it's rained plenty since we arrived. This is the first time it's happened."

Mother shrugged. "You never know when it will stick. Did you need something?"

"I need to use the bathroom." Claire crutched past her and into the hall. Looking behind her, she saw nothing except closed doors. She moved to the restroom.

When she came out, Mother stood outside her bedroom, blocking her path. "So, what are you doing, Mother? I've been hearing noises all morning."

"Noises? What kind of noises?"

Claire waited out a short wave of dizziness. "Knocking and tapping. Things being moved around. Hammering."

Mother watched her a long time. "It might just be the wind. Maybe a tree tapping at a win-"

"It wasn't the wind, Mother." Her voice was louder than she'd intended and Mother stepped back, surprised. "It wasn't the wind. I thought I heard something going on in one of the rooms down the hall. Have you been in one of them?"

"I was in my workroom, darling. Sewing."

The workroom was in the opposite direction of the sounds.

"Perhaps you should lie down, dear. Can I get you anything? Would you like me to bring your breakfast now?"

Claire narrowed her eyes. "No. Maybe later."

"But you must eat right to have a healthy baby-"

"I said I'll eat later." She turned and went back into her room, shutting the door firmly behind her and wishing it had an interior lock. She counted to ten and reopened it - it didn't stick a bit and she was startled to see Mother still standing there, her face wrought with worry. "Would you like me to call Dr. Hopper?"

"Absolutely not. You know I have Dr. Putnam back." Claire shut the door and waited for the tapping sounds to return. Fifteen minutes later, she gave up; the house was silent. *Maybe it* was *part of the dream.*

At her desk, she opened her computer, and checked her email. *Bingo!* Filled with excitement and a little dread, she opened the email from Stephanie Banks.

It's wonderful to hear from you, Claire. Congratulations to you and your husband! I would love to talk with you about Tim and will be coming to Snapdragon toward the end of the week. Paul will let you know when. I look forward to getting to know you (again)! All best, Stephanie. PS I sent you a friend request on Facebook.

Claire smiled and deleted the email, deciding to check her Facebook account later. She hadn't been on in ages and knew if she looked now, she'd be on for hours. It was time to get to work.

***

Babs Vandercooth had decided to skip the Auxiliary meeting. She was working in her front yard in pale green gloves, planting some of the seedlings Carl hadn't gotten to on Sunday. As she worked, she watched for Prissy's car. Finally, the Beamer slid from the Martin driveway and cruised very slowly down the street. Prissy always liked to check out the neighborhood.

Pris pulled over and honked as the passenger window lowered. Babs didn't rise. "Hi, Pris," she called. "Spring is almost here!"

"Have you forgotten about our meeting today?"

"No. The plumber's coming. Can you believe it's already been a year since I've had my pipes snaked?"

Prissy lifted her chin. "I told you that if you put enzymes in all your drains weekly, you wouldn't have to have a plumber in."

"Life's too short to clean drains that often, Pris. A good snaking costs less than all that cleaner, anyway."

"Hmmph. And that's why you have plumbers traipsing in and out of your house and *I* don't." Prissy had never been lenient when it came to servicemen inside her house. She said they'd rob you blind. Babs knew that was her excuse for keeping strangers from seeing the mess she kept behind closed doors.

"You're going to be late, Pris," Babs called.

"See that you come next week. It's important."

Babs didn't even bother to nod. As the BMW disappeared from sight, she stood, stripped off her gardening gloves and brushed off her knees. Then she headed toward Prissy's to have that little chat with Claire, knowing that eventually, Pris would find out she'd been in to see her daughter. *No secrets are safe on Morning Glory Circle. None at all.*

***

Claire, feeling better than she had in weeks, was almost finished with a mock-up of the website for a chain of California funeral homes when the computer chimed the arrival of a Yahoo IM. She raised an eyebrow: she hadn't used that service in a couple of years. *Who could it be?* It was probably just spam ...

Curious, she clicked on the blinking icon and the message box popped up.

How is your leg healing? It was from someone with the handle *Angel4ever*.

Claire stared at the message a long time, considering the possibilities. She could think of no one who would message her.

Who is this? She typed and waited.

An angel.

Claire sighed. *Look, I don't have time for this,* she typed. *I'm working. Please tell me who you are.*

She waited and no response came. Again, she asked, *Who are you?*

She was just about to shut the message box when a reply came: *I've been watching over you.*

Now she was certain it was some sort of scam. The only question was how this person knew about her leg. *What do you want?*

To tell you something.

She stared at the message, not sure she even wanted to bother, but curiosity won out. *What do you want to tell me?*

She leaned close to the screen, resting her chin in her hand while she waited for a response. When it came, Claire froze.

I'm not dead.

"What the fuck?"

A second message came: *I'm not dead. And I'm coming back.*

She'd had enough of this game. If someone was playing a joke, it wasn't funny. Her fingers stabbed the keys. *Tell me who this is or I'm shutting down the message right now and disabling my Yahoo account. Who is this?*

After a long moment the reply came. Her blood iced her veins.

Timothy.

The blood drained from her face.

Timothy Jacob Martin.

"Shut up." She pushed her laptop away from her, but the messages kept coming:

Timothy ...

"Not funny!" She deleted the message quickly, slammed the laptop shut, and stared at it. Her hands began to shake.

***

Prissy had never given her a key, but Babs knew where she hid the spare. She walked up the driveway, toward the kitchen door, pausing at a big pot of holly to fish out the fake rock. It'd been there for thirty years. "You're not fooling anybody with this," she muttered as she slid the key out.

"Hello?" she called as she unlocked the door and entered. "Hello?"

There was no reply, but she thought Claire probably couldn't hear her, so she pulled the door closed and went upstairs then began calling, "Hello? Claire? Frederick?" She hadn't seen Prissy's husband in many years and hoped he was okay. She only knew he was still alive because Pris mentioned him now and then.

Halfway down the hall, she called, "Claire? Are you here? It's Babs."

A door opened five feet away and Claire peeked out. "Aunt Babs?"

Babs smiled, relieved to see her. "I wanted to pay you a visit." She held out a little white Pepperidge Farm cookie bag.

"Chesapeakes! Come in, come in! I'm so glad to see you. You can sit there." She pointed at her desk chair as she sat down on the bed.

"You're a pro with those sticks." Babs nodded at the crutches. Claire really did sound happy to see her, but there was a new frailty about her that shocked Babs. She was thinner and that wasn't usual in a pregnancy. "How are you, darling? Have a cookie."

"I've been better." She set the cookies on the bed without opening them.

Claire looked her in the eye then, and Babs saw more than the ashen complexion and dark circles under her eyes - she looked haunted, and she'd been crying. It was impossible to hide, but she was trying her best, so Babs decided not to ask what was wrong.

"I saw your mother leave and thought maybe we could have a chat." Babs smiled.

"You're a mind reader. I was thinking the same thing. But it's so hard to do with Mother around."

"That's true. That's why I waited until she left before I came over."

Claire's smile was small but real. "She'd never let you come up here if she knew."

"I know. Typical hoarder. They don't like people seeing how they really live."

Claire's eyes went wide. "*You know?*"

"Of course. I've been friends with Pris since our school years. She couldn't even keep her desk neat in school, it was always packed with so much stuff."

Claire laughed. "Seriously?"

"Yes. And you should have seen her room when she was a girl." She paused. "I hope you don't mind me talking about your mother like this."

"Are you kidding? I love it!" Claire's smile broadened. "I've missed you so much, Aunt Babs." The smile fell. "But I never missed my mother. Not once."

Babs stood and gave Claire a gentle hug and a kiss on the forehead, then sat back down. "Thank you. We need to talk about something."

Claire sat up straighter. "Anything. What is it?"

"I'll be blunt."

"Please do."

"Very well." Babs screwed up her courage. "I'm worried about you staying here. I mean, you've already had an accident." She looked at Claire's cast.

"My doctor says she thinks I might be out of here within two weeks. My mother probably told you that Paul Schuyler, Jason's boss at the flight school, is renting a house to us for absolute peanuts. We'd be there already if I hadn't broken my stupid leg."

Babs hoped Claire couldn't see beyond her calm mask because alarm bells were ringing. "Honey, your mother said nothing about you having a new place. Not a word. I'm so happy for you."

"She doesn't want us to go. We even had a big yelling match when I told her. I know she's glad I broke my leg."

Babs' stomach twisted, but she hid her worry and listened as Claire told her about their new home, how they'd already taken a few things over, and that she'd had her injury only a day before they were planning on moving out. "Well," Babs said, "at least you're going to be out of here very soon. That's good. And I'll be happy to come over every day - all day if you want - and help you for as long as you need me to."

"I'd love to have you visit. Just don't bring my mother."

"I won't." Babs chuckled, then saw Claire's expression turn serious.

"Aunt Babs, I want out of here in the worst way, but I need to know why *you* feel it's important we leave quickly."

Babs wished she hadn't led with the statement. "It's not important since you're moving out soon."

"I need to know," Claire said. "I'm a big girl. I can take it." She paused. "I've been reading Timothy's old journals. Priscilla Martin was not a model mother, I know that. Tell me.

"How many injuries have you had in the ten years since you left home?"

Claire looked at the ceiling, thinking. "Does a skinned knee count?"

"No, it doesn't." Babs had nothing to validate her suspicions, so she tried to make light of things. "You had a lot of accidents when you lived here. I guess you outgrew that."

"Except for this." Claire looked at her leg.

"Yes, except for that." Babs studied Claire, unwilling to upset her with half-baked theories. She decided to change the subject. "Do you remember coming to my house almost every day after school?"

"Of course I do. I loved it." She grinned. "We had Chesapeake cookies and milk at least once a week. Why?"

"Did you know your mother only let you come because she claimed you were too noisy and Timothy couldn't do his homework?"

"What?"

"I know, it's nonsense. You were never noisy or clumsy around me; it never made any sense. But I went along with it because I loved having you with me. I always kind of felt like I should have been your mother, you know?" Tears welled.

Claire wiped tears away, too. "I wish you were."

"Thank you. We may not be blood, but you *are* my family, Claire. And let me tell you right now - it was all about your mother, not you. Prissy just couldn't deal with two children. I swear, she was so obsessed with Timothy; that's normal for a first-time mother, but the obsession never wore off, even when you were born. Did you know she breastfed him until he started kindergarten?"

"No." Claire's face lost what little color it had. "I didn't know. Why would she do such a thing?" She paused. "She didn't do that to me, did she?"

"Oh, heavens, no. You were a bottle baby. I probably fed you almost as often as she did." *God, I didn't realize she wouldn't think that was amusing.*

"Why did she do it to Timothy?"

Claire's voice quavered and sounded an octave higher than it had moments before. Babs didn't want to upset her further and wished she'd kept her mouth shut. "I think your mother is selectively OCD. She fixated so heavily on your brother that she just didn't do right by you."

Claire's lip trembled and her pale face blotched red. She said nothing.

Babs had a terrible feeling that Claire was about to crack and thought it best to leave before she accidentally said something to escalate things. She rose, looking at her watch. "I have a repairman coming. I'm sorry, but I need to get back."

Claire looked stricken. "You will come back, right? Mother has another meeting on Friday. She'll be gone for hours."

"Yes, I'll try."

"Please come!" Tears ran silently down her cheeks.

Babs' heart was breaking. "I'll come, I promise." She kissed Claire's forehead again. It was as cold and clammy as a fish. "Are you feeling all right?"

Claire nodded. "It's just been rough being here in this house. Half the time I think I'm losing my mind."

"What do you mean?"

"Just little things. My phone isn't where I left it, then it is. I thought my door was locked this morning but Mother says it must have stuck." She paused. "I think it really was locked." Embarrassment flashed. "Nothing serious. Just little things."

Babs could see that, for Claire, these weren't little things at all, and thought there was more to the story. "Have you spoken to Jason about all this?"

"Yes, I did, but I don't anymore. He thinks I'm imagining things."

"Well, you can talk to me on Friday, okay? Or you can phone me any time you want, day or night."

"Thanks. I might do that."

"Take good care of yourself." Babs hugged her then let herself out of the room. Once the door was shut, tears rolled down her face. Downstairs, she locked the door, replaced the key, and wiped her eyes. She paused before heading home. She couldn't stop thinking of the look in Claire's eyes - frightened, haunted. And she'd been so edgy. She wasn't herself. Not to mention, she was too fragile to talk turkey. But the issues couldn't be ignored any longer. Babs resolved to speak with Jason.

The Secret Life of Timothy Martin

At noon, Jason made his way into the airport cafeteria. He'd packed a sandwich and a bag of Sun Chips for lunch and bought a Coke Zero from the vending machine. He hadn't been watching what he ate since they'd left the apartment in Oakland, and now it was starting to wear on him. He hadn't put on any significant weight, but he was tired, sluggish. It was time to start running again. *And eating better.*

He sat at a table near a large window where he could watch the runway and opened his sack. A sweet little red-and-white Cessna touched down and he felt a pang, wishing he were in the pilot seat, but there was no use dwelling on it. Instead, he pulled out the sandwich. He peeled back the bread, regretting how much mayo he'd slathered on. *Definitely time to get things back in order. I'm going to be a father soon! Gotta get in shape!*

When Paul Schuyler entered the room, Jason raised his arm and waved. Paul smiled and headed over and sat down.

"Just the man I want to talk to." Paul pulled out his own bag lunch, which made Jason's look healthy by comparison: a dozen fried-battered shrimp with tartar sauce. "I got a phone call about a sweet little business class jet I'd like to buy."

"Oh, yeah? What kind?"

"A VLJ. It's a Cessna Citation Mustang 510. Nice and light. If it's as advertised, it would make a perfect addition to our little fleet. Great to teach in. We're getting more and more students who want to learn this class of aircraft."

"Nice," Jason said. "You already have one very light jet. Thinking of expanding?"

"I might be." Paul grinned and ate another shrimp. "Our VLJ is in good shape, but it's quite a bit older. We need something more up-to-date. The thing is, I can't get away to inspect it and there are other interested parties. Would you be willing to go Friday morning and take a look? It's in Denver. I could send you with Jake Fairview and put you up overnight. You'd be home within 24 hours."

Jake was a pilot who taught students in the air. He was about the ugliest man Jason had ever seen, but a great pilot and instructor. "Why not just send Jake?"

Paul smiled. "Because he doesn't have the executive skills you do, and you know your way around jets, big or little. He's strictly a small-plane guy. You have experience none of us have - and I trust you."

"I'd be happy to, then. I just hope Claire understands."

"I'll sweet-talk her into it, if you want." Paul pulled out a tube of Ritz, a small baggie of Oreos, and two Mountain Dews. "Don't judge me," he said, biting into a cookie.

Jason raised his hand. "I wouldn't dream of it." He laughed and took a bite out of his turkey sandwich.

"I deep-fried these babies myself." Paul dipped a cold shrimp and popped it into his mouth. "You can have some if you like."

"No, thanks, but they look great."

"You're not watching what you eat, are you?"

Jason laughed. "As a matter of fact, I was just thinking I probably ought to start."

Paul sighed. "Me too. But not until after I grill up some of my famous ribs for you guys. Those burgers you and Claire had were just the tip of a very greasy iceberg, my friend."

Jason laughed. "I'm looking forward to it, and Claire is, too."

"I'll bet." He popped another shrimp, chased it with an Oreo, then opened a Mountain Dew. "Just a few more weeks, right?"

"Two. Claire has an appointment in two weeks, and as soon as Dr. Putnam gives the word, we're heading over." He paused. "Assuming we get the green light, of course."

Paul stopped chewing. "Why wouldn't you? Everything's okay with Claire, right?"

Jason nodded and took another bite of sandwich. "She's fine." It felt like a lie. "A bundle of raw nerves, but nothing that should threaten her pregnancy."

"Why's she so nervous?"

Jason considered. "Hormones. And, of course, her mother."

"Old Prissy's not making things hard on her, is she?"

"No harder than usual. It's just that Claire's ... well, she's gotten very suspicious of Prissy. Too suspicious, you know? She seems to think she's out to get her."

Paul gave Jason a meaningful stare. "Yeah, well, she may be right." He watched Jason a moment, then said, "You're pretty worried about her, aren't you?"

Jason's throat went dry. He wondered how much he should say. On one hand, he didn't want to put off Paul - though he'd hate for him to think they were going to bring unwanted drama into his life - but on the other hand, a few things *had* been bothering him, and it wasn't as if he had anyone else to talk to. "A little bit. Yeah. She's not ... herself exactly. And I think it's more than the pregnancy."

"She contacted me the other day. She asked me to put her in touch with Stephanie Banks."

"Stephanie Banks?"

"Her brother's old high school sweetheart. She's living in Arizona now."

"Why?"

Paul shrugged. "She said she wanted to talk with her about Tim. Said she's been reading his journals and wanted to clarify some things."

"Shit."

"Eh?"

"I told her to stay away from those damned things. She agreed it isn't good for the baby if she's upset." His sandwich lost its taste. "She was reading Tim's entries from middle and high school, and getting upset about it. Tim wrote a lot about Prissy, and I think maybe that's what's made Claire so ... *paranoid.*"

Paul held his hands up. "Oops. You didn't hear it from me, then, okay?"

"I won't say anything. But I do need to get those journals out of her hands."

They sat in silence, Paul devouring his lunch, Jason poking at his, and then Paul spoke. "You said she was getting paranoid. Was that a figure of speech, or literal?"

Jason thought of Claire pounding her crutch on the floor, shrieking at him to go look at her father. There'd been absolutely nothing wrong with the old man. He recalled her vacant stares, her worrying that her mother was plotting against her somehow. If these things didn't qualify as paranoia, he didn't know what did. "Unfortunately, it's a little more literal than I'd like it to be."

Paul wiped his mouth and started on the Ritz, producing a travel-size can of EZ Cheese to squirt on them. "Stephanie's a psychiatrist, you know."

"She is?"

"Yes. And she's planning a trip here in a few days to see Claire." He blushed. "And me. Claire doesn't want Prissy to know anything about it, so don't tell her. Anyway, do you think maybe Claire would like to ... you know ... *talk* to her or something?"

Jason wondered if that might have been Claire's actual plan. *But does she even realize she's gotten so ... high strung? Or that Stephanie Banks is a shrink?* He didn't think so. "That might be a good thing."

Paul switched subjects, but Jason wasn't listening. He finished out the lunch hour, watching airplanes take off and land, his thoughts hovering around Claire like a swarm of hungry bees circling a flower.

Though he hated to admit it, he was looking forward to his short trip to Denver, to a night off.

***

Mother brought up a lunch tray not ten minutes after Claire heard her pull in the driveway. She had forced herself to work after Aunt Babs left and her good mood had partially returned. Once she'd gotten back to work, her appetite returned and she'd devoured four of the eight cookies. Now she pushed the little white bag behind the laptop screen and forced herself to smile as she accepted the tray. There was a cup of soup, some lime Jell-O infused with cottage cheese, both nestled on paper doilies, a grilled cheese sandwich, and a glass of milk. All in all, it looked like it belonged on the cover of *Woman's Day* circa 1977.

The cookies hadn't dampened her newly returned appetite. "Mmm, this smells good." Claire pushed the computer out of the way, and Mother set the tray on the desk. "Enjoy." She hesitated. "What are you doing?"

"Designing a new website for a funeral home chain."

"That's rather morbid. Should you be doing that while you're pregnant?" She sounded distracted.

Claire looked at her and saw she wasn't looking at the computer screen, but at the cookie bag behind it. *Whatever.* "Thanks for lunch."

"My pleasure, dear. I'll be back later for the tray."

"No hurry, I'm going to work while I eat."

Mother raised an eyebrow. "Don't work too hard. You need your rest."

Claire nodded. Mother left her in peace.

She took the dishes off the tray so she could pull the computer back into position and was soon reading email and eating the tasteless sandwich. Mother favored Wonder Bread and American cheese slices. *Same as when I was a kid.* It was all right, but her son would get real cheese on seed bread and something tastier than Campbell's.

She quickly looked over her email - there were two new client queries and that made her happy. Then she opened Facebook and accepted Stephanie Banks' friend request.

Steffie had only about thirty friends, which made Claire feel special to be asked. She had lots of photos of the Arizona high desert, especially Brimstone, the town where she lived and worked. *Where Tim intended to bring me to after he and Steffie got settled.* It was a weirdly attractive place that mostly clung to the side of a hill. A historical monument, there was very little growth allowed there, and Claire thought it would be fun to visit someday, maybe take a road trip with Jason and the baby. *A family road trip.* She smiled at the thought. Maybe Steffie would show them around.

She clicked through Steffie's profile pictures and recognized her face from childhood. Her rich auburn hair was long now, pulled back in a ponytail in half the photos. It looked good. She'd matured into a beautiful woman, her tall lanky frame softened with curves now.

Claire browsed Steffie's timeline photos, then clicked the albums and stopped at one, titled "Throwbacks."

And there was the Steffie Banks that Claire remembered: the perm, the glasses, the braces. Underneath it all, she could see that Stephanie would grow into her beauty, but at a glance, it wasn't an easy thing to spot. She hadn't been homely by any means, just plain, most of her features concealed by the large glasses and bad perm.

Claire clicked through the pictures and her heart swelled when she saw one of Timothy. He had his cast on - it must have been taken right after the accident. There were several more of him. Her vision blurred by tears, she scrolled through images of Tim and Steffie at an amusement park, hiking a trail, and on Halloween as Bonnie and Clyde. There were even a few photos that featured Claire herself, always smiling, always with one of Tim's arms around her. Tears spilled over; she missed him fiercely. *I wish you were still alive, big brother!*

And then the memory of the terrible IM shattered her.

I'm not dead.

I'm not dead. And I'm coming back.

Her skin crawled. *Who would do such a thing?* Anger swelled and she wished she hadn't remembered. Work had done a fine job pushing it out of her mind, but now it roared back with such vicious determination she felt dizzy. *Who would do that?*

She moved her cursor to log out and paused. An idea struck her; an idea she wasn't sure she liked at all. But it gnawed.

I'm not dead.

I'm not dead. And I'm coming back.

She moved to Facebook's search box, her cursor hovering there as the memory replayed.

Who is this? she'd asked.

Timothy Martin.

Claire shuddered.

Before she had time to overthink, she found herself typing *Timothy Martin* into the search.

There were dozens of them, and as she scrolled past unfamiliar faces, Claire began to feel at ease. And then one stopped her cold. She leaned in close, blood thrumming in her ears, the dizziness returning. *Holy shit. It's him! It's Tim!* She clicked the photo, her hands quaking as she searched his page. He only had one photo up - it was taken a year before he'd died, on Christmas. She moved to the "About" section.

Graduated from Snapdragon High

Worked at Snapdragon Power and Light

Studied art in Brimstone, Arizona

"Oh, my God." Claire clicked to "Details about You." It was blank. She went to "Family." Blank. There was no contact information. "It can't be." She glanced back up at the profile photo. It was definitely her brother. She clicked on "Relationship Status." *It's complicated, with Ashley Perkins* "What the hell?"

She went to Ashley Perkins' page. It was private, so she saw no information except that she lived in Michigan and had Tim listed as a love interest.

It was as if a hole had opened and Claire had tumbled down, down, into a cold and alien place. Blood hummed and buzzed, sweat dampened her brow and upper lip, and she was shaking. *This is too much. It isn't real. It isn't real. I'm losing my mind.* She went back to Tim's page. Nothing had changed. "It can't be." Her mind was a stripped gearshift, grinding, unable to catch. She slammed her laptop shut and sat, unable to move, barely breathing.

I'm not dead.

I'm not dead. And I'm coming back.

Jason in the Middle

"I'm so worried about our little Carlene," Prissy said as she fed Frederick tomato soup. He seemed famished, his eyes traveling to the bowl, urging her to spoon faster. *The poor man.* "Did I forget to give you your Ensure this morning? I'll just bet I did. Shame on me! I'm sorry, sweetheart."

He moaned something around the spoon.

"Oops, you're dribbling again. Let me just get that." She wiped his face with a paper towel. "As I was saying, Carlene isn't herself. Not *at all*. It's probably just pregnancy hormones. That's what her doctor says, anyway. Did I tell you that, against my medical advice, she left Dr. Hopper to go back to that young female physician who was kicked off the staff at Snapdragon General for a while? I don't think she's a very good doctor. What do you think?"

Frederick just looked at her, then shifted his eyes to the soup.

She began spooning again. "Jason and I are both worried about her. She's become paranoid. Just like Timothy did, remember? I wonder if paranoia or schizophrenia runs in your family, Frederick. Do you know?"

Frederick shook his head.

"You're sure? Because there are no mental problems in *my* family." She chuckled. "The Bakers have always been so sane they're downright boring! They rarely even develop a neurosis. It *must* be from your side." She ladled the last of the soup into his mouth.

His hand clamped on her wrist and the spoon clattered to the floor. His eyes on hers, he worked his mouth. "Ooh," was all that came out.

"Well! It's nice to see you responding, Frederick!" She smiled. "You can let go now."

"Ooh!" His hand tightened, but she continued smiling until he finally sighed and released his bony grip.

"That's my good little patient." She took the tray and moved to the door, hoping he wasn't on the verge of a minor stroke. "I'll come right back with your medication so you can relax and have a nice long afternoon nap."

He didn't try to reply, but his hard gaze stayed on her until she shut the door. It disturbed her, that stare, and she hoped he wasn't developing any new problems. Worried, she carried the tray downstairs. Poor Timothy had shown some signs of paranoia as a teen, but she'd only really seen them when he was in his early twenties and she'd brought him home from Arizona after his accident. The accusations, the furtiveness. She'd attributed it to his alcoholism, but now Carlene - who certainly wasn't drinking - exhibited similar symptoms. Perhaps it was something both had inherited from the Martin twins, their fathers. The twins' mother had certainly been a high-strung woman - perhaps it went deeper than Prissy had ever realized. The way Frederick had grabbed her wrist told her she might be treading too close to a family secret. *The poor man is probably ashamed.* She'd have to get on her computer again and see if she could ferret out anything about the Martin family.

***

Jason had been thinking of working late, but Paul insisted he get home to his pregnant wife since he'd be in Denver the following night. As much as Jason dreaded the stress waiting for him at home, he knew Paul was right.

He'd thought about it all day and still didn't know how he might convince Claire to give up her brother's journals. He didn't want to upset her. If he brought up the health of the baby, she'd listen. Probably.

He thought it was likely the journals were the primary reason Claire had been so anxious lately. He hoped Stephanie Banks could help her.

He turned onto Morning Glory Circle. The houses appeared neat and perfect. Windows glowed with golden light: It was dinnertime and families had gathered. The lights were on at Prissy's, too, including Claire's, and as he pulled into the driveway, he saw Hank and Crystal Lowell standing on their front porch. They waved and smiled.

As he locked the car, the Lowells appeared at the edge of the driveway. "Hey, Jason, how are you?" Hank called.

"Okay." Jason, happy for a reprieve, joined the couple. "How are you guys?"

"We're great," said Hank.

Crys giggled and waved an envelope. "Somebody's trying to blackmail us."

Hank chuckled. "They sure are."

"Blackmail? How is that funny?" Jason asked.

"Come under the porch light and you can read the note for yourself. It's pretty pathetic."

On the porch, Crys handed him the note. "Out loud, please." She grinned.

"I know what you did last summer," Jason read. "Seriously?"

"Keep going," Hank said. "It gets better."

"I know all about you and your dirty secrets. Every single one of them. I know about the incident two years ago, and I know why you had to move here from San Diego." Jason looked up. "San Diego?"

"Our blackmailer has done his homework. We did move here from San Diego." Crys grinned. "Totally true. Go on."

"I know about your legal problems and your criminal past. Make no mistake: I can have your children taken away with one phone call to Social Services. I am watching you and your rude dogs and rude children and if you mention this letter to anyone, know that your terrible sins shall be revealed."

Hank and Crystal burst into laughter.

"Why is this funny?" Jason asked again.

"Because, despite my motorcycle and beard and Crys' choice of hair color and tattoo placement, neither of us has even had a parking ticket," Hank said.

"We don't even have bad credit," Crys added. "And our boys are A students."

"Hell, we're not even members of the Communist party." Hank guffawed.

Crys looked at Hank. "Is that even a thing anymore?"

"You got me." He chuckled then looked at Jason. "There is absolutely nothing to dig up on us. We're as clean as the driven."

"So, what does this person want? I mean, blackmailers usually want something, right?"

"We have no idea," Crys said.

"None," Hank added. "And this isn't the first letter we've had. We've gotten pretty much the same thing every year or so since we moved here."

"It's just … bizarre," Crys said.

"It sure is," Jason agreed. "Have you gone to the police?"

"I suppose we should since the guy doesn't want us to," Hank said. "But we haven't bothered. It's bullshit. If I had to say what he wants, it's to rattle our cage."

"Why?"

"Why not?" the Lowells said in unison and laughed again.

Then Crystal looked at Hank. "Maybe we should show it to Roddy sometime."

Hank shrugged. "Not a bad idea."

Crystal turned to Jason. "How's Claire?"

"She's hanging in there, looking forward to moving." He told them a little about their new house, then bid them goodnight.

Entering Prissy's kitchen, he smelled tuna casserole and heard that never-ending Andrews Sisters record. If he never heard that song again, it would be too soon. He walked softly to the stairs and went up, proud of himself for evading Priscilla and her constant questions. Claire wasn't the only one looking forward to moving; Priscilla was okay, just a little too in his face.

Just as he knocked on Claire's door, Prissy called up the stairwell, asking him to come back down.

"Jason? Come in!" Claire called in a no-nonsense voice.

He wished he'd worked late. "Hi sweetheart," he said as he opened the door.

"Jason! Please come down here for just a jiffy, won't you?" called Prissy.

Jason rolled his eyes. "I'd better go see what she wants before she comes up. She's got a tuna casserole on. Do you want to suffer through that? I can run over to Wokamundo and be back in half an hour."

"Whatever," said Claire with no hint of interest.

He really looked at her. "Are you all right?"

She nodded, but her eyes were rimmed in red. "Just emotional," she said.

"You can tell me-"

"Jason!" Prissy bellowed. "Please come see me!"

"Orange chicken?" he asked. "That always cheers you up."

"Yeah, that'd be good. And some kung pao."

"I'll be right back with the food. Hang in there."

He trotted downstairs and just as he arrived on the kitchen threshold, Prissy, her back to him, bellowed his name again.

"I'm right here."

She turned and beamed at him, a snapdragon-printed yellow apron over her powder blue velour jogging suit. "You scared me, sneaking up on me like that." She smiled, reached up, and pinched his cheek. "That's a naughty boy."

"What do you want?"

"I thought the three of us could have dinner together. I have TV trays and folding chairs I'd like you to take upstairs."

"That's nice, but I don't think Claire's in the mood tonight."

"Nonsense. It's just what she needs. She loves my tuna casserole. Olives are my secret ingredient. When she was little, she used to eat olives off her fingers while she watched me make it." Prissy hesitated. "No, I think that was Timothy, but Claire loves olives too. Silly me, mixing them up. I must be getting old."

The Andrews Sisters began fresh instructions about sitting under the apple trees. *God, I wish that record would break in half!* "Let me check with Claire and see if she's up for it. I really doubt she is."

He turned to leave, but Prissy put a hand on his elbow. "I think she'd love a surprise. A tuna surprise."

He managed a smile. "I disagree. She's not in the mood for any kind of surprise."

Prissy's smile disintegrated. "Jason, I'm so worried about my little girl. I was telling Frederick I'm worried. He is, too. He loves her. I just don't know what's wrong with her. I asked Frederick if there's any mental illness on his side of the family tree and he says no, but something's wrong - and I know my side is the salt of the earth."

Jason recalled Prissy telling Claire that Frederick was unresponsive - that though the lights were on, no one was home. Jason and Claire knew better of course, but Prissy had seemed to believe it, and Jason wondered if she was aware of the inconsistency in her logic. "Dr. Putnam has assured her it's simply hormones and stress."

Prissy looked wounded. "But I take care of *all* her needs. There's no reason for her to be stressed."

"Claire is very independent, Prissy. She doesn't like relying on other people; that in itself stresses her out. She needs to be in her own place, in charge. That will make her happy." He spoke gently, diplomatically, but Prissy's eyes welled and overflowed with tears. *Ah, shit.*

"I just want to take care of my baby girl." She looked up at him with teary eyes.

Kung Pao Secrets

Claire's stomach was growling by the time Jason returned with the fragrant Wokamundo bags. Even Mother's vile tuna casserole had started smelling good, but she'd happily told Prissy the fishy odor made her queasy so she couldn't eat it. Even so, her mother had remained for long minutes, standing behind her, staring down at the computer screen, taking in the mortuary website she was building, and not approving of it; Claire could tell by the thin lips and cocked brow.

She drove Claire nuts until a text from Jason arrived saying he was on his way. Then, with a comment that spicy food wasn't good for the baby Mother left before Claire could argue with her.

And, oh boy, was she in the mood to argue. It was a little bit of everything - the revelations in Tim's journals, the instant message allegedly from him, and finding him on Facebook had all served to put her so far over the edge that only by concentrating on work had she avoided a meltdown.

Jason rapped on the door and came in bearing two big bags. It smelled so good that her stomach sang a greeting.

Jason laughed. "You *are* hungry!"

"I am." Claire waited while he dished up portions on paper plates. While they ate, he told her about his day at work and she told him about her mortuary webpage and that Babs had paid a visit. She carefully told him of Babs' concerns, testing his mood. He'd become impatient with talk of Timothy and Mother, and she didn't want to risk an argument. She'd decided not to bring up the IM - it was too weird - but she intended to show him Timothy's alleged Facebook page. "When we're done eating, I'm going to show you proof I'm not crazy."

"I know you're not crazy." Jason smiled and popped a cream cheese wonton in his mouth. "Tell me now."

"Fine, I'll tell you now, but I'm going to show you after dinner."

"Okay. What is it?"

"I was on Facebook today - for the first time in ages - and I decided to look up Timothy Martin."

"Wait. Why would you look him up on Facebook?"

Claire waved the question away. "It doesn't matter." She saw the concern in his eyes, but went on eagerly. "The point is ... he *is* on Facebook!"

Jason's chewing slowed to a stop. "What?"

"He's on Facebook." She saw the concern in his eyes - the look that told her he was worried about her. "It's *him,* Jason. Complete with a bunch of his old pictures, a profile saying where he worked and went to school, and even some friend connections. I couldn't believe it, but it's him!"

Jason stared at her and she understood what he was thinking.

"No, I don't think he's alive, Jase. I think *Mother* must have created an account for him."

"But ... why?"

She shrugged. "It's her sick, twisted form of denial, I suppose. It's just one more way of keeping him alive."

Jason stared at her.

"Here, let me show you. Hand me my laptop."

"And you want to hear the sickest part?" She took the computer.

"I, uh ... sure."

"He's 'in a relationship' with some girl in Michigan!" She booted, impatiently waiting as it came to life and connected to the Internet.

"What the hell?" asked Jason. "How? And *why?*"

"I told you, she's batshit." She'd lost all interest in her food - her only craving now was to see Jason's face when he caught sight of Tim's profile. "She's never accepted his death, and-"

"But to have him on Facebook all these years later? And in a *relationship?*"

"Yep." Jason was finally getting a glimpse of just how crazy her mother really was, and that was more satisfying than all the kung pao in Snapdragon. She logged into Facebook, and typed *Timothy Martin* into the search. A list pulled up and she scrolled down. "There are a few of them." Jason leaned close to watch.

She didn't see her brother's profile and the first spark of panic kindled in her stomach. "He wasn't too far down," she said. "Help me look for his picture." She scrolled further. To the end. And back up to the beginning. And back down. "What the hell?"

Jason remained silent beside her.

She scrolled back up, very slowly. "Son of a bitch. She must have deleted the account." She paused, knowing what Jason was thinking. She looked at him - and his eyes confirmed her suspicion. "And that means she's listening to us *right now!*" She spoke in a whisper and grabbed her cell, turned on Pandora. "Here, put this by the vent. It'll keep her from hearing."

Jason didn't look angry.

He didn't even look worried.

He looked heartbroken, but he took the phone and placed it near the vent. Blondie's *One Way or Another* was loud and clear.

"I swear," Claire said. "Tim's profile was here. It was *right* here!"

Jason swallowed hard and stared at his hands.

.

He can't even look at me ...
She wished she hadn't deleted the IM on her computer.

***

"I'm sure it will sort itself out," Jason said. He saw both earnestness and panic in her eyes - and something else, too: self-doubt. "I think it's time to give up the journals, Claire."

Her eyes narrowed. "You don't believe me."

"It isn't that. It's just ..."

"It's just *what*, Jason? That you believe that *I* believe what I'm saying? And why do you want the journals?"

Jason shook his head but didn't meet her eyes. "I think you're getting very upset over a lot of little things - and I think those journals are at the root of it all."

Claire's jaw flexed.

"Ever since you started reading them, you've become ..."

"Go ahead, say it. Paranoid? Is that the word you're looking for?"

Jason sat very still, knowing he was treading on precarious ground. "I didn't say that, Claire."

Her eyes were glassy, hard ... hateful. "Only because you don't have the guts! You're so damned careful around me - like I'm some kind of ... glass figurine or something. Well, I'm sick of it, Jason. Say what you mean; if you have any respect for me at all, don't mince words."

Anger bubbled inside him now. "Fine," he said. "Yes. Paranoid. That's *exactly* the word I was looking for." He began pacing. "Do you feel better now? Does it make you feel good to hear it?" His face was hot with rage and his hands were fists. "Well? Is that what you wanted to hear?"

Claire blinked at him, and as her eyes filled with tears, his heart sank. "God, Jason. I'm so sorry." She was weeping, her body wracked by sobs.

He sat and put an arm around her. "I didn't mean it, sweetie. I just-"

"No," she said. "You're right! And I don't know what's happening to me!"

"It's just the hormones. Like Dr. Put-"

"Fuck Dr. Putnam!" she cried between sobs. "Fuck Dr. Hopper! Fuck Mother! Fuck them all! And fuck you, too!"

"Claire, please, listen to me. Just calm down. You *can't* keep getting upset like this. You *can't*. You need to take it easy for the baby's sake!"

She looked into his eyes. "I think I'm going crazy, Jason. I really think I am."

"You're not going crazy, babe. You just need to spend less time with things that ... upset you."

Claire sniffed, wiped her eyes, and looked at him. She seemed calmer now. "You're right. Just being here upsets me. I've got to get out of here. I hate that you're right, but the things I read in the journals today ... you need to read them, Jason." Her eyes pleaded. "Do that for me. Read the journals."

"Okay. Then let me have them. I'll keep them safe, and after the baby comes, you can read them all you want - when you're a little more ..."

"God, don't say stable!" She laughed.

He chuckled. "When you're *calmer*."

She wiped her eyes. "I'll give all of them to you. I'm not sure I want to read any more, anyway. Not after today."

"Good." Jason hugged her close and stroked her hair. "Now, I want you to promise me you won't let yourself get upset, okay? The sooner you feel better, the sooner we can leave. Promise?"

"I promise."

He kissed her on the forehead and wondered if this moment of clarity would last, or if in a few hours, she'd be raging on again. He wasn't sure he could take this much longer - wasn't sure *Claire* could - and tried not to think what the next five months might be like.

While she was calm, he decided to take the plunge. "Paul needs me to go out of town overnight - to Denver. He asked me to look over a jet for him."

"Denver?"

"I'll only be gone one night. I leave tomorrow morning."

She smiled. "It sounds like he trusts your judgment. That's wonderful, but I'll miss you."

Relief washed over him. "I'll miss you, too."

PART 3

Mother's Little Helpers

"Oh, what a tangled web we weave,
When first we practice to deceive."

- Sir Walter Scott

By Dawn's Early Light

Claire stretched and drew her curtains wide on a bright Friday morning. She and Jason had avoided topics that could touch off a disagreement and had enjoyed the rest of their evening watching *Murder on the Orient Express*. She'd packed all of Tim's journals in a box Jason then stowed in the Prius with his overnight bag, after she warned him not to leave them in the apartment in case Mother broke in again.

Claire had thought about it all through the movie and decided Jason was right: The journals were part of her problem. Mother, however, was a bigger part but there was no point in saying so to Jason. She would concentrate on working, reading, watching movies, and resting up for the baby's sake. And her own - she needed Dr. Putnam to take her off bed rest so she could get out of this matriarchal prison and into her own house. She thought of Babs, and knew her offer to come over daily would encourage the doctor to decide in her favor. *Maybe Aunt Babs can come with me to my appointment and tell the doctor she'll be helping out. That should guarantee I get out of this damned house!*

Claire was surprised that the journals' absence was such a relief. She also was happy that Jason would be seeing for himself some of the horrible things Mother had done to Timothy.

Tap tap tap. The sounds came from down the hall. *Tap tap tap.*

What the hell is that? She pulled on her robe and headed out of the room, relieved to find her door wasn't locked. First she looked toward the sounds - toward Timothy's room, toward the staircase - but saw nothing. Then she headed for the bathroom, pleased with how easily she used the crutches now. She thought she could make it downstairs by herself if Jason wasn't around to carry her.

Back in the hall, she heard the tapping again and followed the sounds past her room. When she arrived at Tim's room she heard it again. *Tap tap tap.* In full stealth mode, she tried the doorknob. It was unlocked.

"Claire!" Mother burst from the room, pulling the door shut behind her. "What are you doing here?"

"What are you doing in there?"

"I was vacuuming." Mother blocked the door. "That must be what you heard." She looked Claire up and down.

"I heard tapping, Mother. Not vacuuming. What's going on in there?"

"Nothing, absolutely nothing. Why, you probably heard a branch tapping a window, or maybe a woodpecker hammering on the eaves. Little monsters cause so much damage, but we love them, don't we?"

Claire found herself being guided back to her room. She halted midway. "If nothing's going on in there, why can't I see? I want to see that nothing's going on." She felt her insides knotting and willed herself to stay calm.

Priscilla gave her a smile loaded with false understanding. "There's nothing to see. Don't you trust your own mother's word?"

She considered arguing then thought of her promise to Jason, and the health of the baby. *I can't let myself get so worked up about little things.* "Of course I do, Mother."

Mother smiled and led her back to her room. "I'll bring you a nice breakfast in just a few minutes. How do eggs sound?"

"Eggs sound wonderful."

She sat on the edge of the bed for a long time after Mother left, listening for more taps.

But the house was silent.

A Dragon Named Priscilla

"We haven't spent enough time planning the potluck," Priscilla told Babs. They sat at the kitchen table drinking coffee as *Apple Tree* played on and on in the living room.

"We put out flyers announcing it's this weekend," Babs said. "Everyone knows. You don't need to worry." She had reluctantly answered Prissy's command to come over and plan the yearly potluck that celebrated spring's imminent arrival, the block party that meant the Snapdragon Festival was only a few weeks away. Though it was still very cold at night, the snapdragons were already beginning to bloom all around the sac. It promised to be a beautiful spring.

"Without plans, things fall apart," Prissy said. "You know that, Barbara. Why-"

"Of course," Babs cut in. "All I'm saying is that it doesn't need to be policed. I think people should bring whatever they want. There's no need to dictate to them. It takes all the fun out of it."

"And we'll end up with six bowls of potato salad and a few plates of cookies. People need variety, Barbara Rose!" Pris paused. "Without Burke Collins and his barbecue, we don't even have his famous hamburgers. Everyone loved them. Burke wasn't good for much, but those burgers of his were a real treat."

"We don't have burgers," Babs said, "but Carl is going to barbecue. He'll be grilling hot dogs."

"Hot dogs are disgusting," Pris said. "Have you ever read what's in them?"

"People love hot dogs."

"But-"

Out of patience, Babs sat up straight and looked Pris in the eye. "Take them or leave them, Prissy."

"Couldn't Carl consider making hamburgers?"

"No, Priscilla. Be happy he's willing to make hot dogs. And can't we listen to something other than that song? I swear, I hear it in my sleep. It's probably doing something awful to Claire's baby."

"What *are* you babbling about, Barbara? It's a lovely song. My favorite. It's so happy, it can only be good for a fetus to listen to."

Babs sighed. Priscilla had always been ridiculously attached to that damned old song. Even as a child, she played it. Babs had asked Pris why, but all she'd ever said was that it was her father's favorite, and that he played it every time they were alone together. It was "their" song. Prissy's relationship with her father had always been a strange one, though. They were closer than most fathers and daughters. *Too* close, if Babs were to be honest. Right up until he dropped dead.

"How's Claire doing? I'd certainly like to visit with her when we're done." Babs watched Priscilla closely.

"But you just visited her yesterday, Barbara. Remember? While I was at the Auxiliary luncheon you skipped because you had a repairman coming over?"

Babs didn't believe Claire had told her mother about the visit, but of course she knew. Pris always knew. Looking her straight in the eye, she spoke. "Yes, I looked in on her yesterday and I'm very concerned for her well-being."

"No need, she's fine. You're not her mother, after all. Now let's get back to work-"

"I feel like her mother, Pris. She was at my house as often as at home. She came to me for help with everything from making her Halloween costumes to doing her homework. She came to me to talk about growing up, about boys, and just about everything else, including you."

"Well then," Pris huffed. "She was using you because she came to me about all those things, too, including *you*. But I didn't spoil her by giving her bags of overpriced cookies nearly every time I saw her."

The Chesapeakes. Pris saw the bag - that's how she knows. Chesapeakes had been something Babs and Claire had shared since she was a little girl.

"You have no need to worry about Carlene," Pris was saying. "She's *my* daughter, not yours."

"I'll worry about whomever I please. You don't own Claire. Why, you can't even be bothered to remember to call her by the name she has chosen."

"That ungrateful girl," Pris said. "How dare she - how *dare* she just throw out the name *I* bequeathed her when she was born. It's *my* middle name and she's *my* daughter. She has no respect for me, none at all!"

Tears shone in Prissy's eyes as she waited for Babs to tell her it wasn't her fault, that Claire was just a headstrong young woman and she shouldn't take it personally. That's what she would have done even a month ago, but Babs' dislike of Pris had been growing, going into full bloom when Geneva-Marie was murdered and all Pris Martin did was celebrate the fact that her competition for Auxiliary president had vanished.

"I can't believe how ungrateful my daughter is," Priscilla was saying. "And here I've taken her in and fed her and tended to her ..." She hitched a sob. "I just don't understand her. Timothy was so sweet and good, but Carlene-"

"Claire, Priscilla. Her name is Claire. You complain that she doesn't respect your wishes, why don't you try respecting hers?"

Prissy's eyes widened. "What? You're on *her* side? She didn't care how much changing her name hurt me, she did it anyway."

"Get over it, Pris. She didn't like your middle name, and as I recall, when we were children, you complained about it, too. You wished you had a better middle name. And a different first name. You used to say you wanted to be Anastasia Marie Baker-Wellbourne. You kept telling me you were going to change it when you grew up."

"I was just a silly child." Prissy's face was white with red spots on her cheeks. "You can't compare childish fantasies to what Carlene did."

"*Claire* carried through on the name change. You didn't."

"Because I grew up and respected the names *my* mother chose for me."

Pris' hand shook, slopping coffee, and Babs pushed down the instinct to make nice. "Fine. Let's get finished with this potluck nonsense. I have other things to attend to."

Pris stared at her. "What's so important that you call our potluck nonsense? Don't you care about our street's welfare?"

"I'm having lunch with Father Andy," Babs said, rising. "I don't want to be late." It was a fib, but she hoped it wouldn't be for long.

"Oh?" Prissy looked surprised, her manufactured tears forgotten. "Whatever for?"

"I'm thinking of running for president of the Ladies' Auxiliary."

"Against *me*?" Priscilla's face flushed as she pushed away from the table.

"Yes. It's time for a change and since poor Geneva-Marie can't do it, I will."

Priscilla followed Babs to the front door. "How dare you? I'm your best friend!"

"Priscilla, friends care about one another. You only care about yourself."

Pris spoke through clenched teeth. "How *dare* you? After all I've done for you, after all the help I gave you and Carl when he almost lost your house to his gambling addiction."

Babs, her hand on the door handle, looked at Prissy. "We appreciated your help and we thanked you many times. And that was a long time ago - and even then I knew why you really helped us." She depressed the latch.

"Because you were my friend and I was looking out for you."

"No, Prissy, that's not why. You did it so you could keep me - and Carl - in your pocket. And it worked. I've spent years helping you carry out your street parties and just about everything else you plan, and I did it without expectations beyond civility. And how many times did Carl clean out your gutters and help you around the yard? You even asked him to put up your Christmas lights last year. And Carl did it with a smile. But plan on hiring someone this year because when Geneva-Marie was sprawled out there dead in the street, her head blown into a million pieces, all you could do was crow that you didn't have to worry about an opponent this election. I couldn't keep my blinders on any longer. I saw you as you really are. You're ugly, Priscilla. Your soul is ugly. I feel sorry for you. You care about no one but yourself!"

Priscilla's mouth worked, but nothing came out.

"You're only president because everyone is afraid of you, and you know it. You're the only one who wants to put a homeless camp out by the airport, where they're so isolated that they can't even try to get work. You're the only one who wants that, Priscilla. Most of the time, you do right by the auxiliary, but moving the homeless just so you don't have to look at them is too much. You were ice cold about Geneva-Marie and her family, and you're ice cold about the homeless. No one like you should ever be in charge of anything beyond neighborhood potlucks! *That* is why I'm running against you."

"Wait-"

"I'll only wait if you let me go upstairs to visit Claire."

"She's asleep."

"And Frederick? It's been years since I've laid eyes on him. I'd like to see him, too. Is he asleep, as well?"

Priscilla blanched. "He always has a long nap after breakfast! You know that. The poor man," she said, adding a quaver to her voice. "I take the best care of him I can ..."

"Goodbye, Priscilla." Babs left, shutting the door quietly behind her because slamming it would please Prissy. And before she'd even got back to her own house, she'd made a lunch date with Father Andy.

All those years. All those years kowtowing to Priscilla and keeping quiet, just to avoid the inevitable confrontation if she so much as questioned what the woman said. Babs had spent years eating her own words, pushing away anger and resentment. *No more.* She marched into her house and made a cup of coffee - she only drank tea because Prissy did. *Prissy Prissy Prissy!* No more.

She thought of Claire, sweet Claire, stuck up there in that bedroom like a princess in a castle, guarded by a dragon. She had to talk with Jason; he needed to get his wife out of Priscilla's house. If Paul Schuyler's rental wasn't ready, the young couple could stay with her and Carl until it was.

***

Claire, feeling hopeful for the first time since her accident, returned to her desk, intending to go back to work, but she kept thinking about what she had heard through the vent. Sweet Aunt Babs' tone was what first caught her attention and made her move to listen in, straining to hear over the Andrews Sisters; she'd never heard Babs raise her voice before. And she'd raised it to Mother.

At first, it made her happy that Babs wouldn't let Mother push her around. It made her want to cheer. Then, when Babs stood up for Claire, she had to fight back tears.

Maybe I'm not losing my mind after all. Smiling to herself, she realized she wasn't as alone as she'd thought.

She made herself return to work, but kept yawning and finally decided a nap before lunch was in order.

***

The feel of the plane as its wheels lifted from the runway gave Jason a bump of excitement. It wasn't as thrilling as piloting, but still, there was nothing quite like being airborne. He felt like a little boy again. He always did.

He watched out the window as the buildings grew smaller, listened to the muted roar of the plane's engines, and imagined he was in the pilot seat of a 747.

And then Jake Fairview shattered the fantasy by saying, "Denver. Christ, I hate Denver," in that frog-like croak of his.

Jason forced a friendly smile. "Oh yeah? Why's that?"

"I can tell you've never been there in winter, which, by the way, lasts way too long."

Though in no mood for small talk, Jason didn't see how he could ignore the guy without being rude. "Only to the airport. I've never been there long enough to explore the city."

"Well, you're not missing anything. And don't let them fool you with their talk of clean air, green mountains, and legalized marijuana cigarettes. Colorado is just a slightly less Midwestern version of the Bible Belt. And you know how I feel about that." He barked a humorless laugh.

Jason didn't know how Jake felt about the Bible Belt, as a matter of fact, and he wasn't about to ask.

"And Denver is the worst of all." Jake turned in his seat, an undignified pose given his ample size, to stare at Jason with wide, blazing eyes. "Those motherfuckers get eight feet of snow half the year - *half* the got-damn year - and they don't even have the sense to plow the got-damn roads. Hmmph." He straightened in his seat. "Not in the budget, they say. Must be all the marijuana."

"Must be." Jason stared out the window, at the blue-green earth thousands of feet below, and enjoyed a sense of freedom he hadn't experienced in too long. *No wonder they say heaven is in the sky.*

"You know what I think needs to happen," said Jake.

"What's that?"

"I think those fancy Coloradans need to raise the taxes on their handy-dandy legalized pot a little more and use the money to plow the got-damn roads."

Jason chuckled. "You may be onto someth-"

"It's common sense that when it snows, you plow. What kind of fool-idiots build a city in the middle of the got-damn mountains and don't plan for snow? You don't see *that* kind of nonsense in Snapdragon, or anywhere in California. Of course, it doesn't really *snow* in California, not in the cities, anyway, but if it *did* I'd bet my pension *someone* would be plowing the roads ..." and on he went.

Clearly, no amount of apathy was going to stop him. There would be no enjoying this flight and as the man prattled away, Jason found himself suppressing sigh after sigh.

" ... and what *should* have been a *fifteen*-minute drive to the Molly Brown House took forty-five minutes, all because those lazy got-damn sonsabitches can't plow ... "

Jason had an idea. Nothing said *leave me alone* like reading. He reached behind his seat, withdrew one of Timothy's journals, and hoped Jake would take the hint.

"What you reading?" Jake frowned at the journal.

"Uh, it's a ... manuscript my wife wrote. I promised to look it over before she ... sends it to the publishers ... and I really need to get it done."

"She an author, is she?"

"Wants to be, anyway." He opened the journal.

"She any good?"

Jason met the man's eyes. "I don't know yet. I need to read and find out."

Jake sighed and contented himself with piloting the little plane.

Within moments, Jason found himself genuinely involved in the entries. This journal had been on top - Claire said it was the one she was last reading. He saw a paperclip halfway through, marking where she'd left off, but he began at the beginning. It was full of sketches of cars, and poems about Tim's girlfriend Steffie - the woman Paul was flying in from Arizona. *The psychiatrist.*

Then he arrived at the paper clipped page and a knot formed in his gut. *She started lecturing me about abstinence, and I got so mad I talked back and told her that in Sex Ed they said that wet dreams are normal. All guys have them. She got in my face and screamed at me for telling lies in front of my sister.*

"Good stuff?" asked Jake. "Want to read some aloud? I'm a good listener."

"Oh, I don't think my wife would like that. She's very private."

Jake sighed. "Alright, you're the boss."

Lunchtime Confessions

Father Andy smiled at Babs Vandercooth. "I'm glad you'd like to run for Auxiliary president." He sipped his glass of Chardonnay and watched Babs drain hers. He'd been as surprised by the invitation to lunch at the Daffodil Grill as he'd been when she suggested, in no uncertain terms, they start their meal with wine. He happily accepted, in part because he could tell Babs needed to relax. "How long have you been thinking of running?"

The wine pinked her cheeks, giving her a youthful look. "Oh, since this morning when Prissy got under my skin." She paused. "Drink up. I want a second glass."

"Yes, ma'am!" He finished his off. "Maybe you should think it over a while before you decide to run. There's time, you know. I wouldn't want you to do it simply out of spite." But he dearly hoped she would run, and win. After Priscilla Martin's behavior at the Collins funeral, he hadn't been able to make himself have a single kind thought about the woman. She'd flashed Dave Flannigan during Communion, too; and when Andy had given her the Holy Eucharist, the woman had sucked his finger into her mouth, swirled her tongue around it, and looked at him with pure sin in her eyes. *At a funeral!* It was reprehensible that she would dishonor the Collins family that way. Or the church. She didn't deserve to be president, but he'd taken Father Dave's warnings seriously and would not confront her. *God may forgive her, but I don't know if I can.*

"I understand your concerns about my running and I'll sleep on it, but I doubt I'll change my mind." She waved over the server and ordered two more glasses.

"Babs, your disagreement with Priscilla is none of my business, but I would like to know why you've made this decision."

"It's been a long time coming. I've always been Prissy's right hand, and I'm tired of it, but I'll tell you true - what really prompted this ..." She paused while the server replaced the wine glasses. "Cheers. What prompted this was the fact that Priscilla watched them scrape Geneva-Marie's body off the street, calm as you please, then looked me in the eye and told me she was glad she wouldn't have any competition for the presidency. She didn't even pretend to care." Babs sipped her wine. "Father, I don't mean to be a gossip."

"You're not gossiping." Andy watched her. Babs Vandercooth had always been friendly, but shy and retiring, lost in Priscilla Martin's shadow. He'd once overheard someone in the Auxiliary refer to her as Priscilla's lapdog, and he'd secretly thought it apt. Now she had a different look, and he liked it. "You seem very sure of yourself, Babs."

She blinked. "You know, I *do* feel sure of myself. I calmly stood up to Priscilla this morning for the first time in my life - and I've known her since I was a little girl."

"You have the patience of a saint." The words left his mouth before he could stop them, but Babs smiled, a twinkle in her eye.

"Thank you, Father Andy. I think you're right, and I also think I've finally come to my senses. I'd like to explain a little more about what happened."

"My lips would be sealed even if I weren't a priest."

"Yesterday, I visited Claire while Prissy was at the Auxiliary luncheon. That girl doesn't look good, Father. She's too thin to be four months pregnant, and she has dark shadows under her eyes. She'd obviously been crying, and that's not like her. She insisted she was fine, but I know better. She's not fine at all." She swallowed another mouthful of Chardonnay. "This morning when I went back over to talk about the spring potluck we're having this weekend, Pris knew I'd seen Claire, and she wasn't happy about it."

"I would think she'd appreciate you keeping her company."

"No. Prissy doesn't like to share, nor does she like anyone to go upstairs in her house. I've respected that until now. But the point is, for the first time in my life, I argued with her. I'm just so irritated, you know? Between Claire's appearance and Prissy's reaction to Geneva-Marie's death, I can't just stand by any longer. When she began ordering me around - instructing me to tell our neighbors what to bring to the potluck - well, I just lost it."

"I can't imagine you losing it, Babs." He smiled.

She chuckled. "Evidently, for me, standing up for myself is 'losing it'."

They sat back while the server delivered their food. Andy's stomach rumbled with joy at the sight of the spicy chicken burger. As soon as Babs put a fork to her salad, he began eating, and continued until the first hunger pangs were vanquished. "You've known Priscilla a very long time."

"Yes, and she's been good to Carl and me. Many, many years ago, Carl had a flirtation with gambling and we would have lost our house if Prissy hadn't stepped in. I've always felt I owed her for that and I know that debt has been repaid many times over, but I still felt like I owed her - and I recently realized that it's not me being unsure of myself. She encourages it. At the yard and bake sale in January she was bullying Carl, and Quinton Everett overheard." Babs shook her head slowly. "My, oh my. I've never liked the man - we've heard so many unsavory things about him - but he gave her a talking to and by the end of the week, she was no longer a co-signer on our loan. Mr. Everett took care of everything."

"Babs, where did you hear unsavory things about Quinton Everett?"

"Why, I don't know. I've heard them forever. Everyone on the sac knows he has a taste for young men."

"Where did you hear that the first time, can you recall?"

Babs looked at the ceiling, thinking. "Prissy. She told me that years ago when we were taking out our home loan. We were all so young. Quinton was a loan officer back then." She paused, her eyes on him, opening wider in realization. "You don't think she made that up, do you?"

"Let me tell you about Quinton Everett," Andy said. "It's not exactly common knowledge and I don't think he likes to talk about it, so please keep this to yourself."

"All right ..."

"Quinton Everett is a war hero and has a purple heart for an injury he sustained." Andy hesitated. What he was about to say wasn't from the confessional, but it still felt as if he were talking out of turn. *But it's for the good of Quinton and everyone else.* "Quinton's injury destroyed his, uh, testicles."

"Oh, my. I had no idea."

"Of course you didn't. And neither does Priscilla. But she made up the rumor about pedophilia. It's patently untrue. The man has no libido at all."

Babs nodded. "Poor Quinton. But Father, he does always seem to be involved with young boys."

"And girls," Andy said. "Quinton loves kids and can't have any of his own, for obvious reasons. He loves coaching them, teaching them, seeing to it they have what they need. He donates to our Orphaned Children's Fund and many other kids' charities. Big donations. He grew up in the Midwest with three brothers - all of them died in the war."

"But-"

"Volunteers. They all joined willingly to serve their country, but only Quinton came back. He has a great nostalgia for his childhood with his brothers and friends. They were into Little League in a big way. And their church choir. Altar boys, all of them. What he does, he does out of love, not out of lust."

"I never should have taken Prissy at her word."

"You couldn't know."

She hesitated. "Father Andy, I'm ashamed of myself for being a coward."

"What do you mean? I don't understand."

"I hate confrontation so much that I've kept my mouth shut many times over the years. I never had children of my own, so I felt I had no right to say anything when I thought Prissy didn't pay enough attention to Claire - but she was happy to let me take care of her and that made *me* happy. But before that, with her son, Timothy, I really should have spoken up. She was too, um, protective of him."

"Protective?"

Babs nodded. "She never wanted him out of her sight and tried to discourage his friends. She wouldn't let them stay over or let him stay at their houses. But there's more." She finished her wine in one swallow. "When Timothy was about ten she mentioned that when he had nightmares, she had him sleep with her."

Andy raised his eyebrows. "Ten seems a bit old to share a bed with a parent of the opposite sex."

"One day, when he was fourteen, she mentioned it again. Fourteen, Father! But she said it with such innocence that I never questioned it, until one day when I asked Claire if she ever had nightmares. She said she had plenty, so I asked if she slept with her mother on those nights. She looked shocked and told me Prissy had said only cowards have nightmares. Can you imagine saying that to a child?"

Andy gulped down his wine. "That's deplorable. Her treatment of Claire was wrong, but her treatment of her son ... to say the least, it's inappropriate. Seductive." He paused. "Do you think she's tried to seduce other, uh, inappropriate parties?"

"I think she's the reason Father Dave retired early." Babs looked him straight in the eye.

Andy knocked over his empty wine glass. "Excuse me. I wish I could address that." He heard himself stammer. "I can tell you that she tried to entice at least one other ..." He couldn't say it.

"You, Father?" She didn't sound at all surprised.

He gave a bare nod. He wanted to tell her about Priscilla's flashing and finger sucking at the Collins funeral but that was too much like gossip. "She's a rather aggressive woman."

"Prissy thinks that if she wants something, she can have it. Nothing will stop her." The server brought two coffees. Babs stirred hers. "She has always used sex to get what she wants. As handsome as you are, Father Andy, she was only out to get something from you, or to put you in her debt. In her younger days, she was a stunning beauty and it was a rare man who could refuse her." Babs lowered her voice. "Why, she tried to seduce Quinton Everett for years because she wanted a lower interest rate on her house." She went thoughtful. "I think I know now why she hates him so much. Why she spread that vicious rumor. He ignored her."

"No doubt. I suspect that in my case, she wanted me to support her plan to move our homeless shelter out of town."

"Likely," Babs agreed. "And she's hoping you'll stuff the ballot box for her."

Andy nodded.

The server brought the check and Babs snatched it. "My treat."

"Thank you."

She put her Visa on the tray, then sat forward even though there was no one nearby. "Thank you for talking with me about all of this."

"Thank *you*. We've both benefitted, I think."

"We have. I know I'm right about my concern for Claire. Yesterday, I meant to have a frank talk with her and tell her she needs to leave her mother's house, but she seemed too frail, so I didn't bring it up. Tonight, I'm going to phone her husband about it."

"That's a wise decision."

Babs nodded. "I think so, too. I can't give my loyalty to Priscilla anymore. I need to help Claire and Jason, and their baby, and that's what I'll do."

"Good."

"I also want to tell you that I don't need to think overnight about throwing my hat in the ring for the Ladies' Auxiliary. I'm ready to make it official."

"Indeed, I agree. You'll make a fine president."

"I'll run in honor of Geneva-Marie." Babs filled out the check and stood. "Father, are you planning to come to the potluck this Saturday? Carl is going to be grilling hot dogs, much to Pris' displeasure. She wants hamburgers."

Andy chuckled. "Tell Carl to save a couple for me."

Snapping Dragons

After giving Frederick and Carlene their lunches, Prissy, bearing notes addressed to her neighbors, began a brisk walk around Morning Glory Circle. She was still in shock, unable to believe Barbara had thrown a tantrum - even as a child, she had been placid and easygoing. *Must be menopause.* Priscilla could think of no other reason for her recent behavior. None.

The Sachs had a profusion of seedlings lining their walkway, and some were beginning to bloom - all pink, like their garish house. It wasn't creative - they never tried to win the street contest - but perverted as they were, at least they made an effort. Prissy had no desire to speak to that tawdry Audrey, Candy Sachs, so she left a note in the mailbox asking them to provide coleslaw for the potluck.

Duane Pruitt and his houseboy hadn't planted a single flower yet. She stared at the unadorned yard. It wasn't like them. She strode up the front walk as their damned dog barked at her from behind the backyard gate. She rang the bell, then knocked. Finally, the Oriental opened the door a few inches and peered out. "Yes?"

"Would you ask Duane to provide a platter of cookies for the potluck this Saturday?"

The man scrutinized her. "I'll mention it to him, but don't count on us. You must understand that Duane is in mourning."

"Oh, yes, I suppose he would be, but perhaps this will snap him out of it. I see you haven't even planted yet." She tried to see inside, but the house was dark.

The Oriental boy - she'd heard he was thirty-five, but you just couldn't be sure with those people - stared at her, and not in a friendly way. "We won't be participating this year," he said. "Obviously." The word was a coda, cold and unpleasant. He started to shut the door.

"Wait."

He stared at her with suspicious eyes. "What do you want?"

"Is Duane here?"

"He's at work. So am I."

"Oh, how nice. You work from home?"

"Yes. What do you want?"

"What do you do for a living?" She cracked a friendly smile. "I've always assumed you just take care of the house, and cook, and things."

"We both work," the Oriental said, and closed the door right in her face! Fury heated her cheeks and she almost knocked again, but decided it wasn't worth it. This afternoon, she'd spend a little time researching Duane Pruitt's boy toy. She didn't care for the rude little man, not one bit. Not one iota.

She passed the empty Collins house. At least the crime tape had been removed, and she'd seen a van load of Spaniards go in with cleaning tools the other day. Hopefully, it would go up for sale soon and some nice family with a little class would move in.

She swept past Barbara's house without even looking at the snapdragon garden. *Ungrateful woman.* Prissy couldn't believe her behavior. *After all I've done for her, how could she turn on me like that?* Maybe she'd apologize before the potluck, but Prissy was prepared to make do without her and her hot dogs. *She'll come to her senses sooner or later.* Barbara had shocked her with talk of running against her for president, but it was talk and nothing more. Barbara didn't have that kind of backbone.

Young snapdragons shot up around a tree on Lance Etheridge's front lawn. Nothing special, but an attempt, no doubt by Iris. She left a note instructing them to supply pizzas and a warming tray, then crossed the street and left a note for the Crockers, telling them to bring a three-bean salad. She noticed that Bettyanne had done a pretty good job with her snapdragons. Even if she was a klepto, she was good in the garden.

***

Something tickled Claire's nose. She batted it away and turned her face deep into her pillow. *What is that* awful *smell?* She opened her eyes and gasped.

Eyes, glossy and black, like pools of motor oil, stared back at her. She recoiled, shot up and instinctively pulled the bed sheets tight. The stuffed shih tzu - Chopsticks - tumbled off the bed. Placid and freeze-dried in their eternal positions, the other two dogs rested at her feet. *Why? Why are they here?*

Her eyes darted across the room. *Mother? Did she bring them? She must have. But why?* It seemed unlikely. Dead or alive, no one was allowed to touch those dogs. Claire couldn't imagine Mother doing this. *But who?*

She glared at the dead pets. Both faced her, positioned so the marble eyes could pin her in their vacant, glassy, black stares. "Fuck you." She kicked and both fell to the floor.

What's that god-awful smell? It hung in the air, thick and cloying, the chemical fumes burning her nose and making her eyes water. She got out of bed, stared at the stuffed dogs scattered on the floor, and headed toward the door, toward the source of the sharp smell. She peered out. There was no sign of Mother, but the scent was stronger here. It wafted from Timothy's old room.

She looked both ways, then tried the knob, turning it with care. It moved a fraction of an inch and stopped. *Locked. Of course Mother locked it.* Claire jiggled the knob, then knocked, lightly at first, then harder. "Hello? Is anyone in there?" Tim's room, like her own and the bathroom, had an old-fashioned skeleton key lock, so she balanced carefully and bent to look through the keyhole. She saw nothing - Mother had covered the opening. *To keep me from looking inside!*

Only silence from within.

She stood there, enveloped in the fumes wafting from the locked room, trying to make sense of the smell, the dogs. It was useless. In order to complete a puzzle, you had to start with the pieces. But the pieces of this one were blank and held no discernible shape. There wasn't even a starting point.

I'm losing my mind. The recurring thought was a hot spark from a popping fire, and she recoiled from it, pushed it away. *No. I am not going crazy. I am not!*

She returned to her room, half expecting the stuffed dogs to have mysteriously disappeared, but they remained. There was bittersweet comfort in that, and it occurred to Claire that this was a strange thing to take relief in; a signal of how abnormal her life had become.

She sat at the edge of the bed, trying to think; but no matter what route she took, her mind kept bumping into the same thought: *I'm losing it.* Like bumper cars in an overcrowded rink, bumping and colliding into the same horrible thought:

I'mlosingmymindI'mlosingmymindI'mlosingmymind.

She needed to keep herself busy. Though Jason probably hadn't even landed in Denver yet, she felt his absence - a sense of being alone, exposed, unsafe. It bothered her that she'd become so vulnerable, so ... weak.

She gathered the dogs and carried them back to Mother's room, no easy feat with crutches. She placed them carefully on the bed in the same positions she'd seen them the first time. After that, she returned to her room. Deciding to throw herself into work, she opened her laptop and booted up.

I am not going crazy and I won't check to see if Timothy has reappeared on Facebook.

***

The Dunworth sisters were obviously home. Priscilla surveyed their property with distaste. They had a pot of snapdragons near their front porch, but they hadn't planted a thing in the soil. Their yard was stark with bald patches on the winter-yellow lawn. Only a few juniper hedges under their picture window graced the house, which was badly in need of paint. She'd have to talk to them about that, but not today. Instead, she left a note asking them to bring cases of water and soda pop. Surely, they could afford that.

Next door, she saw Earlene Dean's Range Rover in the driveway. Glancing across at Duane's house, knowing it was unlikely he'd do his part, Prissy walked to the Deans' front door and rang the bell. She could hear a TV babbling. There were no snapdragons anywhere to be seen, but that was typical. She knocked and waited. *Enough's enough! They shouldn't live on Morning Glory Circle if they can't participate in our events.* She would ask them to donate some cookies and candy to the potluck. She knocked again and the television snapped off. She waited.

No one came to the door. *Is she trying to pretend she's not there? Is she really that stupid?* Tapping her foot, Prissy rang the bell twice more, then heard a door opening and closing at the rear of the house and the beeps of a car door being unlocked. Earlene, in her Fudge Depot uniform, stepped into the vehicle, not even bothering to look her way.

Prissy went down the walk and blocked the driveway. Earlene backed toward her, and laid on the horn until Prissy stepped aside. When Earlene was even with her, she put her hand on the open window ledge. "Did you not hear the bell, Mrs. Dean? Or my knocking?"

"I don't answswer the door," the woman said, her odd brown eyes not quite looking in the same direction. "I have to get to work." She tapped the gas, but Prissy hung tight.

"This weekend is the spring potluck block party."

Earlene stared at her. "What'sss your point?"

"We would appreciate it if you would contribute something to the event."

Earlene stared hard then finally spoke. "We don't have time for that. Sssaturday is our busiessst day." She sounded like a tire losing air.

"You live here and-"

"Yesss, we do. And we pay our taxess and mow our lawn, ssso leave usss alone." She revved the engine and started backing again.

Prissy stepped back and spoke under her breath. "I know all about you and your husband and those kids of yours, you filthy depraved abomination. You'll change your tune, or *everyone* will know." Earlene only blinked at her like a placid cow and pulled onto the street. Prissy watched the SUV turn onto Daisy Drive, then moved on.

Aida Portendorfer's snapdragon garden was Prissy's only real competition, but as she approached the front door, she didn't worry about it - she would win. Mayor McDonald would see to it. Smiling, she knocked on the door and after a moment, Stan opened it. He smiled but the dog, Poopie-Head or something, started barking. "Hello, Prissy," Stan said. "Aida's in the shower. What can I do for you?"

"Two things. Our little spring potluck is this weekend and I wanted to remind you that if you're inviting extra guests, make sure each one brings something to share. I also wanted to confirm that Aida's making her famous chili. And cornbread, of course."

"I think she's planning on it," Stan said.

"Planning on what?" Aida, her hair wrapped in a towel, shushed Poopie-Head - *thank heaven!* - then joined Stan.

"Chili and cornbread for Saturday?" Prissy asked.

"Of course, wouldn't miss it. Prissy?"

"Yes?"

"Is your daughter alright?"

"Of course. Why do you ask?"

"I ran into Babs yesterday, and she was worried about her."

Prissy saw red, but bit it back. "Carlene is fine. I think Barbara is having a little trouble with the change of life. It's affecting her judgement. Don't take her too seriously; I'm sure it will pass, the poor dear."

"Good. She's such a sweet soul, isn't she? I hope she's not having the night sweats."

Prissy nodded. "I need to get home and see how Carlene's doing. Talk to you later."

She turned and headed to the Stine home. Phyllis' car was in the driveway, but she didn't even want to look at Phyllis with her stretched-out mummy skin. Instead she left a note asking for an extra-large lasagna.

The Halloween house was the last one. She couldn't stand the Lowells. They were slippery and ugly and had motorcycles. Their flowerbeds were blooming as well as Prissy's and Aida's, but that didn't mean much when people lacked class. She put a note in their box asking for an assortment of chips and cupcakes, then returned home.

Prissy poured a big glass of icy cold milk, then headed upstairs with it. Carlene had napped after breakfast, and mentioned she might nap again after lunch. Prissy knew that such exhaustion was normal during pregnancy. Sleep was important, but so was her afternoon milk.

Upstairs, she tapped on Carlene's door.

"Come in." Her voice was clipped and when Priscilla entered she realized her daughter was hard at work - and that, indeed, she did not look well. *Too thin. And her pallor is disturbing.*

"I hope I didn't interrupt you, dear. I just wanted to bring you your milk. I'll be back with a snack as soon as you tell me what you'd like me to make." She set the milk down on the desk beside Carlene, who kept her eyes on her computer screen.

"I'm not hungry, Mother. But thank you."

"You have to *eat,* Car-Claire. You-"

"I said I'm fine." Carlene turned and met her eyes for the first time and Priscilla saw something in them: a spark of anxiety. "Do you smell that, Mother?"

Prissy frowned. "Smell what, dear?"

"I don't know. I've smelled it all morning. It comes and goes before I can identify it."

Prissy sniffed the air. "No, honey. I don't smell anything unusual at all. Tell me, dear, are you ... smelling anything *else*? Oranges?"

Carlene shook her head. "I'm not having a seizure, Mother. You're confusing me with Jason."

"Well, there are a lot of things that can cause this kind of-"

"I'm fine, Mother. I need to keep working. I'm sorry, but I'm on a deadline. Thank you for the milk."

Prissy watched her daughter a moment, but when she sensed Carlene growing impatient, she left the room. She stood in the hall, straightened the wreath - dried white roses - on Carlene's door, then took a few steps and paused to straighten a framed photograph of Timothy's graduation that had been knocked askew. She *tsk*ed, kissed her fingertip and touched her son's handsome smile, then headed into her bedroom where she got out a change of clothes. That's when she noticed the dogs.

General Tso, Chopsticks, and Won Ton were right where they belonged, but something wasn't right, and as she neared, she realized the problem. Chopsticks *always* faced the closet. Now he faced the dresser.

***

Claire turned in her desk chair when the door opened. Mother, face red, nostrils flaring, stared at her.

"You forgot to knock." Claire kept her voice steady, neutral, just like her gaze. She would not let her mother see the anxiety that was eating at her like a cancer.

Mother opened her mouth, then shut it. Long seconds passed before she spoke. "Why were you in my bedroom, Claire?"

Mother's voice was calm, but Claire knew it was an act. It had to be. "I was returning the stuffed dogs that, for reasons I *cannot* comprehend, you brought into my room." Worry tightened its metal bands around her skull. She felt dizzy.

Mother blinked. "Excuse me? *What* are you talking about?"

"Those damned stuffed shih tzus. They were here when I woke up, so I think the real question is why did *you* come into *my* room?"

The hard glint in Mother's eyes dimmed and turned into something worse: concern.

"Oh, Claire, darling." She wrung her hands. "Why don't you take a break from work and tell me what happened? I think you're overdo-"

"Do you mean to tell me you're going to *deny* it, Mother?" Her thoughts raced. This couldn't be happening. *Is she lying to me? She has to be lying!*

Only silence from Mother until, "Did Babs come over again?"

Claire shook her head. "No. And even if she had, I'm certain she wouldn't have touched your precious pets." Her voice shook.

"You don't need to be so angry, Claire."

Claire laughed. "Angry? Me? *Why* should *I* be angry?"

"Well, you sound very angry, dear. And that's not good for the baby."

Claire's eyes bored into her mother's. "You're lying." Her voice choked. "You're lying. I know it."

Mother gasped. "I most certainly am *not*, Claire. Why would I bring my dogs into-"

The thread that held Claire's self-control snapped. There was a flash of white, then the world went red. Her entire body blazed with fury and her own voice was distant and foreign in her ears. "Because you're a liar, and that's what liars do! They lie!" She pounded her fist on the desk, barely missing her computer, feeling no pain.

The hard glint in Mother's gaze sparked back. "Now, you listen to me, young lady." Her voice shook with controlled rage. "I will *not* be called names in my own home. If you think you can just waltz into my bedroom, move things around, and then accuse *me* of lying to you, you've got another think coming. I did *not* do any such thing and I will *not* be accused or insulted."

Claire could see the truth of Mother's words, could hear the conviction in the woman's voice. *I'm losing my mind.* "Then who, Mother?

Who would do this?" Tears spilled and her face collapsed. "Why is this happening to me? Why!"

Mother rushed to Claire and hugged her to her bosom, nauseating her with Opium. "It's okay, dear. It's all going to be okay. Trust your mother."

The touch reignited the flames and Claire jerked away, shrugging out of her embrace. "Don't *touch* me!"

Mother stepped back, her hands worrying the hair necklace. "Honey, please calm down. You aren't supp-"

"Shut up and get out!" Claire slammed her fist on the desk. "Get out, get out, get out!"

Startled, hands shaking, Mother retreated. "I think we'd better call your doct-"

"No!" Claire grabbed the first thing her hands found - a notepad - and hurled it. It struck the wall. "You're lying! You're *lying* to me!"

Mother's face went white and she let out a strangled sob and left, shutting the door hard behind her.

Shrieking, Claire grabbed her glass of milk and chucked it at the door. Milk and glass exploded. "You're lying!" Claire screamed into the empty room. "You're lying!"

She looked down at her broken leg, wishing she could get up and run - away from this house, away from this town - but she couldn't. Her face was wet with tears, her hands quaked out of control, and her heart was a desperate prisoner, beating against her ribs.

Claire wrapped her arms around herself, hunched into a tight ball and rocked, weeping, barely aware of her wails pealing through the house. She considered calling Aunt Babs, but couldn't bear the thought of being seen like this. *I'm losing my mind.*

***

In his room, Fred Martin raised his head and listened to the tormented cries of his only daughter. He wanted to go to her, to comfort her and tell her everything would be okay. But he couldn't, so he prayed to a god he'd long ago forsaken. *If you won't help me, at least help my daughter.*

Then he heard the key in the door. Priscilla had come to call at long last. She bustled in without a word, uncovered him and pulled him sideways on the bed.

When she had him where she wanted him, she spoke. "I'm sure you heard Carlene's little tantrum, Frederick." Priscilla powdered his bottom then snapped the fresh diaper's tapes around his waist. "I want you to know you don't need to worry. Pregnant ladies can get emotional sometimes."

He stared past his wife, unable to ignore the humiliation he felt as she finishing changing him. The anger. He wasn't incontinent and could handle a portable urinal himself - years ago he'd even wheeled himself into the bathroom and onto the toilet. Then she began locking the door because she hadn't liked him going down the hall or looking in on the kids. She claimed she was afraid he'd roll down the stairs, but that was utter nonsense.

She just wanted to keep him out of her hair. So she gave him the urinal and helped him with a bedpan. That had been humiliating and he'd complained, but that was about the time speaking became more difficult. She brought Dr. Hopper over, but he only said something about deterioration of the muscles in his face. Fred knew this was a lie, because it always improved … for a time. Then the medications became stronger: Prissy got a prescription from Hopper that had to be injected and he could barely move his mouth. She said it would help him. It didn't. It helped *her*.

Finally, it had come down to adult diapers, the biggest humiliation of all. Prissy had things to do, she said, and the diapers were just a precaution in case she wasn't home to help him; but he knew better. Her visits had become rarer and, lately, so rare that he usually ended up wetting himself - the urinal had disappeared to a high shelf in the bathroom. When he'd asked for it back, she'd just smiled and told him this was better. Now, she sometimes didn't check on him for twelve hours or more, leaving him to starve, leaving him to shit himself.

"All done, Frederick. You're nice and clean." She glanced at the unplugged TV then back at him. "Let's put you in your chair for a while."

Thank heaven. He was so sick of lying in bed that he wanted to scream. She'd begun keeping him there for days at a time and he hated it. He had bedsores.

She lifted him and slid him into his chair. "Would you like me to open the drapes and the slider so you can get some fresh air?"

He nodded, grateful. He wanted to ask her to plug in the TV, but couldn't. He couldn't even ask for a pen and paper. *She wouldn't give them to me anyway.*

"I'll bring you your dinner in just a couple of hours," Prissy said as she wheeled him to the sliding glass door, opened the screen, then pushed him onto the narrow balcony. Chilly winter breezes caught in his hair and made goose bumps rise on his thin arms. "There we are. Fresh air. It's good for you. I'm making you a special treat tonight - mashed potatoes and pureed chicken and peas. Mmm." She went inside and he thought she was fetching his sweater, but instead, she pulled the screen door closed behind her, and left.

Frederick shivered, crossed his arms for warmth, and stared at the empty apartment over the garage. *This can't go on much longer.*

***

Babs Vandercooth couldn't stop thinking about Claire. Talking with Father Andy had been a good thing, and she knew she would not change her decision to oppose Priscilla Martin in the Auxiliary election. She felt good about that. Standing up to Prissy had made her feel even better. A weight had been lifted, and looking back, it felt like she'd willingly spent her entire life as Priscilla's indentured servant. Now it was over. Self-confidence coursed through her. *Never again.*

She might have danced for joy except for her concern for Claire. That weight would not lift. She'd already gone out several times to look today, and each time, Prissy's BMW was in the driveway. She had phoned twice but Claire hadn't picked up. Now, she looked again as she pretended to check her mailbox. *The car's still there.* It was already past four and Prissy rarely ran errands this late, so Babs hoped she'd at least get a chance to check on Claire in the morning. She promised herself she'd call again later.

"Babs!"

Aida Portendorfer waved at her - she had just come out to survey her huge snapdragon garden.

Babs waved back then crossed the street. "How are you today, Aida?"

"Just fine." They exchanged pleasantries, then Aida mentioned the spring potluck and the huge batch of chili she was making. She glanced at the clear blue sky. "I hope Saturday is as beautiful as today."

"I hope so, too."

"And you, Babs, what are you going to serve up at the potluck this year?"

"Carl has volunteered to grill hot dogs."

"That's wonderful! They'll be the hit of the sac. Would you like a quart or two of chili to put on them?"

"If you have any to spare, that would be lovely." Babs smiled. "Prissy is *not* pleased about the hot dogs."

Aida's eyes lit up. "Why not? They're perfect."

"She wants Carl to make hamburgers, like Burke Collins always did."

Face darkening, Aida said, "That's very thoughtless of her. It's bad enough all of us will think of that poor family every time we glance at their house. Hot dogs are more appropriate."

Babs nodded. "We think so."

Aida studied her. "Good for you."

"What?"

"Good for you. May I be frank?"

"Please."

"I would have expected Priscilla to have talked you into hamburgers."

"She tried but I was so irritated with her this morning that I stood my ground." Babs smiled. "And I'm ridiculously proud of myself for it. Guess what else I did," she added, trusting that Aida would be on the phone spreading the word before dark.

"What?"

"I've already spoken with Father Andy and gotten his blessing to run for president of the Ladies' Auxiliary. I'll officially announce it at next week's meeting."

Aida grinned, then she threw her arms around Babs and crushed her in a long, warm hug. "I can't tell you how happy I am you're doing this. It's what we need. I'm so happy you've found the strength to stand up to Prissy. Except for Geneva-Marie, none of us have." She frowned. "And look what happened to her."

Bab shivered and pulled her sweater closed. "Poor Geneva-Marie."

"Amen. I keep her in my prayers." Aida paused. "Does Prissy know you're running for president?"

"She's the first one I told. It just popped out of my mouth, before I even realized I was serious."

"How did that happen?"

Aida liked details, and Babs was perversely pleased to provide them. "She figured out that I'd been up to see Claire and she wasn't happy. You know how she is about people wandering around in her house."

Aida laughed. "I think she must have a lot of bodies hidden up there."

"No doubt. And a lot of junk. You know she hoards, right?" Saying that made Babs almost giddy. *Everyone's going to know now. Take that, Prissy.*

"Really? I've wondered, I must admit. Once I offered to help her carry some supplies to her basement and she reacted oddly. She actually guarded the door when she said no."

"Oh, it's not just the basement. It's almost all those rooms upstairs. There are only a few that aren't stuffed to the gills with junk." Babs spoke, knowing Hell was coming to call in the form of Prissy, and didn't care at all. "There's a reason she never opens that garage of hers, too."

"There is?" Aida's eyes widened.

"Stuffed to the ceiling."

"I'm surprised. She seems so organized."

"I suppose she is, in her way. Take a peek in her trash cans some morning. You won't believe how organized they are. Or how empty." Babs could see Aida filing all the information away. *No secrets are safe on Morning Glory Circle,* Babs reminded herself. And for the first time, she was glad.

"About Claire," Aida said. "Pris wouldn't let you visit her again?"

"No. And I'm very concerned. Prissy has never been sensitive to her daughter's needs. She's never really had any understanding of them."

"As far as I can tell, she lacks emotional intelligence," Aida said.

"I agree. There's a reason Claire was always at my house when she was a girl - Prissy didn't want her bothering her brother. She told me Claire was too boisterous and daring for her very sensitive son to bear."

"I remember," Aida said. "Excuse my French, but that was a crock of shit."

"It still is. I'm calling Jason tonight. I want them to come stay with Carl and me until they can move into their own place." Instantly, she regretted saying so - that was one thing she didn't want getting back to Prissy. "Aida, please don't repeat that. If Prissy finds out, I'm afraid of how she'll treat Claire. "

Aida smiled. "I understand. I won't repeat anything you've told me."

"Oh, please, repeat anything you want - but that one thing."

Colorado Rocky Mountain Low

Claire couldn't concentrate on her work and had finally stretched out on the bed and tried to read an Agatha Christie novel. It wasn't working, because she couldn't believe her own behavior. She'd never thrown anything harder than a pillow in anger, and that only once - when her college roommate decided to have sex on the couch in their apartment while Claire studied for finals. She hadn't even thrown a pillow at Jason - she just didn't get that angry. Now she stared at the drying milk and the shards of glass on the carpet in front of her door. *I did that. I can't believe I did that.* She'd yelled and screamed and cried - all the things she hated most. There was no point to that kind of behavior yet she'd indulged in it. Pregnancy hormones, frustration, boredom, and the fear that she was losing her mind had all contributed - but that was still no excuse for throwing a fit.

And she couldn't even clean up her own mess; the broom and dustpan were downstairs and there was no way she could get them on crutches. She couldn't even get down on her knees to pick up the glass. And Mother knew it. She hadn't come back. Claire had heard her upstairs a couple of times, and she'd smelled the fumes from Tim's room again, but Mother never showed. She wondered if the milk and glass would still be there for Jason to see when he returned tomorrow.

"Claire?" Mother's voice came from the other side of the door.

Speak of the devil. "I'm awake."

"May I come in?"

Claire considered saying no, then said, "Yes, Mother."

Mother entered wearing yellow rubber gloves and carrying the dustpan and a bucket of soapy water. She didn't look at Claire. "I'm just going to clean this up and I'll be out of your hair, dear." Her tone was distant, cautious, but not unkind. She bent down and began placing broken glass in the dustpan.

Watching her mother clean up after her filled Claire with gnawing shame. She almost apologized, but was afraid of somehow causing another confrontation.

Mother began sopping up the milk. "I owe you an apology, Claire."

Claire wasn't sure she'd heard her right. "What?"

"I know better than to get upset. I reacted poorly, and I'm sorry."

"Mother, I ... I'm sorry. It wasn't your fault."

Mother turned and gave her a humorless smile, then wagged a gloved finger at her. "It takes two to tango," she said in a singsong tone. "I'm every bit as much to blame as you."

Claire felt tears welling. *God, not this again. I'm so tired of the freaking tears.* She bit them back.

"It's hard enough being pregnant, Claire. It's been a long while since I was in your position, but I remember it well. It's a difficult time, and I'm afraid I haven't made it any easier on you. I'm sorry for that."

"No," said Claire. "I haven't been myself."

"You're not *supposed* to be yourself right now, dear. Your body is changing in ways it never has before." She paused and sighed. "While I've always admired the work of the Lord, I can't help thinking He might have ironed the kinks out of this whole procreation process by now. I intend to give Him a thorough talking to when my time comes." She smiled as she wrung milk from the towel.

Claire laughed. It felt good. She'd rarely seen Mother's cheeky side, and she liked it. "I guess that's how they know God is a male."

"Exactly," said Mother. "Believe me, some things are going to change when *I* get up there."

Claire smiled and had no doubt that even in the afterlife, Mother would be trying to take charge. "Did you ever feel … crazy … when you were pregnant, Mother?"

Mother stopped scrubbing. "Of course I did. Every day."

"I mean, like … really, *truly* crazy."

"I know exactly what you mean. And the answer is yes. One minute I was up, the next I was down. I'd laugh, cry, and I even became a bit paranoid."

"Paranoid?" Claire asked eagerly. "How so?"

"Oh, this and that. I thought my friends were talking about me. I was convinced everyone was trying to make things harder for me. I felt unattractive, unlovable. I sometimes saw things that weren't there." She resumed scrubbing.

Claire leaned forward. "What do you mean? What things?"

Mother shrugged, her eyes on the task. "Just little things."

"So … this is *normal?*"

"It was for me."

"Why don't they talk about paranoia and feeling crazy in the books and on the websites? There's no mention of these things at all, and I'd swear I'm seeing things!"

"I don't think it's *usual,* which is *not* to say it isn't *normal,* Claire. Everyone's pregnancy is different. Some women feel euphoric throughout. Others become clinically depressed. I guess the women in our family get very anxious." She faced her now, offered a little smile. "But the good news is, it gets better. The first half was the worst of it." She looked at the floor.

"I'm going to give this a couple of hours to dry then I'll come back with the vacuum and get all the tiny pieces of glass so no one cuts their feet."

"How long did it last? The, uh, hallucinations?"

"Oh, I don't know. It was such a long time ago. A couple of months, maybe?" She stood, lifted the bucket, and inspected her work.

"How bad did it get? I mean, what kinds of things did you ... see?"

Mother sighed. "That's enough for now, Claire." She glanced at the laptop. "And I forbid you to get on the Internet and read about bad pregnancies. It will only make it worse, and you *need* to relax. No more upsetting yourself."

"But I-"

"No, Claire." She used her mom voice. "You need to relax. My pregnancies weren't easy. Yours hasn't been either. But it does get better from here. That's all you need to know. And I *mean* it about the Internet. Those sites will only make you anxious, and I think we can both agree that there's been enough upset for one day. You need to think of the baby now."

Claire knew it was true. She nodded.

"I'll be back to vacuum and bring you supper in a couple of hours. Do you need anything else until then?"

"No," said Claire, thinking, *A new head perhaps? A new set of genes?*

Mother smiled, kissed Claire on the forehead, and left the room, her perfume lingering like an unwanted ghost.

***

The little jet turned out to be just what Paul hoped for, and Jason had emailed him the mechanic's report and a load of detailed photos before going for a steak with Jake Fairview. After, Jake wanted to hang out and watch football in a sports bar, but Jason had begged off. All he'd wanted was to go back to his room, call Claire and read more of Timothy's journals. He hoped Jake wouldn't stay out too late - they had an early morning takeoff, because a fast-moving snowstorm was due to hit Denver before noon.

He'd hung up with Claire half an hour before, relieved. While she sounded a little fragile, she seemed more like her old self and even said she and her mother were getting along. Prissy was making one of Claire's favorites - roast chicken with mashed potatoes - and they were going to have to have dinner together. Claire sounded, if not happy, okay.

This was a great relief, because he hadn't been able to get the journal off his mind ever since he'd read Timothy's entry about "boy stains." The way Prissy humiliated her son was unconscionable, far too personal, and set off alarm bells in Jason's mind. The rest of that particular journal had mostly been full of sonnets to Steffie, rants about teachers, and a few drawings of Prissy in the form of a gargoyle. Tim had been a good artist, and it was easy for Jason to see his mother-in-law's features on the creature. He'd asked Claire if she'd seen them, but she hadn't. She wanted to though, and he promised to show her when he got back. In turn, she thanked him for taking an interest and was happy he'd slipped a few journals in his overnight bag. He pulled off his shoes, undid his tie, and stretched out on the bed, smiling to himself and looking forward to seeing his wife tomorrow. He'd be there in time to bring home orange chicken from Wokamundo - Claire couldn't get enough right now.

He nabbed another journal off the nightstand. This one was from Tim's sophomore year and he could tell by the way it opened that Claire hadn't cracked it yet.

He flipped past a couple of blank pages then found hard, angry-looking writing, cramped and small.

I will never forgive her.

Of all the things she's done to me, this is the worst. It's happened before, but that was a long time ago. I'd hoped it would stop when I turned thirteen, but I'm fifteen now, and the Bad Punishment happened again.

I was in my room getting ready for church. I gave myself lots of time, and dug out one of the Penthouse *magazines Paul gave me from his dad's collection. I keep them in the back of my closet, beneath a bunch of shoeboxes, where Mother wouldn't look. Ever since she barged in on me in the shower, I only look at the mags in my closet. And I do more than look at them in there. I do what every normal guy likes to do and I don't even feel guilty about it. It's not a sin, that's bullshit.*

So that's what I was doing this morning in my closet. I didn't hear Mother come into my room, but as soon as I was done, before I had a chance to clean up, there she was, staring at me - I think she'd been there a long time, listening. Anyway, she screamed at me that she's suspected I've been doing this for years and asked if that was true.

I didn't say anything. It's not like I could deny it. I had my pants down, a dirty magazine in one hand, and a wad of wet Kleenex in my other.

She slapped the magazine away and yanked me out by my hair before I could even pull up my pants. She hit me on the bare ass with the magazine and threw me on the bed on my stomach and was shrieking about me being a dirty boy, and how dare I do such a thing on Sunday, and that I needed to be cleansed - from the inside out. She made me give her the dirty tissue. I don't know what she did with it, but she took it, and told me to leave my pants down and wait for her. I don't know why I did, I should have run away, but that would only make it worse. And I was just so embarrassed I couldn't move, I guess. I knew exactly what was coming, too.

Outside the church, there's a faucet where parishioners can get water that's been blessed by the priests. Mother has always kept a big bottle of it in the cupboard that no one's allowed to touch. She says it's for 'emergencies,' but it's what she uses for the Bad Punishment.

I should have fought her off. I should have punched her in her ugly face, kicked her in the groin and twisted her fucking tits off. But I didn't. I just let her do it. She took me into the bathroom - made me walk with my pants down, had me bend over the bathtub, then filled me up with so much holy water that my insides felt like they were going to explode. Then she made me hold it while I said twenty-five Hail Marys and while I did, she kept slapping my balls, yanking them, and flipping them and saying they were the devil's playthings. I wouldn't show her my pain so she twisted and squeezed them until I screamed. She stopped and made me finish the Hail Marys before she let me go to the toilet to squirt it out. Then she made me do it again. Twenty-five Hail Marys with my ass full of holy water - and when she ran out of that, she started using really cold water from the tub faucet. Then I had to do it again, and again, until I'd said one hundred Hail Marys and made four trips to the toilet.

She yelled at me for making her late for church. At least she let me stay home - she said I was too dirty to go - but then she said she was going to drive me to church after the service, and I had to confess my sin to Father Dave. I wasn't to mention the enema, of course, just that I'd masturbated on a Sunday before church. She dug out all my magazines and made me watch her tear them up and burn them while she told me I was disgusting, those women were disgusting, and the devil put a curse on women's vaginas and that's why men liked them so much. But only weak men succumbed. Men who were strong in the Lord understood that a woman's vagina was created for procreation, not pleasure. She's so full of shit. I hate her fucking guts. I wish she'd die.

So she drove me to church and told Father Dave I needed to make a confession. I did, but I didn't keep her secret. I told him what Mother had done, too. He acted really funny about it, but didn't really say anything except that I'd already done my penance and was forgiven. Then he asked to speak to Mother while I waited in the car. I know priests can't repeat confessions, but Mother was gone so long I got worried that he might be telling her. When she came back out, I expected her to be mad, but she wasn't.

She didn't say anything the whole way home, and when we got there, she just made me go up to my room and read Scriptures.

That was Sunday. It's Wednesday today and it hasn't come up again.

I hate her. I wonder what Father Dave said to her. I hope he told her she was wrong. I hope he told her SHE had sinned too. I hope he told her she was going to hell.

And I hope she does.

"Holy shit." Jason set the journal aside and rose, grabbing a bottle of water from the ice bucket. He wished it was a beer. "Holy shit." *Priscilla Martin is a child abuser.* He wondered if Claire knew about the Bad Punishment, but doubted it - she hadn't read that far yet. *But what does she know? What does she remember?* All at once he felt like a monster for making light of her hatred of her mother. *My God, what did she do to my wife? That woman will never lay eyes on our son!*

Jason sipped his water, looking out on the city lights beneath the lowering sky. *What did she do to her?* He'd never felt so far from home. He texted Jake that he needed to be ready to leave for the airport by five a.m. to make sure they avoided the storm, then as he was about to call Claire, his cell rang in his hand. It was Babs Vandercooth.

There's Something about Priscilla

"Six in the corner pocket," Father Andy told Dave Flannigan.

The old priest looked at him from across the table and smiled. "You'll never make that shot."

"Have faith." Andy took the shot and the balls bounced and went in the wrong direction.

Dave chuckled. "You're lucky you didn't tear the felt. Let me show you how an old pro does it."

He missed, too. "Another beer? Maybe a sandwich? I have pastrami. It's getting to be that time."

"That sounds great."

Andy followed Dave into his small, neat kitchen and sat at the equally small dining table. "I had lunch with Babs Vandercooth today."

Dave handed him a Killian's Red and he twisted off the lid. Tangy mist curled into his nostrils. It felt good. And tasted better.

"Babs without Priscilla Martin?" Dave said over his shoulder. "What kind of cheese?"

"Whatever you're having. Yes, it seems they've had a falling out."

Dave laughed. "Has hell frozen over?"

"Possibly. But I think Babs has simply had enough. She's running for president of the Auxiliary." He filled in details while Dave made the sandwiches and put them in the oven to toast.

"I'm glad to hear all this," Dave said as he brought the food to the table. "I always liked Babs, but even when she was young, she seemed afraid of her own shadow - especially when it came to Prissy."

"True," Andy said. "I'm curious. When Claire Martin - Carlene back then - was little, was she something of a hell raiser?"

Dave chewed thoughtfully. "As far as I can recall, she was always well-behaved. She used to draw quite well."

"She's a graphic artist now."

Dave smiled. "As she should be. What I recall most about the girl was how much she loved her brother, Tim. He carried her around on his shoulder and doted on her." He looked at Andy. "I dare say Priscilla was rather jealous of the two of them. She was always separating them and I recall wondering why."

Andy nodded and told him about Claire being sent to the Vandercooth home so as not to disturb Timothy.

"Nonsense," Dave said. "Nonsense typical of Priscilla. The woman was obsessed with her son. She probably felt her own daughter was her rival. I've seen it before."

"That feels like the truth to me." Andy picked up the other half of his sandwich. "While she ignored her daughter's nightmares, she took the boy into her bed when he had bad dreams - and he was far too old for that sort of thing. The entire story made my skin crawl, but I'm not sure that means anything."

Dave held his gaze. "The fact that she exposed herself to us during the Collins funeral tells us her morals are corrupt."

Andy nodded. "True. But that doesn't mean she actually abused the boy sexually."

"Andrew Pike, let me tell you something and you take it to your grave." He paused. "And I'm only repeating this because you're part of the priesthood and the boy is long dead now."

"I understand. Go on."

"When he was a young teen, Priscilla forced Timothy to confess to me that he'd masturbated before church. The poor boy was humiliated, and he told me what Priscilla had done to punish him."

Andy forgot to eat as Dave recounted Timothy's story. When the old priest finished talking, he couldn't find his own words. "That's ... just wrong."

"It was technically a confession, so I couldn't say anything, but I spoke to Priscilla immediately afterward. Since she knew about his so-called self-abuse, I sat her down and explained that while the church didn't condone it, that it was an old-fashioned stance, and part of growing up. She argued that it was a sin. I told her that I felt a sin was something that hurt yourself or others, and asked how Timothy's actions had hurt anyone. She just stared at me for a moment - I think she was hatching a plot - then told me that because I was a priest I knew nothing about lust. Then she started unbuttoning her blouse with one hand and touching her thigh with the other. I had never been so shocked in my life."

"Is that when..."

"She seduced me? No, but I watched. The woman opened her blouse and opened her legs and displayed herself to me. I'm a normal man. Between my excitement and my shock, I just sat there. I really didn't know how to react. Then, she dropped her skirt and came toward me. She wore hose held up with a black garter belt, and no underwear. She walked straight up to me - I was sitting down - and pressed her privates to my face, and said, 'This isn't hurting anyone, is it?'"

"And? What did you do?"

"I might have succumbed right then and there but her genitals reeked of that terrible perfume she likes to wear." Dave made a face. "I was very polite - too polite due to my surprise - and I carefully moved out of range, stood up, and asked her to leave." He shook his head. "I wish I'd been that strong later when she became really serious about seducing me."

"Why do you suppose she did that?" Andy asked.

Dave set aside the last of his sandwich and took a long pull on his beer before replying. "My answer may surprise you."

"I doubt it."

"I think that Priscilla was sexually excited."

"Priest as forbidden fruit?"

"No, not that time. I was simply handy. I believe she was excited because of what she had done to her son."

"That's sick."

Andy's stomach knotted. "What did you do?"

"I avoided her as much as possible and tried to make myself available to Tim, but he never spoke of it again. He avoided me. There was something about the way he looked at me after that … I suspect she told him I was a pedophile, or something equally heinous. I would put nothing past her. Nothing."

"She's the one who spread the rumor about Quinton Everett. You're lucky she didn't say that about you, too." Andy's stomach clenched as he realized he was also a prime target for such an attack. "Babs told me she wants to help Claire move out. She feels it's dangerous for the girl to stay there."

Dave studied him. "She's probably correct. Prissy Martin is poison. Poor Timothy. He turned to drink. He left town to be with his girlfriend, but had an injury and Priscilla brought him home. He ended up committing suicide not long after."

***

"Babs?"

"Hello, Jason. I wondered if you might have a few minutes to talk."

Worry kindled in his chest. "Sure. Of course. Is everything okay?"

Only silence. And then, "Are you somewhere private?"

Jason looked around the empty hotel room. "As a matter of fact, yes. I'm in Denver on a short business trip. I'll be back tomorrow, but I'm alone, yes. Is everything okay, Babs?"

"It's nothing to worry about right now, but I …" She sighed. "I went to see Claire yesterday. I wanted to talk to her about some things, but decided against it when I saw her. She looked so frail that I didn't dare risk upsetting her."

"Is this about-"

"It's about Priscilla. I should have spoken up sooner."

Jason's heart beat faster, his chest tightened.

The line was silent a moment, then Babs spoke in a rushed tone. "I know you're planning on getting out of Priscilla's house, and I think that's a very good thing. But I also think you need to leave as soon as possible. I realize Claire's on bed rest but I don't think you ought to wait. As I told Claire, I'd be happy to come and tend to her at your new place while you're at work. She'll never be alone. I want you to get yourself, your wife, and your unborn child out of that house as soon as you can. I'm happy to have you all stay with Carl and me until your house is ready."

Jason wasn't sure what to say. After reading some of Tim's journals, he felt the same way, but why was Babs telling him this now? "What happened? Has something happened?"

"Not yet, but I'm afraid it might. I just don't want to see Claire hurt."

"Claire hasn't been herself, Babs. She's been seeing things. Her emotions are all over the place and I think it goes beyond hormonal shifts. If there's anything you know that might help me understand, I promise it won't go further. Claire isn't *Claire*, lately."

"No, she's not. Jason, I think of her as my little girl. I dare say I know her as well as you do - perhaps better, because I witnessed her childhood, up close and personal."

Jason's hand was tight around the phone. "Babs, please, can you tell me more? I don't understand."

There was a long pause, then Babs cleared her throat. "The first thing that really worried me was how Prissy clung to Timmy. She nursed him up until the day he went to kindergarten."

"What?"

"You heard me. Kindergarten. She claimed he had an allergy to milk, and she had to. She told me she stopped nursing him once he was in school, but I'm not even sure that was true. But I do know that Claire was a bottle baby. She had no interest in nursing her. When Timothy was little, I offered to babysit him, but she refused, saying she couldn't bear to be away from her boy. Yet she was happy to leave Claire with me - the first day home from the hospital, she had me take care of her baby girl so she could take care of Tim - who was ten and didn't need any special care. She was horrible to Claire."

"I've been reading some of Tim's high school journals, and they back up what you've said. Prissy did and said things to Tim that were abuse, plain and simple. But what does it have to do with us leaving the house right away?"

"There were a lot of ... accidents and illnesses like food poisoning. Claire and Timothy both had an unusual amount. I've always suspected Pris was behind many of them. I think she enjoyed the attention it gave her when one of her children was hurt. I wasn't worried when I heard you and Claire were moving back. Claire told me you were planning to leave the house long before the baby came - if she hadn't, I would have suggested it. In fact, I would have insisted. I thought things would be okay until Claire's leg was broken. Now I don't. When I saw Claire the other day ... Well, something's wrong, Jason."

He was paralyzed. Stricken. Was it true? *And what has Prissy been doing to Claire? And how the hell did I miss it?*

"Babs, are you saying Prissy had something to do with Claire's broken leg?"

She hesitated. "I want you to promise me something, Jason."

"Anything."

"As soon as you get home, you pack your things, and get out of that house."

After hanging up, Jason went to the window. The stars were hidden by incoming clouds from the north. He got online and checked for commercial flights. None was available. He'd have to wait till morning.

"Shit."

He called Jake Fairview to tell him they needed to fly out tonight, but as soon as the guy picked up the phone, Jason heard the alcohol-thick slur in his words. There'd be no flying out now.

"Shit, shit, shit!"

***

"Tomorrow is great." Paul Schuyler smiled at Steffie Banks. They'd been Skyping for an hour, as they had almost every night since their first conversation. "I'm glad you can get away a day early."

"I am, too, but if this is an inconvenience for you, I can catch a commercial flight. Or wait until Sunday."

"No, no. It's fine. I'll be all finished with work and I can be in Brimstone in time for dinner. We'll fly back tomorrow morning. You *will* let me take you to dinner, won't you?"

"No, it's my town, I'll take *you* to dinner." She smiled back, making Paul feel just a little too happy. When Steffie had texted about being able to come a day early, he'd instantly rearranged things at work so he could accommodate her. He'd already cancelled the day's classes so Jason could go straight home to Claire. Schuyler Flight School students would have the day off. He didn't think they'd complain. *Easy peasy.*

"How's Claire doing?" Steffie asked. "I was thinking of emailing her and saying hello."

"I'm sure she'd like that. I haven't seen her recently, but Jason's a little worried about her. She told him she saw Timothy on Facebook."

"What? That's impossible."

"She said she saw him, all the details were right. The pictures were old. He had a girlfriend on Facebook, too."

"Well, that account has to be a fraud. If you know the girlfriend's name, I'll check her out."

"Jason didn't say, but I'll ask. Claire insisted he look, but there was no account like that. Claire thinks it's been removed. Jason thinks Claire may be imagining things. She's been saying some odd stuff the last few days, I guess."

"Like what?" Steffie looked concerned.

"He didn't tell me, but he thinks she's having trouble, with, you know, reality. He says Priscilla isn't nearly as bad as Claire thinks she is, but that Claire seems to think her mother is Satan incarnate."

On the screen, Steffie's eyes went dark and she leaned in close. "Paul, listen to me. Seriously, Priscilla is probably *worse* than Claire thinks she is."

"I don't know how she could be worse. You know what that woman was like."

"I do. I know more about her than I want to, Paul. Once Tim was away from her, when we were in Brimstone before his accident, he opened up. She did things to him. Bad things. She hurt him. And she hurt Claire, too."

"Hurt her? How? Physically?

"Yes, and mentally. You've heard of Munchausen's Syndrome?"

"Is that the one where people harm themselves to get medical attention?"

Steffie nodded. "Yes. And unfortunately, there's a worse form of it - where the person harms their children, or others in their care."

"Oh, my God."

"And they not only get attention, they get to be seen as heroes of 'saving' the person they've harmed."

Suddenly, the pieces fell together, and Paul felt a tight, cold sickness in his gut. "I never thought about it before, but she was always keeping Tim home from school. He was sick a *lot*. And she loved nursing him back to health."

"And Claire had a lot of injuries. I remember Priscilla always saying Claire was a klutz."

"I remember that, too. I thought that was a mean thing for a mother to say about her own daughter." He paused. "Claire was always falling down the stairs, off swings and monkey bars or tripping. Broken bones. Seems like she had new bruises every time I saw her. Sometimes she limped. And I remember her having her arm in a sling several times."

Steffie nodded, her mouth a firm line. "You were around her a lot, Paul. So was I. Now tell me, did you actually *witness* any of this clumsiness?"

Paul's mouth went dry. "No. Not once." He was having a hard time wrapping his head around this, but it rang true. Too true.

"If Tim hadn't died, we were planning to bring Carlene to Arizona to live with us. After his death, I even called Social Services about her, but I don't know what became of that. Nothing, I assume. They don't like taking children from their parents, and I doubt they were able to find anything - if they even tried. Priscilla Martin is an expert at keeping up appearances, and she's got that whole town in her pocket."

"How could anyone hurt their own children?"

"You ask that like a truly normal person." Her chuckle lacked humor. "Priscilla Martin obviously has narcissistic and sociopathic tendencies. Believe me, I've seen it too many times."

"But she loved Timothy so much," Paul said.

"That was obsession, not love. Big difference." Steffie didn't smile. "Sure, it's possible Claire's having trouble with reality. And the pregnancy could well be affecting her stability, but I seriously doubt she's imagining things. I'm just glad Jason is there with her - it helps keep her safe from Priscilla."

A chill ran down Paul's back and the cold knot in his stomach tightened. "Jason's away overnight. I sent him to Denver to check out a commuter jet." He paused. "Good Lord, I had no idea. I wish I'd gone myself."

"Don't worry too much. Jason will be with her again tomorrow, right?"

"Right. I'll send him home as soon as he lands. There's a big storm coming down from Canada that will be hitting Denver early, so they're heading back before dawn."

"Good." She watched him. "Don't worry too much, Paul. If I know anything about Priscilla Martin, it's that she'd never do anything too obvious - nothing that would cast suspicion on her."

Paul nodded, but he couldn't escape the cold sense of dread that had wrapped its hands around his lungs. He decided he'd give Claire a call before leaving town … just in case.

Heinous Liaisons

"Frederick! What are you doing out here? You'll catch your death of cold!"

Fred heard Priscilla *tsk* as she unlocked the screen and yanked his wheelchair over the threshold so hard he bounced in the seat. He clung to the armrests, afraid of falling.

His wife had shut the screen and locked it after she'd pushed him outside a couple of hours earlier. It was an old trick of hers. Last time was in August, during a record heat wave. He'd suffered a bad sunburn and she'd acted like he'd locked himself out. *Just as she's doing now.* He wondered what was going on. Priscilla pulled such stunts when she was agitated. She took out her aggressions that way.

"I brought your dinner. Have you urinated, Frederick? Do I need to check your bum?"

He shook his head.

"Well, good for you! I'm so proud of you, even if you were a naughty boy sitting out there in the cold. Honestly, I don't know what possesses you! You'll catch pneumonia and I'll have to take care of you! Let me get your urinal, then it's time for chicken, mashed potatoes, and peas! Your favorites."

His favorite was spaghetti, but chicken wasn't bad - he could smell it and it made his mouth water.

Priscilla had left the room without offering him so much as a sweater, but was back quickly, her hands at his pajama bottoms, reaching for his business, yanking it out and shoving it into the urinal spout before he could stop her. He tried to say "No" but it came out "Oo," and she ignored him, pressing his penis painfully against the plastic rim. He put his hand on her wrist and squeezed as hard as he could. With a little yelp, she let go and he took over.

"Why, Frederick, you want to do it yourself! That's so precious!" She smiled. "But please don't squeeze my wrist like that again! You hurt me. You don't want to hurt your little Pris-Pris, do you?" She shook her head. "I don't know where you got the strength."

He did - his legs might not work, or even his mouth these days, but he'd been exercising his hands and arms more and more since his daughter had shown up and given him a reason to live. His arms were beginning to respond almost normally now and his hands were in great shape. He'd never let Prissy see that, though.

"Dinner time!" she announced when he put himself away. After setting the urinal on the dresser, she picked up a bottle of hand sanitizer and a covered platter and brought them over, setting them on the tray she'd snugged up to him. He cleaned his hands, noting she didn't bother to clean hers. She never did. His stomach growled until he saw a large tumbler with a straw and a smaller cup beside it. Within the big one was his dinner, a pale yellow mass with pea-colored swirls. The small glass held something white. *Tapioca pudding.* It was always tapioca. *At least she didn't blend it into the chicken.*

"I know you'd like your meal on a plate Frank-Frederick, but Carlene is having a very bad day and is waiting for her dinner, too. I promised to eat with her tonight. Isn't that nice?" She pulled a sad face. "I'm so sorry, but I just can't be here to help you eat. I'm sure you understand. And it's so yummy this way. Think of it as a chicken dinner shake."

She'd been blending most of his meals lately; at least she offered an excuse this time. He grunted. He was fully capable of feeding himself, though lately, he was having more trouble moving his mouth. She did it for herself, not for him. Priscilla never did anything that wasn't for herself.

She was smiling down at him in that condescending way of hers. "Just let me put on your bib, and then I'll leave you to eat in peace."

***

"I miss you," Jason said. "And I love you."

Claire smiled. "Really?"

"Really. I can't wait to get home. And I'll be earlier than I thought. A storm is hitting Denver, so we're hightailing it out before it hits. I should be home sometime tomorrow afternoon."

"That's wonderful!"

There was silence. After a beat, Jason asked, "Claire, how's everything? Are you okay?"

The concern and care in his voice surprised her. "Yes. Mother is on her way up with dinner. She's being nice to me. Probably because she thinks I'm losing my mind."

"Claire. I've been reading the journals."

"You have?"

"I believe you."

Her heart swelled. "You do?"

"Yes. Listen to me. I don't know what's going on, but you are *not* losing your mind. Stop thinking that. Claire, I'm so sorry I didn't believe you. Babs Vandercooth phoned me and tomorrow, when I get home, I'm going to get the rest of our stuff moved to Paul's. This weekend, we'll be out of your mother's house for good and-"

"Wait - what did Babs say, Jason?"

"I'll tell you the details later, but basically, she said she'll come stay with you until I get home every day."

Tears of relief surged into Claire's eyes. "Aunt Babs is the best, isn't she?"

"She *is* the best. She offered to have us move in with her immediately, you know, until the house is ready. I thanked her and said the house *is* ready - that tomorrow night will be our last night under your mother's roof. "

Claire laughed. "Plus, I'd hate to see how Mother would react to us moving down the street. She'd punish Aunt Babs severely."

"I wouldn't worry too much about Babs - she can hold her own. But I *am* worried about you. Babs and Carl offered to come get you tonight. Do you want them to?"

"I ... well, as nice as that sounds, it'd be difficult. Mother's behaving. She really is, and I don't want to rock the boat, especially with you out of town."

"That does make sense. It'll be a cleaner break if we don't give her any warning. I'm just worried about you."

"Why?"

"Because you're not imagining things."

"Jason, there's something else."

"I'm listening."

"That night I was so upset, I'd gone to see Dad and he had makeup on, even false eyelashes."

"Huh?"

"Seriously. Makeup. Like a drag queen or ..." she shuddered, "a clown. He couldn't have done it to himself. I think Mother drugged him."

"But ... *why*?"

"I don't know." She couldn't bring herself to say anything about the defiled teddy bear or the incessant *tap-tap-tap* sounds that came at all hours, not yet, but telling him about the makeup was a load off her mind. "It was horrible."

"I wish I could get back tonight," Jason told her. "Maybe you *should* go to Babs' place."

"I think it'll be okay, Jase. It's only one night. I'll just keep my mind on work. Knowing you believe me makes me feel so much better!"

"If you're sure. I'll check in with you before bed, okay?"

"Please. And Jason?"

"Yes?"

"Thank you. Thank you so much for believing me."

"Don't thank me - I should have listened all along. Call me anytime. And if anything weird happens again, you call Babs and Carl and they'll come get you."

"I'll be fine, Jason. Knowing it's not my imagination is an incredible relief."

"I'm sorry I ever questioned you. I never will again. I was a fool."

"I love you, Magic Man."

"I love you, too."

The moment she ended the call, the cell rang again. It was Paul. "Hello?"

"Hi, uh, I'm just calling to see how you are."

Claire, confused, didn't know what to say. "I'm fine, Paul, how are you?"

His laugh was uneasy. "It's just that ... I'm going out of town tomorrow and I know Jason's not there tonight ... so I wanted to see if you, uh, needed anything."

She wondered if Jase had told him to check in on her. She smiled. "I'm fine, Paul. Really." And it was true. Things were finally looking up. She considered telling him that she and Jason were planning to move in this weekend, but wasn't sure if Jason had run it past him yet. "I just talked to Jason," she said, "and everything is *wonderful,* in fact!"

Paul blew out a breath. "Oh, good!"

"Claire?" Mother rapped on the door.

"I'll talk to you later. Mother's here with dinner."

***

Dave Flannigan sat forward in his easy chair and sipped his beer. "Priscilla Martin took me down a depraved road. A road I'll never forgive myself for having traveled. I knew better."

Andy watched the old man, who was lost in a different time and place, and could see his anguish. "So you took early retirement."

Dave didn't respond, and Andy wondered if he was going to. *Am I crossing a line, pressing him like this?* But the beer had loosened the old priest's lips - Dave had brought up the subject of Priscilla Martin himself, so Andy plowed on.

"Tell me the rest, Dave."

His eyes misted. "It wasn't just the affair. It went beyond that. An affair, I could have lived with, but this ..." He sipped his beer. "Priscilla continued going out of her way to catch Timothy masturbating. She admitted to listening outside his door, watching through keyholes." He paused. "The worst part was, she told me these things in such a way that ... As I told you before, I got the distinct impression it aroused her - and she hoped it aroused me, as well."

"A voyeur." Andy cleared his throat.

Dave Flannigan's small blue eyes wandered the tabletop. "Worse than that. She became convinced Tim was thinking about one of his teachers while he did it. Then students, one girl in particular. I think what bothered Priscilla was that he wasn't fantasizing about *her*."

"Dear God." Andy's beer curdled in his stomach.

Dave nodded and went on. "When we began the affair, it was all right at first. It was exciting, and God help me, I enjoyed it. You might say I was addicted to her. But as time passed, her son became a constant presence - even in our intimate moments."

"What does that mean?"

"At first, nothing, really. She'd just talk about him a lot - ask questions about how to deter him from self-abuse. But then ..." he swallowed. "Then she started talking about ... other things."

Andy wanted to press his friend, but thought it best to let him reveal the story at his own pace.

"When threats of brimstone and hellfire proved useless against Timothy's activities, Priscilla came to me with a new idea - one I should have reported right away. I didn't, because I would have lost my position at Holy Sacramental." His watery gaze touched Andy's for the briefest moment, then lowered. "When she first suggested it, I couldn't believe she was serious. But she was, and the more I denied her, the more insistent she became."

Andy was riveted, sitting forward, tense, as if he were in a theater, watching a drama unfold.

Dave's eyes met Andy's; this time, they stayed. "She wanted us to perform for her son."

Andy's mouth fell open and his throat went dry. "What? Why?"

"She said he needed to learn what sex really was, and that seeing it firsthand would straighten out his misconceptions and show him that masturbation was an offense to the Lord, because He intended sexual intercourse to take place between a man and a woman - not a boy and his hand."

"You've ... got to be kidding me, Dave."

Dave shook his head. "I'm afraid not."

"You didn't ...?"

Dave's stare was not kind. "Of *course* not! I did no such thing. The trouble was, when I refused, and she realized I wouldn't budge, she threatened to go to the police ... and claim that I raped her. She said she could go to the station right then, file a report, and there would be evidence of my semen inside her to prove it. DNA testing was relatively new then, but I had no doubt they'd believe her." He was silent a long moment. "And that's why I resigned from the priesthood. Not because I had an affair with Priscilla Martin, but because I couldn't bring myself to go to the police and turn her in for child abuse. I knew if I did that, the affair would come out." He gave Andy a tight, grim smile. "I was a coward."

The Ones that Mother Gives You

"Do you want another piece of chicken, dear? I've got more downstairs."

"No, thank you, Mother. I'm stuffed to the gills. It was delicious. I'd love some cold chicken for lunch tomorrow. I'm sure Jason would too. He might be home that early." Claire leaned back in her desk chair and patted her belly.

"I'll bring you both all sorts of goodies from the pot luck." Mother studied her. "You're starting to show."

Claire pulled at the elastic of her sweats. "I've been wearing fat pants for a couple of weeks now."

"As soon as you're able, I'll take you out to shop for maternity clothes."

Claire wanted to refuse, but there was no point in stirring up trouble. "That's nice, thanks." She thought of Jason's last call, his newfound belief in her, and smiled.

"You look happy," Mother said.

"I am. Jason will be home soon, and I feel like things are getting better. And my appetite's come back." The taste of homemade gravy on mashed potatoes was so wonderful that, in her head, it played like a melody.

"I thought you and Jason were having a little trouble. I guess you've patched things up?"

Claire smiled. "He's wonderful." Her mood soared, and the melody in her head became audible. It came from the leftover mashed potatoes and gravy on her plate. It sounded like *Margaritaville*. She cocked her head and giggled. "What the hell?"

Mother smiled. "What's so funny?"

"My food is singing to me. I swear! Can you hear it?"

Mother's smile widened. "When you were a small child, you used to sing to your food."

"And now it's singing to me!" More giggling. Mother had been so pleasant, the food so good - and Jason's call so welcome, that her stress had melted, leaving her with a feeling of such lightness that she thought she might float away. It was incredible.

"Mom?"

Prissy stared at her.

"Yes, I called you Mom. Do you like that?"

"I'm charmed. What is it, dear?"

"Those canned peas I ate."

"Yes?"

"Are they from this century?"

"Of course. Why do you ask?"

Claire giggled. "This decade?"

"What? Why? Is something wrong?"

"I'm in such a good mood, I thought maybe I'm high on aged peas."

A smile. "There's my silly girl. You're in a good mood because we had a lovely dinner together."

"Maybe the peas will sing to me, like the gravy is. But they'll sing *Marching to* Pea-*toria*." Claire began singing but couldn't remember the words. "Mother, Mom, Mommie Dearest." She giggled when Mother glared at her. "Do you have *We are Marching to Pretoria* downstairs? I'd love to hear it if you could crank it up nice and loud so it really comes through the vent." Her own voice sounded strange in her ears - hollow, distant.

"I'm sorry, I don't have that one."

"What about *Margaritaville*?" She could still hear it playing behind *Marching to Pretoria*.

"Sorry."

"Mama mia?"

"Yes, dear?"

"Why do you play *Don't Sit Under the Apple Tree* so much?"

"It was my father's favorite song. He used to sing it to me. Later, I sang it to your brother. It was his favorite, too. Why, every day after school, he came in and put the record on. Every single day." She dabbed her eye with a napkin. "I guess you could say it makes me feel close to him. It helps keep him here."

"He's here?" Claire looked around. "I don't see him, but I've heard you talking to him."

"I don't know what you're talking about, Carlene. Don't be silly. I don't talk to Timothy."

"Why not?"

"Are you okay, dear?"

A dark cloud crossed Claire's bright mood. "Is Timothy *really* still here?"

Mother stood and put the dirty dishes on the serving cart, then folded the two dinner trays before pulling her chair up close to Claire's so they were knee to knee. She took her hand. "Are you feeling all right, dear?" As she spoke, her red lips streaked the air, like the blur of a slow-exposure photograph.

Claire shook her head and giggled. "You have a wonderful complexion for a woman your age. Your pores are *so* tiny." She saw the tiny, inconsistent clumps of her mother's makeup, the jagged details of her eyeliner. "You wear a lot of cosmetics." She couldn't think of anything else to say, because Mother's face was all there was, all she could see.

"Carlene, darling, I think it's time for you to rest. You seem a little … distracted. Are you sure you feel well?"

The thought of her beloved brother haunting the house swooped back into her mind and frightened her. She didn't know why - maybe because of that thing she saw on Facebook. "I'm scared," she said.

Mother took her hand. "Of what?"

Her mood flickered, like a failing light bulb, light and dark, light and dark. "Of Timothy."

"You don't need to be afraid of your brother. He loves you almost as much as he loves me."

Claire's train of thought had wandered. "What do you mean?" *Marching to Pretoria* was drowning out her thoughts. She wondered if the iced tea had a theme song, too. "I'm not afraid of Tim. I just don't know the iced tea's song. I need to know that. Do you know what it is?"

Mother stood and kissed her on the forehead. "Do you have to go potty?"

"No. Jason says I'm a camel." She inspected her mother's hair, seeing every strand, every fiber. It was like shining onyx - or a spider's web. "Wow, did you know your hair is so black it's almost blue? Black and blue! Your hair is bruised!"

"Okay, Carlene, I think you should lie down and have a little nap. I'll check in on you later." Mother smiled and pushed the serving cart out of the room. "Get some rest. I'll put on some music for you."

"See you later, alligator."

"Yes, you will."

"You're supposed to say, 'After a while, crocodile.' Timmy always said that."

Mother didn't reply, just closed the door.

A sudden feeling of dread, of being closed in, pressed hard against her. *Did I say something wrong? Is she mad at me? Why did she leave?* "Mom?"

Mother didn't reply. Claire stood and hopped to the window and looked out. The streetlights glowed, bright balls of gold, like the beaming halos of a dozen angels. She looked down and felt a sudden rush of vertigo. The ground rippled, seemed to move up to meet her, but when she focused her eyes, it was normal. *I'm fine. Everything is fine.* But she felt closed in.

If she didn't have a cast on, it would be easy to climb out the window - she'd done it many times as a teenager, leaving her bed stuffed with a body made of pillows. It had been easy to shimmy down the trellis. *You can't do that now. You have a baby in your oven!* She giggled and returned to the desk chair. She wasn't going to rest; she was going to surf. It was the first time in a long time that it sounded like fun. *We'll have fun fun fun,"* sang the Beach Boys.

Downstairs, the Andrews Sisters started singing. The music filled her senses, and she smelled fresh apples, and then tasted them on her tongue, as sweet as they were sour.

Humming along with the song, she decided she needed to do something to distract herself from the strange state of mind. She opened her email.

***

"Jason," said Paul. "I was just about to call you. That storm is moving toward Denver more quickly than they were predicting. You and Jake might want to be in the air really early."

"Agreed. I was just watching the news. I'll tell Jake. I wanted to talk to you about something."

"Anything wrong?"

"The opposite. Claire and I are moving into your house this weekend. As long as that's fine by you."

"That's excellent. Claire's off bed rest?"

"Not yet, but it doesn't matter. A good friend has offered to stay with her while I'm at work."

"I'll bet Claire's relieved."

"Oh, yeah. She's relieved about a lot of things. We had a nice talk. I brought some of her brother's journals along and started reading tonight. Priscilla Martin did some weird-ass shit to her son. Freaky, creepy stuff. It convinced me we need to get out right away."

"Like what?"

"I'll tell you later, but Paul, I'm really worried about Claire's safety."

"I talked with Steffie and she told me some things that gave me the same worry. But I don't think we need to lose any sleep tonight. I called Claire and she was just fine. But if you want, I can go get her now. She can stay at my place until you land. She'd only be alone a few hours - or she can invite a friend over."

"Thanks, Babs made the same offer, but Prissy would probably freak out, and that would be worse."

"I'm bigger and stronger than anyone named Babs. I'd be happy to take on your mother-in-law." He laughed. "She's been a pain in my ass since high school."

"Claire says she'd rather wait, that her mother is playing nice. And if Claire thinks it's okay, I'm going to trust her. But thank you." He paused. "If something does come down, Babs and her husband - and a neighbor who's a cop - can be there in minutes. But again, thank you. You're a good friend."

"The offer stands if you need me. I'm taking off for Brimstone this afternoon. Steffie's schedule cleared early, so we're going to spend the evening together and fly back tomorrow morning."

"You like her, don't you?"

"I've liked her since we were kids, but she only had eyes for Tim." Paul paused. "I gotta tell you, some of what Steffie told me tonight really backs up your feeling about getting Claire out of Priscilla's right away. Steffie says she's worse than Claire thinks. That's gotta be pretty bad."

Jason felt a chill. "I'll call Claire again and see how things are. Just to make sure."

"I think that's a good idea. Let me know."

***

Claire marveled at the beauty of her email page. She'd never noticed it before, but the background was such a brilliant shade of blue that it glowed, and the darker blue-gray of the toolbars complemented it perfectly. She wasn't quite so fond of the black Arial font. *A serifed font would look better. Maybe Cambria.* She made a note in her desktop Stickies to try the color combination on one of her website jobs, then lost focus when the computer made a short but fascinating musical chime and a new email appeared at the top of the box.

It was from Stephanie Banks. Excited, she opened it and read: *Hello, Claire. I just want to let you know that I'll be arriving Saturday and am looking forward to seeing you again after all these years. Paul has said such nice things about you and your husband. It will be wonderful to talk about old times, and swap stories about Tim. My phone number is in my signature below. Don't hesitate to call if you need to talk before I come. Paul has told me a little about what's going on and I guarantee you, it's not in your mind.*

Claire squinted, fascinated as the words waved and slipped from their places. If she focused her eyes, they stayed in place, but if she relaxed, even a little, the letters moved, rolling as if riding waves.

Paul told me about the fake Facebook page for Tim, and that he had a girlfriend listed. Do you happen to recall her name? I'll check it out.

Stephanie's words turned from black to purple to blue on the screen and the font flipped between Arial, Times New Roman, and Trebuchet. *Hmm. Ashley? Yes. In Michigan. Ashley Perkins. That was the girl's name.* She focused on the keyboard and began pecking at the wavering letters.

How about a nice Lucida? Stephanie's words lilted through her mind, imbued with a soft Irish brogue that suited her red hair perfectly.

I'm using Lucida because it's graceful, like you. But not me. I'm a klutz. Mother says so. But anyway, Tim's girlfriend on Facebook is named Ashley Perkins. She's in Michigan. Claire retrieved the link and pasted it in. With the changing of every screen, bright colors bloomed, distracting her - *I think I need to lie down or something* - but she got the job done.

***

"You're sure you want me here?" Carl Vandercooth said as Babs rang Prissy's doorbell.

"You bet I do."

"Why? Prissy's your friend, not mine. I can't stomach that old witch. What she did to us was reprehensible."

"I told you, Carl, she's not my friend anymore, but I'm worried about Claire. If you stand tall and cross your arms like you mean business, Prissy may let us go see her. Or me, at least."

"Oh, no. I'll go up and see Claire with you, but you're not leaving me alone with that woman."

"You're afraid of her?" Babs smiled. "A big strong man like you?"

"I'm not afraid. I can't stand her. Big difference."

The porch light came on and then Prissy Martin opened the door a crack. The usual Andrews Sisters song poured out of the house. "Good evening, Babs. Carl." Her voice was haughty and ice-cold. "I wasn't expecting you. Do you need something?" She didn't take the security chain off the door.

Babs spoke up. "We're here to visit Claire."

The old record ended and began again before Prissy answered. "Claire is having an after-dinner nap. I'm not going to disturb her."

"We'll wait." Babs ignored Carl's look of dismay. She'd told him she was worried about the girl, but she hadn't told him enough. She'd remedy that later. "Aren't you going to invite us in, Prissy? We can chat." Babs ignored Priscilla's glare and smiled sweetly. "A visit would be nice."

Priscilla looked even more surprised than Carl. "It's not a good time."

"Why is that?" Another surprised look. Babs, proud of herself for finding her backbone, smiled.

"I'm shampooing the carpets."

"At night?"

"They need it, if it's any of your business. I'll see you later."

"Very well. We'll be back in an hour."

"Sorry, no visitors tonight. The carpets will be wet. You understand." With that Priscilla closed the door and locked it.

"Damn it," Babs said as they left the property. "I'm going to try to call Claire again." She pulled out her phone and pressed Claire's number. Within moments, Claire answered.

"Claire, sweetie? It's Aunt Babs. I hope I didn't wake you. Your mother said you were napping."

"I'm not sleeping, no." She sounded fine. Distracted, but fine.

"Is everything okay, sweetie?"

"Yes. As a matter of fact, it's great!"

Babs smiled. "Good. You'll call me if you need anything, right?"

"I sure will, Aunt Babs. Thank you for thinking of me. Don't worry about me. I'm fine. Honestly." She lowered her voice to a whisper. "Mother's even being nice to me!"

Babs laughed. "That's good, sweetie. Call me if you need anything."

Carl put his arm around Babs' waist as they walked. "I've never seen you like this before, Babs. I like it."

She smiled. "You haven't seen anything yet. I'm going to make sure that little girl is safe."

You Give Me Fever

Claire watched in fascination as words floated out of her phone. She heard them first, and then saw them. *Call me if you need anything.* They streamed like smoke, each letter a swirling mass of white steam. She wanted to laugh, but wasn't sure it was funny.

The words rose, hovered, then slowly dissipated, like vanishing ghosts. She reached out and tried to touch them. Her fingertips passed through the final G, breaking it apart and sending it swirling into invisibility.

Something's not right. What's happening to me? For a moment, she thought she spoke the words aloud, but the more she thought about it, the more certain she became it was only a thought. *If I can hear my own thoughts, what if other people can hear them, too?* Worried, she tried to keep from thinking, but it didn't work. And then her thoughts began coming out of her head as fractured words and random letters, and floated in the air.

Panicked, she tried to gather them, frightened that they'd drift downstairs and Mother or someone else might see them. But she couldn't catch them. The scattered thoughts floated around the room and rose to the ceiling, bobbing there. Beyond them, she was able to make out every grain of plaster, every fiber of paint, every stroke of the brush. The hovering thoughts forgotten, she gazed at the ceiling, lost in its intricate patterns. It was amazing. She'd never seen anything like it. *It's beautiful.*

A startling cacophony of sound blared from somewhere close. She turned and saw notes, strong and hard, bold and black, dancing and bouncing toward the ceiling.

Claire searched for the source. "What?" she asked. Listening very closely, she recognized *Magic Man* by Heart. It took her a moment to make sense of this sudden music, then she realized it was Jason's ringtone. *He's calling me. Where's my phone?* She realized she was still holding it. For a moment, it was a tiny ship, sailing on the storm-tossed sea of her hand. She blinked, and it resumed its natural form.

"Magic Man?" She laughed, thinking of Ann Wilson's mama crying that it was time to come home. *That poor woman. What those rude Wilson sisters must have put her through! Brava!* She laughed and answered.

"Claire? Is that you?"

"Jason! You're not going to believe it! I was sitting here and all of a sudden, there were words. *Words!* All over the place! And then I looked at the ceiling and-"

"Whoa, whoa, whoa. Claire! What are you talking about?"

From thin air, a clawed hand reached into her vision and clutched the phone. Claire looked up and gasped when she saw a lithe, wavering snake flickering like the tiny flame of a candle. And then the creature resolved, like a Polaroid, and she was looking at her mother, who began speaking into the phone. Claire watched, fascinated, as a stream of spidery black letters flowed from her mother's mouth.

"It's nothing to worry about, Jason. Just a bit of a fever. I'm taking care of her right now."

Insistent noise from the other end - Jason's voice. No letters, though, only tiny black sparks from the phone as his voice fluctuated.

"Of course." Mother ended the call and smiled at Claire. But it wasn't a normal smile. It stretched too wide, passing the perimeters of her face, stretching, stretching, those red lips, white, perfect teeth, stretching beyond Claire's line of sight. *Cheshire Mother!*

A fever? Mother said I have a fever.

The word *fever* came out of her head in pink bubble letters and circled Mother like a flock of buzzards homing in on dinner. Mother, whose smile was okay now, paid no attention to the *"fever"* hovering right in front of her face, but Claire knew she'd seen it. *She has to see it! And surely she could also see the green fumes and stink molecules that radiated from her skin. God, I hate that perfume!*

"Let's get you to bed, Claire. You aren't feeling well."

"You give me fever, Mother. Fever."

***

Jason couldn't stop worrying about Claire. She sounded happy, but had talked nonsense and when Priscilla said she had a fever, alarm bells rang. If she was delirious - and that's how it sounded - the fever had to be bad. He tried not to think of the things Paul had told him.

It was past one and he lay in bed glued to the Weather Channel. He'd already told Jake they now needed to be at the airport at four for a five a.m. takeoff, and was beginning to worry they might need to leave sooner. The storm was hurtling toward Denver and blizzard conditions were expected by dawn.

He punched in Priscilla's number, not caring if he woke her up. She picked up on the first ring. In the background music played. He couldn't make it out, but it wasn't *Don't Sit Under the Apple Tree.*

"Hello?"

"This is Jason."

"Why, hello, Jas-"

He cut her off. "I'm worried about Claire. You said she has a fever and she sounded delirious. If it's that bad, she needs to go to the hospital."

"She's fine. I called Dr. Hopper and he came by. She's sleeping like a baby."

"What was wrong?"

"Dr. Hopper says there was no fever." She paused. "He said it's likely the symptoms are psychological. He'll be by to check on her again in the morning."

"Psychological? What do you mean?"

Prissy sighed. "Now I want you to be calm, Jason."

"Just tell me what's going on!"

"Fine. It appears she's had a minor psychotic break. I think we've both seen this coming for some time. Gerald - Dr. Hopper - doesn't think it's too serious and-"

"Not serious? Prissy, she needs immediate medical attention!"

"Dr. Hopper's on top of it, Jason."

His stomach knotted. "I'd rather hear a diagnosis from Dr. Putnam."

"Doctors don't make house calls anymore, Jason. Dr. Hopper did it as a favor to me because we're old friends and coworkers. I would think you'd be pleased he came."

Jason, irritated by Prissy's voice, silently counted to three. "I'm glad he came. But you need to get her-"

"What she *needs,* Jason, is to take it easy. Doctor's orders. And don't forget. I *am* a nurse. We aren't amateurs here. The best thing you can do is trust us to take care of her. If the symptoms worsen, we have one of the best psychiatrists in Snapdragon waiting for our call-"

"We have our *own* psychiatrist."

"-but right now, she needs peace and relaxation, and that's what she's getting."

Jason's insides tightened and anxiety bloomed like a flower made of glass. *Something isn't right about this.* "Listen Prissy, I'll be back tomorrow and I'm coming straight home to get Claire to her own doctor and then I'm going to finish packing."

"Packing?"

"Yes. We think it's best to get Claire settled into the new place right away."

"Oh, Jason, sweetheart. You don't seem to understand. That isn't possible."

"Bullshit, Prissy."

She gasped.

"We're moving out as soon as-"

"Now you listen to me, young man. First of all, I won't be cursed at. Second, Carlene is still on bed rest, per *your* Dr. Putnam's orders, and finally, my daughter is experiencing a psychological disturbance that is *very* precarious, and if you think for one moment I'm going to stand here and-"

"We're moving out. Don't concern yourself."

"I beg to differ, Jason. I'll call the police if I have to."

Jason's jaw ached with tension. "Fuck you," he said. He heard Prissy gasp just before he ended the call.

Within seconds, Prissy called him back. "Fuck you," he said to the ringing phone. He had to find a way back to Snapdragon. Right away.

He rang Jake repeatedly, but the pilot wasn't answering - no surprise. When he'd called to tell him they had to leave for the airport at four, he'd had a hard time rousing him. Jason checked in again with Denver International, but nothing had become available. Now he tried private flight services, but no one was picking up at one in the morning. Renting a car was out - he couldn't drive over a thousand miles overnight. *There has to be another way!* He looked at his phone, thought of calling Paul, but decided against it - he needed him to go to Arizona. If Claire did need psychological help, he wanted Stephanie Banks there, not some douchebag in Priscilla's pocket. *Damn you, Priscilla Martin.* He knew she was behind this somehow, some way.

On the edge of his bed, he bounced his knee as his mind raced. He'd never felt so helpless in his life. Then it struck him. *I need to call Babs.*

***

Babs' phone jarred Carl from a deep sleep. He sat up and looked at the clock as Babs switched on the lamp - it was after midnight. The phone stopped ringing but began again almost immediately. She grabbed it and said, "Hello?"

Carl heard a man's deep voice on the other end but couldn't make out the words. Something was terribly wrong, Carl could see it on his wife's face.

Babs gasped and clutched her bosom. "Is she-?"

The man's voice cut her off.

"Yes," said Babs in a frantic tone. "Of course." She looked at Carl, her eyes wide with worry. "I'm on my way." She ended the call and got out of bed. "We have to go, Carl, right now."

"What's wrong, honey? What's happened?"

Babs was headed for the bathroom. "Get dressed. We need to go to Pleasanton."

"Pleasanton?"

"My sister. She's had an accident. It's serious."

"Blanche?"

"No, it's Dorothy. We have to leave right now!" She shut the bathroom door.

Carl hopped out of bed and rummaged for his pants. It was at least a two-hour drive to Pleasanton. If they left now, they'd arrive just after three.

As Carl struggled into his trousers, Babs' phone rang again.

"That's probably Blanche. Let her know we're coming," called Babs.

It was. She'd just gotten the call, too, and was already on her way to Pleasanton. Carl sighed. Dorothy was the littlest sister, a school teacher, and a wonderful person. He hoped she'd be okay, both for her own sake and for Babs, who had always doted on her.

***

"Shit!" Jason chucked the phone down on the bed. Of course Babs hadn't answered. It was after midnight. Head in hands, he tried to think, tried to clear his mind. *I need to get there.*

He picked up his phone and tried Claire again.

It rang and rang.

***

In the kitchen, Priscilla Martin frowned at Carlene's phone as *Magic Man* rang out. *Jason. Again.* After his disrespectful little tirade earlier, she wanted to answer and give him the what-for, but decided it was best to leave it be. He'd been calling all night, and Carlene needed her rest. Prissy herself wouldn't be getting any for the time being. She sighed and finished slathering light mayo on her ham sandwich and when Carlene's phone stopped ringing, she set it to silent mode.

She took a bite of her sandwich and sighed. *A woman's work is never done.*

Laugh, Clown, Laugh

Claire sat in her desk chair looking out the window. Street lamps that were more decorative than useful studded Morning Glory Circle and the sickle moon hung in the sky, surrounded by stars in the cold clear night. Nothing moved, but the houses seemed to throb in place, to breathe in and out, in and out. *That's what a hamburger is all about.*

A hamburger with onions, pickles, catsup, and peanut butter. *Peanut butter fries!* She wanted some right now.

Movement caught her eye. Down the street, an SUV pulled out of the Vandercooths' driveway. She watched, fascinated, as twin streams of red light followed the car down the cul-de-sac and onto Daisy Drive. *Maybe Aunt Babs is going to In-N-Out Burger! I hope she brings back something for me!* Happy-faced burgers bounced merrily around her head, singing the In-N-Out song. Claire smiled and watched. They smelled wonderful.

Then the music came again. She'd thought she'd heard it earlier, but it had been so soft she hadn't been sure. Now it was easy to hear. Goosebumps rose and her stomach knotted as the scratchy old record played downstairs. The singing hamburgers vanished abruptly.

"If you go..." She recognized *Teddy Bears' Picnic* and felt a stab of panic. Though only the words drifted up through the vent, she felt like the picnicking teddy bears were in the room with her. A vivid memory broke the surface of her awareness, like a bubble rising and popping: *Mother is telling her that if the bears catch her listening, they'll tear her from limb to limb and eat her guts and play Ping-Pong with her eyeballs.*

Listening to what? Claire tried to remember, but the memory dissolved.

She shuddered as the sudden sour scent of potato salad filled her nose. Salad left in the sun, poison salad. The smell was so thick and heavy it filled her lungs like curdled sludge. And then there were ants - dozens of thousands of them, marching up the walls, onto the ceiling, clamoring over each other, dripping to the floor in erratic zigzags. She shuddered and heard the buzz of flies, hundreds, thousands of them, buzzing everywhere, and then she saw them, black and emerald, bloated and logy, circling her like drunken bumblebees. She swatted, but the flies were impervious.

"... Mommies and Daddies take them ..." The music continued drifting up from the vent and one huge fly, the size of a football, hovered in front of her face. She stared into its eyes, two gleaming pools of black tar, captivated by her own reflection staring back at her. The massive fly blinked and Claire gasped, backed away. It wore a straw Panama hat and a long

brown cigarette dangled from a mouth that looked like a puckered wound, its sutures prematurely removed. The raw, lipless orifice moved. "I'm not dead, Claire. I'm not dead." Timothy's voice tumbled from the thing's mouth and Claire screamed.

The fly buzzed closer, inches from her face. It reeked of black licorice and Opium perfume.

Claire dropped her crutches, flopped onto the bed, and covered her eyes. "Stop!"

"I'm not dead." The fly slurped the words like a wet strand of spaghetti. "I'm not dead and I'm coming back. I'm coming back."

I'm losing my mind! I'm losing my goddamn mind!

The buzzing stopped. The room was silent except for the faint echoes of the record player downstairs.

"... safer to stay home ... " the scratchy song played on.

Claire opened her eyes and gasped.

On the floor near her bedroom door, which seemed miles away, a man's lifeless body lay heaped in unnatural angles, his clothes rotted and torn. She sat, hand to her mouth, tears blurring her vision, and saw the yellowed ribs where the skin and shirt had disintegrated. A piercing sound, like an infant's shriek, shook the room.

Claire looked up and saw a massive American eagle circling overhead, its golden-bronze plumage glinting, its white head a shining dot lost in its vast wingspan. It shrieked, and from somewhere within, the great bird ticked - *tick, tick, tick* - and Claire saw the American flag emblazoned on its breast ... and the clock embedded there. In its claws, it gripped a small green laurel. It was the awful eagle clock she'd been terrified of as a child. *"If it catches you awake, Mother tells her, "it will find you and peck your eyes out!"* Claire remembered that now; she hadn't imagined it after all.

It circled above the dead man, cried out, and dived, perching on one of the corpse's yellowed rib bones. The eagle looked at her, blinked its glistening pinprick eyes, and cocked its head to one side.

"Go away." Claire's words trembled and she felt their vibration in the soles of her feet. "Go away."

The bird turned its attention to the cadaver, glutting itself on the red, stringy innards, plucking at its intestines. The reek of death fermented the air.

Her stomach heaved as crunching noises and wet, sloppy sounds vibrated through the room, loud enough she felt it in her teeth.

"... lots of things to eat ... " crooned the record player from the vent.

Another memory crashed down on her:

Mother tucks Timothy into bed as Claire watches from the hall. Mother bends to kiss him goodnight. He gives her a quick peck and she slaps his face, fists his hair, and says, "No! You do it like this ... kiss Mommy like this," and crushes her son's mouth to hers. The pink tip of her tongue is writhing like a wet snake around Timothy's lips, seeking passage into his mouth. He tries to push her away and Mother's hand is at his groin, squeezing until he whimpers and stops fighting her. "Kiss Mommy like this ..." She squeezes again, and Timothy allows the kiss as tears leak from his eyes.

The vulture's harsh cry shattered Claire's trance. It flapped its wings, steadying itself as the dead man began to move. The face, a gangrenous ruin of rot and corrosion, grimaced as the cadaver struggled to sit up on decaying, ruined limbs. Leathery gray skin swung from the jawbone as the corpse turned its head to fully face her. When the eyes opened, Claire recognized him. "Timothy. My God ... *Timothy!*"

Her dead brother worked his fleshless jaw back and forth, as if testing its ability, then said, "I'm not dead. I'm not dead, and I'm coming back."

Claire screamed until she thought her throat might bleed and her lungs might burst.

***

On the sofa in the living room, Prissy looked at the ceiling. *My goodness. What is she* doing *up there?* "Carlene?" she called.

Silence.

Prissy set her plate down, stood and made her way to the record player where she started the song over - the 1932 version of *The Teddy Bear's Picnic* by Henry Hall and His Orchestra - and raised the volume several notches.

***

Jason tried Claire again. It rang then went to voicemail. Next he called Priscilla. "Prissy," he said when the voicemail picked up. "Please answer. I can't get hold of Claire and I need to know everything's okay." He paused, sighing. "Look, I'm sorry about earlier. I didn't mean to be disrespectful. I'm just ... I'm freaking out over here and I need to know everything's all right. So please, please, call me back." He ended the call and stared at the phone, and considered giving Babs another try. *She'll call you right back as soon as she sees you've called.* Plus, he didn't want to wake the poor woman. *It's not as if Priscilla would let her in to see Claire anyway.*

Idly, he opened the nightstand drawer, more to give his hands something to do than anything else. There was no bible. *When did they stop putting bibles in hotel rooms?* Not that it mattered - he wouldn't have read it anyway.

"She's had a minor psychotic break." Priscilla's voice broke into his thoughts. He took a slow deep, breath.

Maybe I should just get to the plane and fly home myself. I haven't had any seizures in ... well, it hadn't been that long. And he couldn't bear the thought of dying and leaving Claire and the baby alone with Priscilla Martin. "Claire. I'm so sorry. Please be okay."

"She's had a minor psychotic break." It was more than that, he knew it. He felt helpless, trapped, as if the hotel room were growing smaller and smaller. Before full panic could seize him, he dropped to the floor and began doing push-ups. He didn't know if he was overreacting, but if he didn't burn off some of this nervous energy, he was going to explode.

Let it go, let it go, let it go. This was his mantra as he shoved off the floor, again and again. *There's not a fucking thing I can do until tomorrow. Let it go.*

***

Clowns. Clowns were everywhere. Claire was in a gallery of clowns; she couldn't stop seeing them. It was the same ones she'd thrown out. They leered at her from massive portraits that hung along the hall. She could smell them - cotton candy that had fallen in dirt and straw, cotton candy covered with feces and blood, rank, rancid, moldy. Others smelled like sewer water, like Pennywise. She'd hated Pennywise ever since Mother made her watch *IT* with her when she was five.

Why did you make me watch that, Mother? That really fucked me up. She worked her way down the hall, her crutches seeming to sink deeper each time they touched ground. The walls moved in and out, breathing and rasping, but the shrill giggles of the clowns kept her moving.

Somewhere in the dark corners of her awareness, she knew she was imagining everything, that none of it was real - *I've lost my mind! I've totally lost it!* - but she couldn't stop to think about that. She needed to get ... *Where do I need to get? Where am I going?* She turned a circle on her crutches and stared in the direction she'd come. The hall telescoped on and on, an endless length of closed doors, dried-flower wreaths that pulsed with hunger, and a shifting kaleidoscope of clown portraits that heaved and swayed and changed position with the labored breathing of the walls.

She gasped as a clown dressed in a green Bozo suit unicycled its way into the hall, its blood-colored smile expanding to impossible proportions as it pedaled toward her on a squeaky wheel. A colorful balloon bouquet - red, yellow, black, blue - trailed behind it, each one twisted into the shape of a teddy bear.

"... their piiiic-nic ..." The music in the living room floated up the stairs and appeared as a cluster of wet moldering notes behind the giggling and fast-approaching purple-haired clown.

"No!" Claire turned tail, hobbling back toward her bedroom as sweat poured from her face and into her mouth. She tasted the horrible, cloying sweetness of cotton candy - *it's coming out of my pores!* - as she bustled down the hall, heard the squeak of the unicycle - the honk of a toy horn, the giggle of the thing itself - right behind her, so close she could smell the plastic of the balloons, taste their bitter talc.

The clown cackled and the force of its laugh became a pair of hands shoving her to the floor. "Get off me! Get off me!" She writhed, felt the thing clawing at her clothes, giggling, giggling, giggling. She rolled onto her back and stared into the monster's face - plaster-white skin, blue triangles for eyes, its nostrils like stab wounds, and its mouth a gaping red crater. It smelled of *Opium.*

"Carlene!"

Claire smacked at the thing, trying to knock it away with her knees.

"Carlene! Stop it! It's me!"

Claire shrieked. "Get off me!"

"It's me! Your mother! Carlene! Stop it!"

Mother? Claire lowered her hands, watched in horror as the clown's face rearranged itself, melting and shifting until she stared at Prissy Martin. "Mother?"

And then Claire was on her feet, her crutches at her sides. Mother, wearing a green satin robe, had an arm around her waist. "We need to get you into bed. It's okay now. Mother's here."

Claire was astounded to realize she'd gone only a few feet from her bedroom door. They entered and Mother helped Claire under the sheets. "My goodness, Carlene. I don't know *what's* gotten into you!"

"The clowns. They're everywhere!" She tried to sit up but Mother's arm braced her down.

"Now, now, darling. Be calm. I'm calling Dr. Hopper to come see you."

Dr. Hopper? "Is it ... it is my fever?" Peggy Lee's face formed in front of her, then dissolved into smoke.

"It must be," said Mother. "Just be still. I'll be right back with a mug of warm milk."

Claire watched Mother bustle from the room and sat, staring, listening to the melody that rose from the vents: *"... games to plaaay ..."*

Games to play.

Games to play.

Games to play.

A new memory, as concise and acute as a bee-sting, pierced her. *This song. This is the song Mother played when she ... when she ... did things to Timothy.* In her mind's eye, she saw Mother pinning Tim down on the dining table, securing his wrists and ankles with soft nylon rope.

He's nude ... and screaming. Mother looks up and sees her. "Look at him, Carlene! Look at him!"

Carlene tries to turn away, but Mother's hand is a vise around her wrist. She drags Carlene close to him, yanks her. Carlene cries out and Mother slaps the back of her head. "Look! LOOK!" Carlene looks at her brother's nude body through a blur of tears.

"He's been looking at the girls," says Mother. She stuffs one of Tim's socks into his mouth to muffle his cries, and says to him, "How dare you sneak into a theater with a girl! I told you never to do that." She grabs his no-no and pinches hard.

Behind the gag, Tim shrills.

"Let him go, Mommy, please." Carlene weeps.

"I will when he learns what that dirty, stinking thing between his legs is for." She flicks his no-nos - all of them - with her fingers.

"Mommy, please-"

"You shut up, Carlene. Just shut up!" Mother's grip tightens on Carlene's arm. "Now you listen to me, Timothy. No girl is allowed to touch you except your mother. Do you understand me?"

Timothy nods, tears streaming in rivers down his face.

"I'm going to show you what happens when you let a girl touch you there." She looked down at Carlene. "Carlene. I want you touch your brother's no-nos."

Carlene wails. "No, Mommy, no. Please let him go!"

"Touch them! Touch them!" She yanks Carlene's arm, forces her hand toward her brother's groin. Carlene squeezes her eyes shut and tries to recoil when her fingertips touch coarse, curly hair and soft skin, but Mother squeezes tighter. "Open your hand, Carlene."

Warm, springy flesh fills Carlene's hand. She chances a peek through slitted eyes and sees his no-nos in her palm. "Mommy, please ..."

"Now close your hand and squeeze them!"

"No!"

"Squeeze them or the teddy bears are going to come and eat you!"

Carlene squeezes.

Timothy squeals.

Mother releases her and says, "Now go upstairs and wash your hands." She turns to Timothy. "That's what girls do, Timmy. They hurt you. But not me. Mother doesn't hurt you. Mother makes it all better."

Carlene runs from the room, out of breath, wracked by sobs.

Circle of Hell

At 2:30 in the morning in his hotel room in Denver, Jason finally began to nod off. The alarm would go off at 3:30, but an hour of slumber was better than nothing. He closed his eyes, welcoming sleep, never noticing the snowflakes that began falling just before three.

***

The miles rolled by too slowly. Babs and Carl had been on the road over an hour and Carl figured they'd be at the hospital in Pleasanton by three if their luck held. *Please, no fog. Please, no fog.*

Beside him, Babs stared silently at the road as a rebroadcast of Coastal Eddie's show played. The jock was talking about conspiracies in the town of Devilswood, down near Lompoc and Solvang, where pea soup and Danish pastries reigned supreme. Coastal Eddie was talking about Devilswood's early 19th-century witchcraft trials.

"If you'd like to visit the odd little village of Devilswood," he said in his smooth, ironic voice, "I suggest you go in August to attend the Founder's Day celebration. Why is it special, you ask? Because, dear listeners, the celebration is a murderous one - they're observing the anniversary of their early witchcraft trials. Yes, my babies, my friends and neighbors, witches were executed old-school style right there in the early 1800s in Devilswood. And the celebration is quite a show - they have an execution reenactment that's not to be missed … unless you're a witch of course." Eddie silenced as the first notes of The Eagles' *Witchy Woman* began playing.

Carl hadn't heard about Devilswood before. *Maybe we'll time our next trip to Solvang to coincide. Babs might get a kick out of that witchcraft stuff.* He glanced at his wife. She was a sweet, kind woman, but had a decidedly dark sense of humor. He nearly said something, but now wasn't the time. She was too upset about her sister. He patted her knee and kept driving.

***

Phyllis Stine lay shaking in bed, listening to Clyde grumble and snore. Sleep evaded her. She couldn't get her mind off the letter she'd received today:

I know what you and your husband do when you think no one sees you. I see everything, Ms. Stine, including the years you've tried to hide beneath all that expensive plastic surgery.

There was no threat, and no demand, but it made Phyllis uneasy, nonetheless. It wasn't the first anonymous letter she'd received that boasted knowledge of Clyde's cross-dressing habits, but it *was* the first one that mentioned her age. *Nobody knows how old I am. Nobody.* She'd ransacked her memory and come up blank. *I've never told a soul.* And she knew Clyde wouldn't. He of all people would not have bragged that his wife was nearly old enough to be his mother.

It ate at her.

She prided herself on her beauty. Natural or not, beauty was beauty, and up until six months ago, she could have easily passed for a woman of fifty instead of seventy. *I need to have Dr. Loopus tighten up my eye bags.* Yes. That would help a lot. Things were getting a little loose around her mouth, too.

She rolled over. *So help me God, if I ever find out who's writing these letters, I'm going to kill them with my bare hands.* She closed her eyes, finally stopped shaking, and fell asleep.

***

Nelly and Bertie Dunworth had received a letter as well. Unlike Phyllis Stine, however, neither lost a wink of sleep over it. The letter, in short, had announced knowledge of their secret professions as phone-sex operators. The sender also called them cheap dime-store hussies and threatened to expose them if they didn't fix up their yard.

Neither sister gave a squat about any secrets getting out. If the Almighty hadn't wanted them to get men off over the phone for a living, He wouldn't have given them such sultry, feathery voices. And they'd manage their yard however they saw fit, thank you very much. If they wanted to have old tires, rusted soup cans, and fifteen cat bowls on the porch for strays, then by God, they would. In fact, before retiring for the night, they'd talked about doing just that. It had given them quite a good giggle.

Tonight, the Dunworth sisters slept in peace.

***

Friday night at the Dean house meant one thing: passion.

Due to Delphi and Daphie's clarinet practice, chess tournaments, and piano lessons, Friday was the only night Earl and his beloved Earlene could engage in intimacies. Consequently, Friday nights went long and late. He thanked heaven for his little blue pills: after all these years, he could finally keep up with Earlene's voracious appetites - and they were definitely worth losing a night's sleep over.

He knelt behind her as the strains of *White Wedding* played in the background - *"Hey, little sister ..."* - Billy Idol's gruff voice turned Earlene into a maniac.

Earl clutched a handful of each of her buttocks, shaking them about, and enjoying the show as her flesh rippled and rolled.

"Ohhh ... Earl ..." cooed Earlene, wagging her backside, begging him to enter.

"Are you ready, baby doll?"

"Yessss. Pleasssee. Yessss."

Earl entered her, and not conventionally - *They don't call me the Fudge King for nothing!* - and continued slapping Earlene's backside as she huffed and puffed.

Every time with Earlene was like the first time - exciting, frightening, taboo. That first time had been so long ago, and they'd been so very, very young. Not many couples had as much passion after all these years as the Deans did, but then again, few couples dared to travel down such forbidden roads.

"It's ssso exciting!" cried Earlene. "Harder!"

Earl plowed into her, deep and unforgiving.

She took him like a champ and begged for more.

***

"I'm going to be up all night if we drink any more hot cocoa," Paul told Steffie Banks. He'd landed at the shiny new Brimstone Airport at five p.m. and Stephanie had been there to pick him up in her red Land Rover. Her hug had thrilled him.

After a sublime dinner in the restaurant at the Brimstone Grand, she'd taken him back to her neat, modern adobe home. The Saltillo tile floors were softened with southwestern-style throw rugs and the rocky fireplace crackled and kept the place warm. Her furniture and decor were earthy browns and greens. Paul thought it was the coziest, most welcoming home he'd ever stepped into. Only Steffie herself was more welcoming.

"It's late," she said. "I guess you're right - we should stop with the cocoa."

"Probably. And if we're leaving for Snapdragon in the morning, we'd better get our beauty sleep."

"We don't have much time, but we'll get up early and see a few things before the flight." She paused. "We haven't talked too much about the situation in Snapdragon."

"We will tomorrow," Paul said, not wanting the evening to end. He and Steffie had taken up as if twenty-plus years hadn't passed. Conversation flowed, so did laughter. Paul felt selfish, deflecting questions about Priscilla Martin, but he needed a few hours without worry. "There's plenty of time on the flight home to discuss everything." He paused. "I know I'm being selfish."

"No, you're not. There's no point in dwelling. We'll deal with it when the time is right."

"Sounds good," he said thinking of Jason's last phone call.

"Something wrong?" Steffie set her mug down.

"I'm hoping that storm doesn't hit Denver. Jason is frantic to get home to Claire."

She nodded. "I think it was really nice of you to offer to take her to your place. I wish she'd taken you up on it."

"Yeah, me too, but like I said, there are neighbors ready to get her out of there if necessary. One's a cop."

Steffie nodded and rose. "I'm glad they're there for her. And I'm glad Jason's listening to Claire with an open mind now."

Paul stood up. "What time are we getting up?"

"Meet me in the kitchen for breakfast at 5:30."

"In the morning?" He followed her upstairs. They paused in front of the guest room.

"Yes, in the morning. I have my reasons." Stephanie smiled. "I'm glad you're here."

"So am I." He held her gaze. "I can't believe it's been so many years."

"Way too many." She came closer and he leaned in, his eyes closing, his heart beating like a teenager's.

She kissed him on the cheek. "See you bright and early."

***

Candy had gone to bed hours ago, but Milton Sachs couldn't sleep. He sat at his desk staring at the latest anonymous letter. It had arrived in their mailbox today and Candy had, as usual, left it unopened on the hall table with the other deliveries. She was happy to have Milton handle the mail, and he was grateful because she didn't need to know that, once or twice a year, some reprobate threatened to spill Candy's secret. He himself had no problem with her past, but he wanted to spare her worry and possible humiliation, so he'd never said a word.

The thing was, the sender of the typed letters didn't make threats or try to extort money, and as long as that was the case, Milton preferred not to bring the law into it. That would humiliate Candy even more. Their friends were fellow attorneys and people involved in the city government, not to mention the country club crowd, and Candy loved the socializing and the parties. Sometimes, over the years, on other nights like this one, he'd considered telling her. He stared at the paper a long moment before putting it through the shredder. Then he went upstairs to join his wife in bed. *The most beautiful woman on the sac. Maybe even in the entire town.*

***

Aida listened to Stan's soft, rhythmic breathing and wished she could fall asleep that easily, simply turn off worry like he did, but it wasn't to be.

She couldn't stop thinking about the threatening letter they'd received. Aida's heart had nearly stopped when she'd drawn it from the mailbox and seen the nondescript envelope with the equally non-descript typed address.

The sender never named their crime, only claimed to know what they'd done and said they should pay for their sins. Of course, they wouldn't go to the police, and Stan no longer got excited - it had gone on so many years he felt it was a paper tiger, somebody's idea of a joke.

She wanted to believe that, to be like Stan, but she couldn't help worrying. She lay in the dark and stared at the ceiling, her stomach sour and knotted.

***

Duane Pruitt's dreams were little more than fractured images that haunted him between bouts of consciousness. He could hear Geneva-Marie's soft voice whispering unintelligible words. He saw images of her smiling, laughing, touching his chin the way she had when they were alone together. And then he saw the blood.

It was everywhere. On his clothes, in his hair, on the walls ... and on his hands. Upon waking, he knew blood on his hands was surely symbolic of guilt, but didn't understand the reference. *Do I feel guilty about her murder? Why would I feel guilty?* The answer came easily: If not for his relationship with her, Burke never would have lost his temper and done what he did. *He found out. He had to have found out, or he wouldn't have come here after shooting the boys and Geneva.*

The knowledge burrowed into the pit of his stomach, twisting like a rusty corkscrew, niggling its way into the deepest trenches of his soul. *Geneva is dead because of me. And the kids.* He couldn't bear to think about them, not yet.

Beside him, Jerry rolled over and opened his eyes. "You need to get some sleep, Duane," he said in a groggy voice.

"I know."

Jerry watched him a long moment. "It wasn't your fault. You know that, don't you?"

Duane's eyes blurred but he managed a smile for Jerry's sake. "I know."

***

The house stood, a massive sepulcher bathed in darkness. All around Morning Glory Circle, porch lights and streetlamps marked each house, but the streetlight in front of the Collins house had gone out and no lights burned within. It was a tomb.

Downstairs, some of the dishes and small appliances, books and paintings, had already been boxed up by Geneva-Marie's bereft first cousins from San Jose, but the furniture remained. The cousins had told the real estate agent to sell the furniture with the house, or donate it to charity.

Upstairs was another matter. A cleaning crew had removed the blood-sodden beds and stripped the bloodstained carpets and scrubbed the wood floors in Barry and Chris Collins' rooms. A hungry mouse scavenged for food, nose twitching, whiskers vibrating as it sniffed at the floorboards, scenting blood no human could detect. It peered at the bare walls and trembled. Despite fresh paint, the memory of the murders lived on in the wood and plaster of the room. The mouse ran.

***

Dave Flannigan sat at the kitchen table. He'd been unable to sleep, his mind on the past. Before him lay his revolver, a solid little .38 Special he'd bought after a thief had broken into his mother's house, and stolen her money and jewelry. His mother, long gone these many years, had never gotten over it. Oh, she claimed she had, but he could always see the terror in her eyes when he left for the rectory after their Monday night dinners. He'd bought the gun for her, but she'd refused to learn to use it, so he'd kept it locked in his nightstand ever since. He'd never used it himself beyond a few trips to the police range for target practice.

While his mother had never recovered from the burglar's invasion, Dave had never gotten over Priscilla Martin's. Now, the gun lay on the table because he couldn't forgive his own cowardice. It rarely bothered him - he was good at compartmentalizing - but tonight's talk with young Andy had brought it all crashing back, as fresh and horrifying as it had been after Timothy Martin committed suicide and Dave realized he might have prevented it if he'd come forward years before. *What else did that woman do to that poor boy?*

He poured a shot of bourbon and tossed it back, grimacing, trying to find his courage. *Dear God in heaven, what should I do?*

God wasn't answering. Dave wasn't even sure there was a God anymore, but he wasn't sure there wasn't one, either - and for a Catholic to commit suicide was a mortal sin, a quick ticket on the train to brimstone and hellfire. He didn't know if he'd ever believed that, but it had worried him enough to stay his hand after Timothy's death.

He dropped the empty shot glass and it rolled off the table, shattering on the floor. Uncaring, he picked up the gun, hefted it. There was one bullet in the chamber. *One is all I need.*

He raised the revolver, opened his mouth, and put it to his lips as tears streamed down his old, seamed cheeks. The metal was cold and metallic against his tongue. He could taste the gun oil.

He put his finger on the trigger, felt the resistance. All it would take was a little more pressure. "God forgive me," he sobbed.

But he doubted God would forgive him.

He lowered the gun, thinking back to when he and Priscilla Martin had had sex. As he told Andy, she always got what she wanted and she'd wanted to rut with him, to use him, and the flesh was weak. And then she asked him to copulate in front of her boy. Before that, he'd tried to convince himself she was sincerely worried about Timothy's self-abuse, but he'd sensed perversion early on. He began to feel repulsion toward her, but still, it had been easier to continue the assignation than confront her. She'd found small ways to remind him that if he didn't do what she asked he could lose his position. Those threats had kept him in line for a long time. When he finally refused outright, Priscilla had accepted it, but only because he'd told her that blackmail goes both ways and her sick obsession with her son would be revealed.

Time passed and he convinced himself that Priscilla had quit sexually abusing her son for fear of exposure. As the years went by, he found peace; and even after Timothy died, Priscilla hadn't come after him.

Then, six years ago, she'd wanted him to stop Snapdragon's first annual gay pride parade. He'd refused, saying it was not his place to judge, nor was it hers. That's when the threats began again. Dave was too old and tired by then to contend with the constant anxiety, so he'd arranged to have his assistant, Andrew Pike, put in charge of Holy Sacramental. When the bishop granted his request, he retired. Andy had been in charge ever since. It no longer mattered if Priscilla told on Dave; he had little to lose.

He looked at the bourbon, nearly picked it up. *Just one more shot before I eat my gun.* Only ending his life would end his guilt. But then he had a thought: *If I off myself, she'll rejoice. She'll have won.* And if Priscilla's grave were ever to be dug, he wanted to help hammer the nails into her coffin.

Filled with new resolve, he rose and locked the gun away. He would not give Priscilla Martin the pleasure. He would go on living, and if she gave Andy a drop of trouble, he would reveal her perversion.

***

Father Andrew Pike slept in fits and starts and conscious or asleep, *Don't Sit Under the Apple Tree* was on a constant loop, haunting him.

When he slept, he dreamed of Priscilla Martin.

She stood in a lush garden of blooming flowers and green vines that climbed looming trees. Stone statues of gods and goddesses punctuated the grounds.

Priscilla Martin stood behind the green curtain of a weeping willow's sweeping limbs. She was nude, her private parts obscured by leaves and foliage. She saw him approach and her crimson lips curled up.

Andy was struck by a wave of the woman's perfume - smoky, thick, and cloying.

Priscilla raised her hand and beckoned.

Andy shook his head. He did not want to join her.

Her smile fell, and Andy felt her gaze slithering over his body. He, too, was naked. And fully erect. After searching for something to cover himself, he settled on a leaf plucked from a nearby fig tree.

Priscilla laughed, a high tinkling sound that reminded him of shattering glass. "Come here, Father."

"No. I can't."

She batted her lashes. Her pale amber eyes were lined with thick kohl, giving her a deranged, Cleopatra-like appearance. "I never take no for an answer, Father. Come to me." Priscilla stepped out of the hanging branches, exposing herself.

He swallowed.

"Please," she said, and Andy heard hiss-like sibilance in her voice.

"No. It's wrong."

Priscilla held his eyes and brought her hands to her breasts. She stroked them and Andy felt himself nearing climax as she brought her hands down to her genitals. She pinched her labia, spread them, and giggled, moaning as something wriggled out of her opening.

Andy gasped as a long gray serpent slid out of her, hit the earth, and coiled between her feet. It raised its wet head, its tongue flicking in and out. It hissed and slithered up her ankle, leaving a slick trail as it twined around her calf, her thigh, her waist, finally wrapping itself around her arm.

She stepped closer to Andy and though he wanted to run, he couldn't move, couldn't even pry his eyes away from the woman and the serpent that bound her arm, like the sleeve of some horrid medieval armor.

Priscilla stood before him. "Kiss me, Father, for I am sin. Taste me. Take me into your mouth."

"No!" His feet were blocks of cement.

From the heavens, the Andrews Sisters sang, *"Don't sit under the apple tree ..."*

"With anyone else but *me*," said Priscilla, taking his now flaccid manhood in her hand.

He stepped back, moved from her scaly, dry touch, and realized there were no weeping willows now, only apple trees. As far as the eye could see.

"With anyone else but me ..." Priscilla's words were a snake's hiss. Her pupils turned to narrow black slits. "With anyone else but me ..." A forked tongue spilled from her mouth.

Down the Rabbit Hole

Claire watched the ceiling ripple. It was like watching the sea. *A perfectly white, beautiful sea.* Mesmerized, she barely registered the rapping on her door until the knocks became insistent.

Fear shot through her and she sat up. "Hello?"

"Carlene?" Mother entered, carrying a big white night owl. "It's just me, Carlene. I've brought you some warm milk, as promised."

"Who?" called the night owl. "Who?"

As Claire stared, the owl transformed into a glass of milk. "Milk? Why?" She looked at the clock on the bedside table. The numbers bounced and whirled, but she was finally able to make them out. "It's almost three."

"Yes, it is. I haven't been able to sleep." Mother sat down on the bed and Claire felt as if she were sinking - it wasn't unpleasant exactly. "I just need to know you're okay, dear." She held out the glass. "Drink up."

She drank quickly then said, "Three in the morning."

Mother gave her a sad smile.

"You know what Ray Bradbury says about three in the morning, don't you, Mom?"

Mother shook her head. "No, dear. What does Ray Bradbury say?"

Claire thought. The words were butterflies, fluttering just past her grasp, but then she recalled them. "He said, *'Three in the morning ... Doctors say the body's at low tide then. The soul is out. The blood moves slow. You're the nearest to dead you'll ever be, save dying.'*"

Mother shook her head. "You always read too many frightening books when you were growing up."

"Ray Bradbury knows everything."

"He's dead and gone. Come now. Drink your milk." Mother shoved the glass toward her and for a moment Claire saw wasps and bees floating up from the bottom, bobbing at the surface. "There's something wrong with it."

"It's just milk," said Mother. "Pure, white, warm milk. It's good for you and the baby."

"Yes." Claire took the glass and watched as the insects disappeared. "The baby." She drank it. It was like swallowing silk.

***

Moments before the alarm sounded, Jason awoke to silence. He heard no cars out on the highway, no planes in the sky. The world slept, muffled and blanketed by the night.

The alarm went off, startling him. He silenced it and hopped from bed.

After using the bathroom, he padded out, intending to call Jake, but the silence was so thick he went to the window and pulled back one drape.

A kaleidoscopic flurry of snow danced outside. It lay heavy on the ground, quilting the world in white. Even in the darkness, it was bright.

"Shit. Shit, shit, shit!"

There was no way they were making it out of Denver - not for several hours, even if they were lucky. "Son of a bitch." He found his phone and tried Claire.

There was no answer.

"Shit!"

Outside, the wind began to howl. The blizzard had arrived early.

***

Claire lay on the bed watching a movie on the ceiling. John Wayne, in a tutu and cowboy boots, was getting a pounding from Batman. Big Technicolor words - BAM! BOOM! ZOWIE! PURR! - flashed over the images, then a yellow submarine plowed through them as Gomer Pyle sang *Rocky Raccoon*. She watched in fascination, knowing none of it was real. It couldn't be real.

What the hell is happening to me? She'd never had a fever high enough to do this to her, and she felt fine, except for these hallucinations. *I'm not sick! I know I'm not!*

Then she heard music rising up through the vents.

"... the woods today ..."

Panic seized her. She squeezed her eyes shut, suppressing the memories that threatened. "No. Shut up. Please shut up." She clamped her hands over her ears, but it was too late. A memory came, crushing her beneath its weight.

"Drink it." Mother stands, arms crossed.

"Please, Mother, no." Timothy grimaces at the glass she holds out to him. Though nearly a man now, he cowers from Mother, avoids her eyes.

She smacks him. Hard. His head jerks to one side. "I said, drink it."

Carlene stands in the kitchen doorway, weeping. Mother turns and smiles. "Your precious little sister has come down to join us, Timothy. Now show her what happens when you take the Lord's name in vain in Mother's house." She smiles. "Potty mouth deserves potty mouth."

"I can't. I'll get sick. I'll throw up."

"I don't care if you do, Timothy. This is a punishment, and punishments aren't meant to be pleasant."

"Stop, Mommy." Carlene sobs and Mother takes her by the arm, yanks hard. Carlene hears a Pop! *and pain shoots up her arm, into her neck. She screams as Mother shoves her into a chair to face her older brother.*

"Be still and watch, Carlene." Mother faces Timmy. "I'll ask you one more time, Timothy, and then I'm going to give you the Bad Punishment, too."

"No, no, no!" Timothy takes the glass, drinks it down in heaving gulps.

Carlene can't tell what's in the glass, only that it's yellow. The pain in her arm is agonizing. It won't move. She bites back her anguish, bites her lips so hard she tastes blood.

Timothy puts the empty glass down, then vomits on the table. It splashes on Carlene's pajamas and she recognizes the smell: pee.

Mother laughs, grabs a roll of paper towels and tosses them to Timmy. "Now, clean up your sick. And if I ever hear you talk like that again, I'll drink a whole pitcher of water and you'll drink every drop of Mommy's potty!"

The memory dissolved, and as it faded, Claire recalled her mother's words that night, after she'd jerked Claire's arm back into its socket: *"You've hurt your shoulder again, Carlene. You're just lucky Mommy can fix it herself so we don't have to take you to the big, mean doctor. You're such a clumsy little girl. You didn't get that from Mommy's side of the family! I wish you'd been born with Timothy's grace."*

On the bed, Claire gasped. *So, that's why my shoulder aches so often. How many times did she dislocate it?*

On the ceiling, new shapes began to form, distracting her from her anger. There were clicking sounds and the images flickered as if she were watching an old film reel. Claire saw herself, age six, giggling and smiling as Mother pushed her on the backyard swing. Tim was in high school, too old for swings, but he usually pushed her, not Mother. He was way more fun.

Carlene pumps her legs, moving faster, and the swing goes higher and higher as Mother pushes. Carlene loves it. She's coming almost even with the crossbar on the swing set and she wants to see over the top. "Higher, Mommy, higher!"

Mother pushes hard and Carlene laughs, delighted, as she swings back and forth.

She sees above the crossbar but the swing jitters and swoops, too hard, too fast. "Stop now!" she calls. "Stop now!"

But Mother doesn't stop. "Don't you want to swing all the way over the top, Carlene?"

She wanted to before, but not now. "No! Make it stop! Make it stop!"

Mother laughs as the swing set shakes and jolts. She pushes harder and harder.

Carlene screams as the swing flies over the top of the rail. Time goes into slow motion as she watches herself lose her grip on the chains and fly through the air while Mother looks on, smiling. Carlene sees images from her brief life as she flies, Timmy's last birthday party, an award at school for a picture she drew, Mother spanking her. And then she crashes to the ground so hard it takes her breath away.

She lies in a crumpled heap, trying to catch her breath as Mother approaches, hands on hips, and looks down on her in disgust. "Clumsy girl," she says. "Let's get you up and clean you off."

She bends and puts her hands under Carlene's arms, then lifts. Carlene screams in pain, then faints when she sees a jagged bone sticking out of her wrist.

On the bed, Claire realized she was sobbing. She forced herself to stop as she sat up. Lifting the sheet, she looked down at the cast on the leg she couldn't remember breaking.

Could Mother be behind my leg? No. *No, that's ridiculous. Isn't it?* She'd simply fainted in the shower and fallen wrong. It wasn't like the fall from the swing. She remembered clearly that Mother had pushed too hard, and though it was technically an accident, for that, Mother *was* to blame. She knew better than to push a little kid so hard, to encourage her to swing in a complete circle. But she'd done it anyway, and the look in her eyes... *Glee. She was happy!*

Claire wished Jason were here. He'd know what to do, wouldn't he? A sudden wave of colorful dizziness washed over her, taking away her clarity, blasting her with an explosion of salty tastes, high-pitched sound, and neon colors. She blinked it away. "It isn't real, it isn't real."

Her eyes lit on her cast and she caught strange movement. Her breath stopped dead when she saw fingertips working their way out from beneath the cast. With dirty, cracked nails, the fingers clawed at her skin, pulling themselves along, crawling like spider's legs. "No!" She slapped at it - it was a full hand now, a white, bloodless hand with dried blood and dirt crusted under its nails. It crept up her thigh.

Claire shot to her feet and grabbed her crutches. She looked down. The hand was gone, but now the room swayed, tilted to one side then the other, like a funhouse. The floor beneath her felt like marshmallows.

Downstairs, the teddy bears continued their picnic at full volume.

"I'm not dead."

Startled, Claire swiveled her head and saw no one.

"I'm not dead, and I'm coming back."

Almost sure the voice wasn't in her head, she hobbled to the door. It was locked. Claire screamed. "Let me out."

"I'm coming back." The low voice came from the closet. It was Tim's. It had to be.

With trepidation, Claire moved toward the closet. She pulled the door open ... and saw nothing. "Timothy?" Her whisper shook. "Are you here?"

A deep voice spoke behind her. "It's me. Timothy. I'm here."

Claire turned and saw him. He stood in her bedroom doorway, not the closet, and he was wearing his favorite red baseball cap, blue jeans, and a black windbreaker, zipped all the way up. For a moment, he seemed shrunken, too small. Then the air swirled around him and filled out. Yes. It was Timothy. It had to be. "Tim?"

"Hey, little sister. How are you?"

His voice sounded too deep. But maybe not. It had been so long since she'd talked to him.

"Tim, is it really you?"

"In the flesh." For a moment, his skin seemed to drip off of him. "It's me, Claire." He looked normal again.

Claire shook her head, squeezed her eyes shut. "No. You're ... you're dead."

"But I'm coming back."

She opened her eyes again. It was Tim all right. The ants appeared on the wall behind him, marching up, down, and back and forth, as the walls changed from yellow to sky blue to pink, shifting colors like a basket of Easter eggs. "But how?"

"I don't want you to leave. Not ever." Timothy smiled. His lips were too red. "I want you here, where I can see you every day."

"But-" Claire looked up. Timothy was gone. "Tim?" She stumped to the open doorway, saw nothing. "Hello? Hello?"

She peered down the hall in both directions. It was empty. "Hello?"

"I'm down here, Carlene." Mother's voice drifted upstairs. "Did you need something?"

Claire waited to see the words come bouncing up the hall and for a moment thought they did - but they vanished before she was sure she'd seen them. "No, Mother. I'm okay."

"You're sure?" called Mother. "Is the baby keeping you up again?"

The baby? Again? What? Claire retreated into her room and sat down on the bed. She touched her stomach. "It's too soon for you to kick, isn't it?"

Then she felt it. The baby was knocking - *tap, tap, tap* - from within her. *Qu'est-ce que c'est?* it asked. *Qu'est-ce que c'est?*

Then it kicked. Hard.

Her stomach bounced beneath her shirt. She pulled it up and saw a small face pressing against her skin from within her belly. Then she saw the outline of a hand, then a foot. A cloven hoof. Claws. The points of horns. Claire whimpered, eyes filling with tears of terror, and she raised a shaking hand to her mouth. *It's going to rip me open!*

"I'm coming back." She heard the words in Timothy's strange gruff tone, saw them appear from between her legs, rising to swirl around her head.

Claire squeezed her eyes shut. "I'm going mad. I'm losing my mind."

"Now why would you say that?" Mother's voice startled her.

Claire looked up and saw her approaching the bed. Her face began to melt, dripping off her bones like wax down a candle. Her hair was a Medusa of writhing snakes that matched the green of her robe.

Claire screamed, pressed herself against the wall, and kicked. "Get away from me! Get away from me!"

"Carlene!" The Mother-monster grabbed her wrists, pinned them, held them. "Calm down!" The words were liquid, cold, hitting her face like buckets of freezing water. "Calm down!"

Claire screamed, writhed, kicked, watching as the monster pinned her down and tied ropes around her wrists, then her ankle, securing her to the short bedposts. "No! Stop it! Get away from me!"

"Be calm," said the Mother-monster. "Everything is okay. Right as rain. You're safe. The doctor's coming." She pulled a phone from her pocket.

Claire's heart pounded, then within seconds it slowed, and her thoughts turned to sludge. Ants zigged and zagged across the Easter egg-colored ceiling. *Mother's favorite colors.*

She heard the monster's voice - it sounded like a record set to slow. "Sorry to call at this hour, Gerald. Mm-hmm. She's gone over the edge. I need your diagnosis and something that will calm her down, then we can take it from there." The droning voice sped up, up, until it was like the chirp of a chipmunk. "Yes, I think you're right - it might be a psychotic break. I only pray she can stay at home where I can care for her. My poor little girl." The monster, who now looked like a younger, prettier version of Mother, studied Claire and frowned. "The doctor is on his way, Carlene. I'm sorry. I didn't have a choice. I'm afraid you're going to hurt yourself or the baby. We can't have that, can we, honey?" Mother-monster changed form again, its eyes glowing red, fangs dripping venom. It peered down at Claire and stroked her hair with its talons. "Now, now, don't struggle. Everything will be all right." Mother-monster grinned and its teeth went up to its temples. "Doctor will be here in a little while. Just close your eyes and rest. I'm going down to open the door for him." The monster's face split, right down the middle. Blood and gore and goo oozed from the raw, wet gash.

Claire screamed and writhed in her constraints.

Mother shut off the lights. "Monsters live in the dark," she said, and closed the door.

***

Downstairs, Priscilla made herself a nice cup of Sleepytime Tea, then started *Teddy Bear's Picnic* again and sat down near the vent that allowed her to listen for Carlene. Smiling to herself, remembering how much she enjoyed Timothy's infancy, she couldn't wait to hold her new grandson in her arms.

Twenty minutes passed. She thought about the potluck in the morning. While Carlene was raving, Prissy had made a gallon of potato salad that was still cooling on the counter in the kitchen. She was happy Carlene hadn't been terribly loud. It was all rather humiliating, how her daughter was coming unhinged and it wouldn't do for the neighbors to come poking around, to hear her daughter ranting and raving and talking to Timothy's ghost. *As if Timothy would be spending his time floating around upstairs!*

"Isn't it sad, Timothy?" Prissy said. "Your poor sister is trying so hard, but I don't think she's a very capable girl. It's a good thing Mother is here, isn't it?"

Timothy didn't answer, but she knew he was there. He was always with her.

"I love you, Angelheart," she murmured, sipping tea. "Where is that damned doctor?"

As if in response to her question, she heard a car turn onto Morning Glory Circle. A moment later, headlights flashed as Gerald Hopper, M.D., pulled up in front of her house.

"It's about time!" She rose and opened the door and waited while Gerald gathered his medical bag and strolled up the walk. "Can't you walk any faster?"

"Priscilla," he said, "this is highly unusual, even for you."

"You're a doctor, you make house calls."

"I don't. My wife-"

"Your wife what?" Priscilla laughed. "Does she think you're having an affair?"

"You dragged me out of bed at an ungodly hour. If your daughter needs medical help, you should have taken her to the emergency room."

"What am I supposed to do, Gerald? Carry her down the stairs by myself?"

"You could have called an ambulance."

Prissy drew herself up to full height, straightened her shoulders, and glared at Hopper. "I called *you*, Gerald."

The neat little man, his bald head shining, his brown eyes blinking behind wire-rimmed glasses, stared back. "What is it you want from me, Priscilla?"

She smiled. "I need you to examine Carlene. I do believe she's had a psychotic break."

"You're very quick to dole out a diagnosis, Priscilla, and I don't think an RN is qualified to make psychiatric evaluations. Nor am I."

"You'd best watch your mouth, Gerald. It might get you into trouble."

"Your games have gotten old, Priscilla."

"Games? I've kept my mouth shut all these years about the games you've played."

"The games *you've* made me play."

"Me? Nonsense. As you said, I'm only a nurse. The doctor is *always* in charge. And don't forget: You made at least one medical error that was all your own. That first error."

He broke eye contact. "I should have admitted it to the board. Then you never would have had anything to hang over my head."

Priscilla patted his cheek. "What about *all* those other things you did after that? The drugs you've prescribed that weren't called for and-"

"I know what I've done and if those things were to come out, you would be guilty as well. And, rest assured, Prissy, I would no longer keep your secrets. All those accidents your daughter and son had? The illnesses? All of that? We both know you forced me to cover for you." He paused. "I must admit, I've wondered about your daughter's current injury."

"I don't know what you're talking about. You're the doctor. I wouldn't forget that if I were you. And how dare you imply anything about Carlene's broken leg? I wasn't even there when she fell."

Refusing to meet her gaze, Gerald Hopper spoke. "I'd better examine her now."

Prissy smiled. "Follow me."

***

Claire's bed floated toward the ceiling. She couldn't see it, but she could feel the gravitational pull of the darkened overhead light. It was a black hole sucking her in, and when she was close enough, it would enter her body, crushing through her chest.

She closed her eyes, waiting for death and wondered if that's how her brother had felt when he kicked away the chair to escape Mother once and for all. She closed her eyes and saw him hanging from the belt he'd used as a noose. His skin was blue-gray and bloated. His eyes popped open and Claire gasped.

His mouth moved and he spoke around a swollen purple tongue, but his words were clear. *"You're remembering, little sister, that's good. But you need to remember more. Let me help you."* Tim sounded the way she recalled - not like he did in her bedroom doorway, deep and weird and slow.

"No," said Claire. "I can't. I don't want to remember."

"You have to, little sister. Do it for me."

"Please, no."

"You found me this way," Tim said. "Remember?"

The memory was an unstoppable train.

Carlene is ten years old. She knows this because she just had a birthday and Timothy had sent her a new doll, one she had secretly yearned for. She'd told him she was too old for dolls, but they both knew better. Her big brother had mailed it from Brimstone, Arizona, where he'd been living with Steffie Banks for well over a year.

But he's home again now, because he had an accident and hurt his leg. Mother went to Brimstone and brought him back. Carlene is glad he's back, but she is also sad for Tim because she knows how happy he was with Steffie.

Tim hasn't been himself since his return, though. Someone turned off the lights in his eyes - the lights that had always shined so bright. Mother says he has been drinking a lot. Carlene believes this because she has smelled it, and she has heard him slurring his words and saying funny things. Mother gives him lots to drink, leaving it for him even though he asked her not to.

He says he's going to move back to Brimstone to be with Steffie when his leg heals, but there's something in his voice when he says this - something that tells Carlene he doesn't quite believe it. He hasn't been very talkative and Carlene thinks this is probably because his leg hurts. She feels like there's something more, but she doesn't know how to define it.

Today, she goes down to the basement to get a new box of detergent for Mother. When she reaches for the box, it falls, and knocks several items off the shelf beneath it. Carlene spots something she's never seen before and, standing on a stepladder, sees jars of liquid and other things. She pulls them out and unscrews the lids. Sniffs and recoils. It's pee! And in the other jars, she finds fingernail and toenail clippings. In another, she finds wadded tissues, crusted with something yellow-white. It doesn't look like snot.

"Carlene?" Mother calls from upstairs. "What are you doing down there?"

"Coming, Mother." Carlene replaces the jars just as she found them, takes the laundry soap to Mother, and heads to Tim's bedroom to tell him about the jars of pee and fingernails. They must be his - they aren't mine! - and she wants to ask him why Mother would keep such things.

Tim isn't answering his door.

Carlene knocks once more, steps inside. The room is empty. "Tim? Hello?"

Only silence answers.

She notices his closet door is cracked, and as she nears, is able to make out the metal of his wheelchair. Somehow, he has managed to wheel himself inside. "Tim, what are you doing in there?" She opens the door, thinking he's playing hide and seek.

And screams.

Tim is hanging by his neck from his belt. He's like a rag doll, limp and boneless, and Carlene knows he's dead.

Her tears are a torrent, hot and gushing. The screams are ripped from her lungs as if by a pair of hands. But she's frozen in place.

On the seat of the wheelchair, Carlene spots a small sealed envelope. With trembling hands, she grabs it. It's a letter from Timothy addressed to Mother.

"What's going on?" Mother's voice shatters Carlene's trance before she can open the letter. She stuffs it in her pocket.

Mother shrieks, grabs Carlene's arm and yanks her out of the way. She's screaming, crying, trying to get Tim down. When she does, his body falls hard onto the wheelchair. Mother is slapping him, blowing into his mouth, screaming at Carlene to call 911.

Carlene races down the hall, taking the stairs two at a time. She stops at the bottom, looks up, and thinks, 'This is Mother's fault. She killed Tim. She killed my brother.' She hears another of Mother's cries - a heartbroken keening, a fierce and primitive wail, unlike anything she has ever heard before. She sprints for the phone.

In the dark, Claire was paralyzed. For a fleeting moment, she remembered where she'd hidden the letter, but like a dream upon a rude awakening, the recollection shattered and fled.

The door opened and light from the hall spilled into the room.

**

Babs Vandercooth ran into the Pleasanton hospital while Carl parked the car. They'd made it in record time, thanks to Carl's skill behind the wheel and a lack of fog.

"I'm here to see my sister, Dorothy Meyers. She was admitted earlier tonight."

The nurse turned to her computer and looked up as Carl arrived at Babs' side. "I don't have any record of a Dorothy Meyers."

"Dorothy Winchester Meyers. Or Dorothy Winchester?" Dorothy'd been divorced for a decade so maybe she'd dropped the Meyers.

"No, ma'am. Nothing matches."

Carl put his arm around Babs' shoulders. "Was a woman in her late forties brought in last night after a traffic accident?"

"I don't think so, let me check." The nurse went back to the computer.

"Maybe she didn't have ID on her, Babs," Carl said, his voice low and gentle.

Babs leaned against him, unable to speak.

"Babs!"

They turned to see Blanche, her older sister, come through the door. She trotted up and hugged them both. "Well?"

"We're waiting. They can't find her."

"I'm sorry," the nurse said. "There were no accident victims brought in last night."

"Are you sure?" Babs asked.

"I was here. It was a very quiet night. I'm sorry."

"We were both called to come here," Blanche said. "Someone called."

The nurse looked from one sister to the other. "I'm sorry, but I think they told you the wrong hospital. Maybe you should try phoning your sister. If she doesn't answer, I'll give you a list of other local hospitals to call." She turned back to her work.

The three of them left the nurse's station and huddled in a corner of the silent lobby. Babs pulled out her phone and hit Dorothy's number.

On the sixth ring, Dorothy answered, her voice full of sleep. "Babs, what's wrong?"

"Are you okay? Where are you?"

"Its 3:30 in the morning. I'm in my bed. Where are you?"

"We - Carl, Blanche and me - are at John Muir Hospital."

"Why?"

"Someone called and said you were hurt in an auto accident. We just got here."

Silence on the other end of the line. "I'm fine. I stayed in last night watching an *NCIS* marathon. Sounds like somebody was pulling your leg. Listen, I'd love to see you all. You remember how to get here?"

Babs glanced at Carl. "Of course we want to see you. I'm so glad you're okay! We all are."

"Well, drive on over and I'll make breakfast."

"We'll be there in fifteen minutes," Babs told her, "but Carl and I can't stay long. Don't worry about breakfast."

"You need to eat. It'll be ready when you get here," Dorothy said.

"We'll see you soon," Babs said, then looked at Carl and Blanche. "She's fine. We're invited for breakfast."

"But the phone calls," said Blanche. "Who would have done such a thing?"

"Someone with a terrible sense of humor," Babs said.

Blanche, always the optimist, laughed. "Well, at least we get breakfast out of this wild goose chase!"

They walked to their cars. "I'll follow you two. I haven't been here since Dot moved."

A moment later, Carl and Babs were pulling back onto the highway. "I hope your sister doesn't mind if I get a few hours of sleep before we head back," Carl said.

"I'll drive," said Babs. "We need to be back by eight a.m. You can nap in the car."

"You didn't sleep either. What's the hurry? Don't you want to see your sisters?"

"Yes, but I'm worried about Claire. And there's the potluck."

Carl nodded. "I understand. We'll do what you think is best."

***

Claire thought Dr. Hopper looked like a little pink bullfrog as he listened to her heart and lungs. He smelled like toothpaste. "There's nothing wrong with me," she told him. She was glad to see him because the first thing he did after turning on the light was untie her.

"Your mother says you've been having hallucinations." Hopper looked concerned as he rubbed her wrists, smoothing away the rope marks, easing out the pins and needles.

Mother-monster stepped up and loomed over the bed, her red fangs dripping yellow venom in thick mucoid drops. "Be quiet, Carlene. You need to rest."

"I will *not* be quiet, Mother-monster. I'm fine. Please leave the room."

Mother shape-shifted into a humongous Pez dispenser, her mouth a giant maw that flapped and clicked as she spoke. "I'm your nurse, Carlene, I must stay and assist the doctor."

"If your daughter is more comfortable-" began the froggy little physician.

"Get out, Pez-head," Claire ordered. "Now. You're scaring the frog."

"You don't know what you're saying, dear," Pez-head intoned in the same syrup-slow voice the Mother-monster had used. "A nurse never leaves a doctor alone to examine a female patient, isn't that right, Doctor?"

The frog-doctor's cheeks blew up red and his tongue came out and snatched a few ants off the ceiling.

"That's a really long tongue you have there," Claire said.

Pez-head's broad smile broke her face in two.

"Excuse me?" the doctor said between *ribbits.*

"Tong," Claire said, suddenly clear. "Tong - my husband called stethoscopes tongs when he was a little boy."

"He never told me that, Carlene." Mother's head flipped back up and the Pez body turned into a hula girl, hips swaying above Mother's face. It looked normal now, except that her pale skin gleamed and shimmered like a snake's. Something rattled under the hula skirt.

"Why would he?" asked Dr. Hopper, looking normal again.

Maybe the hallucinations are going away!

"Why wouldn't he?" Mother huffed before looking down at Claire. "We've had some very nice long talks, you know." Her tongue flicked out, forking over Claire's body. It felt like electric sparks.

Claire watched in fascination, remembering that serpents used their tongues to taste things. *Mother's tasting me. I wonder what I taste like.*

Dr. Hopper stared at Mother and let out a big *ribbit.* Mother hissed at him. There were words, too. Claire could see the letters tumbling toward the ceiling, but she couldn't make them out. She stared at the doctor, wanting to know what was wrong with her, but she didn't trust him, even if he did seem annoyed with Mother.

She watched the ants on the ceiling. They were in formation now, like a band on a football field. They were spelling out words. "I'm not dead. I'm not dead and I'm coming back."

"What's that?" asked the doctor. His head reformed into that of an ant and he had shiny blue mandibles. He kept them nice and clean, too.

"I'm not dead," Claire repeated. "I'm not dead, and I'm coming back."

"Of course you're not dead," said Mother, looking upset. Her amber eyes had turned deep yellow, and her pupils were long and thin, as reptilian as her skin.

"You're such a snake," Claire told her, then turned to Hopper. "I'm not dead and I'm coming back. That's what I keep hearing."

"Psychotic break is a definite possibility," Mother said. "Don't you agree, Doctor?"

Dr. Hopper had turned into a lizard and his neck fringe shot out around his face. "Please don't try to make a diagnosis." He looked to Claire. "Your pupils are dilated. Have you taken anything?"

"What do you mean?"

He glanced at Priscilla. "Has your mother given you any drugs today?"

"Of course I haven't given her any drugs. My God, she's pregnant, Gerald. What do you think I am?"

"Mother-monster," said Claire as a googly-green eye sprouted on Mother's forehead.

The doctor studied Claire. "Well, your blood pressure is up a little, but not enough to worry about. Just stay quiet and rest. Can you do that for me?"

"Yes."

"Dr. Hopper." Mother looked like her pissed-off old self again, except for the bloodshot third eye. "She's been violent and she's obviously having hallucinations that are *not* drug-induced. What are you going to do about it?"

Hopper looked at Claire. "Are you having hallucinations?"

"No." She tried to set Mother on fire with her glare. The third eye blinked.

"Your brother talks to you?" he asked Claire.

"I was dreaming," she lied.

"Well?" Mother asked Hopper.

"I don't see anything wrong here, Priscilla. If you want, I can arrange to have her taken to the hospital for psychiatric evaluation."

"Yes, I want to go," Claire said.

"No!" Mother spoke over her. "Carlene will stay at home under my care. Just please give her something to help her sleep. I can't risk her attacking me again."

"What?" Claire said. "You're lying!"

"Why would I lie about my own daughter attacking me? It's humiliating enough to admit it, I certainly wouldn't lie about it, you selfish girl."

Hopper raised an eyebrow but said nothing to Mother. Instead, he looked at Claire. "You do look like you haven't had much rest." He started digging around in his medical bag.

"What are you doing?" Claire asked.

He sat back up. "It's just something to help you sleep a little while. Won't hurt the baby."

"No-" but he injected her before she could say more.

"Now, Doctor, about that psychotic break," Mother said.

"She needs to see a psychiatrist, not a GP. He looked out at the growing gray dawn. "As I said, I can make arrangements-"

"No." Mother's voice sounded harsh. "I won't have my pregnant daughter institutionalized when I am perfectly capable of caring for her."

Claire stared at her mother, then snickered. "I see what you did there."

Mother gave her a look so venomous she recoiled. Then the third eye disappeared as Mother's face flattened into that of a serpent's again.

"Don't bite me," Claire said. "Don't bite me and don't shed your skin in my room!"

Hopper was staring at her, but Mother hustled him out, her angry rattles so loud that Claire heard them all the way down the stairs. Then she heard Mother and Dr. Hopper arguing but they were too far from the vent, so she couldn't make out the words. By the time the front door slammed and Hopper drove off, *Teddy Bear's Picnic* had started up once again. She yawned.

***

"Sunrise over the mesa," Paul said. "You know, I thought you were nuts when you said we had to get up at 5:30, but this was definitely worth getting out of bed for."

"Thought you'd like it." Steffie refilled their coffees from the Thermos, then turned to gaze out at the colorful sunrise. They sat in her Range Rover on Cemetery Hill, where they could see the entire town and the desert and the dark mountains that hid Sedona from view.

"I do. I love being here."

She smiled. "I thought we could go back to my place for breakfast, grab the luggage, then head for the airport."

"Sounds like a plan." Paul looked out over Brimstone. "I feel like I'm in the Old West."

"That's because you are." She laughed. "Have you heard from Jason yet?"

"No, he's probably in the air by now. I hope - I was having so much fun last night, I forgot to check the Denver weather. Hopefully, the storm didn't interfere with their flight."

"I hope not. I'm looking forward to meeting Jason and seeing Claire again."

Paul smiled at her and she felt an unexpected flutter in her belly. She smiled back.

Approaching Dawn

The storm had begun to ease and Jason had finally located a flight, a private commuter jet going straight to Snapdragon. It was scheduled to take off at 10 a.m., weather permitting. Jake would wait until the skies were clearer before flying his plane home.

Jason tried Claire once more, but there was no answer. It was only four in California - she was probably fast asleep. Too tired to think, Jason set his alarm for seven-thirty and flopped down on the bed. He was asleep in minutes.

***

In Claire's dream, she stood barefoot amid at least a hundred thousand puzzle pieces, all scattered in various directions spanning as far as she could see. She was in a white room with no doors or windows, and she wore no clothes. Staring, she tried to make out any evidence of walls, floor, or ceiling, but wasn't able to. It was just white … for miles … in all directions.

She looked down at the puzzle pieces that littered the floor. "Help me," she whispered. "I don't know where to start."

Only her own echo answered her.

"Please. Tell me what's happening."

A sudden *bang!* Her world, a sheet of blank paper, was ripped in two.

Bang!

A biting chemical scent and *Opium* perfume filled her nostrils, bled into her lungs, and set her head spinning.

Bang!

The puzzle pieces jumped, and the invisible floor opened.

Claire lost her footing and fell through empty air, clawing at emptiness, heart in her throat.

And then she was awake.

Bang!

That hadn't been a dream. It was real. Claire sat up, listening. *Bang!* The scents were real, too. *Or are they?* She couldn't tell anymore.

Bang! She turned in the direction of the sound, and the world became a smear of colors, dragging as her eyes shifted.

Bang!

"Stop. Please, just stop." She sank into her sheets - her warm, safe sheets. "I'm okay. I'm in my room, in bed, and everything's fine." The lie tasted like burnt toast on her tongue. Everything around her was still a blur of colors and shapes that moved and swayed, and even sometimes talked to her. "Please stop," she cried, but the room only giggled. The lamp on the nightstand became a goose with an impossibly long and rubbery neck. Its black eyes gleamed as its head swayed toward her, its long, sharp beak aiming for her eyes. She screamed and pulled the pillow over her face.

A new noise came. A melodic, tinkling sound. She stopped breathing, listened hard to the notes. It wasn't *Teddy Bear's Picnic* or *Don't Sit Under the Apple Tree*. It was something else, something new. Her eyes firmly shut, she removed the pillow. The melody clarified. It was *The Magic Flute*. The music seemed to come from all around, sweet perfect notes tinkling and twinkling in the air. She saw Mozart's back as he conducted his invisible musicians. He wore a blue velvet waistcoat and breeches and a black tricorne hat emblazoned with a peace sign.

The music faded and as the room filled with applause, Mozart turned to take a bow, sweeping his tricorne off as he bent. Claire clapped and cried "Encore!" He rose from his bow and looked at her, and there was something amiss. His face was changing. Melting. Like wax. White bone gleamed beneath his flesh and pieces of his face, his neck, his hands, dripped to the floor, sizzling and stinking of sulfur and *Opium*.

Mozart's fleshless skull grinned at her. "You're never going to leave this place! Never going to leave! Never!" His shrill words were followed by a lunatic cackle, and the composer's smoking skeleton drew close, teeth clacking with chaotic laughter.

It poked her stomach with its bone-finger, taunting her.

But Claire didn't respond. Something inside her shifted, like the snap of a branch, and she was no longer afraid. The music faded and Mozart's bones fell to the floor, but Claire didn't see anything now except the blank ceiling above her.

I don't care anymore. I've lost my mind ... and I don't even care.

She sank into the warmth of her bed, shut her eyes, and disconnected herself from the hissing sounds and acrid smells of burning flesh and perfume. The world around her faded and she slipped into someplace new, someplace safe. Someplace far, far away.

***

Carl didn't wake up until Babs pulled into their driveway and killed the engine. She'd fretted through the entire drive, worrying about Claire, wondering about the person who'd called her and her sister to Pleasanton. It was all too much.

At least the sac looked peaceful in the early morning light. No one was out setting up for the potluck yet; it wouldn't even begin until 11 a.m., and she was glad because she might be able to get some sleep.

Carl stretched and yawned. "You should drive all the time, Babs. I slept like a baby." He got out of the car and headed for the house. Babs exited too, then paused, and punched Claire's number in. It went straight to voicemail and she hung up, then, girded herself and called Prissy.

"Hello?"

Priscilla sounded like she'd been asleep but Babs didn't apologize for waking her. "It's me. I just wondered how Claire is feeling this morning. She's not answering her phone."

"Oh, she's fine now," Prissy said. "And how are you?"

The chill had left her voice. Evidently, Babs was forgiven. "She wasn't fine earlier? What happened?"

"She was having hallucinations," Prissy said. "I was scared to death for her, poor thing, so I called Dr. Hopper. He came in the middle of the night. I was so relieved."

"What did he say?"

"He gave her some medicine to calm her down and says he thinks she might be having a psychotic break." Prissy paused. "I'm not even sure what that is. Do you happen to know?"

You know exactly what it is. That's what Babs wanted to say, but she refrained. "I have no idea, but it sounds terrible."

"Yes. I'm so worried, I'm beside myself. I'm just sick from worrying. My head aches. All this stress - I guess it just put me right to sleep."

Babs put on her friendliest voice. "It must have, since you haven't looked up his diagnosis yet."

Prissy hesitated. "Dr. Hopper said I was too exhausted and gave me half a Xanax. You know what those do to me. Out like a light. At least I had an hour of rest."

"Is he coming back to see Claire again this morning?"

"What? Oh, the doctor! Yes, unless he has an emergency or something. But he told me exactly how to take care of her. After all, I *am* a nurse. He has full confidence that I can handle the situation. It's best for everyone." She sighed. "Between Carlene and Frederick, I'm very busy. Despite everything, I did make my special homemade potato salad for the potluck."

The last time Prissy had made potato salad, she'd forgotten to refrigerate it, and more than one neighbor had come down with the trots. Babs hadn't had the nerve to rat Prissy out back then, but today, she would warn people to avoid it. She smiled to herself. "I'd like to visit Claire. Perhaps I can stay with her while you're seeing to the potluck?"

Prissy's voice fluttered like a palm frond. "I- I'll ask the doctor if it's okay for her to have visitors. I'll let you know."

"When does Jason return?"

"Oh, I doubt he can even leave Colorado for hours yet. I watched the weather last night and Denver had a big snowstorm. I don't even know if they'll let a little plane fly today."

Babs knew all about the storm. "I hear it's clearing."

"You know about it?"

"I had the radio on."

"Oh," said Prissy. "Well, I hope he can get home. I don't how he's going to take the news."

"I'm sure once you explain her condition, he'll handle things and find a good doctor to help her." She thought of Steffie Banks, knowing she'd arrive within a few hours. *Thank heaven. Prissy's going to have a hissy about that.* Babs smiled to herself.

"No," said Prissy. "I've already told him about her mental state. I was referring to the news that they won't be able to move out as they planned." She clucked her tongue. "Who *knows* how long they'll have to stay here! I just hope I'm strong enough!"

Prissy was trying to sound disappointed, but Babs heard something that sounded an awful lot like triumph in her tone.

"Coming in, Babs?" Carl called from the front door.

"Just a minute." Babs said goodbye to Prissy then looked up Gerald Hopper's office number and punched it in, telling the nurse it was an emergency.

Within three minutes, Hopper came on the line. "What's your emergency, Mrs. Vandercooth?"

"I'm not sure if I have one or not. Did you diagnose Priscilla Martin's daughter as having a psychotic break?"

There was a lengthy pause before Hopper spoke. "I can't discuss my patients. Surely you understand."

"I'm sorry, Doctor, I do understand. I'm simply concerned about the girl. Can you at least tell me if I may visit her later today?"

The pause was even longer. "I prescribed a sedative, but ... I think a brief visit would be ... okay." He cleared his throat. "You'll need to check with Priscilla, though. As a nurse, she'll have a better idea if it's appropriate." The man sounded like he was in pain as he searched for words. "Yes, I'd have to say you need to ask her."

"If Claire is so bad off, why isn't she in the hospital?"

"I can't discuss-"

"Prissy didn't want her to go, did she?"

Hopper's silence told her everything she wanted to know.

Shattered Thoughts

The storm had moved through so quickly that patches of blue were showing between the dark clouds and spitting snow as Jason boarded the small commuter jet. He thought about pulling out a journal and reading during the flight, but decided it would only add to his stress. He popped a couple of Tums and pulled out his phone. He couldn't call Claire, but he could open his Kindle app and read the latest John Sandford novel.

***

Most of the time, Fred Martin felt like a mind trapped in a rusted machine that was on its way to the junkyard; but having palmed the last three tranquilizers that Prissy'd given him, he could already feel his body and mind beginning to function better. This wasn't news to him, he'd done it before - simply opened the capsules and let the powder flutter onto the blanket - and felt clearer within a matter of hours. He knew exactly what was going on, what Prissy was doing to him, but until now, he'd rarely had reason to skip the pills. He'd long ago given up any hope of a tolerable existence, and the pills at least allowed him a reprieve from the assault of awareness, from the deadly boredom. He glanced at the dark television. Prissy had unplugged it two months ago as punishment when he'd refused a meal and never plugged it back in. She'd removed all his books and magazines six months ago for another infraction. At that point, the pills had become his friends. He was certain she'd recently upped the dosages of whatever she was feeding him, so she could keep him in a near-vegetative state.

But now, he felt it was important to keep his mind clear. Though his body was mostly broken, he at least had his wits.

He'd heard screaming last night. It brought back terrible memories, memories long sublimated to that drugged haze Prissy had induced for more than two decades. Timothy, screaming. He'd gone to his room to see what was wrong and seen him tied to his own bed, naked and blindfolded. Priscilla hovered over him, something in her hands. He crept closer, and saw she had a string tied to one of her fingers. Fred stared, following the line of string to its end. Mortified, he saw it was tied around their son's genitals.

Prissy was giggling, tugging his privates this way and that, the mistress of her own perverse puppet show. As Tim's privates leapt and bounced, she taunted him, telling him he was dirty, that only *she* could determine the activity of his "boy parts."

Furious, Fred had grabbed Prissy by the shoulders and shaken her, hard.

She'd whirled, eyes on fire, and he'd expected her to lash out. But she didn't. Instead, she'd done something Fred had never - not in all the years he'd known her - seen her do before: She'd wept, apologized, and fled the house.

Fred had tried to talk to Timothy. Even then, the boy defended his mother. The poor child was humiliated, traumatized. He'd begged Fred not to tell anyone what he'd seen; told him nothing like that had ever happened before. But Fred knew better ... and he knew he wasn't going to keep quiet about it.

He should have called the authorities that night, but he hadn't. For Timothy's sake, Fred decided to first speak privately with his old friend, Curtis Hocking, a retired cop who might advise him on how to handle the situation with minimal damage.

Prissy came home after midnight and locked herself in their bedroom. Fred had slept in Tim's room, guarding him until he could have Prissy removed from their lives. The next morning, Fred sent Tim off to school without allowing Prissy to even tell him goodbye. Anxious, Fred phoned Curtis, but his wife said he was out of town on a fishing trip and wouldn't be back until later that afternoon. Fred busied himself cleaning out the gutters, trying to keep a calm, clear mind. He was still in shock and though he'd dreaded the conversation, he was eager to get it off his chest - and eager to get Prissy away from their children.

He'd never had that conversation with Curtis. An accident on the ladder had prevented it, and since that day, he'd been here in this room, unable to walk or speak. He could never prove Prissy had been behind the accident - but on an instinctual level, he knew. Over the years, he'd tried and tried to recall the day's events, but he'd always come up blank. One moment he'd been on the ladder, and the next ... he was here, in this wheelchair. *It was her. She did this to me, to keep me quiet.* And it had worked.

Now, something was happening to his daughter. He needed to help her, but getting out of this room was impossible. Prissy kept the door locked at all times and nothing he tried would get it to open. And he'd tried everything; there was no way around a double deadbolt.

He sat straighter in his wheelchair then pushed himself to the sliding door and slowly opened it to let fresh air into the stale, dark room. His body might be a broken-down machine beyond repair, but his mind was still as sharp as a razor's edge, and if Prissy hurt their daughter, he'd make damn sure she paid for it. He began flexing his arms and hands, exercising his muscles.

***

Priscilla Martin checked herself in the mirror by the front door and repinned her bright yellow snapdragon brooch so it didn't disappear into the pale yellow snapdragons in her custom-knitted sweater. *Much better.* She smiled, saw a speck of red lipstick stuck to a front tooth, and quickly scrubbed it off. Satisfied, she backed away until she could see her entire outfit. The new bright yellow pants, brighter than any of the pastel pants she owned, went perfectly with the pin on her sweater. She felt bold today, ready to face the world.

Outside, it was clear and chilly, with a brisk breeze. She looked out at the cul-de-sac and saw several neighbors setting up tables for the Spring Potluck, but not many were out yet. It was less than ninety minutes until the potluck began - people were not taking their duties seriously enough.

She looked over her flower beds, pleased with the snapdragons' growth, then almost began her walk to check in with the neighbors, but decided to set up her own table first. *A good example is the finest form of leadership.*

Hoping Jason would arrive to help her, she walked up the driveway and unlocked the big potting shed to fetch the card table and chair. She had more seedlings growing now - marigolds and zinnias. They were just beginning to sprout under the big skylight. The shed was the best thing Frederick Martin had ever created, bar none.

"Timothy?" she said. "Are you here? I wish you could help me move this big heavy table." She sighed. "You know, it was very selfish of you to take your own life like that. I hope we can get you into heaven when it's time for us to go. Angelheart, I love you so much that if I can't talk the Lord into letting you in, I will go to Hell at your side. That's what a good mother does."

She pulled a folding chair out and carried it to the front yard then came back to the shed. Glancing up, she saw Frederick watching her from the open slider. "You'll catch your death of cold in that breeze," she called. "I'll come up and shut that door for you in a minute."

"Nooooo!"

Startled, she looked up again. Frederick had pushed himself onto the balcony and was glaring at her. "Very good!" she called to him. "Your speech is improving!"

She stepped back into the shed. "Timothy, help me remember to have Dr. Hopper prescribe some more Botox. Your stepfather's is wearing off. It seems like my work is never done, doesn't it?" She tugged on the folded card table and it slid easily out of its slot and halfway out of the potting shed before it caught on something. "I wish Jason would get here. I need him to help me move this."

"Can I help you, Mrs. Martin?"

She whirled to see Hank Lowell standing not ten feet away.

"I heard you saying you need some help," he said, an untrustworthy smile on his face. "I'll carry that for you."

She stared at him, taking in his beard and the tattoo of a motorcycle on his bicep. He was so uncouth, but at least he looked clean. "That would be lovely, thank you."

He pulled the table out and waited while she locked the shed, then carried it to the front of the house and set it up at the curb.

"Thank you," Prissy said. Next door, Hank's wife, with the fire engine red hair, was setting up their own table. Two tables, she realized. *Even though they make a bad impression, at least they participate.* Still, it was difficult to be polite to such gypsies. "What are you and your wife serving today?"

"Homemade tamales. Crys spent two days making them. They're amazing."

"I'm sure they are." Prissy wondered if the health department would approve. She certainly wasn't going to taste anything that ethnic. "Two tables full. How impressive."

"No, just one table of tamales. We thought we'd provide some salads, too. We made coleslaw, three-bean, and my world famous potato salad."

Priscilla nodded. "*I'm* providing the potato salad. Everyone loves it, so you may as well put yours away."

Hank just grinned. "We made too much to eat up ourselves. There'll be plenty for everybody. So many neighbors have invited friends that we figured we'd make some extra, just in case." He smiled. "Mine is hot German salad, with vinegar and bacon. What kind did you make?"

"American!" Prissy wanted to slap the man, but controlled herself, as Hank tipped an invisible hat then walked back to his yard to help his Slutty Susie wife, who was now setting up a big umbrella and a half-dozen chairs. Each table held a napkin dispenser and a stack of paper plates - and boxes of plastic forks and spoons. *What showoffs!*

***

"I love little planes," Steffie Banks said. She sat in the co-pilot seat, smiling.

The takeoff had been smooth as glass, and Paul was proud. "This plane may be little," he said, glancing at her, "but it's a jet, a VLJ, not a plane. Big difference."

"More macho?" Steffie asked, grinning.

"Damn straight! And much faster."

"Coffee?"

"Please." Paul reached his assigned altitude, adjusted his course, then settled in. He had finally gotten hold of Jason and was glad to know he was boarding and would be on his way back to Snapdragon, too. They'd arrive around the same time.

Steffie handed him his coffee. "It's so beautiful here, isn't it?"

Below, the high desert and mountains spread out in uncrowded splendor. "It's a shame to have to leave."

***

Babs watched Prissy as she began her meddlesome walk around the sac. It was ten now and many of the neighbors were all set up for the potluck, but she and Carl had napped and were only getting started. He'd just wheeled his gas grill into the driveway, and now they set up a table and two chairs next to it. They'd bring the ice chest of dogs and condiments out soon.

"Look at Priscilla," Babs told Carl.

"Do I have to?"

She poked him in the ribs. "Have you ever seen pants that yellow?"

He looked up. "I'd better slather on sunblock if she gets too close."

Babs laughed. "No kidding."

Priscilla had passed by the Lowells and was talking to Phyllis and Clyde Stine. They must have passed muster, because she quickly moved on to Stan and Aida's house. Their voices floated over. Pris had tasted Aida's chili and had given it her blessing. She chatted with Aida a moment, no doubt gossiping.

"Carl, while Prissy's making her rounds, I think I'll try to sneak in to see Claire. Cover for me?"

"You're leaving me alone with that old witch?" He grinned.

"She'll be a while. When she and Aida get to talking, it's time consuming." She shook her head. "I've always said that no secrets are safe on Morning Glory Circle, and that's why." She nodded toward Pris and Aida.

Carl chuckled. "Sure, I'll cover for you. But you better step on it - she's already heading up the Deans' walk."

"I'll be right back. I just want to look in on her." Babs took off at a fast walk but just as she approached the Sachs' house, Prissy's voice bellowed from behind.

"Barbara! Over here!"

Babs turned and realized Prissy had been watching all along. *Stay cool.* "Why, there you are!" she said, using everything she'd ever learned in high school drama class to disarm the woman. "I was just coming to see if you needed any help."

Prissy eyed her. "You didn't see me on the sidewalk?"

"No, I didn't. Sorry, I'm a little sleep-deprived this morning and obviously not very observant. My, those pants certainly are yellow!" She fluttered her lashes, knowing butter wouldn't melt in her mouth. It worked. Prissy was staring down at her pants.

"I just bought them. I thought they went really well with my snapdragon pin. The pants are the same shade of yellow."

Banana pants! "They certainly brighten up that pastel sweater."

Prissy tried to stare her down. "It looks to me like Carl may need your help, Barbara. Why don't you go give him a hand?"

Babs gave her a tight smile and headed toward Carl, who was setting out plates and condiments. When she arrived, she glanced back.

Prissy stood in place, staring. *Making sure I stay far away from Claire.* Babs sighed. *Jason, where are you?*

***

Behind the bedroom drapes, Claire sat up in her bed, staring straight ahead into the darkness. She saw nothing, heard nothing, and felt nothing. Wherever her thoughts were, they weren't here, they weren't now.

In the back of her mind, something niggled, trying to make its way to the surface - something important. Something she needed to know. Something she needed to *remember.* But like a knock on the door of a vacant room, it went unheard and unheeded.

Potluck Surprise

There was no parking on Morning Glory Circle, and Father Andy didn't find an open space on Daisy for a block and a half. The potluck looked to be the most crowded he'd ever attended. Prissy always asked him to bless their flowerbeds, and he always did because no other street in town had such good chow.

But this time he'd only come because of Babs Vandercooth and her concern for Claire. When he'd told Dave Flannigan his plans - to help Babs get past Prissy and visit Claire - the old priest had voiced concern, then volunteered to come along. He wasn't sure if Dave was coming to help him get in to see Claire or to protect him from Priscilla Martin's priest-eating appetite. Probably both.

He and Dave walked to Morning Glory Circle; and when Andy saw the barricade closing off the street, he shuddered.

"Someone just step on your grave?" Dave asked.

"There was a barricade like this the day Burke Collins murdered his family. It brings back memories I'd just as soon forget."

Dave patted his shoulder. "Understandable. But today, we have a mission: to visit Priscilla's daughter and then to eat lots of free food." He spoke lightly, but something in his eyes was deadly earnest. His clerical collar spoke of business as well.

"Indeed." Andy started up the north side of the cul-de-sac, heading for Babs' house, but paused in front of the first residence on the corner, where a goateed man and an attractive young woman in a sweatshirt and short-shorts tended a table loaded with water, sodas, coffee, tea, and more.

They approached and the young woman smiled. "Coffee?"

"I'd love a cup," Dave said.

"Do you have any hot chocolate?" Andy had a craving.

"Of course. Here you go, Father."

"Why Ace Etheridge, you old son of a gun, how the heck are you?"

The goateed man looked up, then grinned and stood. "Dave Flannigan, I haven't seen your ugly mug in a decade! I'm great. How the hell are *you*?"

"I'm good."

"What are you doing here?"

"Just seeing to it that my replacement is praying over the food in a proper manner."

"I'm Iris," the young woman told Andy while Dave and Ace talked. "Father Dave presided over my parents' wedding about a zillion years ago. They used to golf together."

Dave and Ace had gone up to the front porch and were sitting down in wicker chairs, obviously talking over old times. "Would you tell Dave I'll be right back, Iris?"

"Sure."

Andy started toward the Vandercooth house, when he heard Dave call his name. The priest was trotting, red-faced, in his direction. "Trying to ditch me, are you?"

"I was going to come right back. I'm only going next door." Andy paused. "You looked like you were having fun. I didn't want to disturb you."

"I was. I will. Don't worry about it. I'm not letting you out of my sight today."

"Okay." Andy smiled. "Let's go see Babs."

***

When Paul and Stephanie stepped out of the hangar after parking the little jet, the first thing they saw was Jason Holbrook crossing the tarmac, overnight bag in hand.

"Hey, Holbrook!" Paul yelled.

Jason turned, then trotted over. "I'm glad to see you, Paul. And you must be Steffie. I'm *really* happy you're here."

"I am, too," she said. Jason was a handsome young man, but right now, he looked worn down, with red-rimmed eyes that carried too much baggage beneath them.

"You don't look so good, my friend," Paul said.

"I didn't get much sleep. And I can't get hold of Claire. I need to get to the house right away. I'm worried." He looked to Stephanie. "I wish I'd listened to her from the beginning. The things she was saying - I thought they were just too crazy. I was an idiot."

"Steffie," Paul said. "Why don't you ride with Jason - he can fill you in. I'll follow you guys over."

"Sounds good," Stephanie said. She picked up her pace and they practically ran to Jason's Prius. A moment later, their bags were stowed and Jason pulled out.

"Paul knows the way," he told her.

"Of course. Jason, Paul told me what he could about the situation. What can you tell me?"

"I thought Claire was losing it - I mean, having psychological problems - because she hates her mother so much. It got really bad when she broke her leg and had to stay in Priscilla's house, under her care. She started telling stories I thought were fabricated. And things happened. One day, there was a teddy bear in her room with eyes painted red and she swore she hadn't done it. Lots of other things, too, and she kept telling me her mother was behind them. I just didn't believe her. Sure, I could see Prissy was overbearing, but I thought Claire was becoming paranoid because she kept blaming everything, including the bear, on her mother." His voice cracked. He wiped away a tear.

"It's okay. Would you mind driving just a little slower? We want to get there in one piece."

"Sorry." He slowed to the speed limit.

"Listen, Jason. Your reaction was exactly what Prissy wanted. She engineered it. She wanted to own you - she always wants to own everything and everyone and she's so jealous that she needs to win everything, too - including her own daughter's husband. She treated me like she's treating you - she was jealous of Tim and me. It's all her. Trust me, Claire is *not* paranoid."

Jason glanced at her. "I read some of Timothy's journals last night. There were things ... horrible things ... "

"I know. Tim told me about his mother's punishments after he came to Brimstone. He never said anything when we were kids, but even then I knew something was wrong. I always knew." She paused. "Jason, when Priscilla Martin looks at you with those amber eyes of hers, even if she's smiling, how does it make you feel?

"I've never thought about it. I've just concentrated on trying to keep the peace between her and Claire."

"Think about it now."

He paused. "She has dead eyes."

"She does. She ... she reminds me of some sort of demigod or something who demands sacrifices."

Jason nodded. "I talked to Priscilla last night, very briefly. She told me the doctor said Claire had had a psychotic break."

"What doctor?"

"A guy named Hopper?"

"Shit."

"She tried to get Claire to use him as her obstetrician. Claire wouldn't - she doesn't like him."

"Neither do I. He's in Priscilla's pocket. She's got something on him." She shook her head. "She's got something on everybody."

They were nearing the neighborhood and Stephanie's stomach twisted in anticipation. She hadn't ever wanted to come back, or see Priscilla Martin or her creepy house again. And now she was about to walk into it to try to help Tim's little sister. She swallowed. "Jason, I need to be more specific about Priscilla."

"Go ahead." Mouth set in a grim line, he drove on.

"You're familiar with the term 'sociopath'?"

"You mean like Hannibal Lecter?"

"Kind of. Except Hannibal seemed to have empathy for Clarice; that was his only real flaw, and it made him human. That's the difference between fact and fiction. In real life, it doesn't happen. A sociopath is someone without conscience, no sense of right or wrong. I can't officially diagnose since she's not my patient, but I do know for certain that Priscilla Martin is unstable - she has definite sociopathic and narcissistic traits. Along with a few other issues. It's all about her, all the time." She paused. "She's incapable of love."

"What about her love for Timothy?"

"It was all about power. Ownership, not love. She doesn't know the meaning of the word." She hesitated. "She's the reason Tim committed suicide."

Jason looked at her. "Really?"

Stephanie nodded. "He wanted to be free of her, but she wouldn't allow it. He'd started drinking in high school. She knew it, and didn't get him any help. Instead, she *supplied* him with alcohol - even when he was trying to quit. See? Power and ownership. Not love. If she couldn't have him, no one could. It's typical sociopathic thinking."

"A sociopath," Jason said under his breath. "And that's your … psychiatric assessment?"

Stephanie nodded. "Without having professionally analyzed her, yes, it's my personal opinion. Based on my education as well as my experience with the woman. Make no mistake - she's a monster."

They were in the neighborhood now and Stephanie realized she was clutching the armrest so hard it hurt. She took a deep breath and told herself to be calm, then glanced at Jason as he turned onto Daisy Drive. He looked in control, his mouth a grim line. His knuckles, on the steering wheel, weren't as white as hers. That was good.

As they approached Morning Glory Circle, Daisy Drive was filled with parked cars. "The potluck," Jason said. "We'll have to park out here and walk."

Stephanie was relieved they weren't going to drive right into the dragon's lair.

Jason found a tight spot and eased in, while Stephanie rang Paul and warned him about the parking.

Feeling a little dizzy, her head light, her stomach queasy, Stephanie stepped from the car. Her memories were getting the better of her. She bent and put her hands on her knees, taking deep breaths.

Jason watched her and when she stood upright, he nodded. "I feel the same way. Now let's go get my girl."

Stephanie put a hand on his arm. "We need to do this carefully, Jason. If Claire's as fragile as it sounds, we want to keep everything low-key. Any more stress, and she might really snap."

"I have to get her out *now*."

"I know, but you mustn't let her see you're worried. It isn't good for her. We need to plan this, just a little, and avoid confrontations with Priscilla. We have to take it nice and slow. Trust me on this." She paused. "And it's not just Claire - it's her mother. If something sets her off, well, that could be dangerous for Claire, the baby, and for you."

"Prissy can't do anything to me."

"Maybe not, but trust me on this." She caught his gaze. "You and I will go in together while Paul stands guard. Okay?"

He stared at her a long moment. "Okay."

She hoped she could keep him from bolting.

The Scent of a Woman

When Hank Lowell had shown Roddy the typed not-quite-blackmail letter he'd received the other day, Roddy had been riveted. While it was anonymous as far as paper and printer (and fingerprints) were concerned, it bore a striking similarity to the letter Burke Collins had received before he went on his rampage. Both letters had extremely wide margins on both sides, making the typing look as narrow as a newspaper column.

Now, Roddy Crocker sat on his front steps looking over copies of both letters as well as two more, typed with the same wide margins. Quinton Everett had brought one, and the Dunworth sisters had given him the other an hour ago. He knew that once he turned them in, the detectives would come to the same conclusion he had: The perp lived on Morning Glory Circle. He just needed a little more proof.

He rose and went back in the house to stash the Dunworth's letter in a Ziploc bag, then came back out and approached his wife, who was manning their table. She ladled vegetable soup into a foam bowl and handed it to the Sachs' boy, Billy. "Thanks, Mrs. C!" He strolled away. Roddy liked the boy. He was going to be a fine man.

"Roddy!" Bettyanne said, giving him the same smile she had the day he'd fallen in love with her. "Pull up a chair!"

"I will in a little while, honey." He gave her a quick kiss. "I need to talk to a few neighbors."

"Business?"

"Always. It won't take too long."

She smiled. "That's what you always say."

***

"Just a minute," Stephanie Banks said to Jason and Paul. "Priscilla Martin's observational skills were always scary, and I assume they still are." She tucked her auburn hair into a khaki sun hat with a floppy brim then slid her sunglasses back on. "It's been over twenty years," she said. "I've changed a lot, but Priscilla may still recognize me without a disguise. We didn't exactly end things on the best terms. She hated me for stealing her son."

"We were careful not to mention you," Jason said. "We think it's best to keep her in the dark, too."

Paul grinned. "Boy, I'd like to see the look on her face when she finds out."

"Stick around," Steffie said. "You just might."

"Go the other way if you see Priscilla," Jason said.

"That's right," Steffie agreed. "Don't let her see you - that'll open up a whole new can of worms and we don't want to further stress Claire."

Jason nodded then led them around the barricade, into the throng of hungry people. Neighbors and friends of neighbors strolled, bunching in front of each house, sampling the wares. Jason, Paul, and Steffie reached Babs' house. He didn't see Babs, but her husband was grilling dogs to the sounds of Frank Sinatra. Old Blue Eyes was crooning about strangers in the night taking chances. It seemed appropriate.

Paul nodded toward the table. "Gotta eat."

"Go ahead." Jason scanned the yard for Babs.

"I'm staying with you, Jason," said Steffie. "I want to hear what Mrs. Vandercooth has to say."

Jason nodded at Paul. "Bring us a couple dogs. Let's find Babs."

They walked up the driveway, and just as they were about to knock on the back door, Babs opened it. Startled, she dropped a stack of paper plates, but Stephanie swooped in and caught them before they hit the ground.

"Steffie," said Babs, accepting the plates. "Steffie Banks, I'd recognize you anywhere."

"Nice to see you again." Steffie reached up and found a stray lock of red hair. "Is this what gave me away?" She tucked it back under the hat.

"That auburn hair is a dead giveaway," Babs said. "I'm so glad you're back, Jason. I haven't been able to talk to Claire at all. Prissy just says she's sleeping. The doctor was there in the middle of the night, or so she claims. I got called out on a wild goose chase and didn't get back until this morning."

"Wild goose chase?" Jason raised his brows. "Something related to Claire?"

"I didn't think so at the time, but I'm beginning to wonder. I kept calling, and I don't think she appreciated it. But the call I received was from a man, not a woman."

"There are phone apps that change your voice," Stephanie said. "They're very common."

Babs nodded. "I know it sounds a little paranoid, but I think maybe Prissy wanted to get rid of me."

"That's not paranoid," Stephanie said.

"I need to see Claire," Jason said. "And Steffie has to come with me."

"How can I help?" Babs asked.

"Can you run interference?" Jason glanced around, and saw no sign of his mother-in-law. "Can you keep Priscilla busy while I sneak Steffie into the house?"

"It's vital - absolutely vital - that Priscilla doesn't see us," Steffie said.

"You bet I can keep her busy." Babs hesitated. "Do you have a plan?"

"After I make sure Claire's okay - and apologize on my hands and knees for not believing her - my plan is to carry her down the stairs and take her to our new house."

"That might be difficult, since cars aren't allowed on the street until after five."

Jason nodded. "Good point. It'll give us time to pack." He rubbed his chin. "Do you know where Prissy is right now?"

"She could be just about anywhere, but I guarantee you she's on the street. Stay here while I take a look." Babs strode down the driveway and up to the hotdog table. Setting down the plates, she said something to her husband, then greeted Paul and pointed. Paul trotted up, extra dogs in hand. Jason didn't know he had an appetite until he took a bite. He was ravenous and that made him feel guilty because he hadn't seen Claire yet.

"Eat," Steffie told him. "You can't rescue a maiden from a fire-breathing dragon on an empty stomach."

"Thanks." He finished the dog in two bites then tried to spot Babs. Not seeing her, he slowly walked down the driveway, Steffie and Paul following. Near the sidewalk, he spotted Babs across the street talking with a woman tending a table that had a half dozen helium balloons tied to the edge. The woman pointed toward Prissy's house.

Babs came right back, pausing only to fetch two men who'd been talking by the grill. Jason did a double take when he saw they were priests.

"I'm hoping she's not possessed or something."

"Bad joke, Paul," Jason said.

"Not a joke," Steffie said. "Priscilla once called the elder priest - Father Dave - because she said Tim was possessed. She tried to make him perform an exorcism. He wouldn't do it."

"Jesus Christ, is there no end to her madness?" Jason said. "I need to get in there now."

Babs arrived and introduced the priests. "Father Andy and Father Dave are here to help."

"Thanks. You know Claire?"

"Slightly," said Father Dave. "I knew her brother." He shook his head sadly.

"And I've spent a little time with Claire," the younger priest said.

"She didn't mention it, Father."

"I'm not surprised. It was the day of the Collins murders. I was upstairs with her when we heard the shots." He shook his head. "We both saw too much."

"I'm glad you were with her."

Andy nodded. "Babs says you need distractions. I may be a pretty good one. Priscilla has made a number of ... flirtatious moves toward me."

"She flashed him at the Collins funeral," the old priest said.

Andy blushed and shot him a dirty look.

"She flashed me, too," Father Dave added. "And she's done worse."

"It's not surprising," Steffie said. "Priscilla Martin always wants what she can't have."

"And she always wants something to hold over your head," Father Dave said.

Babs nodded. "Just like death and taxes."

***

"I'd love another taste of your wife's wonderful chili, Stanley." Prissy Martin watched as he ladled some of Aida's best into a paper cup and added a spoon. "Thank you, Stanley. You know, you probably should keep those spoons in a covered container, in case of flying insects."

Stan cocked an eyebrow. "This time of year? I don't think that's an issue, Prissy."

"Still, it would be more sanitary." She nodded at the small cups he was using. "Don't you think it would look nicer if you used bowls?"

Go pester somebody else. "Take it up with Aida. I just work here." He tried to smile, but it had become more and more difficult to take the woman's condescending remarks. He reached over and turned up his iPod. Priscilla Martin made a face when she heard Coastal Eddie's voice.

"Take up what with me?" Aida asked as she joined them.

"Nothing important Aida."

"Priscilla doesn't like our cups," Stan explained.

"You don't?"

"Or our open spoon container. She thinks they'll be covered with flies."

"Stan! I'm sure Prissy didn't mean-"

"Stanley is just a little Grumpy Gus today." Prissy smiled at him. "I'm sorry Stanley, I meant no offense."

"It's Stanford."

Prissy, spooning chili into her mouth, ignored him.

"How's Claire?" Aida asked.

"She's sleeping a lot. Carrying a baby is exhausting, you know." Prissy looked down the crowded street. "Aida, this looks like the best Spring Potluck we've ever thrown. We should have charged the guests admission! Next year, maybe we'll do just that."

"What would we charge for? It's a potluck!" Aida laughed. "Everyone brought dishes with them."

"I think an admission charge might be a wonderful way to donate to our street's well-being. We could add theme decorations, like at Christmas, and get a nice sound system so we can dispense with this horrible cacophony of radios. Show our unity." Prissy sneered at Stan's iPod, then turned and studied Aida's lawn-gobbling snapdragon garden. "Why Aida, once the blooms really get underway, your pink, white, and blue U.S. flag will be quite a hit. What a patriotic idea." She chuckled. "I'll bet Duane and his little Oriental friend will just *love* it."

"I don't understand," Aida said. The snaps will come in red when they're ready. You know there are often a few mixed up seeds in the packets. You're judging my garden by a single pink bloom." She said it with a smile.

Stan listened. He liked it when Aida got fed up. He cleared his throat. "Priscilla, why would Duane and Jerry like a pink, white, and blue American flag?" He used his most innocent tone.

"You know why, Stanley."

"No, I don't. Please enlighten me, Prissy. I really want to know." He glanced at his wife. Aida was trying to fight back a smile.

"Because, you know. They're pansies."

"Pretty little flowers," Stan observed. "I didn't know they preferred those to snapdragons, but to each his own, as they say."

Prissy opened her mouth, no doubt to explain, but before she got any words out, her expression changed to a big grin. "Why hello, Officer Roderick! How nice to see you today."

Roddy's given name was Rodman - he was named for Rod Serling - but Prissy didn't care. Another reason Stan couldn't stand her, and was only polite for Aida's sake.

"Cup of chili?" Stan asked as Coastal Eddie's voice gave way to *Strawberry Fields Forever.*

Roddy grinned. "Lay it on me. It smells incredible. The hint of cumin and dash of brown sugar really does the trick." He waved away the spoon Stan offered. "I like cups because I can drink my chili like a man."

He and Stan laughed and shot the breeze about the Warriors' current line-up, then Roddy said, "Hey, I want to ask you folks a question."

"Shoot," Stan said.

"The department's had several residents of Snapdragon, including one or two living here on the sac turn in anonymous letters."

"Letters?" asked Aida.

Roddy nodded. "Typed, unsigned, no return address. Each one says the author knows what the recipient did, but usually lack specifics. Generally, they stop just short of blackmail. But not always."

Stan looked at Aida. Her face had gone white. Before Roddy noticed, he spoke. "Aida honey, would you run in the house and get some more napkins? I'm about out."

She nodded and hurried up the walk. Stan looked at Roddy. "And you want to know if we've received any?"

Roddy nodded.

Stan considered telling the truth, but knew Aida would be humiliated if anyone ever found out about their two years in the hippie commune up north, about the flowers she wore in her hair and the henna tattoos on her titties. "Can't say we have," Stan said.

"Mrs. Martin?" The cop took a step back from Priscilla, no doubt to put some distance between his super-sensitive sniffer and the woman's cloud of extra-strength perfume.

"Me? Oh, no! That's horrible. Our poor neighbors! May I ask who was threatened?"

"You can ask, but I can't answer." Roddy looked her up and down, probably blinding himself on those neon yellow stretch pants. They were so bright, tight, and ugly they belonged on a three-hundred pounder in a Wal-Mart somewhere. The Dean Twins walked by and Stan smiled at the peculiar little creatures, happy they didn't stop.

"Well, that's just terrible!" She looked from Roddy to Stan. "I'd better go check on my potato salad."

"Is your son-in-law watching the table for you?"

"No, I wish he were, but he's out of town. My table is on the honor system. I just have so many projects going on that I can't spend all my time there." She sighed.

"Hopefully there aren't any potato salad thieves on the sac today," Stan said.

"Don't call Morning Glory Circle 'the sac,' Stanley. That's vulgar."

Stan watched her walk away, then said to Roddy, "Those pants, now those are vulgar."

Roddy grinned. "No shit."

***

"Do you need a fresh diaper, Frederick?" Priscilla's voice worked a cold finger down his spine.

Fred stared over the edge of the balcony at what he could see of the festivities below. Hank Lowell looked up, shielded his eyes from the sun, and waved. Fred could have returned the wave, but he didn't want to risk being drugged by Priscilla, so he only gave a slight nod.

"Frederick, are you listening to me?"

Fred groaned and turned his head to the side.

Priscilla placed a clammy hand on his shoulder. "I asked if you need a diaper change." She bent down, sniffed, and satisfied, said, "I'm going to be busy, busy, busy with the potluck for hours, so if you need to relieve yourself, tell me now." She crossed her arms and, after a long moment, said, "Suit yourself, Frederick. But I won't be back for a while, and if you end up with a rash, you'll only have yourself to blame." She sighed. "Why don't you come inside?"

"Noooo."

"You want to stay out here? All by yourself on the balcony?"

He nodded.

"Well, all right, but I don't see what good it does you to sit there and look at all the people enjoying themselves. It can only make you feel worse. Be grateful for what you have, I always say, and pay no attention to the things you never will." She turned and clicked out of the room on sharp, noisy heels.

Frederick listened and when the lock clicked into place it was just another nail in a long-sealed coffin. When the coast was clear, he wheeled himself to the railing, reached inside his pajamas and yanked the adult diaper down, then urinated off the balcony. It felt great. *There you go, Prissy. I watered your plants.*

***

Roddy Crocker inhaled, enjoying the festival of tantalizing aromas drifting across the sac. He was sure the Stines had received one of the letters - neither could lie their way out of a parking ticket, but they claimed no knowledge. He'd moved on, pausing briefly to eat a perfectly spiced, incredibly fragrant pork tamale and shoot the breeze with Hank Lowell; then he moved on, passing Priscilla Martin's godforsaken bowl of potato salad just as the Dean twins approached it. He came even with Candy Sachs, and asked her, but she denied all knowledge. Her husband, Milton, looked troubled. Roddy decided to come back and have a chat when Candy wasn't around. He passed Duane's place - no one was home - and then the empty Collins house. He walked by the Vandercooths'; their grilled hot dogs were the hit of the potluck, and there was no point trying to talk to them - too crowded. They even had a couple of Catholic priests munching down.

When Roddy arrived at Ace Etheridge's, he accepted a soda from Iris and shook hands with Ace. He and Ace had been neighbors for almost a decade. "Can we talk a minute?"

"Sure. Let's sit down." Ace led him to the porch and Roddy asked if he'd received any letters.

Ace looked at him for a long time. "Sounds like somebody's sniffing for secrets around here."

"It does," Roddy agreed. While Ace was the editor of the newspaper, he was also good at keeping quiet. He'd proven himself many times over and had been instrumental in helping catch several criminals.

"I have received such letters, yes. At least once or twice a year for - I don't know how long. Since before you moved in."

"You never reported them?"

"No. I figured bringing them to light might actually cause me to be outed on the Internet. Whoever writes those things doesn't make threats, they just want me to know they know *all* about me." He stroked his goatee. "Which is bullshit. If they knew my pen name is Kathryn McLeod, I'd already have been outed."

Roddy laughed. "Exactly. Do you have any of the letters?"

"Are you kidding? I've got them all. You never know when you might need to show something like that to your lawyer. You want them?"

"Please."

"You know Iris signs in my stead." He laughed. "She looks a hell of a lot more like a romance writer than I do."

Roddy nodded. "That she does."

"The only thing that truly bothers me is that if it got out, it might be really hard on her. Humiliation is a bitch she doesn't deserve."

"I bet your publisher would be pissed if it got out that Kathryn McLeod's a man."

"What can they do? It happens. Doesn't matter to me, except I don't want the fame. I just want the royalty checks. And I like writing those damned books." He laughed. "But let's keep that between ourselves."

"Hey, I like reading them. Got anything new coming out?"

"This summer. A brand new series - *Moonflower*. First book is called *Evening Primrose*. I'll get you an advanced copy as soon as they're available."

"Thanks."

Ace stood up. "I'll get those letters. Be right back"

Dean Martin sang about love and pizza as Roddy sat on the porch and watched the neighbors and their friends milling around, talking, laughing, having a good time. And he wondered which one was the anonymous letter-writer.

Ace came back out with a manila file folder and an envelope. "Here are the old ones." He gave him the folder. "And here's the one that came yesterday." He handed over the envelope.

Roddy took it by the corner and slipped the folded paper out. It had the same wide margins ... and something the others didn't possess. His sinuses tickled unpleasantly and he held the paper under his nose. *Opium* perfume.

"Gotcha," he said.

Ace's eyes lit up. "You know who wrote it?"

"Smell it."

Ace did. "I can't smell anything."

"I can." He stood up. "You'll be the first to know, Ace. Now, if you'll excuse me, I need to drop by the station."

Sunday Morning Recon

Priscilla Martin rounded the corner of the house in time to see Daphene and Delphine Dean, in matching plaid skirts, white button-downs, and ribboned pigtails, digging spoons into her potato salad. She watched in horror as the little twits slapped sloppy globs of it on the table, both expressionless, as if sent on some mundane mission just to irritate her.

Prissy's temper came untethered. "You little *shits!*"

The twins turned, their pale faces blank, their mouths agape.

"Get! *Scat!*" Prissy waved her arms and broke into a trot. "What the hell do you think you're *doing!*"

The neighbors' heads turned and someone killed the volume on one of the radios. *Thank heaven!*

The Dean twins' eyes went wide. They wrapped their arms around each other and stood there, slack-jawed, as Prissy approached, then broke out in an arm-flailing dash, pigtails and skirts flying behind them.

"I'm telling your mother!" shrieked Prissy as the brain-dead duo darted down the sidewalk. She looked around and saw several neighbors snickering. "What the hell are you staring at?" she yelled at Candy Sachs, who'd buried her face behind a pink handkerchief. "Scarlet harlot!"

The insult only made Candy fall apart with laughter. She hugged her son close and pointed at Prissy - not at those dreadful twins - and both laughed.

Prissy ignored them, staring at her table. Frowning, she began scooping up the globs of salad. If the whole neighborhood hadn't been watching, she would have returned it to the bowl - certainly there was nothing wrong with it since the little cretins had used spoons - but instead, she bundled the goop into napkins and, face hot with fury and humiliation, stalked toward the garbage can.

"Pris?" Barbara Vandercooth, in black pants and matching sweater, both lacking a single decorative flower, approached.

Prissy straightened her shoulders and willed her face to remain placid, hoping it wasn't as red as it felt.

"What happened over here?"

Prissy sighed. "Those retarded little monsters thought they were being funny." She wiped her hands on the last napkin. "I'm going to have to talk to their parents about this, though I wouldn't be a bit surprised if the parents didn't send them here. Either way, their lack of respect for other people's property must be addressed!"

"Would you like me to watch your table for you while you go do that?"

"Well, I wasn't going to do it *now,* necessarily."

"Oh, I think you should," said Babs with a knowing smile. "While the crime is still fresh."

Prissy thought about it. "You're right." She sighed. "I'll be right back."

"I'll be here." Babs' cheery smile annoyed Prissy, but right now, she had more urgent matters to attend to.

She felt the eyes of the neighborhood on her as she stalked toward the Dean house. From someone's yard, *Chariots of Fire* began to play. Giggles broke out from all directions.

"Fudge you," she muttered under her breath as she patted her hair into place. "All of you! And your brothers and sisters, too! And your dogs. Fudge your dogs, too!"

***

"She's after those little girls," Paul Schuyler said, before biting into another hot dog. "See her? Across the street?"

"I believe those are the Dean twins." Carl handed Father Dave a chili dog.

Paul shielded his eyes from the sun and watched as the flailing, shrieking girls disappeared up their driveway. Priscilla didn't follow them, but marched up the front walk, as stiff as a soldier, and knocked on the door, non-stop. Father Andy cringed. Steffie went to the curb and looked toward the Martin house, then came back. "Babs is on guard. Ready, Jason?"

He nodded. "Let's go, Paul!"

"Coming." He could barely tear his eyes off the scene unfolding across the street.

Earlene Dean had stepped onto the front porch and if Paul read her body language right, she was fixing to punch Priscilla in the tits.

"Paul, are you coming?" Jason asked.

"Yeah, yeah."

"Father Andy?"

"I'll stay here and interfere if it gets physical. Priscilla will respond well to me, I think."

"She will," Father Dave agreed.

Paul, Jason, and Steffie stayed on the sidewalk, slipping in and out of clusters of chatting people. There were just as many in front of the dark Collins house, looky-loos more interested in death than food. The trio passed them by and made it quickly to Priscilla Martin's house. Babs smiled. "What took you so long?"

"Sorry," Jason said, his eyes on Claire's bedroom window.

Paul blushed. "My fault. It's like a train wreck down there. I couldn't look away."

"It is?"

"It will be," Jason said, "if Father Andy doesn't get over there quick."

"Okay," Babs said, looking at Jason and Steffie. "Paul and I will keep watch down here while you two go up. Stay in touch. Use the kitchen door. I already checked - she didn't lock it."

"Great, thanks." Jason and Steffie trotted up the driveway. The bearded next-door neighbor watched.

"He's a good guy?" Paul asked Babs.

"He's fine, don't worry about him."

Paul reached for a paper bowl and the serving spoon. Babs swatted it away. "Don't eat that. Last time Priscilla made potato salad, half the street got sick."

**

"Claire?" Jason sat down on the bed next to his wife and took her hand. If she noticed his presence, or Steffie's, she gave no indication. She sat up, pillows behind her, staring into space. Her hair was a mess, her face pale, and her eyes were hollow. Haunted. "Claire, baby, talk to me." Jason heard the quaver in his voice.

Claire made no response.

He looked to Steffie, who eyed his wife with clinical intensity. "Do you hear us, Claire?" she asked. "It's me, Stephanie Banks. And Jason." She sat down on the other side of Claire, and without looking away said, "She's in some kind of stupor."

"What does that mean?" Jason sounded more forceful than he meant to, but Stephanie didn't seem to notice.

"I'd say she's suffered some kind of trauma and has ... well, checked out."

"Checked out?" His voice sounded high and thin.

Stephanie put a hand to Claire's face, peeled back one of her eyelids. She frowned, felt Claire's forehead, then lifted her arm and checked her pulse. "There's something else going on here."

"What do you mean?"

For the first time, Steffie looked at Jason. "Her pupils are dilated, for one thing. I think she's on something."

"*On* something? On what?"

Steffie shrugged. "I'd imagine Priscilla has drugged her."

"That fucking bitch." Jason spoke under his breath. He palmed his wife's face, kissed her cheeks, his own tears brimming. "Claire," he said. "Talk to me. Please, baby, talk to me."

***

In the distant reaches of her mind, Claire thought she heard Jason's voice, but it dissolved before she was able to wrap herself around it.

She was with Timothy. He spoke to her in such low, quiet tones that she had trouble making out his words. Behind his voice, she kept hearing a distant tinkle of sound - music - and occasionally she saw flashes of a tiny plastic ballerina, arms overhead, turning a slow circle.

"... the truth ..." Tim's voice insisted. "You have to know the truth."

Claire tried to find him, tried to *see* him, but the world was black. She wanted to communicate with him, but even here she was voiceless.

" ... the truth ... You know it ... remember ... try to remember ..."

Then another voice. "Please, baby. Talk to me."

Jason?

Then the tinkling music came closer.

The plastic ballerina spun faster.

***

Jason broke down. He let Claire's arm fall limply to her side and, burying his face in his hands, he wept without shame.

Stephanie leaned toward him, took his hand. "She'll come out of it, Jason. She will. When a person experiences something traumatic, they sometimes detach temporarily. That's what this is. I'm almost positive."

"What am I supposed to *do*?" he asked.

"Just keep talking to her. Tell her she's safe. Tell her to come back. We need her to come back."

Jason raised his head but one look at his hollow-eyed wife restarted silent tears. "What did she do to you, Claire? What the hell did she do to you?"

They both talked to her for long minutes. Finally, there was a flutter of eyelid, then Claire blinked.

"Claire?" Jason moved close, taking her hand.

Steffie's eyes remained fixed on Claire. "Claire, can you hear us? We need you to come back."

Claire blinked twice more, slowly, then turned her head and looked at Jason. He saw the knowledge, the *awareness,* filtering into her eyes. She blinked again. "My music box. The one Timothy gave me." Her voice was a dry, papery whisper. "Water."

Jason turned to lift a full water glass off the desk.

"No," Steffie said. "Here." She pulled a bottle of water from her jacket, unscrewed the lid, and put it in Claire's hands. Claire drank greedily until Steffie gently pulled it away. "Not too much, it'll give you cramps. You're very dehydrated."

Claire nodded.

"What?" Jason kissed her face, over and over. "What about your music box, baby?"

"That's where it is," said Claire. "In my music box."

She turned and looked at Steffie and, for the first time, smiled. It was like the sun breaking through the blackest clouds Jason had ever seen, warming, and soul-soothing.

"Steffie?" Claire asked.

Stephanie smiled back. "In the flesh!" She put an arm around her and they hugged for a long time.

Claire turned to Jason. "Magic Man. I missed you." She kissed him, pulled him into an embrace.

When he released her, she looked at him, then squeezed her eyes shut. "I'm still having ... I'm still seeing things."

"What?" asked Jason.

"Things."

"Tell us what you mean." Stephanie brushed sweat-damp hair off Claire's forehead.

Claire shook her head and pinched the bridge of her nose. "I don't know." For a long moment, she didn't move, then she looked up. "My music box, Jason. I need you to go get it." She paused. "It's already packed, but it's still in the apartment."

"But honey, I-"

"It's important, Jason."

He looked at Steffie and she nodded at him. "I'll stay with her. Go."

Jason kissed his wife one more time, feeling horrible for leaving her but wanting to fulfill her wish, whatever the reason might be.

"It's in one of the boxes in the bedroom," said Claire.

"I understand."

"And don't let Mother see you, okay? Especially don't let her see the music box."

"I won't." Jason took off, hurrying for fear she might slip back into whatever state she'd been in before he returned.

Secrets

Earlene Dean and Priscilla Martin were standing off on the Dean lawn like two cats sizing each other up for battle. Their movements were stiff and slow, their postures rigid. Near the house, the twin girls watched, eyes wide, fingers stuffed in their mouths. Half the street was staring.

Father Andy approached, hoping his collar would keep him out of the fray that, in his mind, was about to turn into a cartoon whirlwind of arms and legs. As he neared the women, he imagined he heard them growling and hissing.

"Your children need to be taught a lesson." Prissy snarled. "They are evil, undisciplined brats and you people don't belong here."

"You don't talk about my kidsss that way, you nosy old bitch. You never talk about my babiesss that way unlesss you want me to kill you." Earlene Dean's wandering eye made her appear even fiercer than Priscilla.

"Kill me? I'll have you arrested for making threats, you inbred good-for-nothing … cunt!"

Andy Pike stopped dead, startled.

"What did you sssay to me?" Earlene's voice rose. Neighbors gathered.

"Cunt! I said you're an inbred cunt! And your children are retards!"

Earlene's face went white. "I am *not* inbred!" she cried.

"You married your brother and you … *copulated* with him until you created those abominations against God! You are a sinner. Your brother-husband is a sinner! Your blood is tainted and your children should be sacrificed to the Lord to atone for their misbegotten time on this earth!"

"If it was good enough for our parentsss, it's good enough for usss!"

Their hands curled into tight fists and they approached each other on stiff legs.

"Ladies," Andy called. "Ladies, please!"

"Are they really inbred?" Phyllis Stine gasped, clutching at her pearls and looking around the crowd, making clicking, huffing noises. "Oh, sweet Jesus!" She looked like she might faint, and was quick to light a cigarette, corking it in her mouth like a pacifier.

Earlene stepped close enough to Prissy that their noses nearly touched. "Lisssten to me, you dreadful, horrible woman …"

"No," said Priscilla, spittle flying like tiny sparks. "*You* listen to *me!* It's high time everyone knows what you really are! I've kept my mouth shut until now, but-"

Andy saw it, but was too late to stop it.

Earlene's fist shot out and the subsequent *Pop!*, as it connected with Prissy's mouth sent a collective gasp through the crowd. Phyllis Stine's cigarette tumbled from her lips. Andy threw himself between the women, but it wasn't necessary. Prissy flew back, landing ass-over-teakettle on the lawn. She shot up, held a hand to her bleeding mouth, and faced the gaping neighbors.

Stan Portendorfer threw his head back and laughed. "Great right hook, Earlene!"

"You all saw that!" Prissy shrieked. "You're all witnesses! And yes! Earl and Earlene Dean are brother and sister! I've known it for years! And their children are the product of this unholy union!"

Another collective gasp rippled through the crowd.

Earlene lunged for Prissy but Andy caught her and held her in place. She got an arm free and thrust her finger at Priscilla. "So *you're* the one who sent the blackmail letters! You!"

Now the crowd was silent.

All eyes shifted to Priscilla.

***

"I think you've been given a hallucinogen," Stephanie told Claire after she described some of the hallucinations she'd been suffering. My guess is LSD."

"Oh my God!"

"It hasn't been shown to be harmful to fetuses," said Steffie. "I'm almost certain your mother has been giving it to you."

"LSD?" Claire could hardly wrap her mind around it.

"Probably. Somehow, despite how horrible she is, I don't think she'd want to hurt the baby. But where would she get it?"

Claire stared at Steffie. "Anywhere. She's got this whole town dancing on her strings, drug dealers included, no doubt. It wouldn't be hard for her to get. She's a monster."

"Yes, she is. When did she leave that glass of water here, do you recall?"

"I don't remember. I don't think I've had any. I started feeling funny right after dinner. It was passing, and then it got worse again in the middle of the night."

"But you don't remember sipping that water?"

"No, but Mother brought me a glass of warm milk around three in the morning."

"That woman should be in prison," Stephanie said. "She did the same thing to Tim."

"Drugged him?"

"I don't know, but you know he had an alcohol problem, don't you?"

"I smelled it on him, but I was just a kid. I didn't think about it until …" Tears streamed down her face. "Until last night, I'd forgotten I found him. You know… In the closet. There was a big bottle of booze sitting there." She wiped away tears.

Stephanie held her in her arms, stroking her hair, kissing her forehead, and let her grieve.

***

Her mouth hurt, but Prissy stood tall and stared down at the neighbors surrounding her. "Did you see what that inbred cretin did to me?" She touched her bleeding lip. "She assaulted me! Where's Roddy? Get me Roddy! He needs to arrest her now and take pictures of my mouth!"

"He took off for the police station a while ago," Bettyanne Crocker said. "He'll be back soon enough."

Prissy glared at her. "He'd better be, you little sneak-thief! You goddamn klepto!"

Bettyanne looked aghast.

"So you're the asshole who's been sending us letters!" Nellie Dunworth's voice rang out as she pushed through the crowd on her scooter, Bertie right behind her. The plump sisters glared at Prissy.

She glared back. "Whores like you shouldn't live on this street, any more than perversions like *her*!" She pointed at Earlene Dean. Her idiot children peered out from behind her and Andy. "They need to be put down!" Prissy cried. "It's the Christian thing to do."

Father Andy straightened his shoulders. "Priscilla-"

"Shut up, you milquetoast minister," Prissy growled. "You don't live on this street. Stay out of it."

Then grizzled old Dave Flannigan appeared next to Andy, saying nothing, just staring at her. She ignored him, and looked around. Nearly all her neighbors were there. She pointed at the Dunworth sisters. "Do you know what Nellie and Bertha Dunworth do?" She glanced around. "Do you?"

"We operate a phone sex business." Bertie's voice was strong and defiant and she came closer, fixing her gaze on Prissy.

Nellie gunned her scooter and shot forward. "And we're proud of it!" She looked around. "Does anyone have a problem with that?"

Stan's laugh rang out. "Hell, no!" Others tittered, but no one objected.

"You are prostitutes who use your mouths instead of your genitals for sex!"

Nellie and Bertie's faces went blank for a fraction of a second, then both began laughing along with the rest of the neighbors.

"Don't you laugh at me!" Prissy shrieked. "Don't you *dare* laugh at me! I keep this street running and I know *all* your dirty little secrets! You'll be sorry!"

Phyllis Stine began sobbing. "I'm not laughing at you, Prissy! You're my friend!"

"Thank you, Phyllis. What about you, Aida? Are you laughing at me?"

***

"I'm still seeing things, but not as bad as I was," said Claire. "Mostly just streaks of colors now. But what I did see ..." She shuddered. "It was horrible."

"The effects of LSD can last up to twelve hours," said Steffie, "but they usually only last about eight. I'd say you're coming down right on time."

"I just can't believe it. How could she do this?"

"Because, Claire, your mother is a very sick woman. She always has been. To be honest, she's probably the main reason I became interested in psychiatry. I saw what she put Tim through ... and I wanted answers." She looked at Claire a long moment, tears welling. "I wanted to get you away from her, Claire. I even called Social Services after Tim died. I didn't know what else to do. I was so young then. I'm sorry."

"It's okay," said Claire. "I don't think she was nearly as hard on me as she was on Tim."

Steffie nodded. "She always seemed to have a preference for boys." She stared a moment, lost in thought. "I contacted that young woman, Ashley Perkins, the other day."

"The Facebook girlfriend?" Claire sat forward, eager to hear.

Steffie nodded. "Apparently, 'Timothy' and she met about nine months ago." She made air quotes around his name. "They'd exchanged pictures and talked at length about meeting. It was pretty serious. But then they started talking about their families and upbringing. The way he went on and on about how wonderful his mother was - it turned her off, so she cooled things down; she didn't want to date a mama's boy."

"Did you tell her that ... that Tim's been dead for twenty years ... and that my mother ... was ... posing as him?" The words were hard to say, like glue on her tongue.

"I told her and she was stunned. I felt very sorry for her. She wasn't sure she believed me at first, and assumed I was a jealous ex or something. But I explained the whole ... situation and emailed her Tim's obituary."

Claire closed her eyes, trying to imagine that poor woman's betrayal. It was just too much. And so humiliating. "How did I come out of that woman? I'm so ... ashamed! She's a monster."

"You're not her, Claire, You're not her at all." Steffie touched Claire's hand.

"I just can't wrap my mind around it. It's crazy."

"Truly. She was, and still is, obsessed with Tim. His death was just a minor technicality - it changed nothing. She still thinks she owns him."

"We've heard her talking to him quite a lot. Of course, last night I was talking to him, too." Her laugh was humorless. "But I don't think it's the same thing."

"Not at all. Your mother never accepted Tim's death," said Steffie. "And if she couldn't have him, then she'd become him. As evidenced by the Facebook affair."

"And to think, I used to envy the attention she lavished on him. If I'd only known how bad it really was." She looked at Steffie. "How much did Tim tell you about what she did to him?"

"Not much. I suspected something was very wrong, and as I got older, it started making more sense. But he never really told me anything back then. I imagine he was ashamed of her, too. All I really knew was that she wouldn't let anyone get close to him. I suspected abuse, but had no way of knowing how far it had gone."

Claire closed her eyes against the sunburst of color that had formed around Steffie's hair. At least the effects are diminishing. "When Jason gets back with my music box, I think we'll know a lot more."

"How do you mean? What's the deal with the music box?"

"It's something I'd forgotten until last night." Claire chewed her lip. "You'll see."

***

Aida stepped forward, Stan behind her, still trying to control his chuckles. Aida's arms were crossed and she had a look on her face that didn't belong there. Eyes narrowed, she frowned. "I don't see anything funny about this, Priscilla. We've been getting threatening letters for years." She raised her voice. "Does anyone else think that's funny?"

The crowd murmured.

"I never expected *you* to be disloyal to me, Aida! I never thought you-"

"Then why did you send those letters? Tell me why!"

"I remember when they started, Aida-honey." Stan's smile fled. "About twenty years ago, Prissy asked me to light the pilot on her water heater. I did … and then, well, she tried to seduce me."

The crowd gasped.

"I did *nothing* of the sort!" exclaimed Prissy.

Aida turned to Stan, gaping. "Why didn't you tell me?"

"Because I didn't succumb to her, and it would only have upset you."

"I made it clear I loved my Aida," he told the crowd. He turned back to Aida. "She ran up the stairs and I left. It was never spoken of again."

"Liar!" shrieked Prissy. "He's a liar!"

He pointed to Priscilla. "If she'd tried it twice, I would have told you, sweetheart."

Aida stared at Prissy with cold eyes. "So you threatened *my* husband for rejecting your advances?"

"This is just a diversion from the truth! A red herring! I know your *real* secret, Stan! And Aida!" She looked around and announced, "You two used to live in a commune! You were dirty hippies! In a dirty commune!"

Stan broke out laughing. So did Aida, who leaned against her husband as he put his arm around her. "We joined a commune after college," Aida said, realizing that in light of the recent events, her "dark" secret wasn't so dark after all. She shook her head. "You're showing your ignorance, Priscilla. It was a farming commune and we-"

"Grew marijuana! You were drug dealers!"

Stan belly-laughed. "We may have smoked some occasionally, but we grew produce and did it so well that Greentown Farms - the commune - became a business. Today, it's the supplier of the best organic produce in Gold Country. In fact, Prissy, I believe your snapdragon seeds come from Greentown Farms, don't they?"

Laughter rippled through the crowd. Clyde Stine stepped forward. "Phyllis and I have gotten letters too, so I may as well confess my secret. I've been known to wear ladies undergarments. I like the feel. And, evidently, Prissy's the real pervert on the sac. She's a peeping Tom!"

"I am *not!*" Prissy cried. "None of you people have any idea how to use the Internet, do you?" She laughed, high and cackling. "I don't need to peep to know about your sick habits. And Morning Glory Circle is a *cul-de-sac*. Not a 'sac'!"

Phyllis stepped forward, her hand in Clyde's. "I," she said, voice shaking with effort, "am a little older than my husband."

"A little older?" Prissy asked. "A *little* older? You're-"

"Priscilla," Father Andy said. "Stop this now." He stepped forward. Earlene and her girls stayed put. "Priscilla, you need help-"

"And *you* have no sack!" Prissy screamed. She pointed at Dave. "At least that old reprobate is a *real* man!" She eyed Andy, looking him up and down. "I suppose you prefer choir boys to women!"

"Shut up, Prissy!" The circle parted as Babs strode into the center of it, Quinton Everett and Stan behind her. "You've made us all suffer. For years, you've been saying Quinton was a pedophile!"

Excited whispering commenced all around. Prissy smiled. Babs knew that Prissy didn't believe a virile-looking man like Quinton would never admit the truth.

But he did. "I exchanged my ... equipment - and my sex drive - for a purple heart, many years ago." Quinton looked at Prissy. "That was a vile rumor you spread, and now you're trying to say the same about Father Andy. But no one believes anything you say anymore, Priscilla Martin. No one."

"You people think you're so high and mighty. But there's more!" Prissy whirled to face the crowd. "Why don't you tell us about your gambling problem, Carl?"

Carl stepped forward, a little smile on his face, and began his confession.

***

At the bottom of a carton, packed neatly away, Jason found Claire's music box. He saw nothing unusual. It was old but well cared for, and he found nothing inside except the plastic ballerina that teetered and circled on a spring as music tinkled. Closing it, he left the apartment, locking the door behind him.

Fred waved from his balcony and Jason raised his hand in return, then glanced around to be sure Prissy wasn't in sight before darting down the steps and into the main house. His pulse thudding in his chest, he held the music box in a death grip as he walked through the kitchen, past the empty living room, and up the stairs. In the hall, he noticed evenly spaced nail holes on both sides of the wall that he hadn't seen before, and many of the dried wreaths were missing. He paused, running a finger across one of the holes. It was new, and on the carpet below it was a small mist of white dust, as if pictures were going to be hung.

The strong odor caught his attention again. *Turpentine? Paint?* He recalled Claire saying she'd smelled chemicals. She'd also said she'd heard tapping from a nearby room. He'd written it off as delusion and paranoia, but it was undeniable now - pungent, bitter proof that his wife was as sane as the day he'd met her. He kept walking, following the acrid scent. And stopped in front of Timothy's old bedroom, where it was strongest.

He tried the knob. It was locked.

He almost ignored it - *Just get Claire's music box to her* - but his sense that he'd find something important behind that door overpowered him. He bent, tried to peer through the keyhole, but saw nothing. Setting down the music box, he dug into his back pocket, withdrew his wallet, and found his debit card. It wouldn't take much to jimmy an old lock like this. After just a few moments he felt and heard the *click* of success. The door cracked. *Piece of cake.*

He pushed the door. It swung slowly open and Jason stepped into Timothy's bedroom.

His breath caught. His feet and thoughts were frozen in place. He stared, unable to make sense of what he saw.

And then, as if by one swift stroke of the brush, the bewildering picture before him became horribly, dreadfully, hideously clear.

"Oh, my God ..."

The music box fell from his hand.

***

"I have something to say." Candy Sachs stepped forward, her son and husband behind her.

"You wouldn't dare." Prissy stared at her. So did all the neighbors.

"I'm a transsexual. My name used to be Conrad."

The onlookers went silent.

Milton Sachs took his wife's hand. "And she told me well before I proposed. I love my wife. It's no secret."

Billy stepped in front of both. "And I'm adopted! Duh!" He stuck his tongue out at Prissy.

Dave Flannigan stood with Andy, and stared steadily into Prissy's eyes. "I wonder what you had on the Collins family," he said. "Everyone knew you didn't care for Geneva-Marie."

Andy nodded. "What did you know about Burke Collins, Priscilla?"

Prissy tried to stare him down. It didn't work. "His business was failing."

"We all knew that."

"And he was a drunk. He abused his wife and children."

Roddy Crocker pushed through the crowd. "Priscilla," he said.

"Roderick, thank heaven." Prissy touched her split lip. "Earlene Dean assaulted me. I want to press charges."

He glanced at Earlene, then looked back at Prissy. "I have to ask you not to leave town. You're under investigation as an accessory to the murder of the Collins family."

Prissy's jaw dropped. "What the hell are you babbling about?" She stepped closer to the cop. "I had nothing to do with what Burke did to his family."

"We may not be able to arrest you, Priscilla," Roddy said evenly, "but we're virtually positive you lit the fuse that started his rampage. So don't leave town."

"I don't know what you're talking about!"

"The letters you wrote to your neighbors match the one we believe you wrote to Burke Collins."

"I did nothing wrong! I merely told him the truth about the boys he was raising. He had a right to know that Duane Pruitt was their father!"

The neighbors gasped, started to chatter, then shut up, straining to hear as Roddy began speaking. "Whether or not that's true-"

"It's true!"

"That's neither here nor there. What matters to us - your neighbors - is that you chose to inform him of this while the man was going to AA and trying very hard to get his life back on track." He paused. "And what matters in the eyes of the law, is the homeless woman we located who claims you paid her to deliver both the note and scotch to him. She's agreed to testify, if it comes to that."

Father Andy cleared his throat. "It's time to let go of your anger and hatred, Priscilla. It's not Christian. You need help."

"I don't need your prattle, you ... you ... sexless ... *priest!*" Priscilla wanted to punch him in his self-righteous face. "I saw you staring at me at their funeral!"

"We tried not to, Priscilla," Father Dave said in a voice so calm and pleasant that she wanted to slit his throat. He turned to the crowd. "Priscilla was exposing herself to us throughout the service. Even during Communion. It was quite unbecoming."

More gasps.

Bette Midler's voice started belting out *I Put a Spell on You* from a nearby radio.

Prissy felt the many stares boring holes into her, burning her with their accusations. "It's not true. None of this is true! This is a conspiracy! Why are you doing this to me?" She paused, wiped spittle off her cheek, and glared at her neighbors. "I made you! You're *nothing* without me! None of you! This street would be *nothing* without me! I have given and given and given to *all* of you!" Her wild eyes raked over the crowd. "Well, no more!"

Revelations

Jason grabbed the music box and backed out of Timothy's bedroom. His throat was dry. His head spun. It was as if someone had torn a hole in reality and he was tumbling through the empty air with nothing to cling to, nothing to grasp.

Swallowing, he headed to Claire's room.

On the bed, Claire and Stephanie looked up.

"You found it!" said Claire. Her face was still blotchy from crying, but Stephanie had helped her dress and comb her hair. There was a fire in her eye that told him the old Claire was back.

Jason looked down at the box, his mind still reeling from shock. He handed it to Claire. She didn't notice his trembling hands.

She opened it and started peeling back the purple satin lining. "In the … uh, vision I had … I remembered that I'd found Tim's body - and that I found a note he meant for Mother." The satin lifted as she tugged. "Before she arrived, I took it and hid it, but I didn't even recall doing so until-" she paused. "Until, well … Until Tim told me. When I was … unresponsive." Her eyes flicked to Stephanie then to Jason. "It sounds crazy, right?"

Jason said nothing. He was still trying to wrap his mind around the things he'd seen in Tim's old bedroom … and wondering how he was going to tell Claire.

"Yes!" Claire's exclamation startled him. She pulled a yellowed envelope from behind the lining. "I never even opened it." She turned it over, then tore it open.

***

Prissy stared at Roddy Crocker. "So," she said. "I'm not under arrest, am I?"

His gaze hardened. "No, ma'am. But don't leave town."

She smoothed a hand over her hair, drew her shoulders back, and stomped off, the crowd parting like the Red Sea. On the sidewalk, she paused and turned. "You people need to open your eyes!" She brought her hands up to the sides of her face and splayed her fingers. "*Open* your eyes!"

All of Morning Glory Circle stared on, whispering as Priscilla Martin stalked toward her house, as dignified and blameless as ever.

***

"None of her neighbors know what she's capable of," Dave said to Andy. "Maybe we'd better go in after her."

Andy spotted Paul Schuyler, who came trotting over. "Thank God you guys are here. She just went inside. We've got to go in. She's a danger to Claire."

"And everyone else in that house," Dave said.

"You're right," said Andy. "Come on."

Andy, Dave, and Paul headed into Prissy's house.

***

"Oh, my God." Tears slipped from Claire's eyes and the letter shook in her hands.

"What is it?" asked Stephanie.

"I can't ..." she handed the letter to Steffie.

The torture in Claire's eyes brought Jason to the present. Tim's bedroom forgotten, he put an arm around his wife.

"Read it, Steffie," said Claire. "Please."

"Okay." Stephanie looked at the letter, her heartache obvious as she recognized Tim's scrawl.

"Mother,

"First things first, I don't care what becomes of my body. If you feel compelled to give me a 'proper' burial, that's your business, but know that as far as I'm concerned, you can cremate it, put it in a box, or, for that matter, toss it in a river. That's how much I care about the life you gave me.

"I can't live knowing the things I know. I can't live having done the things I've done. And I can't live without Stephanie. You ripped her away from me the same way you ripped away everyone I cared about. You won't allow me to love anyone but you. Not even Carlene is allowed to be with me anymore, because you know how much I love her.

"You are a sick woman, Mother, and I hope that if my death does nothing else, it forces you to look at who you are and what you've done. If I believed I could get Carlene away from you, I would. But I know now that you'll never let that happen. I only hope she never knows how deep your sickness goes. She's witnessed many of the horrible "punishments" you've given me over the years, and I hope she forgets them all. I hope she locks them in a box somewhere deep and never has to think about them again. But, most of all, I hope she never knows that you were carrying my child."

Stephanie's breath caught. "Oh, my God."

Jason felt like someone had punched him the gut.

"Please," said Claire. "Keep going."

Stephanie took a slow breath, then continued.

"*When you told me today that you miscarried, you were heart-broken, but for me, it was a miracle - a second chance. So, no, we will not 'keep trying' as you said, Mother. My death will make sure of that. I'm horrified, I'm ashamed, and I'm sickened by what I've done. And I'm sickened by who you are.*

"*I hate you, Mother. Live knowing that. With every cell in my body, I hate you and I always have. I only wish I'd strangled you in your sleep, or slit your throat, or slipped you an overdose - believe me, I've thought about it many times - but somehow, I could never do it. But I CAN end my OWN life. And I will.*

"*My death is just a formality, though. My life has ended a thousand times before today. It ended when I was five years old and I saw the look in your eye as you told me that you'd never let anyone take me away from you. It ended when I was ten and you started giving me enemas while fondling me. It ended the first time you pushed my hand up your skirt and said I was a good boy for touching you there. It ended when I was fifteen and you showed me what oral sex was. It ended when you took me away from Stephanie. It ended when I realized that even leaving the state wouldn't put any distance between us - that you'd always find a way to bring me back. But most of all, it ended when I became so sick myself, and so desperate for freedom - that I allowed myself to believe you when you said you'd let me go back to Steffie if I gave you a baby - a permanent piece of me.*

"*But sitting here in this wheelchair, listening to your ugly lies, I realized there IS another way out.*

"*I don't know where I'm going. Maybe there's nothing after this life, and that would be fine with me. The only thing that matters is that, wherever I'm headed, you can't follow.*

"*And in a way, that doesn't make this the day I died. It makes today my birthday.*

"*Timothy.*"

The three of them sat in silence. Jason's mind whirled. Claire wept. Steffie's face was a mask of shock.

"I can't believe it," said Steffie. "I had no idea ..."

Now, more than ever, Jason knew he needed to tell Claire about what he'd seen in Tim's bedroom, but he wasn't quite sure how to say it. *I'm going to have to* show *her.* But not yet. He had to let the shock of the letter sink in first. He didn't want to risk sending his wife spiraling into another fugue. Not after she'd just come back to him.

***

After locking both the front and kitchen doors, Priscilla started the record player. After taking a moment to calm her nerves, she took the stairs to the second floor. She had no interest in Frederick or Claire. What she needed was some time alone in Timothy's bedroom. *Those ingrates!* she thought as she walked down the long hall. *Every last one of them! After all I've done for all of them!* But it didn't matter. The only thing that mattered now was Timothy. She couldn't wait to tell him all about it.

She pushed his bedroom door open on darkness and closed it gently, then turned on the light and crossed to the newly painted crib she'd been working so hard on. She had painted it the same beautiful sky blue it had been when it was new; redoing it three times before she got the shade of enamel just right. The paint still smelled - she'd done the third coat last night - and the smell of thinner traced through the room.

She looked around. In every corner was something from Timothy's infancy - his *first* infancy. Except the changing table. That was new. "Timothy," she murmured, "Your room is almost ready for you." Oh, what a chore it had been putting his old crib together again. "But, it was worth it wasn't it, Timothy? *You're* worth it, my sweet little Angelheart." She smoothed the blue blankets that she'd carefully stored away all these years, then touched the frayed ears of the little blue stuffed bunny he'd loved so much - the one with brown eyes. She'd considered replacing it, but was afraid he wouldn't be as happy with an imitation. "You're going to help him remember," she whispered to the bunny. "You're going to help Timothy remember who he is when he's born."

She lit a scented candle that sat on the dressing table. The smell of baby powder softened the stench of paint. She caressed the white mobile hanging over the crib, touching the musical notes and blue and yellow ducks and chicks that hung from it. Unable to resist, she wound it up, smiling as the first notes of *The Magic Flute* began tinkling. "Do you remember your mobile, Timothy? I've kept it for you all these years. Oh, how it made you smile, and it will again very soon, I promise."

The walls were pale blue with colorful wallpaper borders that were almost identical to the ones she'd put up nearly forty years ago - cavorting ponies and baby cowboys, edged above and below by coils of western rope. Calves with smiling faces branded on their backsides appeared every six feet or so. The new paper didn't have the brands, so she'd painted them on herself, using old photos to make sure they matched the original. She'd done a good job. "I hope you'll appreciate all I've been doing for you, Timothy."

Moving toward the bassinet, she lifted the baby blue curtains and stared down at the street, thinking of her neighbors, of the humiliation they'd put her through. She wanted to tell Timothy all about the trouble they'd caused her, but being in this room calmed her nerves. She didn't want to tarnish the room with such negativity. *Soon, my baby boy will be back, and none of it will matter.* She pulled the curtains closed and continued on, running a lingering finger along the lip of the blue bassinet - her favorite item. It was a roomy wicker cradle that, as soon as he was born, she'd move into her own bedroom, so he could sleep with her. "Timothy, I'm so glad you're *finally* coming home again." she murmured. "So glad. I only wish I could have carried you myself and nursed you like I did the first time. But we can buy you formula and you'll be mine - all mine - from the moment you emerge from Carlene's womb. All mine. It's going to be just perfect."

"Mother?"

Prissy whirled and locked eyes with her daughter.

Carlene, Jason, and that tawdry Audrey, Stephanie Banks, all stood, watching her, listening to her.

***

"It's locked." Andy shook the knob on the front door.

"What now?" Dave Flannigan stared at the door and windows. "We need to get in there."

Andy knocked on the door. "Priscilla," he called.

Babs Vandercooth headed toward them. "There's a key," she said in cheery tone. "It's in a holly planter by the back door." She smiled. "Come on, I'll show you."

***

"My God." Claire looked wildly around the room. *This is what she's been doing in here?* She stared at the crib, caught the sickening-sweet scent of baby powder that came from a burning candle on the dresser, and the sharp tang of paint thinner coming from a tin that stood next to it. She saw the bassinet, the changing station, the new wallpaper, all the old toys, and it began to make sense - yet she couldn't quite wrap her mind around it. "What in the name of God are you doing?" Her voice was thin, weak.

"Carlene ..." Mother's smile was placid but her eyes were crazed.

"A *nursery?*" Claire's voice bordered on a shriek. "You've been building a nursery in here?" *She never intended to let us leave!*

Mother smiled. "Yes, dear. For Timothy when he comes." Her gaze roamed over the faces that stared, darkening when it lit on Stephanie. "Don't you see? That was God's plan, Carlene. To bring you back to me so you could give me my Timothy back."

Claire crutched into the room, closer to Mother. "You want to ... *steal* my baby?"

"Of course not, dear." Mother raised a hand to her throat, toying with the hair necklace.

"You think my baby is Timothy?"

"Of course he is. It's God's will, dear, that he come back to me." She paused. "You aren't fit to raise him. I'm sorry, but it's the truth. You're not stable. Everyone knows that."

Hearing the words was like a kick to the gut. "This is why you drugged me? To prove I was unfit?" Her mind raced. "And you broke my leg. I don't know how you did it, but I know you did. It was your plan to keep me here all along, wasn't it?" Her voice took on a hard edge, and she felt Jason's hand on her waist.

She stumped forward several paces. "Oh, poor put-upon Priscilla Martin, stuck nursing her daughter back to health. Poor Priscilla, thank heaven she's a fucking nurse so she can oversee her daughter's recovery."

"Claire?" Jason's voice was low, cautious.

Claire ignored him. "What were you going to do, Mother? Deliver the baby yourself and make sure I didn't survive? And what were you planning to do about Jason? Pump him so full of drugs he can't speak? Like you do Dad? You're behind Dad's accident, aren't you?"

Mother gasped. "Carlene! You're being so paranoid! How could you even *suggest* such an appalling thing?"

Steffie Banks stepped forward and spoke through clenched teeth. "Because you're not sane. And when your husband recovers from the drugs and damage you've inflicted, I'm betting he'll tell us plenty that backs that up."

Mother laughed. "Well, well, if it isn't little Stephanie Banks all grown up. Finally grew into your teeth, did you?" She crossed her arms. "Given your expression, I take it you think your presence in my home comes as a surprise to me. Don't you think I know what goes on in my own house? I've been expecting you for days now, Ms. Banks."

Steffie's eyes didn't waver. "It's *Dr.* Banks."

"You look ... different," said Mother. "Though I can't say it's much of an improvement." She looked at Claire. "You need to get back to bed, young lady. You aren't well. All of this upset isn't good for little Timothy." She reached out and ran her fingers over Claire's abdomen.

Claire slapped her hand away. "Don't touch me, Mother."

"Oh, Carlene. Don't act up in front of your friend. You always were so *eager* to please Ms. Banks. You seemed to think she walked on water." She sighed. "Unfortunately, your brother wasn't quite as taken with her."

"You. Are. A. Crazy. Bitch." Steffie spoke between her teeth.

Mother's spine went rigid. "Excuse me?" She pinned Steffie in a cold, furious gaze.

Steffie stepped forward. "You heard me."

***

Paul, Andy, and Dave entered the kitchen. Andy led the way upstairs, walking quietly, listening hard. The muted voices they'd heard from the kitchen sounded louder now - and angry. He glanced at Dave and Paul, a finger to his lips as they reached the landing.

***

The block party had ended abruptly, though the music from Hank Lowell's radio played on. *Stand By Me* filled the air as potlucks were solemnly disassembled. Stan and Aida's chili table was neatly folded, the leftovers put in the refrigerator for tomorrow's lunch. Bettyanne's vegetable soup and Candy's salads had been put away. Others followed suit until, at last, Carl and Babs' hot dog grill was closed and rolled back up the driveway.

The neighborhood began the cleanup, removing trash and banners and balloons, pushing trash cans up driveways until, finally, there was no evidence anything unusual had happened on Morning Glory Circle.

When they were done, the residents remained outside, silent in the clear afternoon, listening to music and watching the big white house that presided over the street.

***

"How dare you?" Prissy said to Stephanie Banks. "Haven't you done enough damage to this family?" A vein pulsed on her temple.

But Claire felt no fear. "Tim would be alive today if you hadn't dragged him back to Snapdragon, Mother. He's dead because of *you*!"

Prissy whirled. "You bite your tongue, you vicious little brat!"

"It's the truth," said Steffie. "And you can't bring him back, Priscilla. He's gone."

Tears welled in Mother's eyes, but Claire had no remorse. "This baby isn't Tim, Mother. And it doesn't belong to you." She touched her stomach.

Mother's eyes blazed. "You would *deny* me what is rightfully mine? What the *Lord* himself has commanded?"

"The Lord has nothing to do with this, Mother. And I assure you, if Tim *could* come back, he wouldn't want to."

"Timothy *wants* to come back!" Mother shrieked. "How dare you say-"

"This letter says otherwise." Jason stepped forward. "It's to you, from Timothy on the day he died. Claire stored it away."

Prissy's mouth worked. Her eyes darted. Her voice was a rasp. "Give it to me."

Jason did.

Prissy's gaze ravaged the letter. Her hands began to shake. The color drained from her face, and tears raked ragged patterns down her powdered cheeks. "Lies. These are lies. My Timothy did *not* write this!"

"Yes," Claire said. "He did. And what you did to him is inexcusable." She couldn't even bring herself to name the crimes. "You're a child abuser. A molester. And you're going to pay for it."

Priscilla Martin threw her head back and shrieked. "LIARS! All of you! *LIARS!*"

From the corner of her eye, Claire caught sight of Paul and the two priests, Andy and Dave. Motionless, but tense, they listened.

Jason made a move toward Priscilla, swiped at the letter, but Priscilla jerked her hand away. "Give back the letter, Priscilla."

"No!" She stepped back. She had the look of a cornered rat, her eyes wild and darting, unbelieving. Her mascara was smudged, her mouth was tight, and the veins in her neck and forehead stood out. "Get away from me! All of you! Get away!" She backed toward the dressing table, swatting at them with the letter. Her entire body shook and her perfectly-coiffed hair was falling from place, standing out in rough cowlicks.

***

Jason looked from Claire to Priscilla and saw red. He took a deep breath. He needed to get that letter back. It, along with the journals, would incriminate Priscilla and send her to prison, and that was the punishment she deserved. He stepped closer. "Give me the letter, Prissy."

Paul stepped into the room, standing at Steffie's side, while the two priests moved to flank Jason.

"Priscilla," said Father Andy, his tone gentle. "Listen to me-"

"Listen to you? *Listen* to you?" Prissy held the letter up. "Carlene wrote this! Isn't it obvious? She's lying to all of you! And you're fools for believing her!"

"No, Mother. I didn't write it."

"My Angelheart would never say these things about me. Never!"

"He did," said Jason. "And I don't blame him. Holy water enemas, Priscilla? You gave your teenaged son holy water enemas?"

The priests looked at each other. Dave nodded, then both stared at Prissy.

"Lies!" Prissy swiped the open tin of paint thinner and threatened to douse the letter.

"No!" Jason lurched forward but Father Dave got there first, wrapping his hand around her throat, shaking her. The thinner tin fell to the floor, spilling, but Prissy had the letter in a death grip.

"Enough!" said Dave, tightening his grip. "Enough!"

Prissy's eyes bulged. She made gagging sounds. Her face went purple.

With his free hand, Dave Flannigan went for the letter, missed.

Jason swiped at it, and missed.

Priscilla wrenched out of Dave's grip. Screaming, she pistoned her fists down on his head and shoulders. Jason and Andy tried to pry her away. Forgotten, the letter dropped to the carpet.

"You filthy, godless liar!" Prissy whaled on the priest, trying to claw his eyes out.

Her sharp nails slashed across Jason's cheek, and Andy took a fistful of her hair, and wrenched her off Dave. She writhed out of his grip and shoved Andy against the dresser. The candle rocked, then fell. It hit the floor, kissed the spilled paint thinner, and the carpet blazed. The flames crawled up the crib's legs, starved wolves on fresh meat. It flared, melting the mobile, as *Magic Flute* tinkled out death knells. Fire raced across the room, licked the curtains, then climbed them.

"No!" Prissy lunged for the crib, beating at the blaze. Her sleeves caught, and Jason pulled her away. Then Andy grabbed her, pressed her to him, extinguishing the flames. He shoved her toward the doorway, toward Paul.

"Where's the fire extinguisher?" Paul screamed in Prissy's face. "Where's the goddamned fire extinguisher?" He shook her.

Prissy stared at him with uncomprehending eyes.

"We've got to get out of here!" Steffie yelled. "Now!"

Paul and Steffie yanked Prissy into the hall and moved back, letting Claire stump from the room. Jason and the priests followed. Andy slammed the door as flames spread and jumped, knocking a dried wreath off the door.

"Go!" Jason yelled. He followed Claire on her crutches toward the landing.

Claire halted in front of Fred Martin's room. "Dad!" She yelled. "Someone get my father!"

Prissy shrieked. "My baby! Timothy's jewelry! His baby pictures! My baby's things!" She wrenched out of Steffie's grip. Dave lunged at her, but she was quick, running toward a room at the far end of the hall.

"Priscilla!" Steffie yelled.

Dave turned to her. "Go. I'll get her! You two," he said to Andy and Paul, "get Fred out of here!"

Flames licked beneath the door. The fallen wreath caught and was devoured. The fire climbed the side table, seeking the massive arrangement of dried flowers. Within seconds, the flowers exploded and flames grew to consume the walls and carpet.

Andy grabbed Dave's arm. "It's spreading too fast! If you go after her, you'll be trapped!"

Dave yanked his arm, but Andy's grip was a vise.

"Don't," said the younger priest. "Let her go. She's not worth your life."

Dave looked Andy in the eyes. "Let me do this." There was something in his voice that left no room for argument. "I have to do this. This is my chance to set things right." A look passed between them that only Andy seemed to understand. "Let me go," said Dave.

Andy, his reluctance apparent, nodded and released the old man's wrist, and Father Dave took off down the hall after Priscilla. Within seconds, the fire spread and rose, building an impassable wall between Andy and Dave.

"Come on, Paul, let's get Fred," said Andy, but for a moment, he didn't move. He seemed mesmerized, shocked. Finally, he crossed himself, and turned.

"Paul," said Steffie.

He looked at her. "I'll just be a minute. Go on down!" He threw himself against Fred's door. Andy joined him.

Jason scooped his wife into his arms and, as Fred's door gave, he carried Claire downstairs, Steffie following, her head turning to watch Paul.

They reached the ground floor and entered the living room. Steffie threw the front door open wide.

As they left the house, Jason had a strange sense of carrying his bride over the threshold.

A Pleasure to Burn

Priscilla Martin, the woman whose clothes never wrinkled, whose makeup was always flawless, and whose hair never dared stray, now looked like a madwoman, a picture of chaos and ruin.

In her bedroom at the end of the hall, she shrieked, threw drawers open, swiped contents off of dressers and desks, shoving her pockets full of necklaces, bracelets, rings, and hanks of golden blond hair tied with baby blue ribbons. *Timothy's hair.* The realization made Dave feel ill. She shoved them into her blouse, down her yellow pants. A dozen framed clown portraits were piled in the corner near the closet. She ignored them.

She clawed framed photos from the walls and when she saw Dave in the doorway, she screamed, "Don't just stand there! Carry these, for Christ's sake!" She crushed photo albums into his arms, piled on clunky pieces of jewelry and more ribboned blond hair, her eyes haunted and wild, her mouth a smeared red gash.

"No, Priscilla. It's over." He let the photo albums and accessories fall to the floor.

Priscilla gaped at him. "What- what are you doing? We have to hurry!"

"It's too late."

"What on God's green earth are you *talking* about?" She shoved him aside, peered into the hall, and gasped.

Dave turned to see. The fire, fed by Priscilla's dried flowers, had progressed rapidly. It was tall, furious, and headed their way, a burst dam of flame. The hallway walls, floor, and ceiling were engulfed, and Dave felt the heat of it, coughed on the acrid black smoke as he slammed the door to buy time.

"The slider!" Prissy shoved Dave out of her way and began pulling at the balcony door. "Help me! It's jammed! We can climb down the trellis!"

Father David Flannigan sat down on the bed, clasped his hands, and closed his eyes. He wasn't praying - it was too late for that - he simply wanted a moment of peace before the pain, before the end.

"What are you *doing*? Have you lost your mind? Help me!" Prissy pounded on the glass. "Help me! Someone, help me! Up here!" But Dave knew no one on the street would see them; they'd be looking at the front of the house. He took a breath and stood. Placing a gentle hand on Priscilla's shoulder, he said, "Come. Let's not make this worse than it is."

She jerked from his touch. "Get away from me! How can you just *sit* there?" She pounded a fist on the glass door. "Help me! Help! We have to break it!"

"That's not going to happen, Priscilla."

Her jaw dropped. "Of course it is!"

"No. It isn't. I'm not going to let it happen. You're not leaving this room, Priscilla. Neither of us is leaving."

She gaped at him. The room was getting hot; smoke curled under the door, choking the atmosphere. "You're mad. You've lost your goddamned mind." Wetness spread across the crotch of her yellow pants, and trickled down her leg.

Dave smiled. "Perhaps." He grabbed her left wrist, then the right, and pulled her away from the slider.

"Stop it! Let me go!" She kicked, flailed, scratched, even bit him, but his resolve was iron.

"No. Confess, and meet your end with dignity." He had no interest in absolving her, but for years he'd yearned to know the secrets hidden in the darkness that was her soul.

"You're mad. You've lost your mind. You can't keep me here! We can get out!"

He squeezed her wrists hard. "Confess, Priscilla, and pray for forgiveness." Smoke grayed the atmosphere.

Prissy's jaw was hard, her eyes like stones. "I'm not confessing anything, and if you think I'm going to die here with you, like this-"

With the strength of pure rage, Dave lifted Prissy off the floor, and tossed her onto the bed. Her long-dead dogs bounced from the mattress and tumbled to the floor. Dave climbed on her, pinned her wrists, using his body to keep her down. She bucked and writhed, kicked and screamed, but she was no match for him. "Confess!"

He heard the fire burning outside the door, crackling and ravaging the dried flowers and carpeting. The house groaned. Even through the door, he felt the heat searing his back. The smoke thickened, made it hard to breathe, and clouded his vision as it grew heavier and blacker. They didn't have much longer.

"No!" cried Prissy. "Let me go! Let me go!"

"It's over, Priscilla. Confess your sins, or risk the wrath of God."

Something changed in her eyes. She went blank. Then tears spilled. "I can't die, not like this."

"But you are going to die," Dave said with utter calm. "We both are. Today."

Prissy's fight had gone out of her. For a long moment, she wept and choked, whispered rapid and unintelligible things.

Dave leaned close and heard her.

"I did it for you, Timothy." Her eyes met Dave's. "I did it all for Timothy."

"What did you do, Priscilla?"

She mewled. "I broke my daughter's leg." Her voice was a croak. "Drugged her. So I could do it. She never knew. And I … I did other things. Things that would make her feel crazy." Her eyes pled with Dave. "I just wanted that baby. That baby is *mine*." Her face crumpled.

"Go on, Priscilla, say it all."

"I hid Jason's medication so he'd have a seizure. I needed to get rid of him, too."

He'd guessed as much. "What else, Priscilla? Tell me what did you do to your son! Tell me what you did to Timothy!"

She cried out. "No! Let me go!"

"Say it, woman! Say it!" He shook her.

"I used to … to hurt him. And Claire, too. And, and … Frederick. Oh, God, Frederick." She wept. "He saw me. He saw me touching Timothy - and threatened to take the kids away. I tried to kill him, but he wouldn't die. He was *supposed* to die." She shrieked. "God *damn* it, why didn't he die?"

"What did you do to Frederick?"

"I loosened the rungs of his ladder." Her voice was that of a little girl. *The Bad Seed,* thought Dave.

"He wouldn't die! I started drugging him. So he could never tell anyone." She coughed. "I'd do it again, and I'd make sure he died this time!"

Smoke burned Dave's lungs, stung his eyes, and the charcoal-gray haze blurred his vision.

"We're almost out of time, Priscilla. Confess before God! What else?"

"I got Claire's doctor suspended, so I could have Gerald Hopper attend to her. Gerald will do anything I ask. Anything. He has to!" She coughed. "And I sent Claire an instant message. I said I was Timothy. And I gave her LSD and put up pictures of clowns to frighten her."

"Why? Why, Priscilla?"

She sobbed. "I wanted to make sure everyone knew she was unfit, so I could keep the baby - otherwise I'd have to kill her." She sobbed. "You don't understand - none of you understand! It's Timothy! He's coming back! That baby is *mine*! He's *mine*!"

Dave felt the heat rising in the room. He was getting lightheaded and could see by Prissy's rolling eyes that she was near unconsciousness.

"What else, Priscilla?" He slapped her cheek and shook her hard, bringing her back.

Awareness filtered into her eyes and she fixed Dave in a hard stare. "I fucked you. I fucked *you*, Father Flannigan." Her voice cracked and she coughed hard. "But you already know that, don't you?" She wept, but the fight had gone out of her.

Dave had waited so long to hear the truth, thinking perhaps he might find some compassion for her after the things she'd done ... but now that he'd heard it all, he felt no pity for the creature beneath him. He willed himself to speak calmly. "You're a monster, Priscilla Martin. Perhaps God will absolve you, but I cannot."

The door exploded open, revealing a wall of flames. Fire snaked across the rug and began feeding on the stuffed dogs on the floor.

"Forgive me, Father, please!" Prissy's eyes begged, and in them Dave saw terror. Terror, and resignation. It was strange to see such vulnerability in those eternally defiant eyes. And he saw his own reflection too, and the fire rising behind him.

"No." He was fading fast. "Your deeds are unforgivable. There is no redemption." He took a deep breath, coughed, and spoke his final words as fire climbed the bedspread. "You're a monster. And so am I. This is what we deserve. I'm going to escort you to Hell."

She coughed, deep in her lungs. The desperation in her eyes was gone now, and she turned her head, went still, resigned to her fate. Her eyes rolled back, and the last thing Dave saw before his vision darkened was her hand, curled into a claw, clutching a golden hank of her dead son's hair.

And then the flames came and turned the bed into a sea of fire.

***

Babs ran toward Prissy's house when she saw the front door open. Jason was carrying Claire in his arms, but by the time she arrived, he had set her down and he and Steffie Banks had their arms around her waist, supporting her. They were staring up at the house from the front walk.

"Claire!" she cried. "Are you all right?"

"Aunt Babs, we're fine. We're waiting for Paul and Andy-"

Just then, the two men appeared. Frederick was in Paul's arms. Andy toted a folded wheelchair and Claire's crutches.

"Dad!" Claire called.

"What's going on?" asked Babs.

American Pie rose from Hank's radio, singing to them about the day the music died. The neighbors began to crowd around. Roddy Crocker pushed his way through. "What's burning? Something's burning."

"I don't smell anything." Aida sniffed the air.

"You will," the cop said.

Father Andy unfolded the wheelchair and Paul helped Fred into it.

"Oh dear God," said Babs looking up at the house. Smoke, thick and black, rose from beneath the eaves.

Phyllis Stine shrieked and fell into her husband's arms as flames shot from a vent on the roof.

"Holy shit!" Hank Lowell said. "Someone call the fire dep-"

"No," said Andy. "Not yet."

There was a ripple of murmurs.

Babs whispered to Carl as they watched smoke seep from windows and eaves and pour from more roof vents until they could see nothing but flames and dark smoke.

Andy turned and faced the crowd. "Not yet." He looked directly at Roddy Crocker. "This is a last request from Father Dave. We'll call the fire department before it threatens any other houses. But not until we're sure it's … over."

Roddy's confusion turned to understanding. He nodded and looked uneasily at the neighbors. "I'm with Father Andy on this. But we *all* need to agree. Right here, right now."

Babs stepped forward. "Listen to them. Do as they say." She nodded at the cop. "I'm in full agreement."

The neighbors looked at each other, looked at Roddy, looked at the priest. No one said anything.

"Do it." Claire spoke up. "As a favor to me, my father, and my baby. Do it."

One by one, heads nodded their agreement. The crowd moved closer together. Husbands put their arms around wives.

Babs was pleased to see there were no children present. Carl put his arm around her and, together, the residents of Morning Glory Circle watched as fire devoured Priscilla Martin's home.

The roof broke open. Black smoke poured out. There were gasps, but no one spoke, they didn't have to. Their silence spoke for itself.

Roddy nodded at Andy. "It's time."

The priest pressed 911.

The neighbors watched solemnly as more of the roof collapsed into the second floor. As the house burned, and the wail of sirens neared, Babs thought of what Morning Glory Circle would be like without Priscilla

Martin. *It's been a neighborhood full of rumors, deceit, and lies, a place where no secret has ever been safe.* But not any longer. Now, finally, it would be home.

And this, Babs knew as she looked at the faces of her neighbors, was one secret that Morning Glory Circle would keep safe forever.

Epilogue: Halloween

It was late afternoon when Jason parked in front of Babs' house, but the jack o'lanterns were already lit and the smell of burnt pumpkin permeated Morning Glory Circle.

"It's Halloween," Claire said, looking over her shoulder at little Michael in his car seat between Paul and Steffie. The infant was dressed in the smallest Superman costume ever and he was adorable.

It was the first time Claire had returned to the sac since the fire, and she found herself avoiding the empty lot where Mother's house had stood. She almost hadn't come, but Babs and Carl wanted to give their honorary grandnephew a special first Halloween - with a walk around the cul-de-sac. Every house was decorated, even the Deans', and once twilight fell, the whole street would be twinkling with lights. Next door to Babs, the Collins house held a new family. Claire was glad.

They piled out of the minivan and Paul scooped up the baby and handed him to Claire, who kissed him on the forehead, then let Jason snuggle him against his chest. Meanwhile, Paul and Steffie helped Fred move from the rear seat into his wheelchair. In the absence of drugs and Botox, Dad was able to smile and speak now. His speech wasn't perfect, but it was the best he'd ever sounded to Claire.

They started up the walk as Babs came outside to greet them. "I'm so glad you decided to come!" Babs hugged Claire, then turned to Jason, who held baby Michael firmly in his arms. "Hello, Michael!" Babs cooed. The baby cooed back and grabbed her finger.

"Would you like to hold him?"

"I thought you'd never ask." She held the baby close and spoke softly into his ear. Michael gurgled happily.

Claire smiled. "What did you tell him?"

"That his Great-Aunt Babs is going to spoil him rotten."

"You can call yourself Grandma if you'd like, Babs. You were more of a mother to me than *she* ever was."

Babs' eyes welled. "Do you mean it?"

"Of course."

"I'd love that."

Claire turned to Carl. "And how do you feel about being Michael's Grandpa Carl?"

Carl grinned. "As long as it's okay with his real grandpa." He turned to Fred. "You don't mind sharing the title, do you, Fred?"

Fred smiled. "Glad to."

"Good." Claire looked down the street. "No one's putting out the witches this year?"

"Nope," said Babs. "Prissy required us all to have matching decorations, but we've done away with that. No more rules. Decorate if you want to, however you want. Mow your lawn, or don't. We're happy these days."

"I can see that." Claire looked at Aunt Babs. The woman positively glowed.

"Happy Halloween!"

They turned and saw Andy Pike strolling toward them.

"Father Andy!" Claire hugged him. Jason held his hand out, but the priest pulled him into a quick hug.

"It's good to see you again, Father," said Jason.

"You, too. How's the business?"

Jason looked at Paul, then back to Andy and said, "Couldn't be better. It's a dream come true."

Paul had promoted Jason to general manager of the flight school, and had just completed work on a new one. This was Paul's last night in Snapdragon. Tomorrow, he and Steffie were flying back to Brimstone where the second Schuyler's Flight School was ready to open. He and Steffie had been inseparable since that night in March, and it filled Claire with joy to see them both so happy.

Carl joined them at the front door, and handed Claire a plastic jack o'lantern. "Here you go. Michael's first trick-or-treat pumpkin. I already put half a dozen Reese's Cups in there - your favorite, right?" He grinned.

"Right." Claire started to fish one out.

"Wait until after dinner. It'll be ready in an hour," Carl said. "Corn chowder, cranberry muffins, and salad. I'm the chef tonight. Why don't you take little Michael around the cul-de-sac before it gets dark? You can gather lots more candy for yourselves." He looked at Paul and Steffie. "Do you two want a trick or treat pumpkin, too?"

"I'm on a diet," said Paul.

Steffie laughed. "Maybe Michael will let us snitch a peanut butter cup or two from him."

"If that's what you want," Babs said. "We have a whole bowl of them inside."

Fred worked the controls of his new chair like a champ. "I'll take one."

"Come around back," Carl said. "You can wheel right in through the sliders."

"Do you need any help with dinner, Carl?" asked Andy.

"No, why don't you go with the kids?" Carl and Fred headed up the driveway, speculating about Dr. Hopper's upcoming trial.

"We'd love for you to come along," Claire told Andy. She didn't want to hear about Eugene Hopper's trial and hoped she wouldn't be called to testify.

"Then I'd love to," Andy said.

They headed to the former Collins house, now the Newcomb house, where Snickers bars were added to the pot, then passed the darkened Pruitt residence, where a *For Sale* sign stood sentry. Babs told Claire that Duane and Jerry had moved a few months ago, unable to live so close to such bad memories. They lived in an older part of town now and were fixing up a Victorian and talking about adopting a child of their own.

At the Sachs', they were invited in and Candy made a huge fuss over Michael, saying he reminded her of Billy when he was a baby.

When they left the Sachs' place, Claire's stomach began to knot. Mother's property was a vacant lot and had just been sold for enough money that she and Jason could buy the huge beautiful house Paul was vacating tomorrow. It was a single-story rambler with easy wheelchair access at one end that would be turned into an apartment just for Dad. He was overjoyed. So were Claire and Jason.

Jason handed Michael over to his godparents, Steffie and Paul, then put his arm around Claire as they paused in front of the property. Claire had stayed away, but Jason had overseen much of the demolition. The basement had remained, for the most part untouched, though much of what was down there had been destroyed by the water from the fire hoses. Before it was filled in, Jason had had a look around at the burst cans of old food, the big boxes of hangers, and piles of lamps. Whatever else was still down there would remain.

Claire leaned against him and he held her close. "It's all gone," she said. "All of it. It's such a relief to know Michael will never see what was here." She looked at Father Andy just as he crossed himself in prayer. His eyes opened and she smiled at him. "I'm so sorry Father Dave died in the fire."

"It's what he wanted. He'd been consumed by guilt for a very long time and this was his penance, his sacrifice."

"I appreciate what he did, but I'm sorry it had to be done. If she had lived … it wouldn't have ended."

"I know." Andy cleared his throat. "I came back after the house was razed and sowed the ground with salt."

Claire kissed his cheek. "Thank you. And bless Father Dave for slaying the beast."

"Amen," said Jason. He paused. "Let's keep moving. I'd love to say hello to Hank. Maybe he'll invite me to have a beer with him sometime."

Claire smiled. "Okay." But for a moment, she couldn't move, couldn't tear her eyes away from the place where the house had stood. *Goodbye, Mother.* She didn't know where souls went after the body died, but she chose to believe it was to someplace happy, someplace where she, Tim, and everyone she loved, would never see Priscilla Martin again.

As she looked at the dark salted earth, a cold breeze ruffled her hair. For a moment, she thought she caught the faint scent of *Opium* perfume; but, like a fleeting ghost, it was gone. *All the ghosts are gone.* She shivered. "Goodbye, Timothy."

Claire took Jason's hand and they joined their friends - their *family* - and continued down Morning Glory Circle.

About the Authors

Tamara Thorne's first novel was published in 1991, and since then she has written many more, including international bestsellers *Haunted, Moonfall, Eternity,* and *Bad Things.* She is hard at work on more projects. Learn more about at tamrathorne.com

Alistair Cross grew up on horror novels and scary movies, and by the age of eight, began writing his own stories. First published by Damnation Books in 2012, he has since co-authored *The Ghosts of Ravencrest* with Tamara Thorne and is working on several other projects. Find out more about him at alistaircross.com

In collaboration, Thorne and Cross are currently writing several novels, including the serial, *The Witches of Ravencrest,* which appears about every six to eight weeks. Together, they also host the horror-themed radio show Thorne & Cross: Haunted Nights LIVE! which has featured such guests as Laurell K. Hamilton, Christopher Moore, Chelsea Quinn Yarbro, Charlaine Harris, and Christopher Rice. Thorne and Cross are hard at work on several upcoming collaborations, including a sequel to Tamara's *Candle Bay,* which will feature plenty of vampy action as the Darlings and Julian Valentyn are joined on a road trip to Eternity with Michael and Winter from Alistair's The Crimson Corset. It's going to be a harrowing ride!

Coming in 2016 from Thorne & Cross

Welcome BACK ... to a little bit of Hell on Earth

Fang meets fang when the vampires of Candle Bay and the vampires of Crimson Cove get together for a road trip to the little California town of Eternity for a family reunion.
Lust.
Blood.
Death.
Disorderly conduct.
Just another day in the family ...

Check out these haunting titles by Thorne & Cross!

The Ghosts of Ravencrest

Darkness Never Dies

Ravencrest Manor has always been part of the family. The ancestral home of the Mannings, Ravencrest's walls have been witness to generations of unimaginable scandal, horror, and depravity. Imported stone by stone from England to northern California over a thirty-year period in the 1800s, the manor now houses widower Eric Manning, his children, and his staff. Ravencrest stands alone, holding its memories and ghosts close to its dark heart, casting long, black shadows across its grand lawns, through the surrounding forests, and over the picturesque town of Devilswood below.

Dare to Cross the Threshold

Ravencrest Manor is the most beautiful thing new governess, Belinda Moorland, has ever seen, but as she learns more about its tangled past of romance and terror, she realizes that beauty has a dark side. Ravencrest is built on secrets, and its inhabitants seem to be keeping plenty of their own - from the handsome English butler, Grant Phister, to the power-mad administrator, Mrs. Heller, to Eric Manning himself, who watches her with dark, fathomless eyes. But Belinda soon realizes that the living who dwell in Ravencrest have nothing on the other inhabitants - the ones who walk the darkened halls by night... the ones who enter her dreams... the ones who are watching... and waiting...

Home is Where the Horror is

Welcome to Ravencrest, magnificent by day, terrifying by night. Welcome to Ravencrest, home of sordid secrets and ghastly scandals from the past. Welcome to Ravencrest, where there is no line between the living and the dead.

The Ghosts of Ravencrest is a serialized novel. The first installment, titled Darker Shadows, includes the first three episodes, The New Governess, Awakening, and Darker Shadows. Christmas Spirits is the novella-length 4th installment which can be read as part of the series or as a standalone.

The Cliffhouse Haunting

When the Blue Lady Walks...

Since 1887, Cliffhouse Lodge has been famous for its luxurious accommodations, fine dining ... and its ghosts. Overlooking Blue Lady Lake, nestled among tall pines, Cliffhouse has just been renovated by its owners, Teddy and Adam Bellamy, and their daughter, Sara.

Cliffhouse has not always been a place of rest and respite, though. Over the years it has served many vices, from rum-running to prostitution - and although the cat houses have been replaced by a miniature golf course and carousel, Cliffhouse retains its dark history; darkest during the Roaring Twenties, when a serial killer called the Bodice Ripper terrorized the town, and a phantom, the Blue Lady, was said to walk when murder was imminent.

Death Walks With Her...

Now, there's a new killer on the loose, and the Blue Lady sightings have returned. The Bellamys are losing maids, and guests are being tormented by disembodied whispers, wet phantom footprints, and the blood-chilling shrieks of mad laughter that echo through the halls of Cliffhouse in the dead of night.

The little mountain town of Cliffside is the perfect hunting ground for a serial killer... and the Blue Lady. Police Chief Jackson Ballou has bodies piling up, and between the murders and the mysteries, he can hardly pursue his romance with Polly Owen. And Sara Bellamy may lose her true love before they even have their first kiss.

The Crimson Corset
by Alistair Cross

Welcome to Crimson Cove

Sheltered by ancient redwoods, nestled in mountains overlooking the California coast, the cozy village of Crimson Cove has it all: sophisticated retreats, fine dining, a beautiful lake, and a notorious nightclub, The Crimson Corset. It seems like a perfect place to relax and get close to nature. But not everything in Crimson Cove is natural.

When Cade Colter moves to town to live with his older brother, he expects it to be peaceful to the point of boredom. But he quickly learns that after the sun sets and the fog rolls in, the little tourist town takes on a whole new kind of life - and death.

Darkness at the Edge of Town

Renowned for its wild parties and history of debauchery, The Crimson Corset looms on the edge of town, inviting patrons to sate their most depraved desires and slake their darkest thirsts. Proprietor Gretchen VanTreese has waited centuries to annihilate the Old World vampires on the other side of town and create a new race - a race that she alone will rule. When she realizes Cade Colter has the key that will unlock her plan, she begins laying an elaborate trap that will put everyone around him in mortal danger.

Blood Wars

The streets are running red with blood, and as violence and murder ravage the night, Cade must face the darkest forces inside himself, perhaps even abandon his own humanity, in order to protect what he loves.

Haunted
by Tamara Thorne

Murders and Madness

Its violent, sordid past is what draws bestselling author David Masters to the infamous Victorian mansion called Baudey House. Its shrouded history of madness and murder is just the inspiration he needs to write his ultimate masterpiece of horror. But what waits for David and his sixteen-year-old daughter, Amber, at Baudey House, is more terrifying than any legend...

Seduction

First comes the sultry hint of jasmine...followed by the foul stench of decay. It is the dead, seducing the living, in an age-old ritual of perverted desire and unholy blood lust. For David and Amber, an unspeakable possession has begun...

Candle Bay
by Tamara Thorne

Vampire Hotel

Shrouded in fog on a hillside high above an isolated California coastal town, The Candle Bay Hotel and Spa has been restored to its former glory after decades of neglect. Thanks to its new owners, the Darlings, the opulent inn is once again filled with prosperous guests. But its seemingly all-American hosts hide a chilling, age-old family secret.

Innocent Blood

Lured to the picturesque spot, assistant concierge Amanda Pearce is mesmerized by her surroundings—and her seductive new boss, Stephen Darling. But her employers' eccentric ways and suspicious blood splatters in the hotel fill her with trepidation. Little does Amanda know that not only are the Darlings vampires, but that a murderous vampire vendetta is about to begin—and she will be caught in the middle. For as the feud unfolds and her feelings for Stephen deepen, Amanda must face the greatest decision of her life: to die, or join the forever undead.

Eternity
by Tamara Thorne

Welcome To Eternity: A Little Bit of Hell on Earth

When Zach Tully leaves Los Angeles to take over as sheriff of Eternity, a tiny mountain town in northern California, he's expecting to find peace and quiet in his own private Mayberry. But he's in for a surprise. Curmudgeonly Mayor Abbott is a ringer for long-missing writer Ambrose Bierce. There are two Elvises in town, a shirtless Jim Morrison, and a woman who has more than a passing resemblance to Amelia Earhardt. And that's only the beginning.

Icehouse Mountain Mysteries

Eternity is the sort of charming spot tourists flock to every summer and leave every fall when the heavy snows render it an isolated ghost town. Tourists and New Agers all talk about the strange energy coming from Eternity's greatest attraction: a mountain called Icehouse, replete with legends of Bigfoot, UFOs, Ascended Masters, and more. But the locals talk about something else.

Yours Truly, Jack the Ripper

The seemingly quiet town is plagued by strange deaths, grisly murders, and unspeakable mutilations, all the work of a serial killer the locals insist is Jack the Ripper. And they want Zach Tully to stop him.

Now, as the tourists leave and the first snow starts to fall, terror grips Eternity as an undying evil begins its hunt once again…

Moonfall
by Tamara Thorne

Halloween Horrors

Moonfall, the picturesque community nestled in the mountains of Southern California, is a quaint hamlet of antique stores and craft shops run by the dedicated nuns of St. Gertrude's Home for Girls. As autumn fills the air, the townspeople prepare for the festive Halloween Haunt, Moonfall's most popular tourist attraction. Even a series of unsolved deaths over the years hasn't dimmed Moonfall's renown. Maybe because anyone who knew anything about them has disappeared.

Evil Nuns

Now, Sara Hawthorne returns to her hometown...and enters the hallowed halls of St. Gertrude's where, twelve years before, another woman died a horrible death. In Sara's old room, distant voices echo in the dark and the tormented cries of children shatter the moon-kissed night.

Girls' School Secrets

But that's just the beginning. For Sara Hawthorne is about to uncover St. Gertrude's hellish secret...a secret she'll carry with her to the grave...

The Forgotten
by Tamara Thorne

The Past...

Will Banning survived a childhood so rough, his mind has blocked it out almost entirely—especially the horrific day his brother Michael died, a memory that flickers on the edge of his consciousness as if from a dream.

Isn't Gone...

Now, as a successful psychologist, Will helps others dispel the fears the past can conjure. But he has no explanation for the increasingly bizarre paranoia affecting the inhabitants of Caledonia, California, many of whom claim to see terrifying visions and hear ominous voices...voices that tell them to do unspeakable things....

It's Deadly

As madness and murderous impulses grip the coastal town, Will is compelled to confront his greatest fear and unlock the terrifying secret of his own past in a place where evil isn't just a memory...it's alive and waiting to strike...

Bad Things
by Tamara Thorne

Gothic California

The Piper clan emigrated from Scotland and founded the town of Santo Verde, California. The Gothic Victorian estate built there has housed the family for generations, and has also become home to an ancient evil forever linked to the Piper name…

He has the Sight

As a boy, Rick Piper discovered he had "the sight." It was supposed to be a family myth, but Rick could see the greenjacks—the tiny mischievous demons who taunted him throughout his childhood—and who stole the soul of his twin brother Robin one Halloween night.

Deadly Family Secrets

Now a widower with two children of his own, Rick has returned home to build a new life. He wants to believe the greenjacks don't exist, that they were a figment of his own childish fears and the vicious torment he suffered at the hands of his brother. But he can still see and hear them, and they haven't forgotten that Rick escaped them so long ago. And this time, they don't just want Rick. This time they want his children…

Thunder Road
by Tamara Thorne

Cowboys and Aliens

Evoking Stephen King's terrifying novel The Gunslinger and the epic adventure film Cowboys and Aliens, Tamara Thorne delivers a tantalizing blend of horror and Western SciFi--in a dangerous arid world from which there is no escape...

Amusement Park Apocalypse

The California desert town of Madelyn boasts all sorts of attractions for visitors. Join the audience at the El Dorado Ranch for a Wild West show. Take a ride through the haunted mine at Madland Amusement Park. Scan the horizon for UFOs. Find religion with the Prophet's Apostles--and be prepared for the coming apocalypse.

Unstoppable Serial Killer

Because the apocalypse has arrived in Madelyn. People are disappearing. Strange shapes and lights dart across the night sky. And a young man embraces a violent destiny--inspired by a serial killer whose reign of terror was buried years ago.

The Four Horsemen Ride

But each of these events is merely setting the stage for the final confrontation. A horror of catastrophic proportions is slouching toward Madelyn in the form of four horsemen--and they're picking up speed. . .

The Sorority
by Tamara Thorne

They are the envy of every young woman—and the fantasy of every young man. An elite sisterhood of Greenbriar University's best and brightest, their members are the most powerful girls on campus—and the most feared...

Eve

he's the perfect pledge. A sweet, innocent, golden-haired cheerleader, Eve has so much to gain by joining Gamma Eta Pi—almost anything she desires. But only a select few can enter the sorority's inner circle—or submit to its code of blood, sacrifice, and sexual magic. Is Eve willing to pay the price?

Merilynn

Ever since childhood, Merilynn has had a sixth sense about things to come. She's blessed with uncanny powers of perception—and cursed with unspeakable visions of unholy terror. Things that corrupt the souls of women, and crush the hearts of men. Things that can drive a girl to murder, suicide, or worse...

Samantha

Journalism major Sam Penrose is tough, tenacious—and too curious for her own good. She's determined to unearth the truth about the sorority. But the only way to expose this twisted sisterhood is from within...

Made in the USA
Middletown, DE
26 November 2016